13 Secret Cities

Cesar Torres

This book is a work of fiction. References to actual people, events, establishments, organizations, or locales are intended only to provide a sense of authenticity and are used fictitiously. All other characters, and all incidents and dialogue, are drawn from the author's imagination and are not to be construed as real.

FIRST EDITION

Cover design by Matt Davis

ISBN: 0991036344
ISBN-13: 978-0-9910363-4-9

To Lino and Elsa.

CONTENTS

ACKNOWLEDGMENTS

This digital serial and its companion paperback would not have been possible without the help of many people. My first readers, Robert Haining Tolar, Jacqui Cheng, Matt Saba, and especially Max Carmona III, provided valuable insights on the manuscript as each installment went into production. The talented Richard Shealy copy-edited the book, and the visualization of the digital and physical book emerged from Matt Davis' mind. I would also like to thank Dr. Lisa Barker and her undergraduate students at Towson University, who did an analysis and reading of the text in October of 2014. Lastly, I would like to thank all my family members for weaving their love into a tapestry of support for *13 Secret Cities* and the books that are going to follow.

PART ONE
RED TEZCATLIPOCA

BURN: RITES MY FATHER TAUGHT ME

"There are thirteen secret cities, but no one knows where they are." –Arkangel, "Plainsong", *The Violet Album,* 2008, Reckless Records.

"The city of Chicago is experiencing a renaissance that outpaces all other North American cities. There has never been a better place to live." –Acceptance speech by Mayor Ron Amadeo, inauguration night, 2010.

"The elders of the Illini and Chippewa tribes explained that their people drew their strength from the immense lake they call Michi Gami. This body of water was the source of much fear and superstitious rumor. In their native tongue, they told me how death hovered above the waters, like a cloud. The lake itself was a place of death, and its scent was that of carrion. Where men tread, death stalked in shadows, made of no discernible form." –Louis Jolliet, letter to Terese Chirac, 1674, Chicago History Museum archives.

A glance into the past revealed to me the simplicity of time: The moments of my life were stars, suspended in the vastness of space, and each one shone bright. But between each one, there also existed a vast darkness, a vacuum that threatened to swallow their light forever. My story began with a single point, a single star: The events that happened on October 4, 2013 in Millennium Park.

I followed the crosshatched dome of the pavilion, moving toward the silver wings that cradled the stage. I shoved my way forward, scared to be knocked over by someone bigger than me.

A hiss and a whistle overhead tore through the din of the shouts. I looked up to follow the noise, above me. I turned my head toward the sky. Small objects streamed through the air, headed north, in the same direction I was moving.

The missiles left white trails as they soared. When they reached the stage, I heard the metal clink like empty beer cans. A white cloud bloomed immediately in three spots.

When those of us who could see the stage saw the tear gas swell before us, our screams grew into shrieks.

The protesters who had already gathered by the stage ran immediately away from the cloud. But they weren't quick enough. The white smoke swallowed them up.

The hiss continued and the cloud grew. The breeze blew toward the north, but Chicago wind was fickle, and it could turn right around, toward the south, at any moment.

I thought about my parents, and my brother, and it occurred to me that right now, my father was probably still at work, at the Botanical Gardens. My mother was also at her office, and perhaps she was texting my brother as he arrived home from school, just to make sure he made himself a snack while he waited for her and my father to come home. This thought shifted and moved beyond my grasp as I ran, until it was gone.

On my shoulders I wore the shawl my mother had given me the day I moved away to college, and I wrapped it around my mouth and nose to keep the gas out. I fished in my pocket for my petrified moss, a good luck charm from my father that I carried on my keychain.

I pivoted and ran toward the south, away from the stage.

As I ran, I witnessed moments from my short nineteen-year-old life flash before me like water rushing down the side of a mountain. I re-lived the awkward pomp of my first communion, the climbs we made on the hills surrounding my grandmother's lop-sided house in San Miguel, Mexico, and the road trips through San Diego when I was a toddler. I lived through these moments fast. In was the girl with the long face and the auburn eyes, a face I could see with precision, as if I were a camera-man shooting these memories. These visions of the past slid downward, vanishing as soon as it had arrived, gone in microseconds.

And I ran. My legs pumped with fury and speed, but they were untrained and clumsy. I was not an athlete and I had never been fit. And now, the pounds of weight in the backpack on my back forced me to run without grace or agility. Now that tear gas was encroaching on the pavilion, slipping out of the straps could cost me precious seconds.

About two hundred feet in the distance, uniformed police were closing this perimeter, shouting and pummeling, and bellowing through megaphones. I would never make it past them without being beaten down by their weapons and their strength. I let my running stride slow down a bit, enough to shake off my backpack, and to give me some time to think of where else I could run to. If I broke out toward the lake, to the east, I might be able to squeeze onto Columbus Drive and perhaps avoid the dozens of officers around us.

My father had always warned us to avoid the lake, and instead I ran straight toward it.

I found the short concrete wall that lined the perimeter of the pavilion, just about forty feet ahead. I zigzagged my way over to it.

My long legs, which I had always been proud of, catapulted me over the short wall of the perimeter. But my legs were too long, in fact. My shoe caught the edge of the concrete wall. I flipped forward and landed hard on my hands and knees. These awful long legs, I thought. But I looked around me. I could see the southern end of the pavilion, and behind it, the glint of the BP bridge. I wrapped the shawl around my head one more time, though the gas was starting to creep into my eyes and sear them with pain. Other protesters were escaping through this very same route, where the police and SWAT forces were a little thinner.

I realized I was free; I was escaping the pavilion.

Just as I came to standing, I heard the crack of gunshots behind me. One. Then another and another.

I heard new voices, full of anger, surging from the crowd. New gunfire exploded, and this time it sounded very different from the first three pops I heard. Their rhythm was calculated, and precise. Perhaps it was an automatic weapon.

The bursts grew louder and moved closer to where I stood. Whoever was firing was cutting through the middle of the pavilion.

I kept on running, away from Pritzker, and I spotted an opening of about thirty feet with fewer officers, where I could run through.

I turned around one more time to look behind me through the open patches of clear air inside the white cloud.

The SWAT officers had now joined the police. They wore gas masks lowered over their face and their Kevlar gear protected them like scarab shells. They formed a dark ring around this cloudy oval, and they moved in tight, choking it out. They fired over and over. Their dark figures and hard helmets rendered them genderless, ageless, raceless.

Soon, the thick gas engulfed the black shapes of the SWAT men, too. The whole Pavilion disappeared under the chemical mist.

The screams were beginning to fade a bit, and I realized that the gas might be taking its effect now, silencing the crowd as it burned itself into their eyes and throats.

More gunfire exploded from the white cloud.

In front of me, I could see the street and the snaking structure of the BP Bridge. Hundreds of people ran in every direction, pleading for help that wasn't going to come.

Though police officers flanked the entrance to the bridge to seal off the area, I spotted an opening I could take. I darted through.

I ran up the curving path of the bridge. By now I had stopped paying attention to the discomfort in my legs and the ache in my throat. I had become a runner. I didn't dare look behind me, though I could hear the cacophony still.

The run over the bridge became a kaleidoscope of fear, my ragged breath, the pointed spikes of sailboats in the marina, and the silvery reflections on the waters of Lake Michigan, where I was headed.

Then I moved toward the exit, relieved. I dashed toward Lake Shore Drive, and I clutched the fossilized moss in my hand.

I felt like a coward. I didn't know how to stay back there in the pavilion and fight, but how could I? Someone was shooting guns in there, and all I wanted was to run far away from this place. And Edgar. I had no idea what had happened to him. I had a cell phone in my pocket, but my mind could not conceive of picking it up and using it. Instead, my legs did the thinking for me, telling me to go far away from this place.

Before me lay Lake Shore Drive. If I reached its underpass, perhaps I could catch my breath for a few moments and then continue toward the lake. If hiding meant I had to jump into its icy waters, I was ready to do it.

I felt a sigh of relief when I ran down the grassy slope that led to the overpass. I was almost there. The flapping beats of helicopters overhead smothered my hearing. I saw three of them circling overhead, vultures against an orange sky.

Just about a hundred feet until I reached the underpass.

At the bottom of the slope, I tripped again, clumsy and unathletic. My knees stung, but I didn't care. I heard more shouts, more gunfire and a strange whistling sound in the air. I ran again.

Just twenty feet left.

My legs pumped harder, and I could see the cool darkness underneath the hard concrete structure.

Just five more feet.

I turned the corner into the safety of the underpass. I was not about to stop running until I was deep inside its cavern, safe.

I made it.

I ran into the opening and turned the corner.

My body slammed into a hard mass and bounced back, losing balance and falling backward. I looked up. Six SWAT team officers, masked and faceless, stared down at me. The one whom I slammed into didn't hesitate. He brought down the baton with a muscled arm.

The black club swept across my face and connected with my cheekbone. A deep crack sent a sliver of pain down from my right eye and down my back. Then another one. And another one.

This was how my cheekbone shattered in two, and the reason why I eventually went blind in my right eye. The nerve damage in my spine because of the blows I endured was also a direct result of what happened to me in that underpass. When the officer's metal wand made contact with my body, I bit down on my tongue, and blood gushed into my mouth. The baton also flayed open my cheek; I knew the liquid that ran down my cheekbones was not sweat, and it was not tears. I rendered my dignity as I curled up into a ball at the feet of the officers.

The dried moss my father gave me didn't stop the violence, and it never could have prevented that officer from crushing my skull. In my pocket I also carried a travel-size icon of the Virgin of Guadalupe, which my mother had given to me three months ago, when I had moved from home to the university. She was a little Guadalupe, drenched in gold and red, boldly stepping over the horns of a demon and radiating light. Her eyes implied safety and love, but the protection I was supposed to receive from the icon never came to be. Even as I fell into a dark sleep and went deeper into shock, I remember feeling cheated by these useless objects, and though I don't like to admit this, I hated my mother and father for instilling this false sense of security in me. I hadn't realized how superstitious my parents were until I thought about how a dried piece of moss and a laminated photo of a virgin could be so utterly fucking useless. That was the hateful little thought that crept into my head, even as my vision burst into white stars and the officer fractured my bones. He shouted many words at me, and his other companions shouted too, words filled with hate and revulsion, for me and for the other thousands of people that had gathered at Millennium that day.

By my count, from the moment I lost Edgar until a SWAT officer split my face, four minutes elapsed. That in itself is a lifetime. That four-minute moment became one of the stars in the firmament of my life.

But that's all it was, just a tiny moment. To dwell on my escape would be as if I asked you to stare up at the sky and fixate on only one star or planet and expect you to understand the full scope of the galaxy that contains it. It wouldn't be fair to you, me, to those who perished in Millennium Park, or my story.

There were other moments in my life that had an impact on those four minutes. They were moments made of interdependency, like a spider's web.

Four days before the riots, I had celebrated my nineteenth birthday.

My parents had picked me up at the dorm in Rogers Park. My brother, José María, flipped me his middle finger from the backseat as I got into the station wagon, and we drove downtown. We ate pizza at Uno's, and I blew out nineteen candles on the cake. Afterward, we decided to walk off the meal. We walked east on Ohio Street until we reached an underpass. We crossed its length, and when we emerged, the dark waters of Lake Michigan greeted us.

It was much too late to be walking down the lakefront, but there we were, all four of us -- I, my parents, and my brother -- alone at the eastern edge of the city, where land meets water.

My father, the tallest member of our family, walked up in front, smoking a cigarette, and my mother walked between me and José María, our arms intertwined, her long straight hair brushing her shoulders. We walked north, along the bike path that ran up the shoreline of Lake Michigan. This part of Lake Shore Drive didn't close officially until 11 p.m., but even now, at 10:31, it was deserted. The lake's waves lashed the concrete wall next to our feet, and up on our right, we could see the tops of the cars as they rushed down Lake Shore Drive. The lake remained black tonight.

I dug in my pocket for my cell and pointed my camera toward the water. From up ahead, my father shouted, "Put it away, Clara. No photos."

His voice rumbled, and the sweetness of the chocolate birthday cake I had just eaten earlier tonight rose up to my throat in acid waves. *Why do you have to yell at me?* I thought. He was always yelling at me. He ignored this expression of rage in my face and squatted down, facing the lake a few feet ahead of us.

I felt a tug on my shoulder and a pat on my arm.

"Put the phone away," my mother whispered. "Do what he says."

The lights that shone from Navy Pier turned my father's profile into a shadow. He sat down on the concrete and patted the ground for us to join him.

"Birthday girl, right here on my left," he said. I sat cross-legged on the cold surface, and we joined him on the other side. My father offered my mother a cigarette, but she shook her head.

"Not now, Adán," she said. "Let's not stay out here too long. We have be back to the car by around eleven; you know that."

It was important for us to run on time. Not only did I want to get back to the car in the parking lot, I also wanted to get back to the dorm as soon as possible. I wanted to celebrate all night. We had spent all week making big plans for the march at Millennium Park, and Edgar had borrowed an ID to buy beer and celebrate my birthday when I returned to campus.

I hadn't told my parents yet about Edgar. I hadn't even told José María, but then again, I knew what would happen if I told my little brother. He'd be sure to notify my parents, faster than the Internet.

During my first week at the dorms, Edgar had asked to borrow my screwdriver to fix his mini fridge, and that's how I had discovered he lived on my floor, on the other side of the dorm. Over the next few days, he kept cruising through my suite, and I kept on traveling to his. We were both freshmen, and both of us held political change high on our list of values. Now we were inseparable in our dorm, in the dining hall, in the two classes we shared, and in our ways of thinking about change for the world. His face was boyish, his voice was not. We both joined the Occupy

Liberation Front on the same day.

The lake pummeled the breakers, and I noticed José María was starting to resemble my father more than ever before as the angles in his face grew sharper and his hair grew out thick, wavy and black.

My mother unfolded her shawl to free up her hands. From her purse she withdrew a small laminated image of the Virgin of Guadalupe, which she placed on her lap as she genuflected. She kissed the image of the virgin, and then she put the image away. I couldn't see what my brother was up to behind her, but I could hear him tapping his hands on the concrete, drumming the beat to one of his favorite metal songs.

There we were, like hippies staring at the dim slice of moon through the clouds. Birthdays were starting to become more and more like this, as the lines in my parents' faces grew just a little deeper, and some of their weirdness got...well, weirder.

"In another part of the world, there is a lake where men once built a city," my mother said. "This city floated on top of the water, like a dream. Its towers reached toward the sky, and its architecture reflected the beauty of the natural world. The city's surfaces were red, blue and gold, like the plumage of jungle birds."

José María leaned over behind my mother's back and twisted his face into a knot. "Here we go again..." he whispered to me. *Shush*, I mouthed over to him.

"Tenochtitlán," I said, speaking loudly enough to make sure my father heard me, to make sure I had this knowledge etched into my memory. "That's the city Mom's talking about."

Tenochtitlán, or in other words, Mexico City. The place my parents were born. I was born there, too, but I only lived there for year. By the time I could walk, we were living here, in Chicago.

"We probably won't live in Mexico City ever again, but it's good to visit Lake Michigan and remember that we once did," my father said.

My father turned back toward all of us, and his face shone clear, despite the shadows cast by night. His skin was deeply grooved by lines and wrinkles, and his hairline had receded, but his eyes looked young to me. My uncles and cousins had always said that my father's eyes looked defiant. In my experience, his eyes were sometimes gentle, sometimes terrifying. Mostly terrifying.

"In any case," my father said, "before your mother interrupted me, I was going to tell you what you need to do when you come to this lake, Clara. You're nineteen -- almost old enough to be an adult."

"Dad, I work and I vote. I *am* an adult. I don't like being dismissed," I said.

"Fine," he said. "In this country you're an adult; I'll grant you that. But your adulthood in other terms is still a long time away. So we come here on your birthday to think about this for a minute and to put our hopes in your future."

José María stirred, crossed his skinny arms. "Mom, you always let him go on and on...I mean, are you listening to this?"

"As a general rule, your father's wrong about many things," my mother said, and I could see José María sit up straight from his own sense of validation. "But in this case, you do need to listen. You may not understand everything we're doing as a family, Clara, but it is your responsibility to grasp it. So, sit back and listen. Yes, this means you too, José María."

My father was a strange dude, and that meant he always carried strange stuff with him. He dug in his coat and pulled out a bundle of twigs and leaves.

"Pay special attention, birthday girl," my father said. Using his free hand, he pulled out a lighter from his trousers.

"I bring both of you here because the lake is a place you should respect. It's a place that's beautiful, but my mother always said that certain beautiful things should not be touched, by any means. Lake Michigan has been here longer than you, me, or the men who built this city behind me. And though the lake gives life, the lake also has also dealt out death over the years. Never dive into its waters. Understand?"

I nodded, so that we could just move on. Over the years, I nodded a lot this way. I got good at scurrying past these talks.

"We live about six miles from here," my father continued, "and that's just about the right distance to show our respect for these waters. If our house was any closer and we would be under its threat."

"Actually, that's not really true," José María said. "Clara lives by the lakefront, so she's really just a few hundred yards away from the shore--"

My mother smacked my brother on the back of the head, and he grinned as he shrugged his shoulders and chortled.

But José María was right. The dorms were very close to the water. But I kept my mouth shut. This was not the time for interruptions.

My father lit one end of the bundle of twigs, and it took a moment to catch fire. Soon its flames were leaping up its length as my father held it away from his jean jacket and over the concrete lip. His hand stayed poised over the water. He spoke no words. He just let it burn until the flames caressed the tips of his fingers and the fire lit our faces. He tossed the bundle into the waters, where the darkness swallowed it up in a hiss.

"Clara, you have to promise me you'll always stay away from this lake." My father said.

"Sure."

My father turned toward all three of us.

"So, that's what you do when you come to show respect to the water," my father said. "Learn it."

Another order for me.

I pressed my lips into a flat line. Impatience burned in my gut. I was feeling ready to leave this place. I wanted to be back in my dorm room, cracking open a PBR. I was over this spooky water and the hippie weirdness.

My mother was the first to stand up, and she reconfigured her shawl, adjusting its length and folds bending to suit her will and keep out the wind. She shooed us along the bike path, toward the parking lot. Pretty soon, we were inside the car, the engine running and the heater roaring to life, and on our way to the dorms. I stared out the window at Lake Shore Drive, and the water was blue, very blue now. Its former black appearance was gone.

Our family was not the most normal of families. I had always thought so, but as we walked back from the lakefront to the parking lot, I realized that not a single jogger, cyclist or even cop had crossed our path while we sat on the concrete in front of the lake's waters. We had spent a half hour at the water's edge without a single interruption, as my father tossed flames into the lake.

Four days later, the Millennium Riot became a reality.

A PLACE CALLED MICTLÁN

"If I should paint my city in red, would you think that I bathed it in sacrificial blood?" – Sodium Chloride Veritas, "Bleed Like Me", *Meditating on the Medusa*, 1995, 5AD Records.

"Nothing about the events that took place on October 4 made sense. For months, we tried to figure out how the riot started and who fired their weapons first. We investigated the question: How could a peaceful march turn so deadly? I was one of the first responders at Millennium Park. I still don't understand the savagery I witnessed." –Interview with Officer Michael Coleridge, *Super Cops: How Technology Changed the War on Terror,* by Haley Phair, Neo Press, 2016.

"The inequities of life: Parents are the first people to teach their sons and daughters shame." – Internet meme. Point of origin circa January 2011.

I fell into a darkness, something denser and thicker than sleep. When I awoke, pain crept down my back and through my jaw, my face and the top of my head. I was a thick knot of hurt, and each breath I took sent deeper pain coursing down my right leg. I tried to move my arms, but they were stiff, gnarled, determined to fight me.

Someone was dragging me along the ground.

The underpass beneath Lake Shore Drive lay before me, and it shrank away as I moved further away. I was moving swiftly, as if riding a sled.

A person draped in shadow dragged me through grass. If I

craned my head toward the sky, I could see his or her head bobbing, like a black bowling ball. We crossed Columbus Drive, and pain ballooned inside me.

All the work I had done to run, to escape the tear gas and the shooting inside Pritzker, was now undone. I was being taken back toward the place where it all started.

We hit a bump on the ground, and my body shook. And then there was worse pain coursing all through my body, in my teeth and inside my guts.

Night was descending, and the orange glow of the streetlights swirled with the sky.

The person carrying me set me down on the ground on my back.

"Listen up!" He shouted into the distance. "No one gets moved until all EMTs move in. Bring the rest and put them here, next to this one. Careful with backs and necks!"

The person got down on his haunches next to me. He kept shouting orders as his gloved hands straightened out my legs beneath me. A hard black helmet and visor kept his face hidden.

Then a strong smell of chemicals and pats on my cheek.

"Stay awake; stay with me," the man in the helmet said. "I'll be right back."

He stood up and ran off into the distance, the letters SWAT glowing on his back as the noise of sirens, shouts and motor vehicles drowned my world out.

The pain in my head had become so intense, I forgot to cry. My pain threshold had always been low, and back then, small bruises and sprains could drive me to tears. But this pain muted me.

The edges of my vision were going fuzzy, and I hoped I could black out, to forget this all, to *unfeel* it all.

Something loosened beneath me, and warmth dampened my jeans. I had wet myself, or I was bleeding, not sure which. I was now on my right side, in a fetal position, wet, and my head and neck on fire in pain.

In the distance, I could see the turtle-shell shape of Pritzker Pavilion, lit by ambulance lights, and I took a moment to glance at the grass around me.

The sight in front of me made me scream.

Just two feet away from me, a tangle of flesh writhed like a living pile of garbage.

The shape the legs and arms made was sloppy, uneven, asymmetrical. Over the top of the heap, I spotted a portion of a torso and a chunk of parka, then one of its arms folded over on its back like a broken doll. The arm poked sharply through the sleeve of the parka, most likely from the break in the bone. The faces at the top were lifeless.

Something moved along the bottom of the pile.

A portion of a face poked out from under the pile. A man's boot pinned the face deep inside the heap, but the eye stared out in wide open fear.

The eyes looked female. The cheeks looked swollen, the pupils frozen in terror. Beneath the chin, I saw her brown arm missing its hand, the wound jagged and ringed in black soot.

Then, a grunt from the mound. It was wordless but filled with pain. Inside its notes, I heard deep sorrow and loss.

"Awwwreh," the voice said.

"AWREEH," it repeated, weeping with every syllable. "SAWWW UHM AWREEH."

My eyes danced in circles, looking for someone to help me, someone to help this person. Her mumbles sent a chill down my neck, and I hoped the red lights washing over the metal skeleton of the park meant that ambulances would come help her soon.

The pain in my body grew white-hot. I swept my hand in front of me to touch the mound of people. I didn't know what I could accomplish by doing this, but I could extend my left arm without triggering more pain.

I felt under the brown boot, and I shoved it aside with the heel of my palm. It didn't move. Beneath, the voice continued.

"AWREEEH."

PUSH.

I used all my shoulder strength to shove the work boot, and the leg inside it finally gave way.

Just twenty inches away from me, I saw her full face. Older than mine, female, and her ebony skin slashed to shreds but somehow still recognizable as human. The eyes flat like paper, barely holding on. Her ragged breaths escaped as steam through her matted hair.

"SAWW UHM AWREEH," the woman said.

There was something in her mouth obstructing her words. I put my index and middle finger between her lips and dug around. I found something firm, and I pulled. A chunk of her tongue, which she had bitten through, fell into my palm. The sorrow in the woman's eyes swelled. Now I could hear her words clearly.

"God, I'm sorry. God, I'm SORRY," the woman said, and she stared out at me, but her eyes looked through me. There was no focus there.

She was dying.

"Gaaa--" she said, and the last plume of steam left her lips.

I had never seen a dead body in my life, and I had never been this close to someone so brutally injured.

I screamed, and I tossed the lump of tongue away from me. My eyes were still making contact with the dead woman's, but now I was sure that she had joined the other three or four bodies on top of her in death.

I could see other injured people like me, laid out flat, some groaning, others silent as stone. The helicopters above me screamed dangerously close to the ground, and the words the woman spoke turned in my mind, downward and in circles, like a spiral.

"God, I'm so sorry," she had said.

Sorry for what? I thought. Sorry for... Sorry for all this death? Sorry for joining the march? Sorry for her sins?

I tasted a bitterness in the back of my throat that reminded me of insecticide, and I realized that traces of the tear gas must still be dispersing through the air. My eyes stung, too, and it hurt to blink. Wind whipped around my legs, and I felt coldness in the spot where I had wet myself. My eyes went there now to my gray jeans, and the stain that ran down their leg. There was no shame left in me, just pain, and a new creeping fear.

The woman's eyes had been online for one moment, and then they weren't. Is this what death was? Just like a circuit moving into the open position?

My father had warned me about these horrors, and I could see him now, seated in the living room, smoking his cigarette, reminding my brother José María and I, that "if you give men weapons, they become butchers."

The word "butcher" had felt crass when my father said it, but I thought of it now, as arms poked through piles of bodies and the metal from the blood scented the air. I didn't need to see the other dead people in this field. I had seen enough. The woman before me had no name, and I didn't want her to have one. The redness of her cheeks invaded the skin, and the matted hair, wrapped in blood around her cranium like a cocoon. It was a shade of red filled with chaos.

The massacre around me felt like it had no meaning, and I feared that this was all there would ever be. Pain, sorrow, the woman's sorrow, her sad apology to God, her body a broken pretzel under her.

I felt a stir in my stomach, and I remembered.

When I was a freshman in high school and José María had only entered sixth grade, he yanked me by the hand to the front porch of our house, away from our father's close eye. José María fished from his backpack one of his treasures — the library books he liked to read. The title, *Devil's Mask: The Richard Speck Story* sprawled in red ink over its grey cover. The nonfiction paperback had gone into great details about Richard Speck, who in 1966 entered a hospital in the South Side late at night and committed atrocious things to eight of the student nurses who lived there.

Eight women, raped and tortured and killed, all at the hands of one man. When I had finished that book, I felt sick inside, as if I had swallowed a dozen needles. I slept in my room with the light on for weeks, and each time I remembered the murders, the sharp pains came back to plunge into my midsection.

The needles of pain solidified. Richard Speck had nothing to do with the massacre before me, but I felt something tenebrous, something sick on this wide lawn beneath the Pritzker Pavilion, and it felt just like on those nights I thought of that awful book my brother handed to me.

The woman's face went slack, and the wind picked up, blowing her hair over her lips.

More voices shouted, and I saw an ambulance creep toward me, driving right over the sidewalk and onto the grass, its red lights dancing like pinwheels. How they whirled.

My vision went grey at the edges, and then I fell into unconsciousness.

My eyes came into focus.

Everything's gone white and blue.

The halogen lights burst in a wash of blue, and they drew sharp shadows over the bed, the machines at my sides, the food on the tray before me, and the pale flowers at the far end of the room. A television hung from the corner like a single black eye staring into the room. The IV in my arm throbbed, and my lips felt dry as dust.

My mother walked into the room, and I felt relief wash my insides.

As far as I could remember, she had always looked this way: rail thin and her hair pulled behind her as if to say, "Let's do this." As she took each step into the room and toward my bed, her eyes widened like saucers, and despair distorted her face into long lines. Her hands flew up to her temples, and her tears came down, the droplets braiding themselves into her hair, staining her blouse and beading up on her leather jacket.

I felt my own tears come up, but something was wrong. I felt a throb inside my chest, and I realized it hurt, a lot, a whole fucking lot, to cry. My face was frozen into a mask. Why couldn't I wince?

My father trailed right behind my mother. He did his best to not let his eyes widen in shock, but I knew by looking at him that whatever had happened to me was a lot to bear.

Every part of my body felt puffy and stiff. I tried moving my arm to prop myself up, but instead, pain greeted me. My parents took places on each side of my bed, their faces hovering over me while machines beeped behind them in a steady rhythm.

"What time is it?" I asked.

"Ten in the morning," my mother said.

She leaned over and kissed my forehead, eclipsing my view of the room. When she pulled away, I could see my father's tears coursing down his face.

She interlaced her hands on mine. I felt the tiny bumps of the rosary beads looped around her wrist as they touched my skin. I couldn't stop staring at my father, though. I had never seen him cry, not like this.

"If it's ten, where's José María?" I said. I really wanted to see my brother.

"José María's at school," my father said.

"But isn't it Saturday?" I said.

"Clara, you've been in the hospital for six days," my mother said.

I looked down at my body in the powder blue sheets. Only my arm poked out. A bruised brown arm. The rest of me lay underneath.

"Pretty soon, your aunts and uncles will be arriving," my mother said. "Your father and I wanted to spend an hour with you alone first."

"Before they take over —" my father said.

"Because they will take over," my mother said.

"They always take over," he said.

My mother checked her phone, ran to the door to see if they were here, and once she was satisfied enough, she came back to the bedside.

"Have a seat, Juliana," my father said. "You know my brothers and sisters never arrive on time. Clara, how do you feel?"

I cracked a smile. It's as close as I could get to laughter.

"Like a champ," I said.

My father chuckled and handed my mother a coffee. From my vantage point, my mom and dad looked small to me, like miniatures of themselves.

"Your injuries..." my mother said. "The doctors say your recovery will be slow."

"Juliana, let's start at the beginning. Clara deserves to know what happened," he said.

My father took shallow breaths, and the wrinkles in his eyes bunched together.

"Dr. Ecker, was just here, before you woke up," he said. "Whoever did this to you broke three ribs. Punctured lung. You also bled internally. That is what almost killed you. The blows to your head fractured your skull in two places. You've suffered a brain injury, and the doctors did their best to work on your left eye. But you may not be able to see out of it again. They have reconstructed your face, and Dr. Ecker assured us their cosmetic surgeon is one of the best."

I raised my left hand to touch my face. The texture of the bandage was soft, feathery. My whole face was a bandage.

This is when the horror movie gets really good, I thought.

José María would like that joke. My parents would not.

"Don't touch it, Clara," my mother said. "The swelling will go down soon. But don't touch it."

"Could have been worse, right?" I said. The face of the woman under the pile of bodies flashed in my mind, and I knew that could have been me, exhaling for the last time on the grass.

My father took out his slender hand from his jean jacket and pointed his index finger at me. His eyes went flat and cold.

"YOU," he said. "You had to go to the march at Millennium. What the fuck where you thinking, Clara? Do you not have a brain up there?"

He tapped the side of his cranium hard enough to make a solid thud. This was a serious matter if he was swearing. He never did so in front of us.

"I was going to tell you," I said.

"When, exactly? At your funeral?"

"I don't even know what happened!" I said.

"The body count right now is at three hundred or so," my mother said.

"Not to mention the thousands of injured," my father said.

"This was the way to make change happen," I said. "I know that, and you know that." It was my turn to push back.

"You think that armed forces gunning down people makes change happen?" my father shouted. "You learned nothing from history, then."

He pulled up a plastic chair, and he propped one leg up on it so I could see it up close. He loomed over the room, his short breaths thickening the air. He tossed his jean jacket over the chair and rolled up his right shirt sleeve. Then he rolled up his pants leg.

I had seen the long scars on his arms and legs before, many times. My father was sixty-three years old, but the strength in his arms and legs gave him the appearance of a man in his forties. The scars bloomed on his skin like dull white veins.

"This is what revolutions bring, Clara. I want you to get a good look at it," he said. "A day doesn't go by where I don't feel pain. Two bullets and a femur fractured in half. And my limp -- you wanted to have a limp, too, didn't you?"

"Adán, calm down," my mother said.

"No, I'm not calming down," he said. He puffed up his chest and my mother sat still as stone. This was their dance. "I thought I could change the world, too."

"Some would argue you did," my mother said.

"And look how Tlatelolco turned out. My country went to the dogs. *Our* country, Juliana."

On October 2 of 1968, my father, together with his older brother Jorge, took the city bus to the plaza of Tlatelolco in Mexico

City. That day, many other students also organized to gather at the plaza to protest the repressions of the Mexican government. This was one of several protests that had taken place in Mexico City. That was a year that was filled with civil action and unrest.

Over that afternoon, ten thousand people, most of them students, gathered. What happened next was unclear, but my father told us helicopters had flown over the plaza, and at some point, someone fired flares from a nearby building.

And then gunfire erupted. The army assaulted the plaza, killing hundreds of people. My father had been sitting on the stone steps of the Aztec ruins at the plaza when the shooting started, and he led Jorge and all of those he could to safety, doing his best to avoid gunfire. As they ran into a nearby apartment building, a bullet shot Jorge clean through the head. Two rounds pulverized my father's leg.

Jorge's death turned my father into a gaunt figure over the decades. There was a pain about Jorge that my mother couldn't describe, and which my father hid from us. To mention Jorge was to summon my father's strongest silence.

I had heard the stories about Tlatelolco from my mother over the years, because my father refused to talk about them. He only ever raised it as leverage during conversations like this one, where he reminded me of how incompetent I was.

My father's eyes shimmered as he bit down on his lips. He rolled down his pants and sleeves again, and he sat down on the chair. His former magnitude was gone now. He shook his head and sank into the white plastic.

"Your mother has something to say to you," he said.

"So you're going to just disengage from this, Adán?" my mother said. "Sure, yell my ear off in the car about working as a team, and now it's just me that's the harbinger of bad news. Mom plays the good cop."

"This was your idea," he said. "So here we go, team. You get to tell Clara the big news."

My mother swept my hair back with her fingers. Unhappy with the results, she pulled out a brush from her purse and ran it in strokes away from my face. Each brushstroke hurt my head a little, but I let her go on. Her eyes went very dark, and she never dropped them from mine.

"They're calling the event the Millennium Riot," she said. "The police and the other troops who were there shot the protesters many times. There are rumors that a few of the protesters in the crowd might have shot back, but it's all on shaky cell phone videos, and the country is in chaos, pointing fingers."

"Really?" I said. I felt a sick dread, but also a sense of victory in my heart.

Change. Was it possible?

"I saw a few clips of the start of the riot," my mother said, "and I had to stop. There was so much gas -- and when the shots started, I kept on thinking, 'She's dead, she's dead.' I had to turn it all off."

"We were very lucky to get you back," my father said. "We had no way of knowing if you were there, buried beneath somebody."

"I escaped the park when the gas canisters hit the stage," I said. "I got pretty far, and then--"

I trailed off. My father had warned me to stay away from the lake, and that's exactly where I had run. My mother's side of the family kept many secrets, and so did my father's. I kept this bit of information from him, at least for now. I couldn't stand to see him lose his temper like he had just moments ago.

"Do you remember who did this to you?" my mother said.

"Men in uniform."

"How many?"

"Not sure. It happened fast. I ran into them, and then I can't remember much after that."

It was true. The dark visors had made the people in uniform anonymous, faceless. And then the baton swung. I did remember the baton.

"I think they were the same people who dragged me back to the pavilion, where they brought the rest of the dead and the injured," I said.

I couldn't keep everything secret. I decided to share this part of the story before my mother had a chance to ask me. "They put me next to a pile of bodies. There was a woman at the bottom and what I saw was horrible--"

I sobbed.

"Clara, you don't have to--" said my father.

"It's okay, Clara," my mother said. "Tell us what you saw. The details matter."

I needed a little space, but my mother would be hurt if I told her not to crowd me in with her body. It was better just to get this over with.

"She was the last one alive under that pile of bodies. Until she wasn't."

"So, you saw her die. That's what you're telling me?" my mother said.

I nodded.

We all fell silent for a moment, and my mother tightened her grip on my hand. My father paced around the room, as if he were formulating something long and intricate. He dug in his brown leather bag. He pulled out a petri dish, which I recognized immediately. He handled these often at his job at the Botanical Gardens, and he kept a few at home for odd projects in our back porch. The dish was lined with clear agar, and white spirals coiled around its surface like the trail left by an ice skater. My father pulled out the tray built into the bed, and he placed the disc in front of me, like some sort of present.

"This is a fungal spiral," he said. He traced the white tendrils over the plastic. "They call this little beauty the Yellow-Gill Damsel. Its job is simple. It thrives off of dead things. Dead wood, dead plant matter, but its favorite is dead flesh. This powerful little fungus spreads itself deep in the ground, and when things go to die, it extends tendrils like these."

The tendrils made me want to puke.

"Don't fear it," my father said. "These swirls, Clara -- this is what death looks like, from a microscopic level. What you saw when that woman died was also death, at a macroscopic level. You saw her take her last breath, and out it went, into the air, possibly in little spirals of air, just like the ones here."

"Hurry," my mother said, and she brandished her phone in my father's general direction. "Dolores texted to say she'll be here within minutes. Clara, be sure to keep your mouth shut when your aunt gets here."

The odor from the petri dish corkscrewed its sweet and musty scent into my nose.

"Thinking about that dead woman is making me sick, Dad," I said. "I wish you would take this thing away."

"That's the whole point, Clara," he said. "I'm afraid I can't. After the riot, the woman that died in front of you, the hospital--I am sure you think morbid events are following you. This very scent is shadowing you."

"No, I think you're putting morbid thoughts in my head."

"That's my girl," my father said. "You don't let anyone push you around."

"Well, I'm pushing this fungus back *to* you," I said, and I put it back in his bag, which lay on the bed. It took me some time to do this, because my arm still ached, but I did it without his help. When I was done, my father reached inside the bag and placed it back on his lap.

I knew we could go on forever like this, taunting each other.

My father stopped pushing the dish back.

"Do you recall the early hours of the morning of your thirteenth birthday?" he said.

"Not really, no. Well, let me think about it," I said.

I thought hard. I still shared a room with José María back then, and my father had painted the walls bright green so we could have a color that suited us both. I went back to that memory, and a small fragment appeared, like a glint of metal inside a cave.

I remembered waking up in the middle of the night, and I had looked at the clock. José María lay curled into a ball, snoring. It was about 4 a.m. My stomach stirred with hunger pangs, and my mouth was dry. At the far end of the room, a light flickered. Two figures sat in the far end of my bedroom, and they watched me from the corner.

I remember wanting to scream.

My parents, my parents--now I remember. They were there with me.

They sat side by side, lit by the glow of a veladora candle. My father waved at me, smiling, and I felt confusion, shock and fear.

"Go back to bed, Clara; there's still more time to sleep," my father had said. We lived in Little Village, where street noise lasted all night, but I remember that night had actually been quiet.

My mother had wrapped her shawl around her shoulders and tucked me back in bed. I wanted to ask what they were doing here, but I was mute, drowsy, inert.

This was not a happy birthday memory, no sir.

My mother had leaned forward into the soft glow of the candlelight.

"When you step inside the Palace of the Skulls, just remember we're always with you," my mother had said.

She had stood up then, and she crossed the room with an odd

grace, as if her feet were being carried by a gust of wind. Her face above mine had calmed my fears a bit. I felt her dry kiss on my forehead, and then I was dissolving into deep sleep again. That cocoon of nothingness that arrives with sleep took over me.

When you step inside the Palace of the Skulls.

When you step inside the Palace of the Skulls.

When you step inside the Palace of the Skulls.

Surely this had just been a dream.

Today was the first time the memory had sprang back into my hands, like a found object.

"That morning, I had a scary dream," I said. "I woke up and you two were in the room with me. You tucked me back into bed."

My mother nodded toward my father in silent approval. He looked eager now, excited. If he could, he would have lit a cigarette. He liked to celebrate with smoke.

"It wasn't a dream. We were actually there with you," my father said. "That night was as important as the day you were born. That night, you survived a rite of passage."

"Come again?" I said.

"A rite of passage," my mother said.

"It was actually your *second* rite of passage, Clara," my father said.

"There's more than one," my mom said.

"The first one is birth itself," my father said. "When a baby is born and arrives into the world alive and breathing, the first rite is complete. The child has survived the emergence from the matter of the universe and exits the womb through the mother."

"And the second one – oh — this is what you talked about. The night of seeking —" I said.

"So she *does* remember," my father said to my mother.

In our family, we began to leave childhood behind at thirteen, but according to my father, true adulthood didn't arrive until the twenty-sixth year.

"José Maria also passed this rite when he was thirteen," my mother said. "It begins in the middle of the night, when the sun is on the other side of the planet. It's very simple. During that night, a dream arrives. Then the rite begins inside a dream."

My father nodded, and my mother continued.

"That night, we watched over you while you dreamt. We were there to protect you. That's what all parents have to do for their children on the thirteenth year. Your dream journey is all your own of course, and no parent can accompany the child *inside* the dream. We simply wait at the bedside, making sure the children are physically unharmed.

"That night you woke up from sleep — just for a minute or so. An interruption like this is normal, but it was our job to make sure you went back to sleep, to make sure you completed your task."

"Which is...?" I was so damn impatient already.

"The task on the thirteenth year -- is the one where each person goes out and seeks his or her tonal. The search can lead you to many places, many of them very dangerous."

My tonal.

I hadn't heard that word in many years. This word also came back to me, like a message in a bottle.

Tonal.

I remembered the tonal, in stories that my father told me about his mother in Oaxaca, and stories of his uncles' travels in the jungles of the Yucatán. All the stories led back to the same word: tonal.

The tonal was an animal or symbol that corresponded to each person's birthday. Some people got the deer, some got water, and some the monkey. There were twenty in total. These had always been the little stories my mother and father told me growing up, but it had been years since they had mentioned *tonal* in my presence.

"And if I went out to find my tonal, then what was it?" I said. I had always wished for the rabbit.

"That is the problem," my father said. "You came back without one. Your mother and I never saw one come back to the room with you."

"Is that like having no soul?" I said.

My father stared out the windows into downtown Chicago and cried in silence.

I tried sitting up. My heart was racing and the aches in my back were roaring back to life.

"Sit back," my mother said. "You're not well enough to sit up yet."

"I want José María here right now," I said. "I'm *not* liking this conversation."

It was true. José María was nothing close to being what I called a "normal," but at least he could corroborate the utter weirdness in our family. I could surely use his backup now. I needed him here to bring some sanity into the room.

"Timing is not on our side," my father said, "The painkillers they are giving you interfere with your lucidity. Normally, we would explain all this history to you without the intrusion of a single foreign chemical in your body. But your mother and I don't have a lot of time."

"Your father and I--" my mother added.

"We're worried you're headed in a very wrong direction," my father interrupted. "Joining the OLF and going to the protest was only a first step. I'm worried that you carry not just my stubbornness, but also my temper, and maybe even my bad luck. I have to ask you to stop your involvement with the OLF."

"What do you know about OLF?" I said. "You'd rather have me stay complacent and superficial."

"These are the same people that hacked the 911 phone system when the Millennium riot started. That disruption kept ambulances from arriving on time. People died as result. Clara, before you fight me on this, you need to get the whole story--"

"I don't need anything."

"They say that the OLF has put a contract out on the city politicians. This information's coming directly from OLF. Do you think you're not going to be bring more violence and anarchy about?"

"What does this have to do with the tonal, anyway, Dad? Get to the point."

My father took a seat on the bed. My mother pulled her chair closer to where I lay, her chin almost touching the rail.

"That night," my mother said, "we saw you go into deep sleep to find your tonal, but when you returned, something was different. You looked afraid, stunned. You did not look happy. That's how we knew you didn't find it. If you had been successful, you would have told us about your animal over the next day, as all children do during the rite.

"Instead, you brought something else back. As far as your father and I know, no one has ever brought anyone, or anything, back during the journey. It's unheard of. Finding the tonal happens in the dream, and the rite ends in a child understanding the knowledge of her tonal. While we waited in your room, we saw this *other thing* that came through. It stared at us through windows. We couldn't make out its size or its shape, except for two eyes that shone like headlights on the highway. The eyes--Clara--they were the size of dinner plates, lit from within. Whatever owned those eyes did not like us, and it fixated on you."

"I don't believe any of this," I said.

"You don't have to," my mother said. "You get to make up your own mind. All you have to do is hear us out."

It had always been this way in our family. Our parents just gave us what they knew and what they believed. But it was up to me and José María to make up our minds. This was the very reason why I still didn't believe in half the tales from the Bible, while they did.

My father dragged out a green disc from his leather bag. It was nothing but a tangle of weeds, coiled like a snail's shell.

"Another fungus?" I said.

"Better," he said.

He drew his finger along its surface.

"We all take the trip to find the tonal," he said. "We take the trip the day we're born, when we are thirteen and when we are twenty-six. On the 26th year we see the tonal and embrace it, whether it's a rabbit, a crocodile or a jaguar. This is how we become full adults. That's three trips from birth.

"Your first trip would be akin to this origin point on this piece of lichen. It's where things begin. They say that lichen like this one have access to the mysteries of the universe--sort of like a key--but it's never worked for me. What's important is the shape that you see here. The second trip is further along the edges here, where the texture is still smooth. When you brought back that creature at the age of thirteen, we didn't know what it meant. But I am afraid I have learned it. You are living close, very close, to death and violence, Clara, and I am worried that you are actually enjoying the chaos. I am worried that the lines that you are creating are closely intertwined with something with terrible and cruel intentions. You like blood."

Get off my case.

I'm so offended.

"You're saying I got...contaminated?" I said.

My father shrugged, shook his head.

"Something has to change in order to cleanse you," he said.

"Your father's proposing that you take drastic measures, Clara," my mother said. Sadness tinted her voice. "He and I both think you need to take your third trip early. Seven years early."

No one spoke for a few moments. The machines at my bedside punctuated time with their chirps.

"Because the thing you brought with you on your thirteenth year--" my mother said, "It was from Mictlán."

Mictlán. That was another word I hadn't heard in years.

A day of found objects. Will the fun ever stop?

I sighed.

"But I thought it was just an old fairy tale," I said.

"Old…but a story with legs," my father said. "What we know about Mictlán we know from what my grandparents taught me, and what they learned from their grandparents, and on and on."

"And I only learned it from your father when I married him," my mother said.

"Direct knowledge of Mictlán is forbidden," he said. "And yet, something drew itself to you when you sought your tonal. I suspect you might have visited Mictlán in your thirteenth-year dreams. It's unusual, but possible. I have lived in anxiety for the past six years, wondering why this happened and where your mother and I went wrong."

Suddenly, I wanted some more hardcore drugs so I could just tune all of this out.

Give me all the drugs, somebody.

But my mom and dad were relentless.

"Cleansing is possible," my mother said. "Handling this type of creature—taming this kind of creature--can only be done by an adult," my mother said. "And you are not an adult yet."

"Far from it," my father spat. "Immature and obstinate."

Heat rose in my face, and I clutched the bedsheets with rage. All the years in school, the work I did for social justice, the volunteering, these meant nothing to these people I called my parents. Perfect grades and part-time jobs--they were nothing, nothing, nothing.

But I am adult. So much more adult than you, with your old ideas and creepy ways.

"I don't want to be here anymore," I said. I was not used to talking to my parents in such a terse manner, but my tongue moved faster than my heart. "Get out of the room. And take your new age superstitions with you."

"See, Juliana?" my father said, his voice gathering steam. My mother started gathering her things as he hovered over her. "I told you this was going to happen. Everything we do for these two, they just toss it aside."

My mother had placed my cell phone next to the bed, and I picked it up, oblivious to my parents' departure, texting José María as fast as I could.

"They've gone completely batshit," I texted him.

My mother and father reached the door.

"Clara, we'll be gone for a couple of hours, but we'll be back with the rest of the family. We'll have more time to talk in the next week or so. Just be ready for the journey. Won't be easy."

Get the fuck out already.

The door shut, and I let out a huge sigh of relief.

That was perhaps the most awkward moment I had ever lived through.

None of this was fair. My body was broken, and my face hurt even through the veil of painkillers. In all this time, it hadn't occurred to me to look at myself. There, along the bottom row of icons, was the camera app on my phone. If I pointed it at myself, I'd get a glimpse of my bandaged face.

I brought the phone up into the air, and I held it there, my hand shaking. In the end, I didn't have the heart to tap the icon.

I set the phone down on the blanket and resented the lack of clarity in my head. Painkillers and fairy tales--these two things made a deadly combination. Why mess with my head? Why? And my father--shouldn't he have thought better of what he said to me about my thirteenth birthday? Why have me recall a memory that felt so hazy, so fragile? It was just a dream, anyway. Just a dream of my parents with a candle in the room on the day of my birthday.

They couldn't just let it rest. What was their urgency? They couldn't wait till I got out of the hospital.

I wanted to get back up from this bed, to heal, so I could get back to the real world. To learn what exactly took place in Millennium Park and, more importantly, what was next.

No response yet from my brother on my phone, but as I flipped toward the bottom of the inbox, I found dozens and dozens of unread messages.

Messages from members of our chapter of the OLF. Dozens of messages from strangers that knew I had been hospitalized, wishing me well. These people identified me by my screen name, "She-Ra" on the Internet forums and Twitter. I didn't so feel alone. I had a lot to catch up on and lots to plan. For the next few hours, I could forget about my parents and come back to reality, where I could touch solid matter, where action was still needed.

I pieced a few things together. The five thousand protesters at Millennium had pushed the lawn's capacity to the brim, and the use of SWAT and military forces had actually been quite routine. In fact, the deployment had looked very similar to that of the May 2012 NATO protests, also in Chicago. According to reports about the Millennium Riot, gunshots had been fired at 4:54 p.m. The media reports said the first shots came from armed protesters in the center of the pavilion, while Twitter reports and bloggers pointed to the sound in the video clips to put blame on the troops situated on the north side of the park, behind the stage of the pavilion. The rest of it--the thousands of bodies trapped and trampled, the use of force from the SWAT teams and the police--was more or less as I remembered.

The mayor's "sit down and shut up" ordinance from 2012 was already kicking into place. Those who could be identified in the video footage were already seeking damages against any organizations that took part in the protest, while the investigations continued. I forgot to ask my parents if the investigators were trying to reach me, but I figured if that was the case, I would know soon.

I saved several images into my camera roll so I could take a better look. An aerial view of the park: It was a high-resolution image that I could pinch and zoom as I needed. Here I could see the places where the aftermath took place. There, along the southern edge of the Pritzker Pavilion, the first ambulances began to treat the chemical burns form the tear gas, and to provide aid to those who had been shot and injured. There, in the middle, was the worst chaos. And then up on the northern shoulder of the pavilion, a span of grass where the armed troops laid out the bodies of the dead.

I stared at this diagram for some time, and I scrolled back, going back to look at the photos of these piles of the dead. The twisted feet, the broken fingers and the bloody heads were so familiar to me now.

That flat patch of grass was the place where I had been dragged.

This was a path carved out in dead bodies, laid out by troops and armed cops. They had placed me in the same zone as the dead.

When you step inside the Palace of the Skulls.

When you step inside the Palace of the Skulls.

When you step inside the Palace of the Skulls.

I let go of my phone and it hit the floor with a dull crack. I was breathing fast, and sweating under the hospital gown. I fought back the urge to vomit.

When you step inside the Palace of the Skulls, my mother had said.

When you step inside the Palace of the Skulls, my mother had warned me.

I considered calling my parents now, to tell them to come back. I would eat my words, but seeing them might calm me down. I was scared. My finger lay on the “call” button, but I never tapped it.

There, on the blanket, lay the coiled lichen my father brought with him. I ran my fingers over it, grasping it with both hands like a tiny steering wheel. Its edges were pebbled, like lizard skin. I turned and turned it in my hand, knowing that the repetitive motion might help me bring my breathing back to normal.

As I spun the lichen, a damp taste filled my mouth. It arrived from the front of my tongue, filling my tongue ad my palate with its oily scent. It was a smell unlike any I had known before, though some of its notes were easy to identify. I tasted copper and sulfur, and a sick sweetness like fruit gone bad. It was a taste that reminded me of shit, but perhaps worse. This was the taste of graves and swamps, and the taste of burning human hair. The tighter I gripped the coil, the more intense the smell became.

I retched, and pain exploded in my back and in my head. I tossed the coil of lichen at the hospital curtains. As soon as it was out of contact with my hands, the taste of rotted meat vanished from my mouth.

I was panting again, while my heart sought to explode from my chest.

A nurse showed up at the door.

"Everything all right?" she said. " I thought I heard something."

"You did," I said. "I dropped my phone. Can you get it for me?"

"Thank you," I said as she slid it onto my palm.

Before she could make it out of the room, I was already typing with fury into the phone, scouring through search engines for the word "Mictlán."

RHINOCEROS

"About the stele that stands at the Plaza of the Three Cultures in Mexico City: It exists squeezed between the church of Santiago de Tlatelolco, rows of mid-rise apartment buildings, and the ruins of the Aztec empire. The stele pushes itself up from the ground like a magical object, filled with men's words and runes that are readable to those of us who speak Spanish. In this stele, we recognize that this plaza was a place of life, and much death. Mexico's ancient marketplace was once converted into a place of violence during the Tlatelolco Massacre of 1968. Today it flourishes as the home of the twenty-first-century Mexico. It is in this very spot that the masked identity of the Mexican people lies hidden, yet also exposed through the power of language." –Architect Carlo Fuente, *Journal of Architecture and Design*, Vol. 56, May, 2012. p.89.

"In the name of the father, the son and the holy ghost. Once your authority, now your parasitic host. Motherfuckers grab their scepter and pull the trigger." –Arkangel, "Lyra Destroys a Shrunken God", *The Violet Album*, 2008, Reckless Records.

"She caught the shawl as she spoke, and looked about for the owner. In another moment, the White Queen came running wildly through the wood, with both arms stretched out wide, as if she were flying, and Alice very civilly went to meet her with the shawl." –Lewis Carroll, *Through the Looking Glass*, 1871.

I ran my card through the reader, and I walked up to the platform to wait for my train. The wind whipped my face, and my hair lashed my skin. It felt good.

This is my strange new skin, and it takes some getting used to.

The Loyola stop on the red line was the place that served as my entry point into other parts of the city. It wasn't the prettiest of stations, but the sun came down in fat yellow beams in the late afternoon.

I was free of the hospital, able to breathe the city air. I wore my lucky brown boots and a plaid skirt that matched my vintage blouse. My makeup was a simple gash of black across my eyelash line and a layer of mascara. I could walk now, though many spots across my back and my legs were still tender to the touch.

I sat near the sliding doors. In my mouth, the taste of Edgar's mouthwash.

The Millennium Riot was weeks behind me now, and since then, I had crept up to Edgar's dorm room in the early mornings, when it was still dark out. His roommate slept right through my knocks at his door. Edgar would open the door, his face a moon in the dark of his room, his boxers hanging low on his hips and the thatch of hair on his chest wild like reeds.

Once I was inside his bunk, the sex was short, sweet, pungent. The pain in my back faded away when I came, and I kept my panting short and shallow so we wouldn't wake up his roommate.

I had been visiting his dorm room in this manner for weeks.

In those moments before the sun came up, we didn't talk about what happened at the Millennium Riot. We didn't talk about the media frenzy around us, and we didn't talk about the heightened security around the campus. Edgar was no longer part of our chapter of the OLF, and I didn't press him for details why.

Today had been different, though. When we finished, and he lay in my armpit, sweating, I decided to ask him to talk about what happened. I needed us to talk.

I asked him what he remembered from the Millennium Riot, but when I did, he just stared at me.

"How dare you ask me?" he said. His body stiffened with anger.

He's trying to simply forget.

It was fine by me. I didn't ask any further. Once was enough today. I left.

I went to my classes later in the morning, then to my job at the library for a couple of hours. At dinnertime, in the dining hall, I ran into Edgar again. He was smiling again.

He looks happy. What a change.

"Maybe we could go to a movie? I can introduce you to my

friends in crew," he said. "We can all hang out."

I had no idea where he got this idea that we could start "hanging out". We no longer socialized anywhere--not in the dorms, not in class. This was new.

"I'd rather not," I said.

"But why? We get together virtually every day. We're always doing *that* together."

Not as together as you think.

"Oh, that," I said.

"I'm fine with the way things are right now," I said.

"You mean where you just use me for sex and then you leave me?"

"I don't know how to answer to that."

"I know things haven't been easy since what happened--but we can still be close, Clara."

"It's just sex," I said.

"Just sex," Edgar said, as he finished a glass of soda. He went up to the self-serve machine for a refill. When he was done, he walked past my table – his smile was gone -- and went to sit on the other side of the dining hall, his back turned away from me.

Maybe when he walked away, he called me a whore under his breath, but I knew that in the past two weeks, I had lost interest in what I had imagined to be my infatuation with him. Before the Millennium riot, I had trailed Edgar like a shadow through the lecture halls, the student union and dorm hallways, but now, I could only think about Mictlán and whatever I could learn about it.

I needed to keep some distance from Edgar myself, now that I had pieced together some of the events of the riot.

I had learned that when we got separated as we held hands, Edgar too ran off to find an exit from the rounds that were being fired in the Pritzker Pavilion, and he successfully ran onto the street before the tear gas arrived. Police officers arrested him on the spot, but he was released later that night. He had survived unscathed by the violence. He never visited me in the hospital, and when I returned to campus, I expected to find messages from him.

There were none.

I learned he had quit the Occupy Liberation Front altogether. He removed my name, as well as that of many others in OLF, from his Facebook account. I asked him in the dorm one day how we had lost hand contact and become separated during the riot, but all he said was "You were the one that let go of my hand, Clara."

Those words hurt me, but the further I pressed him to talk, the further away he moved.

Had I been dumped? Or had nothing been there between us in the first place? And why did Edgar think that my morning visits meant so much?

Maybe I really was a whore. I considered this idea for a second, then I laughed to myself. Of course I was not. But I would probably never find out what Edgar really felt for me.

During my return to campus, I had dealt with police interviews and my classwork, as well as short meetings at our OLF chapter. Our attendance was not the same anymore. Besides Edgar, we lost forty other members. I knew fear kept many of us away, but even after what had happened, I wasn't going to give up. In fact, I knew that the Millennium Riot only confirmed for me my path. I had to continue with OLF and the movement.

I ignored my coursework, putting off my reading and skipping discussion sections. I spent my time instead in a corner of the library, deep in a sea of information. In the mornings, I read every news post about the OLF and the Millennium riot investigation.

I read every blog and every tweet, and watched all the videos I could about the riot and its aftermath. I stayed up till four in the morning, reading, absorbing, and reading some more.

The latest death count was 309, and the debate over who shot first was not over. Those protesters who had brought firearms were either dead or in custody, and a federal investigation was underway.

At night, I slept in pain, my back aching and my skin breaking out in a sweat. When I slept, it was only for a couple of hours. I avoided taking too many painkillers. I had always disliked pills, but as a result, I stared out of my room into the orange-black glow of the city lights and cuddled my insomnia. My roommate Morgan slept soundly, as usual. Fog rolled over the bedroom window each night, and the darkness pressed behind it. Winter was approaching.

But I had still wanted and needed sex. The mornings with Edgar helped me start my day; they helped me feel like I was free, like there were no shadows pressing down on me through the sky and no blades of sharp pain running down my spine and inside my skull.

The train stations whizzed past me, and a gush of cold air filled the subway car each time the sliding doors slid open. On the streets below, the police cars saturated traffic. Since the riots, all eyes were on Chicago, and it was now common for anyone to get stopped and searched during all hours of the day.

Thorndale, Bryn Mawr, Berwyn and finally Lawrence. I had arrived at my destination.

I walked down the greasy stairs and turned onto the street. It was much too early for the doors to open, but there, lined up around the corner from the entrance of the Aragon Ballroom, a hundred fans sat with their backs against the wall, checking their phones, complaining about the wind and the cold, anticipating their entrance into the concert hall. The Aragon eclipsed the whole block with its Moorish architecture style and the deep layers of soot and grime that had tarnished it over the years.

As I walked up to the line to look for my brother, I was already regretting my clothing choices. These were the most hardcore Rhinoceros fans, and here I was, caught in the cross hairs of the fashionistas who waited in line. I didn't have any tattoos to speak of, and the indigo of my blouse and the red checkered pattern of my skirt were all wrong for this crowd. It was too late to go back home and change. It was what it was. I walked quickly down the line, avoiding the pressure of the eyes that bore down on me.

Three fourths of the way back in line, I spotted my brother José María. I had been waiting three weeks for this moment, where he and I could see each other alone, away from our parents' house, and I away from campus.

José María smoked a cigarette under his hoodie, letting out big gulps of smoke, one leg kicked out directly in front of him, the other one bent so he could rest his cell phone on top of it in case. He looked up at me with wet, red eyes. He was high already.

"Grab a seat, reina," He said. That's what my father called me when I was a little kid. *Queen.* Hadn't heard that in a while.

"How much longer till they let us in?" I asked.

"About another hour and a half. This way, we'll be at the very front."

"That's a lot of work just to see some dinosaurs."

"Hey, it's Rhinoceros. Some things are worth lining up for."

Rhinoceros had been playing the Aragon for decades now, and José María had never missed any of their Chicago stops, at least since our parents had allowed him to attend concerts. And that wasn't very long ago—it was barely a year. He was allowed to go if I went with him, and that meant I got to see a lot of shows.

"How much do I owe you?" I said.

"Just gimme thirty," he said.

I handed him three tens. I had ninety minutes, maybe a little more, if we could chat a little inside the Aragon.

"I thought it would take me an eternity to be able to talk to you without Mom and Dad poking in," I said.

"It's no problem; if you want, I can text Dad to turn right around. He just dropped me off thirty minutes ago. He can come hang with us all night," José María said, giggling, threatening to text on his phone.

Oh god, no. Please don't call Dad over here. I'll die.

"Okay, in all seriousness. Let me show you something. Okay?" I said.

I pulled out my phone and brought up all the saved searches I had found online, but also the academic materials I had gathered at the university library since I had been released from the hospital. I found a lot of information, but I organized it as best I could in a folder, because I wasn't really sure if any of it was useful for what I needed. I handed my brother the phone, and he scanned for almost twenty minutes until he handed the phone back to me. He lit up a cigarette and offered me one. I passed.

"So?" I said.

"So what? You know how to Google. Congratulations to you, Stephen Hawking." José María flourished his right hand and took a small bow in my direction. His sleek eyebrows and his hoodie, his thin stubble—they reminded me of a medieval court jester. He would never, ever stop making fun of me, as long as we lived. With a sigh, I turned the phone's screen back in his direction.

"Did Mom and Dad talk to you about their visit to my hospital room?"

"Not really," he said. "Mom stayed up crying every night, and during the whole time you were in the hospital, Dad went up to the attic and reorganized the whole thing. He put every book and tchotchke we have up there into little plastic crates, and he labeled every single one of them. He did this over and over, a real shitload. He did a good job, just like a psycho should, but no, he didn't say anything, either."

"José María, I am still having nightmares about the Millennium

Riot. The reporters won't stop calling me, and they show up on campus, looking for those of us who were there. And my face--"

"What about it?"

José María had never been prone to coddle me when it came to my looks. He awaited my answer.

"I don't look the same. Probably never will. Feels ugly."

He nodded.

"What does your face have to do with any of this?" my brother said.

"Well, you're not going to believe me until I show you, so take a look here, at this image I pulled up on the World Digital Library."

"Ah, you went and dug up the Florentine Codex. Nice!"

José María sat up straight, letting the wall support him. He pulled his hoodie back and spikes of his hair rose into standing, while the longer locks fell back . He grabbed the phone from me.

"The Florentine codex is cool as shit."

"It talks about Mictlán. That's why I wanted to talk to you while it's just the two of us."

"Awww... I thought you came out to see Rhinoceros with me because you recognize a person with great taste. You bitch!"

"Relax, I'm here for the show, too. But you're the only person who obsesses this much about...well, this stuff."

This stuff. Legends of gods, statues bathed in sacrificial blood, deities whose internal organs fell out of their stomachs like a Hannibal Lecter trophy. These were stories of old rituals, superstitious crap.

Three weeks ago, in my hospital bed, my parents had warned me about a place called Mictlán. Up until then, they had never mentioned the word much, except in nighttime tales. Or in some books in their library in our small living room. But that wasn't enough information.

I had started my searches in the university library. I learned Mictlán was the realm of the dead in the times of the Aztecs, a place ruled by the two lords, the god and goddess of death, blood, and sacrificial tribute. Mictlán was the place where souls were said to travel when they left this world.

In the end I found out almost too much information. It was more I knew what to do with. There was so much of it--archeological evidence, scholarly work, Buzzfeed trash--that by the time I finished my research, I felt like I had not accomplished much at all. And as I stayed up at night in the library reading abstracts, I realized I should have consulted José María in the first place.

"Mictlán is the shiiiiit," he said. "It's supposed to have mountains made of poisonous spikes and rivers swimming with monsters. Hades has nothing on this place. It's about as *secret* as you can get. After all, you have to kick the can if you want to see it." He laughed, and his laughter infected me with giggles, even though I was the sober one. Each time we looked at each other, we snorted again. When we were done, José María put his finger on the screen.

"That guy right there is the king - Mictlantecuhtli. He's got this sick blade coming right out of his skull face. He's got a wife, too, and together they govern the place. So fucking dope!"

The figure of this god, whose name meant the Lord of Mictlán, showed a reclining figure with a human skull instead of a face made of flesh. His headdress rose into the sky with bird feathers, and a bloody obsidian blade rose jutted the nostrils in his skull face.

It really meant nothing to me. José María had moved toward all things Aztec, Olmec, Teotihuacán and Maya since he was a kid, but I had been more interested in history, civics classes and math--the things grounded in tangible reality. I preferred the real world.

Tiananmen Square, the crimes of Pol Pot, the civil rights riots--those were concepts I could operate on. And all through the years, José María lived in his little bubble of mythology books, vampire novels and comics. But that's what made my little brother my little brother. The purveyor of all that was weird.

The image we were both staring at was a page from the Florentine Codex, created in the sixteenth century, and its creator, friar Bernardino de Sahagún, had chronicled the beliefs and habits of the Aztecs during their early conquest. In this particular image, a half dozen men surrounded a woman in a grassy field, while a warrior in headdress brandished a club. In the background, green mountains filled the horizon. Floating shapes like ghosts made of stone floated in the air.

"So, I can't stop thinking about this image, and here's why. That day at the hospital, Mom and Dad said there's something wrong with me. That I have been contaminated by something that happened when I was thirteen. This passage describes a grassy field drenched in death, and for some reason it reminds me the Millennium Riot. Mom and Dad said that I brought something full of death back with me. A creature."

José María whistled. He stretched his legs and the grin on his face lit up from ear to ear.

"Wow...Dad's dealer must have gotten him the really good shit."

"You know Dad doesn't smoke. I am serious. They really said this. This is why I was texting you so much over the past couple of weeks. I wanted to talk to you, to see if they mentioned any of this before."

"All they've talked about is your reconstructive surgery and uncle Teo's divorce. Oh, and Mari's ugly baby. Well, that and the mayor cracking down on OLF after the riots; there's that, too. But they don't mention you that much, not that way."

"Every time I look at this picture, with that warrior and his club—my heart begins to race so fast, I think I'm going to die. If I stare at it too long, I feel that panic of what happened in Millennium Park. Why, José María?"

"Those who make the trip to the city of Mictlán don't come back," my brother said. "That's just the way it works. Maybe you're worried about death, after what happened. Maybe this isn't so literal. Maybe our parents just want you to get more in touch with our roots."

Roots feel so far away. My Spanish is barely remedial. I don't even know how to pronounce some of the names of the places and things in this research. Touching roots is a sad understatement.

"That's just it," I said. "Mom and Dad said I have to go on a trip to Mictlán. To reach adulthood. José María, have you ever heard the phrase 'When you step inside the Palace of Skulls'?"

José María considered my words, and he glanced at me sideways, as if I were the one who was high on weed.

"You know, I'm not going to answer that quite yet. Mostly because I think I have heard the phrase, but I can't remember exactly where. But I can help you dig up info on the place. I'll look it up when I get home tonight. Of course, some of the stories conflict, and some details are lost with the people who died in the colonization of the New World. And one more thing--shouldn't you be consulting with some archeologist professor at school? I'm only fifteen, remember?"

"This stuff is so weird that I am embarrassed to bring it up to anyone. All I have done is pull up my own searches. And you are the one that's always reading up on this. You have to help me."

My brother and I had been sitting on the cold pavement for so long, we were going numb. We faced a gray wall that was part of the elevated tracks of the train, and several people had been walking up and down the line, chatting with friends, finding the end of the line or simply killing their boredom with a cigarette. Scalpers orbited the block, too, asking who needed tickets for the show. I was so focused on what my brother was saying that I never noticed the pair of workman's boots stop right next to where we sat.

"After all this time, you fuckers insist on this socialist shit, still?"

The owner of the boots was a short man, packed with muscle, his face taut with tension. He wore a Rhinoceros baseball cap and a flannel shirt.

I knew immediately he was referring to me. I wore an OLF armband on my left shoulder. It was a logo-less design, just white letters on a black background, but unmistakable. The armband usually sparked a lot of conversations around campus, but it didn't occur to me that it would anger someone like this outside the Aragon.

"Hey, we didn't come here to get yelled at," José María said. "We're just hanging out."

"All our taxpayer money gets sunk into doubling up on cops and riot gear, thanks to pieces of shit like the OLF, man. It all starts with the stupid fucks that join in on this shit. Do you really think the OLF is looking out for you?"

I had to say something. I remained seated, though I felt awkward. But I was scared of standing up. What if he started a shoving match, or worse? I remembered the pain I had felt for days inside my bones from being beaten physically. The man in the work boots looked ready to lunge, his thick neck puffed like a cobra.

"Have you looked around this place recently?" I said. "The city is close to being insolvent, and we've got one of the worst murder rates in the country. And our school system's going down the hole and fast. You have faith in the traditional way of doing things, then?"

"This is the same shit I get from all of you fucking hipsters every time I bring this subject up. We wouldn't have this shit if you all you losers just got jobs and we kept illegals from stealing jobs."

José María stood up. I dreaded this moment already.

"You want to watch what you say," he said.

The man in the work boots crossed his arms and laughed in José María's face. He texted on his phone for a second and laughed at us again. "Fucking beaners. I'm sending YOU my damn tax bill next time it arrives."

The man peeled away toward the end of the line, laughing at us as he walked away.

My heart was racing, and the scars inside my cheeks hurt. My back pulsed with electricity.

"I get so angry, and yet I never know the right thing to say," I said.

"Forget it," José María said. "We came here for the show. Look, they are opening the doors. Tell me the rest of what we were talking about inside."

As the line of concertgoers went through the glass doors of the Aragon, I looked over my shoulder to see if I could spot the man in the work boots. He was nowhere to be seen. I felt as if he was somewhere near, watching us. As I handed over my ticket at the door, my hand shook uncontrollably, like the hand of an old person.

"Relax, Clara," José María said off to my left as security searched him. "You look like you've seen a ghost. When we get upstairs, I'll tell you how to get to Mictlán."

Suddenly, the cavernous entrance of the Aragon, with its Spanish motifs, felt like a suffocating tomb. I put my hand on the OLF band on my jacket and considered taking it off, but I knew José María wouldn't let me. I walked through the turnstile. As we joined the hundreds of people in line in the concert hall, I got the distinct sensation that whatever I felt was watching me was not the man in the brown work boots. I was being watched by something or someone feral and dark. I felt an ache come over my joints and face, and it took me several seconds to get my heart rate down through heavy breathing. If I could have bought a beer, I would have.

José María waited for me at the bottom of the double staircase, and we ascended into the dark together.

My brother and I pressed our bodies against cold metal, and

hundreds of bodies closed in behind our backs. We had nowhere to go. This space, our little slice of room right by the stage, was going to be ours for a while, and though other conversations surrounded us with noise, I felt like we had the best privacy I could ask for. This was the anonymity of the city, and I don't know why it hadn't occurred to me earlier to hold important meetings in the pit of the Aragon in between acts while surrounded by thousands of people.

José María pulled out his wallet and unfolded an old concert flier. The image at its center showed a gaping maw filled with white teeth. Inside the cavernous mouth, small stalactites shot upward toward the creature's palate. I looked closer and noticed those stalactites were buildings--little skyscrapers. There was a tiny city in that predator's mouth. Above it, in ragged white script, it read "Arkangel: Murderous Tour, 2009" The lower half of the flyer showed stops in North America, Europe and Latin America. José Maria turned it over and drew a single vertical tube. On the tube, he plotted a single black dot, and labeled it "Earth." Above the dot, he plotted thirteen empty circles, evenly spaced. Below, he drew nine more empty circles, pointing downward.

"It works like this," José María said. "These stories go way further back than the Aztecs. The civilizations before, like the Toltecs and the Teotihuacans, were, in my opinion, even wiser and more interesting than the Aztecs. They had notions about what else was out there in the galaxy and how the planets moved. And they had a very detailed religious belief about the universe. In general, it went like this: There are thirteen levels in the overworld and nine levels in the underworld. The numbers sometimes vary, depending on the source, but what you need to know is that there are nine levels in Mictlán, the world of the dead. The end of the journey is the city of Mictlán. Souls travel down through all nine to meet the lords of death. So, when Mom and Dad talked to you, did they get specific about what they meant by 'going there'?"

I shook my head.

"They want me to take a leave of absence from school so they can train me for the trip. There's no way in hell I was going to take time off."

"I see," José María said, resting his chin in the palm of his hand. If he could have used a pipe as a prop, he would have. I had survived all his affectations for years, including this one.

Little Sherlock Holmes. The thought made me want to giggle, but I stopped myself.

"Surely you don't think they actually mean that it's a literal journey. Right? I mean, Mom and Dad believe a lot of stuff, but surely they can't believe in this underworld business?" I said.

"Why not? They believe in Catholic hell, right? And don't they also believe Jesus went zombie and flew up from a cave, leaving behind his Calvin Kleins, right?"

"Mom does, yeah. I guess Dad does, too. Good point," I said.

"And they still take me to mass each week to remind me not to go there. So, if they can believe in that..."

"José María, if only Mom could hear you, she would flip. And she would flip a table on you."

"Well, the issue is not belief," José María said. "As far as I can tell, Mom and Dad believe in what the Catholic Church says, but also all the stuff they told you and me about over the years. You know, all that *cosmic* shit."

I had stepped through the rites of the Catholic church, just as everyone else in the family did. I was baptized, made my first communion, was confirmed, and so on. But through these years, there were other kinds of trips: voyages to talk to the ocean, cross country drives to visit the California redwoods (but only at night), hikes in snake-covered hills that led up to the cascades in the state of Veracruz. Each time we had made those trips, my father had also performed rites on us. I didn't know what these were when I was a little kid, but my father called them rites. An anointing with sap from the trees, the little packets of amaranth he made us carry for "protection," the emerald beetles he made us hold in our hands in order to connect with the things that lived inside the soil--those little rituals had made José María and me a little different over the years.

I had grown up thinking that my father was simply very close to nature and that my mother had also been a nature lover, but in fact, José María and I had figured out that the truth went much deeper than just a love of trees. It didn't take much more than a glance around my peers to know that most of their parents were not performing rituals of gratitude in the woods. What my parents did with us had never been normal.

That petrified moss my father gave me was still in my pocket, and I felt it now with my hand, like a charm to hold my resentment toward all this superstition. I fingered it while the tech crews did the sound check and set up the stage for Rhinoceros.

I brought out the nugget of moss so José María could see it.

"I cannot believe that of all places in the Aragon, I ended up behind these two shitbags," said a voice behind me. I turned. Four feet behind me, sandwiched between two women in black lipstick, was the man in the brown work boots.

He had no idea we could hear his words. My stomach started to burn. He leaned over to a woman who I presumed might be his girlfriend. "These two..." he said, pointing to my brother and me. "Nothing but socialist pieces of shit. Fucking idiots."

There was no way José María was going to allow us to move from our spot beneath the stage, so I hoped that was the end of the exchange. My gut clenched and I felt anger flush my cheeks, though. I turned back to my brother. He was smiling at me, oblivious to the rage I was sending out with my eyes.

We turned around to ignore them.

"Things get interesting with legends like the one of the city of the dead," he said. "You know, Arkangel's written some good songs about Mictlán."

"I should have known this was coming," I said. "Of course Arkangel wrote about it."

My brother turned over the crusty flyer again so I could look at the ivory city inside the jaw of the invisible monster. He ran his thumb over the logo, tracing its sharp spikes and white lettering.

In the solar system of my little brother's life, there was him, a planet out in elliptical orbit, and at its center, a giant sun called Arkangel: a Norwegian band comprised of four men and one woman. Arkangel always performed in some sort of visor or mask, and they attracted the strangest kind of person to their concerts. From the moment José María heard them on YouTube, his obsession had never stopped.

"It's on an EP, CD-only limited run, I have it at the house. It describes the journey from death as a dance, and it talks about finding the entrance to Mictlán. Mictlán itself is a kingdom, and the song says it's one of the most secret cities a human can ever find. But the narrator of the song can only get a glimpse of it, though, you know? It's fucking dark in there, but they know they have to get to a temple made of skulls, and this temple is located exactly in the heart of the city."

When you step inside the Palace of the Skulls.

"They seriously made a song about this?" I said.

"Is weed green?"

I clicked my tongue at my brother. More superstition, more coincidence. Electronic Norwegian death metal and too much weed equaled José María Montes.

Nothing but coincidence. This isn't rational. Just take in the info but leave it there. Too wacky. And don't forget he's still high.

"So, that's a nice coincidence and all, but it doesn't add up to much," I said. "That's only a song, and it has nothing to do with the legend. I am sure the band took huge liberties when they wrote it."

José María thought about what I said and nodded.

"You're destroying my little bubble, reina," he said. "Don't mess with Arkangel."

Such a drama queen.

This wasn't really getting me anywhere. My mother's request for me to go to Mictlán was nothing more than the fucked-up kind of stuff that I am sure every person went through with parents.

At least I hoped so.

It was time to abandon this wild goose chase. May as well be now.

"I've decided to just ignore what Dad and Mom told me about this 'trip,'" I said.

"Oh, reeeeeally?"

"It makes no sense at all, and it's going to keep me from moving on with OLF stuff. What you told me sounds good for a literature class, but I got bigger things to accomplish. Between you and me, what you heard about an act of defiance against the legislators is really happening. And there's another march in the works. I can't lose time on this spooky stuff. It makes more sense to just get back to the OLF."

"I thought Dad told you to quit OLF."

I wasn't sure if José María was phrasing this as a statement or a question. It made my skin prickle, and the rage that was bubbling in me swelled. In some ways, he was just like my father.

"Dad's not in charge of that decision. He can't stop me from joining the campus chapter, and plus, he can't be there all the time to watch over me the way he'd like to."

"Is it true you guys are looking to target City Hall and the mayor?"

I frowned and crossed my arms, frustrated with José María's naiveté. The ceiling of the Aragon was dotted with tiny lights to give it the appearance of a night sky. How had I never noticed that before?

"Give it up, little brother. You get no info unless you want to get involved with us. The marches are public, you know? And there's plenty of internet groups you can join if you really want to find out."

"Oh, please. I ain't signing up for shit," José María said.

Applause interrupted us as the lights on the stage went dark, and we felt the space around us constrict as people took small steps to get closer to the stage. The sounds of the crowd filled the dome of the Aragon.

"There's still a bunch of other stuff you should know about Mictlán," José María. "But I'll tell you after the show."

Rhinoceros was known to take up to ten minutes to arrive on stage. Tonight was no different. Droning electronic tones filled the air while we waited for their emergence.

José María and I hooked our hands over the safety railing that divided the audience from the stage. Our hands did not resemble each other's, but they did lay bare our history: I wore several rubber bracelets on my right, and a cheap Casio watch on my left. Despite my long arms and legs, I had tiny hands and tiny nails. José María, on the other hand, gripped the steel railing with long talons. His wrist bone jutted out from his arm like a tumor, and the dark hairs on the back of his forearm shone under the powerful blue lights on the stage. Long and intricate designs looped and swirled on the skin of his arms, where he had drawn them using a black gel pen. They were rudimentary, crude images, drawn poorly and with lots of frequency. These were the tattoos my parents would never allow him to have. The primitive and desperate nature of these curling spines, birds and female faces on his skin were out in the open for anyone to see, and I felt an embarrassment for my brother that I could do nothing about. The Arkangel logo he had drawn in the crook of his elbow was now a dull smear. I was so embarrassed for him that I couldn't even tell him to roll down the sleeves of his hoodie.

There was no point in taking any action, because suddenly, music was pouring from the speakers that framed the stage, and the blue lights glowed brighter. We had stood in this crowded spot for two hours, enduring a dismal opening act. Now we finally had the payoff.

Rhinoceros took the stage swiftly, each band member moving with agility despite the fact that all of them were in their mid-fifties by now. The grind of the guitars made my ears ache from the first strum, but the music drenched my bones and my hair with a wave of sound. José María and I shared a love for these shows, and we got lost in the lumbering but sharp sound of the music. The main set lasted seventy minutes, and I don't recall ever lifting my hands off the railing. The air was thick and hard to breathe, but José María and I craned our necks toward the stage, where Cheetah the lead singer crooned their massive hit "Hail to the Chief."

After the main set, the crowd roared for an encore. We chanted and stomped for twenty minutes, until Rhinoceros came back to the stage. Before they started playing again, Cheetah took to the microphone.

"Chicago," he said, and the audience shrieked for almost a full minute. He pursed his lips and continued. "We just want to take a moment to acknowledge the tragedy that took place in Millennium Park just a few weeks ago. We have always loved your city."

The applause and shouting from the crowd went nuclear. It took a full minute for it to get quiet enough for Cheetah to get back to the mic.

"On this visit, we have noticed that the place looks grayer than usual. We feel the sadness and mourning as if we could almost touch it. Too much blood has been shed in this place, and we hope for peace."

The audience applauded.

"Now if only we could bring ourselves together and reject the anarchism that's splitting us apart, man. OLF, and Anonymous, we wouldn't be here today lamenting the graveyard that we created in Pritzker if it wasn't for the bullshit that groups like OLF cause."

The noise from the audience became pure thunder.

"You know who you are, man," Cheetah said. "If you're caught up in this shit, stop it. You're the very root of the problem, and you can take yourself out of it. You can prevent more bloodshed."

A series of boos rang throughout the Aragon, but they were few. Other voices cheered.

"If you're going to push for this kind of anarchy," Cheetah said, "just take yourself out of the equation."

"Take yourself out," chanted the crowd, an echo of thousands.

"Yeah, like this fucking traitor up front," shouted someone behind me. I knew the voice. It was the guy with the brown work boots. "We got two little OLFers right here."

I blushed, and José María turned to me, his face pale with fear. The crowd around us had turned to look at us, and the white lights from the stage burned my skin. Now even the band was looking at us.

"Leave the kid alone," someone shouted behind me.

"Traitors," someone else said.

"Anonymous pieces of shit," rang out.

"Fuck you and your kind."

"Terrorists," someone shouted.

Terrorists.

José María had nothing to do with this, but now people were shouting names at him, too. The man in the work boots came up close and he tapped my shoulder hard with his index and middle fingers. I turned around and looked into his drunken face. The can of Miller in his hand was too likely to become a weapon if he decided to brandish it or toss it at me.

Suddenly, I felt sick, and a gray shroud clouded my vision. I was remembering hazy images, where I ran down a grassy field and shots rang out in the distance like thunder, and around me people kept on falling on their knees, their hands and backs. I could suddenly remember clearly the woman in the pile of bodies next to me, and the way her breath was there one moment, hot under the chilly air, then gone forever in the next. Her glassy eyes stared at me, pulling me in, tighter and tighter.

I felt out of air.

I was going to suffocate to death, and all the pain in my back and in my face came back, stabbing my insides and making me want to collapse to my knees, right here in front of everyone.

But I wasn't going to cry, and I told myself I was not going to pass out. Pain blasted inside my head, and I wondered if I was finally inheriting my mother's migraines.

"They should have popped you and the rest of them in that park," spat out the man in the work boots. I stood as tall as I could, and I spat the thickest phlegm I could find in my throat right onto his face.

"Fuck you," I said, and then he tossed beer in the air as he took a step toward me. He swung a punch near my ear, but he missed. Around us, the crowd was breaking out into shoving matches, and men and women got swept into a sea of bodies. Others were beginning to shove and taunt, and I knew more punches would be arriving soon. I had been beaten in the face once, and the humiliation of this punch by a stranger brought a sense of dread and rage into my gut.

A gnarled hand pulled me back, and I bucked and kicked away at it, until I saw it was my brother José María. He curled his long arms around my arms, and he literally yanked me out of that pit. He dragged me to the sides, where we could leave the crowd and follow the long hallways that led out to the stairs and eventually the exits.

This took some time, and all I could hear as José María dragged me was "We need to get out, we need to get out."

I glanced one last time at the stage, and it looked like the disturbance had dissipated. Rhinoceros was looping their guitar straps over the shoulders and starting up their encore.

As we bolted down the old stairway and down the long tunnel that led to the exit, I wanted to punch out, to tear away at something, anything. Maybe the T-shirt and merch table. Maybe flip the beer cart. I saw a trash can at the end, and I knew I would kick it as hard as I could. Finally, a target. José María still had me locked into his grip, and I got ready to let out my rage through my feet.

It was a long hallway, and now that Rhinoceros was back on stage, the tiled tunnel was virtually deserted.

At the end of the corridor, a final set of glass doors led to the street. These were plain double doors, just as one might find in a department store or office building. In the dim light of the hall, they gave off a strong reflection, almost like a mirror, and as my brother and I approached, I could see our ourselves in fairly sharp detail. Me in my checkered skirt and with my asymmetrical face, my brother's long frame swimming inside his hoodie and his face taut and pale.

"Stop running," someone shouted from the merch table, but we ignored them.

We ran as fast as we could, and time began to slow around me, my blood beating inside my ears like a drumbeat. It grew louder and louder, and the reflection in the glass doors began to change as we approached. José Maria and I were determined to fly out of here, hand in hand, running

(once, long ago, I ran with Edgar on a field of grass beneath a valley of skyscrapers)

(once, long ago, I had my original face)

and now the image in the glass grew black, like a pool of tar invading its surface. Our reflections grew sharper and more solid inside of it. With each step we took toward the glass, I noticed changes in our skin, too. As the glass grew black and glossy, our reflection in the mirror transformed. My skin had gone from brown skin and dark lashes to a bright crimson, wet and raw. As we approached our mirror images, blood spilled from our lips, as if we had just severed arteries or our skin had burst. My left eye, the one that was no longer working properly, was missing from my face in that black mirror, and the hole that remained showed the frame of the skull bone and a glimpse of raw brain inside. My lips had fallen off, and I could see all my teeth outlined in blood. I looked mutilated and severed. I was a body violated and putrid.

But José María's reflection looked worse, as his hair fell away in the image and his full lips receded. His skin had gone dark and black, charred like barbecue. His hands dripped with blood, and his neck split open in the image. His skin had holes in it, and beneath these holes, there was nothing but raw flesh.

I screamed as the reflection grew more solid and we ran toward them.

I was not imagining this moment. José María shrieked next to me. He could see this disgusting reflection, too.

"Jesus Christ!" he shouted.

We were running too fast when we had started down the hall, and under normal circumstances, José María and I would have slowed down our gallop in order to pause, and then exited through the doors with caution. But that had not been the case. The dark reflection in front of us had mesmerized us, entranced us, and we had run toward it with magnetic speed, and now, just three feet away from the glass, we were going to crash right into the doors, possibly shattering the glass and cutting ourselves to ribbons, truly becoming the bloody images we saw in its reflection.

I let out a sound that was part cry, part bellow, but all fear.

José María had not let go of my hand, and his grip got tighter as he also braced himself for impact.

When we struck the glass, the first sensation I felt was that of sound rippling through my whole body, making my bones and organs vibrate and my head ring with tones like bells. The surface of the glass had gone soft, like gelatin, and we struck the double doors without a crash. Instead, we moved through the surface and into the darkness of the reflection inside. A symphony of sound enveloped us, and I thought that this was what it might feel like to be a molecule of air inside a violin. In the microseconds where we crossed through the barrier, sound surged so deeply inside my body that I felt my organs melting away, and the tension that had been in my body fade away into a velvety softness.

We fell forward for what fell like hours, and my stomach fluttered as if I had just leapt from the Hancock tower without a parachute. When we landed, we struck hard, dry earth, and small pebbles scraped my cheek.

I was facedown now, and the only thing that felt solid was my brother's hand intertwined in mine.

I looked up. We were in the dark that I had glimpsed in the other side. I couldn't make out anything, because night had taken over here. This was darkness. This was the kind of dark that had terrorized me as a child. This was the same darkness where the boogeyman lived, where Freddy Krueger slashed his film victims, and where my heart and my brain had always told me not to enter.

The symphonic sound I had heard was coming from a place above me, and in the dark, I got the sense that I was standing on some sort of flat surface, like a desert. Wind whipped around me, and I felt very, very cold. In the dark before me, I finally made out a single object as my night vision kicked in. I still couldn't see José María, or the ground, or anything except for the silhouette of the object in front of us. But I felt his hand, and I squeezed.

The object before us was pyramidal in shape, and possibly the size of a skyscraper. It was a triangle of ink set against a dark blue-black sky, and the symphonic sound was coming from its peak.

From the top, something was peering at my brother and me.

The thing itself emitted no light, and so there was nothing to see. But I knew that it occupied the space at the top of that triangular shape, and it was staring down at us.

When I looked at my brother's hand, all I could see was darkness, but the warmth of his skin was real.

José María, I tried to say.

But I had no words. Each time I opened my mouth to speak, no sound came out.

I tried screaming, and all I could hear was the blood beating inside my eardrums and a soft roaring sound, the breathing inside my lungs.

My heart beat too, very fast.

Do not let go, I tried to scream. Though no sound came out, I hoped at least my thoughts would carry across the dark to my brother. His hand tightened, and I propped him up on his feet. I stood shoulder to shoulder with him now. If I let go of his hand, I might lose him forever. There was so much silence here, except for the melancholy music that came from the shape in front of us.

I knew then that the structure in front of us was not a building. It was a mountain. Taller than any mountain I had ever seen. And up there, in the dark, something was making the saddest music I had ever heard in my life. The sound filled me with fear, and as the music grew louder in my ears, I realized that whatever made that sound was staring at us. The sound stirred sorrow in my heart.

I looked at the peak and searched for its eyes. I only saw a wall of onyx.

But it was looking at us.

And as its tones changed, some of them grew long and harsh, like a growl.

Then it grew silent. After a few moments, it began to emit long brassy knells. It was ringing a bell of some sort, and its tones pulsed long into the space around us.

The owner of those sounds was descending down the mountain.

I tried screaming, shouting, whistling, and nothing came out anymore. My vocal cords were gone, or I had done deaf, or worse. But I couldn't be deaf, because the bells and moans were closer now.

The cold air pressed itself against my skin, and I was thankful I could still feel at least that. This darkness was like nothing I had ever seen. It was the world of the blind.

The bells echoed and their infernal sound banged in my eardrums. It felt so loud that it hurt.

I took two deep breaths to think about what to do, but two breaths were all I ever got. The thing that crept down the side of the mountain came down faster, moaning and murmuring, and its sound flooded my ears. Though I was blind, I shut my eyes as it sprinted toward us.

The bells rang through my whole body, making it shake.

I felt something let go inside of me, like a string popping on a guitar, and my eyes flew open.

I wasn't ready to die.

PART TWO
WHITE TEZCATLIPOCA

9 UNDERGROUND RIVERS

"This is why cities are breeding grounds for the occult: In their streets, sewers, subways and wonders of architecture, man can wear a mask. Inside the city he can trick himself into thinking he can fool nature." –Frederick Law Olmsted, Marginalia, National Park Service Archives, Brookline, Massachusetts.

"*All* experiences are non-local. Most people choose to call these experiences narrative and language. I prefer to call them quantum physics." –Sculptor Vlad Stoppard-Goswani, commencement speech at Northwestern University, Evanston, Illinois, 2007, YouTube.

"They couldn't pronounce her name, but her work was not in vain. Up they rose, in demon form, and her feet crushed their horns. Tow, non-seen. Tow, non-seen." –El Samaria, "Meet Ze Monsta", *Brief Interviews with Singular Women: Remixes and Rarities*, 2011, A-O-T Records.

To live in blindness was to live in fear.

I tried wriggling my fingers and toes, to prove to myself I was still somewhere, *anywhere*.

There they were. My digits made tiny circles, and each ellipse brought me a smidgen of comfort.

Everything was dark.

My eyes and my vocal cords had stopped working.

I focused my attention on my face, and I forced my eyes to blink as many times as I could. I felt their tiny muscles move, but whether they were open or closed, it didn't matter. I was as blind as a mole.

Somewhere up ahead, some massive and feral thing galloped down toward my brother and me,

(You are still grasping his hand, don't let go of his hand)

and whatever it was would be tearing us up soon.

I felt a tug at my wrist, and I knew José María was still there with me. Three tiny squeezes ran up my forearm. He was trying to communicate.

It was time to stop lying on the ground like prey. I remembered the woman whose life escaped on the grass of Millennium, and I knew I didn't want to succumb in such a submissive state.

Running blind would be dangerous. We would be likely to trip or stumble if we ran. I took my right hand and felt in the dark for my brother's reedy shape. I found a forehead, and I felt the tangle of his coarse hair. I patted his nose, and I moved on to his left shoulder. I lifted him up by the armpits, the same way I did when we were kids and we transformed the dinner table into a train, and he needed to ride up front as conductor.

Crawl with me. Crawl for your life.

I yanked the collar of José María's shirt, and we crawled forward, using the sound of the bells behind us to give us direction. The only shape I had been able to make out in the dark was a mountain the size of a skyscraper, and I knew I wanted to get away from it as fast as I could.

The grit beneath us dug into my bare knees and tried to puncture my palms. There were smells down in this darkness, smells that made me want to vomit.

Under our hands, the ground became coarser, like gravel. We scrambled forward. The sound of bells, brassy and full, pummeled my ears, and I felt a presence behind us. It didn't sound like a locomotive, car, motorcycle. It was something animal-like.

It's that thing. The thing at the top of the mountain.

Our crawl was frantic and tedious, and as we moved forward, we felt new textures beneath us. Some were hard and wooden, other soft and dense. Were those eyes beneath—was that human hair? Did I touch a dead hand?

We pushed on.

Then we bumped into something hard and flat. I felt over the surface with my right hand. Luckily, it didn't feel like human hair or skin. My hands explored it.

It was only about three feet tall. I knew we could clear it. I dragged my brother up its surface. Our legs scrambled, and we never let go of each other's hands, despite the clumsy climb.

Once we lay on top, the rock felt smooth, like a brick. Maybe we were on top of a short stone wall.

To continue, we had to move past its edge. I moved my hand through the dark to see if there was solid ground beneath it. Nothing. I had no way to tell if the drop was inches or miles deep.

But the sound of the bells behind us was getting closer.

I wrapped both arms around my brother and we jumped off the edge.

I rotated my body in midair so we could land on my side or my back.

We fell, and the dark made it impossible to know how long we fell.

My shoulder hit the ground, and spikes stabbed my legs through my stockings.

We lay wedged inside a bed of hard objects.

Nothing felt broken, though I had gotten the wind knocked out of me.

My brother scrambled close to me. I felt his hoodie and his arms under my hands.

This time, José María grabbed my bicep, and he brought me close to the wall next to us. He tapped my ears furiously, but without hurting me. He tapped right near the ear canal. What was he trying to say?

He wants you to listen, to listen close. He wants you to listen for both of us.

We moved our hands up the wall, and I tried standing up. The wall ended at about chest level for me, and I peered into the dark, listening, while José María tapped my ear.

He tapped me in sync with the bells.

I had never heard a single sound fill miles and miles of space like this. Each time the bell rang, it swelled into the space, packing it with vibrations. It was a violating sound, revolting. But it had a rhythm. Roughly six seconds would pass, and then another repetition would shake my ribcage and make my gut want to empty itself.

I tried finding that tall mountain again in the dark. Anything that would help me orient myself. Instead, there was nothing. All I saw was darkness.

In between the knells, my brother tapped my head, syncopating his taps to their rhythm. He was trying to tell me something.

There's a sound under the bells, a sound. Something like a rush of air—and José María wants you to hear it.

Then I heard it.

The beast making the sound was breathing. I could hear each breath it took. That was the syncopated beat beneath the bells.

Now that I could hear the breaths, it was easier to assess how close the beast was. By my estimate, it was about fifty feet. I hoped I was wrong about this.

In front of us, the beating of a thousand wings exploded and I screamed as loud as I could. No sound emerged from my mouth.

Screeches tore at our ears, and more sounds burst in patches around us. They reminded me of blue jays from the woods or even monkeys in the jungle. The wings grew louder, then they were gone, moving into the distance in the dark in their flutter.

My legs shook, and the darkness smelled of rot and decay, and something else. Something like flowers.

A hard, metallic musical note broke through the space. Two hard cones of something that seemed like light shot from the dark. The cones spread far and wide, and they remained suspended in the air, pointing up toward the sky, while the metallic tone stretched itself further and further in my ears.

The beams lowered toward the ground. They descended with grace and precision, until they were pointing at us like headlights in a deserted highway. The musical tone they emitted blasted my ears.

Then they stopped. They were pointing straight at us. The strange light from the beams allowed me to make out some details.

That is not light.

Light doesn't look like that.

But what is it, then?

The beams allowed me to *understand* the positions of objects around me, giving me a rudimentary sort of vision. In fact, the beams allowed me to feel the textures and surfaces of the things around me, and in feeling those, I could create a sense that felt like normal vision.

I caught a glimpse of the solid ground. Flat and dry.

Beneath my hands I felt and understood the debris on the ground. The dusty bits clung to José María's hoodie like lint, or like tiny, dusty chicken bones.

Not like chicken bones.

Like bones. They are human bones.

Baby bones.

I squeezed my brother's shoulder. The beams allowed me to see details of his shape and body, though José María remained bathed in black darkness. It felt strange to see all parts of his skin, even his eyeballs, in pure black.

Then another change in the musical tone in front of us. I jerked my head forward.

The tone broke, and then the beams disappeared. The darkness swallowed everything again.

One noise remained: the breathing of the beast.

It took air in, exhaled, and the breaths inched closer toward us. José María tapped out their rhythm.

The breathing stayed steady, and a smell of cheese, mushroom and what I could only think was pus, wafted toward us. No more bells. Just the precise breaths of an animal I would never see.

We were being stalked. I had to hide us.

I yanked José María's collar one more time, and we slid along the low wall, with our bellies pressed tight against the cold surface. How I wished that we could have even just a sliver of moonlight instead of this vacuum where I couldn't even see my hands in front of me.

As we inched left on the wall, I heard footsteps come toward us, and then the sound of rocks and grit shifting. It was so very close. Holding on to my brother for dear life, I turned us around so we had our backs against the wall to protect us, or possibly hide us from the beast.

We slid downward into a squatting position, and I dug my nails into José María's flesh. The wall scraped the back of my arms, but I didn't care. Words were useless, and my urge to scream resulted in nothing but silence.

A roar detonated in front of us, and I realized that hiding behind this wall had been futile. It had somehow leaped, flown or gone around the wall.

It's here.

A long tone burst forth into the air, and the bells rang. The cones of understanding swept over us, and as they spread wider, they amplified my cognition of the topography around me. I could feel every object, its position, its texture and exact shape as if a 3-D map had turned on in my brain. The beams floated about ten yards in front of us, and they allowed me to see through and into the darkness. Their haunting tone droned far and wide.

What is this place?

When I understood what I was seeing, I cupped my hand over my mouth.

Up until that moment, I had spent nineteen years—my whole life—able to see the colors of the world. Red and indigo, emerald and brown, purple and blue, they came to life when the sun or artificial light radiated onto objects that could reflect them. In daylight, back in Chicago, I could see the blue of the lake, the gray of the skyline and the green of the trees. My favorite had always been green.

But nothing about that sunlight and those colors had prepared me for what I could feel and understand now through this dark.

We crouched in a vast place, like a desert. Rocks of all shapes and sizes lined the ground. I felt them in absolute detail. Some were razor-sharp, and now that I could see their jagged edges, I was surprised I hadn't cut myself open when we jumped over the wall.

The ground was littered with little bones. And big bones, too. They resembled human bones, but I couldn't be sure about all of them.

Off to the sides, I spotted crumbling chunks of stone, and a quick glance behind me showed me the wall where José María and I crouched. Its walls also reminded me of coal. The wall's edges were decorated in shimmering runes that I couldn't read.

I let go of José María's hand, and I looked down at myself.

This is not normal.

I turned my palms up and down, over and over. No matter which way I moved them, the skin looked black as night. What's more, I could feel and understand in incredible detail. The narrow ridges on my palms became like maps carved in onyx. Whatever the cones allowed me to see was magnified, allowing my to feel every single thing as if I had an electron microscope.

I turned the hands over, and the skin, with its imperfections and tiny triangular patterns, was as black as the downy hairs on the back of my hand. If this was what the light was doing to my skin—

I jerked my head to the left to look at my brother.

The fifteen-year-old who went by the name of José María

Montes stared out at me through eyes whose irises and pupils were as black as crow feathers. His skin, his clothes and everything on his being looked as if it had been bathed in the thinnest layer of tar. He parted his lips in surprise as he stared at my own black face and skin, and I could see the inside of his mouth, with its tongue and teeth—all of it was black now. He moved his lips, but no sound came through. We could see each other finally, but we still couldn't speak.

And then the creature roared from behind the beams of light. The bells rang again.

The beast had stalked us well, because when it pounced, we had nowhere to go.

Now I was able to understand more about the imminent violence that approached. Though the beast moved with the speed of a jungle cat, I could now understand how the cones had sprung from its head. The creature was the one making the cones with its dreadful musical tone.

The animal lunged.

The beams arced toward the sky, and they traveled over several yards, sweeping a over heaven that bore no stars.

As the beams crossed the air, I saw the beast in detail.

The body was long and ragged but human. Its sinewy arms and legs bare; the skin hairless and smooth. Its coal-black skin shone with the sickly texture of diseased skin. Its toenails were long and curved—talons. It was a body that looked ill and strong at the same time, as if someone had taken a corpse and given it incredible strength.

And the beams floated in front of its shoulders.

They are not headlights, and they're not flashlights. Those beams are coming from its head.

I saw the creature's face and its long jaw, its folded-back ears, the hard skull that tapered.

It was not a human head.

The shoulders supported an unnaturally large dog's head. It was hairless and just as smooth as the human portion. The snarl in its jagged teeth was something I had only ever seen in animals like wolves or jackals.

The black light from those eyes lit up every detail of that monster as it shortened the distance between it and us, and its stringy biceps, its watery skin, the bits of gristle in its sharp teeth—I saw them all like my eyes were a telescope and a microscope.

And then it crashed into both of us.

The creature was even larger than I had expected, easily double the size of an average human, and the jaws of the beast looked wide enough for José María or me to crawl through.

The beast plunged into us, and our senses exploded. We heard the bells go off inside our very cells, and the stink of wet dog and rotted meat bloomed in my nose.

The black cones emanating from the eyes grew wider, thicker and clearer, and though I was living in a world made of night, I had to shield my eyes from the blast of sensation that allowed me to see into this world of coal.

The beast grabbed both of us by the neck, and it did not let go. It thrust its maw in our faces and it tore at our clothes. As it did so, ragged sounds emanated from its tissues. Then it lunged. Its flesh made music as it dragged José María along the rocks. The beast's claws pinched my shoulder blades.

Maybe this is what that woman in Millennium Park felt when she got shot and trampled.

Clara, you didn't look out for her. That woman's death was your fault. You could have tried to save her. You should have found out her name.

God, I am sorry, she had said.

You should be sorry, too, Clara.

My body was tossed and turned, and the notes of the beast's body drifted in the air. Then it dropped us on the rock. The beast roared and stood on its skinny legs. Its strength was incredible.

The dog head licked its chops, and the beast screamed at us. It was a scream filled with music—tinny drums and terrifying screeches.

It had knocked the wind out of me, and I sat up on the ground, trying to get in some air.

The creature darted away a few feet, and it turned around.

Its eyes locked on mine.

It crawled on all four human limbs toward me. My shoulder hurt, and a thin stream of blood poured from my head. I put my fingers to it, and I drew them away. The blood remained as black as my skin.

Behind the beast, I spotted the wall where we had fallen. To the right, I saw a shallow forest running up a small hill, and farther back, the giant mountain I had seen when we arrived.

The beast ran at me and grabbed me again by the shoulder, and it opened its jaw wide. It let out a roar, and it stuffed me all the way up to my waist inside its throat. Thick saliva coated the inside, and rotted meat got in my hair and in my mouth. I could hear its gut growling below. I scrambled to push myself back out, and I felt electric shocks throughout my body.

Then it bit down on me as hard as it could.

The teeth came down on my lower back and then on my belly, but they couldn't even pierce my skin. The jaws came down again and again. It chewed. And each time, it failed. It was as if my body was made of stone.

The stink of death was all over the beast's sandpaper tongue, and I was running out of air. It bit down again, working me over like an old bone, and then it spit me out.

It roared above me and screamed. This time, its shriek sent music into the sky. I saw a flock of dark shapes fly off in the distance.

This place has no stars.

That realization made me shudder.

Behind me, José María was curled into a ball, crying his eyes out, though no moans came forth. Bugs crawled over his shoulders and his legs, and they raised hooked stingers over his bare flesh, right over the long lines of his homemade Arkangel tattoos.

Scorpions.

Hundreds of them.

And then the beast pulled me around by the shoulders to face it.

Its eyes squinted, and it examined me, sniffing me at the same time as it inspected.

The beast stared at me with cold suspicion and rage.

From its thin loincloth, it produced a small knife, a blade that looked so tiny in comparison to his body that I wanted to laugh.

It plunged it into my arm, in the very center of my bicep. I shrieked. It squeezed my body, and blood gushed to my skin in its black inky sheen.

My blood flowed in thick spurts down my arm.

The beast held out its dog tongue. It cocked his hand and

plunged the knife into the tip. He didn't seem to feel any pain in its self-mutilation. It dug into the muscle until black blood sprang. Then it rolled out the tongue toward me.

Before I could struggle out of its grip, It pressed the cold tongue onto my wound.

José María, help me!

My mind blew up into a thousand little bits.

My ears rang and my eyes burned, as if a blast had fried my retinas and blown out my eardrums.

A thousand dots made of shadow danced in my mind while I stared into the black dog face in front of me.

And then the creature spoke to me in *blood.*

"Bitch," it roared.

It sat me on the ground, as if I was its doll, and it got down on its haunches. The eyes remained dark, evil, hungry. From its throat, sound emerged, and it was both music and language all in one.

From the wound in my arm, I heard the creature speak. Its voice whispered, like a lone flute in an orchestra pit. Its blood coursed in me, and mine in his, and now, when it moved its canine jaw, I heard its words.

"Why," it said.

It was not a question, but instead a statement. Its voice was high and thin but distinctly male. Air rushed around its musical pitch.

Tears welled in my eyes, and I wriggled, trying to move away from the being and toward José María, to wipe off the bugs from his skin. The creature held me down, and he spat a word toward the blanket of scorpions. They scrambled away from my brother, who was covering his face with his hands.

"Now speak to me, woman," the creature said. "Why is the word where we start. Why. You must ask why."

I had never heard the language that this creature spoke, but the blood he shared with me tingled inside my veins, and the blood translated the notes of the dog head. I was able to understand through the music I felt and heard.

He had called me *woman.* In this dark, where no color distinguished anything, my concept of "woman" felt thin and artificial, but if he was calling me woman, that meant he knew what humans were.

"Why—" I said. My voice became a new sound under the spell of the blood, and what emerged from my throat was raspy and undulating, like notes from an electric guitar.

"SPEAK," he shouted, and his voice melded with the bell sounds he made from inside his body.

"Why is there no light here? Where are we?" I said.

The beast spat thick phlegm in my face.

"Stupid woman. You've wandered here. You're nothing but a wanderer." He turned his shoulders away and spat again and again. The gobs of spit didn't bring the creature relief. He was furious, frustrated.

"Don't kill us, please," I said.

Those were the words that came from thousands of people inside Pritzker Pavilion. Don't kill us. Now they are mine again.

This smell of rot all around me—it's that final smell of—

"Kill you?" the monster cackled. His laughter sounded exactly like a harp. He grabbed me by the collar and tried taking one more bite of my head. His teeth met resistance again, and he roared in frustration.

The creature scooped me up and reached out with his long arm to pull José María from the nest of scorpions.

He carried us over the wall in a single leap. Despite having nothing but rotting skin, he dashed with grace through the rocky landscape.

We headed back toward the mountain. Now that the twin cones from the creature lit up the terrain, I could see we were in a vast plain where no plants grew and where everything lay flat under the dark. And indeed, the things that had felt like human flesh and bones beneath us were mutilated bodies. I saw them clearly now. Bodies thrown there like trash in a landfill.

I saw the small hill to the right and the mountain towering over us as we approached its foot.

Though we were moving too fast to free ourselves from the claws of the beast, I wasn't going to waste my ability to speak.

"José María," I shouted. "Can you hear me?"

He shouted at me, but we were bouncing off rocks and the terrain below, and I couldn't read his lips. Nothing emerged from his mouth. Only I had the ability to speak, it seemed.

Because of the blood.

Tears streamed down my brother's face like rivers of black ink, and even though he was shaded in the darkest black I had ever seen, he remained familiar—annoying, irritating—but also my brother. I didn't want him to get hurt. I reached out with my left hand to try to get a hold of his hoodie, but I was too far away.

"Stay with me!" I shouted to my brother.

As we gained height in our climb, I could suddenly begin to understand the vastness of this place.

The arid land spread out for thousands of miles. My eyes scanned every detail of the black panorama. The ground was coated in a fine, shiny gravel, and my eyes caught many glints through the vast plains that stretched before me. These were insect or scorpion colonies, I wasn't sure. The rest was emptiness, enclosed by a sky without a single star and without a moon. The desolation of this place suggested to me that it might spread out into an infinity.

Not just infinity.

An infinity. One of many.

That idea felt suddenly more terrifying than if we had been buried alive and left to rot.

Here, the darkness eats everything.

We were now climbing up a slight incline, and the foot of the mountain spread around us. When the rocks became flat, he forced us to walk, keeping his long claws wrapped around our shoulders. When the rocks became too sharp and uneven to clear, he grabbed us by the collar and leapt.

We flew into the air, bouncing from one rock to the next. My ribcage rattled and I screamed. We were not just going up the mountain; we were going *around* it. My sandpaper music-voice sent out futile screams.

We reached a flat boulder, and the creature landed on it with a creak of its bones. He tossed us at its edge, and José María landed on top of me. My brother let out another silent shout.

The creature got down on all fours, and now he was more doglike than ever before. His black eyes showed no iris, no pupil, and his cone of black light let me see the steep slope of the mountain behind his shoulders. He flexed, and the bell sounds rang deep from inside his belly. He pounced on José María, pinning him on his back, and the dog head turned toward me.

"Is this your gift to me, woman?" the creature sang.

"Leave him alone," I said. "Take me first."

"You still don't understand, do you?" the creature said. "You have proven yourself, but no one visits my gate without bearing a gift."

"He's not your gift," I shouted, and I ran toward the beast. I punched him in the eye as hard as I could. Just like he had been unable to chew through me, my own fist didn't make the monster flinch.

You need to distract him; you need to buy time.

"What is your name?" I said.

The beast cocked his head, and our eyes stayed locked. Time passed in that trance we held through each other. I saw the fine wrinkles of his dog face, and the edges of his gums drip with slobber.

Then a single tear ran down his smooth skin.

The musical note that created the twin cones in the air gave the tear extra dimension and detail, and I could see deep within the tear's structure, the way the molecules clung to themselves. Even in this world of no light, I could see the tear was transparent as water.

"No one has asked my name in a very long time," the creature said, and he lowered his head. His human arms and legs went slack, and the decaying skin wrinkled on his thighs as he took in a few sad breaths.

He stared at José María for a second, then slashed his cheek with a talon. José María's scream went unheard in the vacuum of sound around us. Black blood sprang from his cheek. The monster licked the blood with a sweep of his tongue.

"What is your name, then?" I said.

The breath of the beast rolled down over my face. The breath was feces and fetid vegetables. It was maggots and sulfur. He heaved, breathing hard, and then spoke his name.

The word the beast spoke was long and strung together by many syllables. Each one rolled out of his throat as music, like a wet whisper. Its sound was like a flute and a rattle.

It was a word I had no comprehension for.

"I cannot pronounce that," I said.

The beast stared down at his body, as if evaluating a thought.

"That is my name. I can't help you learn it," it said. "I can't help you say it, either."

"Fine. I'll call you X."

"X—" he said, and the single syllable melded with a bell tone. The music the creature made sounded exactly like a letter X, except wet and hollow at the same time.

"And now you can let me feast on your gift," it said.

"He is *not* your gift," I shouted.

What I saw in that monster's eyes filled me with dread.

He's old. He's really, really old.

He was ancient. And he didn't really care about us. That's the reason his stare felt so odd.

"X, you said I was a wanderer," I said.

"Yes, and we send wanderers back from where they came. Last time someone wandered through my gate was six hundred wheels ago."

"Wheels?"

"600 wheels, yes," said the creature.

"How much is that in years?" I said. His harp laughter danced in the air. With each cackle, his teeth bristled.

Those teeth. There's so many teeth in there.

"You, too, have an obsession with time," X said. "Interesting. Many wanderers share that defect. You're a wanderer; you should know how many years there are in a wheel, and how many wheels there are in what you call a year."

"I should?"

The creature smacked his lips.

"Let me show you something," X said.

X scooped us under each of his arms, like kittens, and we walked along the edge of a precipice. As we leapt among the rocks, I smelled the mountain and its metal notes.

We moved closer to the edge of the precipice.

I could see that we were high up, but it wasn't until we came close to the edge that I understood what lay below.

Dear God.

I had never seen a place more vast than this, not even when my father took us to the Grand Canyon. The immensity terrified me, and though I didn't want to, I held on to the bony arm of the creature to make sure I didn't fall.

Up above, a screech broke out—identical to the one I heard when we arrived in this place. A bird swooped upward, headed for the mountain.

On our left, the precipice of the mountain at first looked like outer space. As X approached the very edge of the rocks, his cones grew deeper and their music more melodic, revealing detail. Behind us, the mountain loomed over us. And now I understood that the mountain was minuscule in comparison to the precipice beneath it.

I looked down.

A land lay before us, as big as a planet, deep, so deep. It was a place built out of night.

Inside this deep space, a circular pattern emerged, and it coiled round and round, like a corkscrew. The circular canyon definitely had a topography. It was like a sinkhole with walls that curved in toward the center in a spiral.

This was nothing like the Grand Canyon. It was bigger than planet Earth and filled with a darkness that smelled of things forgotten and forbidden.

The coil moved downward, starting from the mountain where we stood. Thanks to the light from X, I could see tiny knobs of shimmering lights along the ridges of the coil, each one connected to the other by rivulets of black liquid like pearly tar. Those little dots twinkled like torches on top of long towers.

Those are cities. Cities dot the landscape as it curves downward to the bottom.

The cities formed tiny clusters of towers and houses, and the path between them was made of a wilderness. I could see water rushing through the rivers that wound down through the coil, and forests that looked like they were made of sharp needles. I even saw a set of bridges built out of what looked like snakes.

And though I could see these cities, and the roads that connected them downward into the canyon, I saw no cars, no planes, no buggies. No citizens.

My ears were drawn by the very center of the spiral-shaped canyon. It was there that I heard the loudest noise, made of music that seemed to rattle me and cause my teeth to chatter.

At the heart of the coil, a pulsing mass of blackness beat like a heart, bathed in a soft sheen that could have almost looked like blue. That sheen was the only thing even close to a color that I had seen in this world of blackness.

The mass of darkness in the center throbbed and elongated. I spotted slits along its surface, like gills on a shark. The slashes revolted my guts, but I couldn't take my eyes from it.

"So, you know the heart of this world, woman," X whispered to me. "Will you touch the black heart inside the city?"

Could it be?

The city?

José María, why can't you hear me?

I pointed down there so my brother could see the center of the coil, but he had passed out. His eyes were rolled back into his head, and the whites glinted as black marbles.

"You said I am a wanderer. Tell me about that," I said.

X grunted, and he lowered itself onto the floor. With one clawed hand, he pinned José María facedown onto the rocks, while he held me down by the shoulders as I kneeled in front of it.

The dog head lowered itself toward me, and his rheumy eyes approached. He placed his forehead on mine, and then a lone bell rang out into the space, rattling my body like a toy.

Inside the music he emanated, X talked to me.

I saw you, wanderer. You were a half child when I first spotted you. You were the visitor who came here in a dream. You came from a city of concrete, wood and glass.

The night of my thirteenth birthday, I said through the vibrations that rang where our foreheads met.

You know that the number thirteen marks the entrance to my gate, wanderer, X said.

And then the creature showed me a thousand images, each one cutting in front of the other with the speed of a lightning bolt. I saw images of my father, my mother, our house in Little Village, all in the past. And inside these images, I saw myself sleeping in bed, at the age of twelve, tossing and turning. I felt shame and sadness as I saw my old face, my original face. Inside these exploding images, I caught my parents in the corner, watching over me on the night of my thirteenth birthday.

But what brought me to this place? I thought through into X.

The creature snarled, and his stink of rot enveloped my shoulders, my back, with a single embrace.

She doesn't know, X said, and he craned his neck as if he were talking to someone else over his shoulder. *She can wander, but she doesn't yet know.*

Who else is here? I screamed through my forehead. *Who are you talking to?*

X pulled back, and I felt a hot spot where our skin had been touching just a second ago. He was scared.

"They will pull out my innards," he howled. "They will bring me pain."

"Who?" I said.

"They will be so angry," it said. "You shouldn't have spoken when we touched. *They heard you,"* it said.

"They who?" I shouted and my startling voice trilled.

"The Lords of the city. The Lords in the heart of the city," X said.

I heard a bass sound pummel from below, like a steel drum destroyed by a hammer. I peered into the heart of the coil, and it pulled darkness toward itself, like a black hole in outer space. The thousands of slits on its heart-shaped surface parted open, then zipped close in perfect unison.

"What is down there, exactly?" I asked.

"Well, the city, of course. The city that rests under the nine underground rivers."

"Bullshit," I said. Calling his bluff—this was the only way I could tell if what he was saying was true.

His brow furrowed, and his eyes squinted.

"You challenge me," X said. "I do not lie. You, with your red heart and its thin blood. Shall I take you down to the city myself so you can meet the Lords Who Devour All?"

I didn't want to meet any lords who ate anything.

"How do you know my heart is red?" I said. "This world has no light for you to see color."

"Because I have seen it on the other side, in your world."

"Perhaps you'd like to see the Lords now, and experience your evisceration."

"Hell no," I said.

I punched him in the nose, and I wriggled from its grip as he recoiled. The cuts on my legs were ablaze with pain, but I didn't care. I held onto José María's foot to make sure X didn't run away with him.

"How does one get down the coil?" I said. The tension in my voice became like a buzz saw of metallic music.

"Citizens of Mictlán can come and go as they please. I am not sure what you're asking. Wanderer."

There, he had said the word *Mictlán.* Even in his native tongue, it sounded exactly the way I remembered it. It had a musical tone, like the music the wind makes in the trees in the autumn.

"But I am not a citizen of this place," I said.

The creature heaved in laughter, and tiny slits on its chest like the ones in the center of the spiral opened up, then closed. It was like seeing a shark breathe through its gills. He laughed and his eyes rolled back into his head.

"The delusions of the other worlds," X said. "Sadness and laughter."

I had to think of another tactic.

"What I mean, is, if I asked you take me there, how would *we* get there?" I said.

X scratched his armpit, and I realized then and there that he was only humoring me. I was nothing but a plaything for him.

"Enough, charlatan," X said. "You are supposed to have all this knowledge already. If I can't eat you, I can excrete you like the feces you are."

X shouted. The music of that shout rang with hate, disease and despair.

Pain shot through my ear canals. I cried hard sobs, and they emerged from my throat like the song of starlings. Metallic, polyphonic, desperate.

He took hold of my neck again, and we were climbing up the mountain, soaring up its walls as the creature's haunches sprang us forward. He held the limp body of José María in his other arm. We moved at an incredible speed, yet time passed in slow motion before my eyes. At the top, a starless sky and a jagged peak waited for us.

"I'll never tell anyone what we've seen," I said. "I promise."

"You like making deals," X said, and he showed me his teeth. The gums bled in black, and I spotted about six canine teeth. It was a shark's jaw inside a dog head. "But you don't seem to understand. Nothing can be *unseen*. You know this. Do not barter with me, wanderer."

X's voice echoed through the sky, and it occurred to me that I must be dreaming.

You idiot, you know you can snap out of it.

The grit that scraped my knees felt real. My nostrils on fire with the smells of rot and dank water, and the sight of José María, still wearing his hoodie and the tattoos he made on his arms still reminding me of his immense geekdom—they had the solid quality of reality.

Just a dream, is all, in these walls.

We had easily climbed thousands of miles within seconds, and now we rested atop a flat outcropping of the mountain. Black snow fell on X's shoulders, and I heard more music coming from inside his chest. The razor-sharp cuts at its center swelled open, and shut again.

I reminded myself to come out of the dream. And nothing.

Wake up.

But nothing.

X laughed at me as he scraped his claws along the black snow. He drew runes in the powder. He no longer held us down. He knew that if we ran away, he'd capture us again.

"I see what you're doing. You tell yourself you are in a dream," X said. "You are some sort of idiot."

"How do you know what I was thinking?"

"Your mind has a voice and that voice makes its music—they all give you away, imbecile. Stop announcing yourself so loudly. Learn how to quiet your thoughts."

I took a seat next to José María, who was still unconscious. I pulled back his hair, and the loss of privacy—the sheer intrusion of this beast into my thoughts—made me feel as if something big, menacing and unforgiving was ready to take me and kill me for real this time.

My brother came back to consciousness, and his eyes peeled open. He screamed again, but when he made eye contact with me, he stopped. He pointed toward his heart and made looping circles around it with his finger. Then he pointed at X.

What are you telling me? What should I do???

I shrugged my shoulders. I couldn't tell what my brother was saying. I wanted to give him the power to speak, but there was no time.

Then X barked like a real dog, a feral wolf, like an animal.

"All sound and all thought are music, wanderer," he shouted. "You must be careful what sound you make, with your body and mind. Even in your breathing, your music announces you. You know, when they bring the humans to my gate, none of them—none ever—have made such a cacophony as you. They are always silent. You are as loud as the oceans. Vulgar bitch."

"Who brings you the humans?" I said.

"Death, of course. What do you think I have a gate for? Death delivers them to me, and I take them down through the nine rivers to the Lords. Their journey begins with me."

FUCK THE OTHERS, KILL THE MOTHERS

"Do you know what it's like to watch more than 800 people drown, for all that death to pour into Lake Michigan like bile? Lord I pray you are listening. My consciousness will always bear the scar of that cursed Eastland disaster in the Chicago River." –The diary of Jack Woodford, November 1, 1915.

"Every song we've ever written is a fiction, but trust me, it's a lattice work. Our trilogy of albums, starting with *The Violet Album* and ending with *2666*, was written as a map. Thankfully, it's out of Google's reach." –Sergio Andersson, lead singer of Arkangel, "Slicing Deep, Screaming in Quiet: The Rise and Fall of Scandinavian Indie", *Vanity Fair,* 2013.

"In the Aztec cosmos, the god of duality created the world. The god/goddess bore four god children, all named Tezcatlipoca: The red, the white, the blue and the black. These children, too, embraced the power of duality." –Jane Morrigan, *Clara Montes: A Biography in Four Parts,* 2074, Castor Books.

I didn't want this reality anymore.

I didn't think it was possible to find any more adrenaline on which to run. My arms ached, and I waited to catch my breath for a moment. But there was no relief.

Pressure nagged at my temples and ate away at the base of my neck. Around me, every shade of the darkest black brought the world into sharp relief.

My father had wanted to show me something about this place, about this window into the dark, and I had refused. He and my mother had called it Mictlán since I was a little girl. My mother tried, too, and now I stumbled, clumsy and lost. I still held on to the idea that I might actually be dead, but where was the light at the end of the tunnel?

In Mictlán, time was melting.

I felt it. It moved slowly, very slowly. It reminded me of the times I crashed through the deep end of the pool at my high school: the seconds that melted into whole minutes as I waited to break the surface.

Maybe I have been inside this place for weeks. Maybe months. Who knows?

I stared into the eyes of X, a creature that made every nightmare I ever had—every boogeyman I had cringed from—a reality. Those human eyes blinked at me through its dog head, as it took a moment to decide my fate.

A few summers before, my father had saved up his vacation time, and he took José María, my mother and me down to Oaxaca on vacation for four weeks to visit the Montes family there. My father's collection of Luis Miguel and Rolling Stones CDs drenched our ears every mile of the way there. José María blocked it out with his iPod, drumming on the back of my father's seat all the way.

It was the worst trip of my life. The drive took so long—it was endless, in fact. Each time we stopped along the road for a bathroom break or to get something to eat, things got dirtier, more weathered as we crossed over into Mexico.

We arrived on a late Sunday afternoon in the city of Oaxaca. Relatives pinched my face, squeezed my shoulders, examined my hair. At the age of fourteen, the last thing I wanted was touch from anyone. And to top it all off, my mother asked me why I couldn't be more like my cousin Nadia, who didn't seem to mind this physical invasion from every relative. Nadia took me for a walk through he city. We walked under its colonial church towers and cut through the mercados. Nadia's cordiality unsettled me. She was graceful, long-haired and perfectly suited for this place. I was not.

My Spanish language skills were broken, and I felt they always would be. I fumbled in Spanish in Oaxaca, and I felt like no one forgave me for not having a better accent in Spanish. The air had an earthy quality that repulsed me. Nadia left me alone in my guest room, and I thanked her in broken Spanish. I lay on the lumpiest knitted blanket in a room the size of a closet in Oaxaca, overlooking an avocado tree grove.

I didn't know how I could spend four weeks in that place. I cried in silence, and then a smack to my head made me bolt upright in a scream.

José María darted past the doorway like a fox. The object he tossed at me flopped onto the floor. A book. It was his way of giving me a gift without having to speak. Before I could call out his name, he ran off into the maelstrom of our cousins in the courtyard, laughing.

I picked up the book. *The Grimoire*, by Stephen Knowles-Reading. I opened it, and within minutes, I was gone, drifting off into a world of water-based magic, imprisoned fairies and the quest for Merlin's lost talisman, the Gold Finch. *The Grimoire* saved me during my stay in Oaxaca. It yanked me far away from that house on a dusty hill and the daily trips we took to visit every relative in town. Aunts and uncles and cousins stopped accosting me with the question "Do you have a boyfriend in Chicago?" during these visits to their houses during the mornings. In the afternoons, I dissolved into *The Grimoire,* sipping a bottle of Jarritos in the side garden of the house, away from everybody.

Inside the book, Hugh Bright, no older than me at the time, had conquered a dragon from King Arthur's round table with a single kiss to its forehead, rendering her his servant forever after. After I finished the book and I had returned back to Chicago in September, I had preferred Hugh's journey over mine.

That was about four years ago. Since then, I had outgrown that book, and in fact, I had now almost forgotten *The Grimoire.* It was silly information, and I had moved on to harder school work and details that really mattered.

Except that if you read more of those books, you might know what to do when a monster with a dog head tries to kill you.

That was my voice I heard talking to me in my head, but it could have easily been spoken by José María, who remained mute. The beast had been able to speak with me after it performed our blood pact. José María shivered in the blackness.

The monster will gut him. He'll drink his black tears. You know it.

I looked into the canine head above me, its gums lined with black pus, and its breath bearing the scent of violence. Its hairless skin, dull and dry, was parchment, and the bulge in its loincloth a terrifying and ridiculous monstrosity. How I wished now that this thing I named X could be as easily conquered as Hugh Bright had tamed the dragon.

Can't hurt to try. This isn't exactly a place that sticks to the rules. May as well go for it.

X was so bony and jagged that I didn't think much of climbing up his body like a chain link fence. I grabbed the loose skin near his ribs and pulled myself up. As I did so, his eyes went wide as saucers, and he grunted in a flurry of musical beats. His hard nails clawed at my skin, but I didn't care. I used the saggy muscle of his thigh for leverage, and I jumped up onto his head. Its jaws released the reek of dead flowers and fish innards. I pressed my lips onto its forehead, just like Hugh Bright as he conquered the dragon.

"NO!" the beast shouted, and it tossed me off his body. I flew through the air and landed hard on my back. The beast took two steps forward and he leaned over me.

X took his clawed hands and pulled the corners of his canine mouth apart. The flesh came apart like taffy at first, and he opened his maw as his body stiffened. The eyes, those all-too human eyes, jittered and vibrated, and the nimbus of sound that allowed me to see through the darkness turned sharper, moving into a higher pitch. The jaw spread open like a flower as its folds spread out wide. I gasped.

It was a travesty of a jaw. A machine of death. Four rows of teeth curved outward, as his gums rolled forward from his mouth.

José María scrambled in the dark, blind, screaming in silence. He crawled on all fours.

X made the rows of teeth in his jaw bristle, and he craned his neck at an incredibly sharp angle. He shouted once at José María, who curled up into a ball when he heard the musical bellow. Then the creature craned his long neck back toward me.

He shouted again.

My breast shook and my ears felt like they were bleeding. It was a shout made of a hollow sound, hard, everlasting. It was lonely music, like the blues, but bereft of soul. His eyes swelled and threatened to split open.

And then screamed one more time. As he did so, a smell emanated from his body.

X released the smell of the woods, something floral, something made of dirt and rain—

Marigolds. The beast smells of marigolds.

As the smell reached my brother and me, I experienced several visions—several experiences—all at once.

I was a nurse in a dormitory, huddling under my bunk. My lungs burned as I held my breath. I pressed my lips together to not let out any sound, so I could not be heard by the man with the knife who had just butchered the other women in my house just a minute or so ago. Seconds passed, and I couldn't hold it any longer. I let out my breath and took another breath. I held it again. And then I saw his shoes. They cleared the threshold of the bedroom, and then I heard his breath. Heavy, moving closer. When he yanked me by my hair, he tore out most of it, and he had to grab another patch on my head so he could pull me up to full standing. His face was sadly a blur. As he stabbed me, I felt a realization: I hadn't had the chance to get married. When he was done cutting me, I fell to the ground. The last image of my life was a chunk of cheap yellow paint on the wall, and the stranger's calves in front of my nose. This death was not imagined. I was really there. My name was Merlita.

I was a skinny teenager, barely fifteen years old, crossing the intersection of Pulaski and Lake. I didn't react quickly enough to the pops. They went off like soda bottle caps. Pop, pop, pop. My friend Bernard shouted. He shouted hard, and he called my name. None of it made sense. Behind me, a liquor store's glass windows blew out, and then I understood. The black Suburban screaming down the street was shooting, its passenger holding a handgun in each fist. I felt pressure in my gut, in my head, and in my shoulder. Red flowed from me, and it was then that I felt regret and fear. Would Momma be okay? I pressed my hand to my chest and my stomach, and my insides were soft, like gelatin. Momma lived under the fist of my father, who also beat me when he showed up unannounced at our house around the corner. If this blood was true, I would never see Momma again, and I would never get her out of this neighborhood.

I was old, much too old, and I hated it. Ninety-three years old, and my knee ached like the devil. I remember that. I no longer had a reason to live, because my wife's death had left me empty. My many sons tried cheering me up, but my knee tortured me every minute of the day, and the cancer in my liver was winning. My father had come to Chicago from Poland a long time ago, and as I lay on the sofa, drinking straight from the whiskey bottle, I became alarmed. He used to drink like this, too, sideways on the couch, piss stains on his boxers and one eye half shut. I couldn't remember my father's name. I tried. I really tried. His name. What was his goddamn name? There was a blank space in my memory. I wept into my hands, and the stabbing pains grew deeper in my gut, right where my liver was located. It was New Year's Day, and my sons were coming for a visit at four p.m. The pain in my insides grew deeper, sharper, and I knew what was coming next. I died with my hand still wrapped around the neck of the bottle, and wishing I could just remember that name. Since we arrived in Chicago, we had lived on the South Side. I remembered that.

I wrapped my hair in a towel, and I walked out into the back porch to smoke a cigarette. I could hear the son of the Montes down the street blasting Rhinoceros, and I thought, *Don't they ever turn down the music?* My phone rang from the living room, but I let it go to voice mail. I was dreading answering the call from my boss, so no hurry. I'd fake a doctor's note if that's what it took to take another day off. Instead, I went to the kitchen and popped an Eggo waffle in the toaster. I ran down the figures of my credit card debt and the student loan payments I still had left. I was going to get a handle on this problem, and today was the day it all would start. I had spent the past three months hiding the numbers from my Trevor, but he knew I had a problem. $150,000 in debt, and a serious shopping problem. I stared at the stuff I bought and put in our extra bedroom. All of it beautiful stuff, my things, my clothes. A new purse and a silk skirt. Dozens of DVDs. Perfume. I considered going out shopping later today. Why not? Then I put the butter knife into the slots of the toaster to fish out the waffle. The knife came to life, hot to the touch, and suddenly it was glued to my skin. My jaw clenched, and I felt a surge. Cramps in my flesh bent my arm into the shape of a hook. My lips trembled, and fear filled my being. I shook, my whole body clenched, and I felt my own eyeballs cook and my hair begin to smoke. The clock that was plugged into the wall popped, and fire broke out from the socket. I didn't fade out into death. It was more jerky than that. Like a TV set flickering on and off. I tumbled into a place of fear, and the last thoughts in my head were those of that credit card bill for $14,608 that lay on my counter as my retinas and my corneas burned. I smelled my own body fat cooking, and the dark came over.

Each plume of marigold stench thrust these experiences into

me, and my eyes watered. I vomited black liquid onto the dirt, and the bends in my stomach made ghostly music.

"Want more, wanderer?" X said.

I shook my head.

"Then you know not to try touching me like that again. *Never* touch me."

"Am I dead?" I asked.

X was still holding his jaw open from the corners of his mouth, and his tongue rolled out like a snake. He pulled the corners up, and his grin mocked me. He walked toward us again, and in a swift move, he grabbed José María and me by our collars. He leaped over rocks with grace, and as we cut through the darkness, I felt as if I were flying up the side of the mountain.

"I do not want to go up there. Stop it," I said.

The mountain peak felt wrong, all wrong, and I knew we were not supposed to go there. The toes of my shoes grazed the rocks beneath us, and I heard screeches above us. Birds were circling this mountain. They had always been there. I just couldn't see them until X's nimbus of sound lit them with its tone and I could see their textures.

It was a whole flock. It stayed close to us, scanning with dozens of eyes. The birds stared at me with a deep knowledge. These were like no birds I had ever seen. Their bodies were solid but made of the blackest smoke. Their eyes and flat faces stared into me, and they left trails of smoke in the moonless sky.

They are owls.

We reached the peak in what seemed like seconds, and the final point was nothing more than a mound of snow, black and glittering like the same snow I knew on Earth.

"If I cannot keep your guest as my present, you must leave," X said, and he hurled us toward the snow mound. The snow sparkled like volcanic sand, though I knew that if I touched it, its icy coldness would sting my skin. X swelled with rage, and his skinny body filled with wetness, as if his circulatory system had reactivated. His dog face and his human eyes coveted José María. It wanted to consume flesh.

We fell toward the snow, and as we approached it, I saw it magnify before me, as if my eyes contained microscopes inside each eyeball. Inside each black snowflake, I saw myself reflected. It was like seeing a honeycomb of mirrors, and we approached it with speed and fury. My eyes magnified the images, and I know José María saw them, too. We had been here before.

Thousands of mirrors before us. And my brother and I inside each one.

We barreled toward the snow, and when we made contact, we passed through it like bodies through gelatin. Sound swallowed us up, filling our ears and blasting our bodies into ether.

We struck a hard object.

What it feels like to hit the pavement at 1106 West Lawrence Avenue in November: wet and slick. And oh, so good.

I had never been so happy to feel gray water slide on my cheek. I breathed in exhaust, the smells of french fry grease, pho, injeera and motor oil. City air. But what was even better was seeing color. Red stoplights, the emerald tease of the Green Mill off to my right and the gorgeous brown of the back of my hands. Light spread everywhere, and where it shone, color followed.

Things are no longer black.

Tears came to my face and the wind got knocked out of me, but there was glory on my right as José María landed with a thud next to me. I heard a dull crack near his hip. This sound was glorious, because it was a sound from the real world. It felt familiar, and thankfully, it didn't emanate music. We were back.

José María scrambled to his feet and withdrew his Samsung from his pocket. "Piece of shit!" he said, and he tossed the two halves of the phone into the traffic before us. It hit the windshield of an SUV driving east on Lawrence Avenue.

The driver pulled over across the street.

I stood up, straightened my skirt, and I blinked, over and over and over, to make sure I was really here, really back.

The driver of the car stormed toward us. His belly bounced over his belt, and his face reddened.

"What the fuck is your problem? You wanna start something?" he shouted.

José María spat out, coughed, and his voice choked on a syllable. He coughed again, and I heard his voice, loud and clear now.

"Step the fuck away from us! I'll beat your fucking ass!" my brother shouted. Red spots bloomed on thin cheeks and he shivered with anger.

José María ran toward the vehicle. This was nothing I had ever seen him do before. The driver stepped backward, almost stumbling over himself. José María punched the passenger side window, and the window rattled. He then took his closed fist, raised it above his spiky head, and slammed it down on top of the car. He didn't leave a dent, but the noise of his fist slamming on the steel rang out like a gong. The driver stepped back into his car.

He locked himself in his car as José María ran up to the window.

"Step out of the car, asshole," screamed my brother.

José María was still shouting as the car took off.

I heard Rhinoceros's sonic boom rock the building. The show was still on. My brother stood across the street from me, shivering, as it started to rain.

José María held his hand to his throat, and he smiled each time he spoke.

"I can talk," he said.

I felt tears welling up behind my eyes, but I fought them back. A deep sense of confusion was washing over me now, and I felt slightly dizzy. So much time had melted inside that world of darkness. I turned around to face the building looming over me. The glass of the Aragon Ballroom doors looked as innocent and inert as ever.

"This wasn't supposed to happen like this," I said.

"Clara, did you also *see* what I saw back there...back *through there?*"

"Shared hallucination, right?" I said.

"I don't think so."

"Okay, glad you said that. Me neither."

José María pulled up his hoodie over his head, and he sank his hands in his pockets. This meant he wanted something.

"Do you think it's too late to go buy a T-shirt? If I get this one, my collection will be complete."

"You are unbelievable. We just popped out of—what?—Hell? And you want to buy a T-shirt."

"Retail therapy, *reina*. It will make me feel better."

I could see the long tunnel of the Aragon's lower level through the streaked glass.

"No way. No way at all. We're leaving," I said. "Everything is different now."

"But we made it out alive, you see? We're okay!" José María said.

"Talk to me. Dad will be here to pick you up shortly. You saw that dog creature?"

José María nodded.

"And the way it made music, the way the sound allowed us to sort of see in the dark?"

"It was a world made of every shade of black. I saw it too," José Maria said.

My brother lit a cigarette, and we took tiny steps against the wind that whipped through Broadway. I figured we'd walk a few blocks until we got to Little Vietnam. Something about the pho shops and families huddled over the bowls made me feel more comfortable than standing in the presence of the Aragon. The concert hall felt like a mountain in this stretch of Broadway, and the last mountain I had seen had been black, so black, the home of a creature who spewed bell tones from himself....

"Did we die?" I said.

"You still don't get it? You know, for being in college, you are the dumbest person I know," José María said. "This is what Dad tried to tell you about. We peeked into Mictlán."

"So... we should be dead."

"No, no, no, stupid. Not dead. All we saw was a tiny glimpse. Just the gate," he said.

"That's what the creature called it, a gate."

"Exactly. I mean, who else would be guarding it but Xolotl? "

The word escaped José María's lips like an elongated, wet whisper. *Show-low-tuhl.*

He knows the thing's name.

"It was most terrible thing I've ever seen," I said.

"I dunno; I thought it was pretty cool myself. He meets dead souls at the gate and he takes them, you know, down there."

"He told me his name. I don't supposed you heard him say it?" I said.

José María shook his head.

"I heard nothing."

"Me, neither. Not until he shared his blood with me. Then I could hear what he said."

"That was fucking cool, Clara," José María said. I thought about shaking him by the shoulders to rattle some sense into him.

How can that be cool?

"The name was long, full of syllables and musical notes. Maybe it sounded like Xolotl, the more I think about it."

"So, you could hear *everything* down there?" José María said.

"Only after he cut me and rubbed his blood on the cut," I said.

We reached the corner of Argyle and Broadway, and my head pounded with fresh pain. My stomach churned, and I felt nausea rise up my body.

"I think I need some time to think about what happened," I said.

"Why not talk about it right now?"

"You're unbelievable; you know that? You just came out of that place fresh as a daisy? Didn't you just feel all that despair, that rot down there? Didn't you smell all those dead people?"

"Yeah, but, like, whatever. Get over yourself."

How quickly this little shit made me angry. It was real skill.

"What will our parents think?" I said.

"Sooner or later, you'll have to ask Mom and Dad."

"I don't know how you find all this time to try to be a smartass." I said. "And put out that damn thing. You're gonna get cancer."

My words made me pause. Would cancer claim my brother, like the cancer that I saw, heard and felt inside the man who died on his couch in the stench of the marigold? Why would I wish cancer on my brother? And why did I say those words? After the vile things I saw in that kingdom of darkness, words seemed to matter a bit more.

X said, "You must be careful what sound you make, with body and with your mind. Even in your breathing, your music announces you."

I glanced up Broadway, and I spotted my father's Honda racing down the street. Behind us, I heard sirens blaring, and an eerie quiet flooded the streets.

The car pulled up, and my brother hopped in. My father lowered the window and I peered in. My father layered a thick sweater under his jean jacket and wrapped his neck in several coils of his wool scarf. I got ready to tell him a million lies, to create a smokescreen he could never see through. He didn't know how happy I was to see him, but I needed time to unpack what I had experienced.

"How was the show?" he said.

"Sick," shouted José María from the back. "So sick!"

How is he so fearless?

"Come on, get in the car. It's cold."

We fielded questions about Rhinoceros, and we skipped over the near scuffle in the pit as we told it. My father had no idea. During the drive up Broadway, nothing broke the eye contact that José María and I held through the vanity mirror. I pretended to check my makeup, and he and I held our gaze. I kept my mouth shut, and José María knew I'd beat his ass if he said anything. This time, he held the information in.

I had no idea how I was ever going to tell my father about what happened. In doing so, I would admit that he had been right all along about Mictlán.

And if he was right about that, he might also be right about things like the OLF.

The OLF. The thoughts about my real life with the OLF popped back into my head, and I was grateful.

We crossed the intersection at Sheridan, and I remembered I was supposed to host a meeting the next morning for the OLF. I had no idea how I was going to do it. I still felt sick to my stomach from the journey to the dark, but I wasn't going to let anyone down.

I popped the door handle as hard as I could when we arrived in front of my dorm. I glanced back at my brother one last time, and I said, "I'll talk to you tomorrow. Don't sleep in."

"Never sleep again," José María said. "Scout's honor."

He held his hand up, showing me how he crossed his fingers.

"Wait a minute there," my father said. "You're not leaving without giving me a time to pick you up tomorrow."

"What?" I said. Pain throbbed in the base of my neck. "I have an OLF meeting tomorrow. We're marching next week."

"You really don't read your mother's texts, do you?" my father said. "I don't care about your meeting. Your aunt Minerva will be expecting you at her house."

"The baby—"

"Yes, early again. They sent her home today, and that means we can go visit them tomorrow. I'll pick you up right here at two p.m. Don't be late."

José María shook like a marionette in the back seat. He laughed without a single worry.

"See you tomorrow, *reinaaaaa*!"

I crept into my bunk that night, and I tossed and turned, afraid of dreams. Thankfully, none came. Eventually, I slept, but just for a handful of hours.

The next morning, I washed my unease away with four cups of coffee with lots of sugar, lots of cream. The OLF meeting locations were never decided until two hours before, when we each got a message sent through IRC.

Ever since the Millennium Riot, we no longer used university buildings to meet. Coffee shops were also out of the question, thanks to their high visibility and open Wi-Fi networks. Instead, we chose old diners. The greasier, the better. Today, we were told to go to the Golden Nugget on Lawrence Avenue, and we filed in in batches. No meeting could ever be larger than about six to eight members. This also helped keep a low profile.

Most of us were students, some were not.

We filed in around the circular booth, and we poured maple syrup over flapjacks.

The taste of those fluffy cakes and the thick butter that dripped from their edges was heavenly. It was a drastic extreme, the opposite of Mictlán, in fact, and I wanted the taste of those flapjacks to last forever. I couldn't tell anyone how much I appreciated every element of the real world. The most mundane things had become rich and beautiful.

Our meeting kicked off.

Mercy, a lesbian queer activist, the oldest of our group, took a seat across the table from me. She brought two others with her: Julian, and Mauricia. I represented the university, though by now, our numbers had dwindled to a mere fifteen on campus. Today, only three of us attended. Myself, Dennis Cho and Kayla Onayemi. There was no texting, no checking in allowed at these meetings.

"There's more sanctions coming from the feds," Mercy said. "Those new checkpoints on Lakeshore Drive and the Eisenhower Expressway, they're not just for DUIs."

"They're scanning the driver's licenses," said Julian, Mercy's trans boyfriend. "It's a registry."

I felt completely lost in this new information. My head was sticky and tangled with other thoughts. I needed to separate them, but thoughts about Mictlán were winning.

(But Clara, you know you didn't dream about the creature X)

(He was real)

(José María knew the creature's name)

(Xolotl, he who guards the gate)

(Black skin and black eyes and black pus)

But I did my best to focus.

"What kind of registry?" I said.

"The kind you would expect. Just adds to every bit of data on those they think are part of OLF, Anonymous, or any group that came before it," Mercy said. She shifted in her seat and gave a slight nod. Immediately, Mauricia passed the individually packaged tubs of jelly to Mercy.

Kayla, who sat in the economics lecture hall next to me many times, leaned forward into the circular table. She was barely passing her classes, but she was loyal to the group.

"There's not much to it," she said. "They just take any data they can - Facebook check-ins, store receipts, checkpoints on Lakeshore Drive, and they crunch the data. They make models. The models let them predict if any of us are likely to show certain behaviors in the future."

"You mean that they want to know if we're likely to attend protests or to become violent at protests," I said.

"This is some pre-cog shit," Julian added. "Like a Phillip K. Dick book."

"No, too science-fictional," Mercy said, cutting everyone off. "It's just market research. That was my job for ten years. I know."

Mercy's soft voice belied the authority she had.

"How old are you, anyway?" I said. Mercy didn't look older than twenty-eight. Her skin was blemish-free, smooth as stone.

"Forty-two," she said.

I felt out of my depth suddenly. OLF was a decentralized movement, one in which we could all have a voice, a chance to say our piece. But I still admired those who put in lots of time to lead the movement. Suddenly, Mercy seemed to command more than dibs on grape jelly. She had real experience.

"Clara, you grew up in Little Village, right?" said Mercy. Her amber eyes appraised me like a jungle cat in the dark.

"Sure," I said. "My mom and dad still live there."

"It's exactly those people who should be joining our next event," she said.

"I agree," I said. "But we need everyone. The unemployed. The African-Americans. Everyone."

"One group at a time, that's how we get there," Mercy said. "Systematic."

"There's another event planned?" Dennis said. Dennis had come up from nothing—he had been born on a boat coming over from Korea literally on his way to the US, and he absorbed information like a sponge. I could see him work out dates and interlocking thoughts in his mind as Mercy continued.

"The Millennium Riot was just the beginning," Mercy said. "If the city responded with force—deadly force—then we retaliate by coming back stronger."

"Actually, it's still unclear who shot first—" Dennis said.

"Get fucking real, Cho," Mercy said. "After hundreds lay dead on that grass, you have the gall to posit this idea still? STILL?"

Dennis wasn't going to let it go.

"There's been so much analysis. The tear gas on the Pritzker stage. Five minutes pass. Then shots are fired. The YouTube recordings—there's about thirty that have usable footage—they show protesters firing with handguns—"

"But who shoots first, Dennis? Who?"

"There's not enough evidence," Dennis said. He bit into his Monte Cristo, but the cold stare from Mercy stopped him in mid-chew.

"If any of you want to follow these theories to their tired end, you can step," Mercy said. "We came here to cause change, not to side with Mayor Amadeo's political machine."

"So, where's the event?" I said. I wasn't going to let Mercy bully Dennis.

"Parade of Lights on Michigan Avenue." The parade took place every year the weekend after Thanksgiving.

"And the goal?" I said.

"To put on a show. They bring the lights, we crank them up. We make them burn," Julian said.

"Good way of putting that. I'm gonna use that," Mercy said. She jotted a note.

"This time, we're being tailed by the cops, so the plan's different than during the Millennium event," Mercy said. "Everyone breaks up into their own mini-pockets of groups, and they get a few kicks whatever way they want. Shut down web sites, prank the cops, spook the tourists, whatever."

"Whatever," Julian chimed in.

Julian's frizzy hair floated above his shoulders in a wiry mass. The wisps of hair evoked the thin essence of the owls made of smoke who flew inside Mictlán. I shook my head to clear my thoughts.

You need a shrink, girl. Get back to business and focus.

"I think we need to make a statement against the lack of investigative journalism," I said. "Kayla and I were just talking about this recently. When I was hospitalized, I found virtually no decent coverage explaining what really happened to those of us who were there, marching."

"This sounds good to me," Mercy said. "And your plan?"

"Dunno yet; I need to make one," I said.

"Good," Mercy said. "Can't wait to see what you come up with."

I wasn't sure I liked her tone of approval.

"Let's meet here next week. This is enough of a plan to get us started," Mercy said.

We paid for our breakfasts, and when we opened the door, winter had arrived. Ice pelted our faces, and the cars maneuvered just a little more slowly than in autumn. Ice brought on caution on the slick roads.

I felt proud of our little group, but something in my belly stirred. Something I didn't like.

For a moment, I remembered a world made up of darkness, shaded only in the color black. It was a place guarded by a man with a hairless dog head and teeth that bristled in the dark. The images pulled at me, dragging my mind into their world without light.

I made additional plans with Kayla and Dennis on our way back on the Clark bus, which would get us back to campus. December 7th was going to be a significant milestone for the OLF and the movement.

We made a couple of stops along the way, and the police checkpoints along Clark Street made me shiver in my long coat.

When we arrived, I put my key in the front security gate of my dorm, and a horn honked behind me.

"I think it's for you," Kayla said.

There was my parents' Honda. My stomach sank. Couldn't my dad arrive a little late just once? He was always fifteen minutes ahead of schedule.

I took a step closer to the car and realized my father wasn't behind the steering wheel.

"Take your time," my mother said. "I meant to give you a little more time, but your father shooed me out the door to prevent my lateness. As you well know."

I ran up to my room and grabbed a backpack full of stuff for the overnight trip. I also grabbed my hamper full of dirty clothes. On my way out of the suite, I pushed the swinging door and struck something hard.

"Clara," said Edgar.

The door divided the space between us, but I could see his fine stubble, the hard lines of his shoulders, the radiance inside his eyes. Now that I was back in a world full of color, I lost track of time as I studied the way reds and yellows and greens pulsed and throbbed in sync with the shadows.

After everything I had witnessed last night inside Mictlán, I felt like a different person. Edgar put his hand on my forearm.

"I came looking for you," he said. "I heard you went to a meeting today. Dennis told me."

"Of course he would," I said. Dennis and Edgar. Indivisible, held together by the glue of a bromance. "What do you want?"

"No need to be nasty, Montes."

"It's been a rough week."

I'm not apologizing. He has no idea what I've been through.

"I'll be gone a few days from school," he said. "My mother passed away last night."

When I heard the words from Edgar's mouth, the sounds became music again, and I remembered a place

(Mictlán)

(The Lords at the bottom of the coil are waiting)

where the words of a person became notes to a song.

"I didn't know that—"

"It's okay," he said. "I just—I don't know how to say this, but—"

I didn't know what to say to a friend whose mother died. This was the first time it happened to me.

I slowed down for a moment and set down my two bags. The staircase stank of male sweat and beer, as it always did on a Saturday morning.

"Go on," I said.

"I did a lot of thinking last night, after my brother called me to give me the news. I feel I owe you in some way," he said.

"For what?"

"Dunno. I wanted to say I am sorry," Edgar said. His baritone filled the white walls of the staircase.

Edgar had been one of the first people to see my new face when the bandages came off after the cosmetic surgery. I was never going to be happy with the new nose and eyes and lips that the scalpel gave me, and yet—he had kissed the subtle scars under my jawline and kissed my reconstructed lips. Of course, that felt like it was a long time ago, too. We had stopped touching, seeing each other. I understood now that we had even stopped being friends. But on those early mornings, weeks ago, when I had crept to his room, he had seen and touched my new face in a very real way.

"I am sorry, too," I said. "What happened?"

"My mom went in for a routine surgery to remove a cyst. She had complications from the operation. No one saw it coming."

Time began to drip again. I had felt this before. The slow travel of each second, elongating into longer moments. I had never known Edgar's mom. Never would.

I expected him to cry, but he just stared off into space.

"I knew I had to come see you, Clara. My brother's picking me up later today. I'm going back to Ohio to stay for a while," Edgar said.

I bit my lip and gave him an awkward hug. I kept my body mass as far as I could from him. I had lain on top of Edgar and ridden his hips. Now, the touch of his body gave me a sickly chill down my arms and legs that I did not like.

You're supposed to say you're sorry, girl.

His mother is dead. If your hallucinations are true, she's moving down that spiraling valley right now, descending while the smell of rot rises.

Soon, she'll rot.

She'll be sent down into the black chasm, and her innards will float on the water of the nine rivers.

Tell him you're sorry.

Why? Sorry for what? Never knew the woman.

"I don't know what else to say," I said.

I felt the urge to press our bodies together, to kiss with our tongues, to strip off our clothes and forget how we didn't know what to say.

Instead, I took a step back with my left foot. I didn't like feeling horny—it was wrong. I took another step back. to get myself out of that line of thinking. I pulled up my bags by their nylon straps.

"It's fine. You don't need to say anything," Edgar said. "See ya later, okay?"

He walked out of the hallway before I had a chance to do so. He darted out through the heavy doors, like a ferret squeezing through the gap between two tree trunks.

I was more confused than ever. When I got in the car, my mom kissed me on the cheek. Her eyes looked too brown, and suddenly, the dusting of flurries on the ground sparkled too brightly. The colors were making my head hurt.

My mother drove down Ashland Avenue until we couldn't anymore. The snow drifts made our drive slow, dangerous. She chose another route. And the trip became longer.

It gave my mother time to ask me lots of questions about the night before.

"The concert was pretty good," I said. "I think José María had a good time."

"He seemed content today. And you?"

"Glad I went," I said. I played with the radio until I had flipped through twenty or more stations. When I settled on the Top 40 station, she pressed the power button and the sound died.

"You know that deflecting only works with your father. So, let's cut right to it. Talk to me Clara; I am here to help. What happened?"

She knows. How does she always know?

This moment had some of the weirdness of the first time my

mother talked to me about having my period. That morning she had broken into conversation just like this—with the violence of cracking an egg.

How do I talk to my mother about a world of owls of smoke and a crater the size of a planet?

Because she knows, you idiot.

"Last night on our way out of the Aragon, José María and I fell—that's the only way I can describe it, I think—we fell into Mictlán. Just like you said we would."

Her eyes peeled open and she bit her lip. I explained how we ran toward the doors of the Aragon, and how the creature Xolotl found us.

"That's all wrong," she said.

"But I went into Mictlán, you said I had to—"

"You were supposed to do it alone."

"But José María fell through the reflection in a piece of glass; how wouldn't we go together?"

My mother's tears welled up in the corners of her eyes, and the glare of the white snow lit her face up.

"It should have only been you," she said. "How did you learn to go through the glass?"

I was dumbfounded.

"I didn't learn *anything*. It just happened."

"There's ritual, Clara, and you bypassed it. I've never heard of someone entering that world in the way you did. It doesn't even seem possible. Your Abuela Blanca would have mentioned it, if it was an option. In fact, it was your father that wanted to show you the method he was taught by Abuela Blanca."

"When we landed, there was just darkness," I said. "And the Xolotl found us. He hunted us, Mom. He treated us like trespassers—"

Except he called you "wanderer." Why?

My mother took the ramp onto the Stevenson Expressway.

"Your father's family accessed the realms of the gods and goddesses through very simple means," she said. "Through dream divination and magic ritual. Two ways. Not through running into a glass door. You entered illegally."

"All we did was run toward the glass," I said.

That's when my mother's tears broke.

"That goddamn Montes family. If I had never met your father, I would still be safely in the Catholic Church."

"But Mom, we survived—"

"You'll see when we get to Minerva's house today that your father's sisters suspect something. He and I are trying to resolve this problem before the news travels up their channels all the way to you know who."

I had no idea who she was talking about.

"But why; can't my aunts help?" I said.

"Get real."

"But why not?"

"Because they think you've got the stink of death on you. You carry death around you like a necklace. And they will think that your corruption is my fault, for your father not marrying the right woman. They like me a lot, but not *that* much."

"So, that's what this is about. You've made this about you."

"Don't talk to me like that, Clara."

We crossed into the suburbs of Palos Hills.

She was really angry now. The tires slid on the ice as she parked.

"Just be sure not to tell Vanessa a single word about what's going on, ok?"

Vanessa was my father's oldest sister. My mother only used Vanessa's real name when she was really angry.

That's the "you know who" she was talking about.

"You mean La Negra?" I said.

"Yes, La Negra."

We walked up to the driveway of the wide suburban house of my aunt Minerva.

I took a deep breath. Going into the void of Mictlán had been a perilous journey. But entering a party of Mexican relatives during the peak of intra-family conflict was far, far worse.

Clouds rolled above the house in waves. They churned into a black ball as a snowstorm headed our way. I distinctly saw a pair of eyes in those clouds. They examined me, my mother, the rolling streets of the suburb, and they felt as cold and black as those of the Xolotl.

Cumbia music pumped out through the windows. My mother put her arms around my shoulders, and we walked in together.

LA NEGRA

"My husband is white, and I am black. When our son was born, his family never failed to make racist comments about the color of my child's skin. Forty years later, my mother-in-law still talks about what it means to have 'good' skin and hair. See how much we've improved as a species?" –Political Scientist Kyra Driskell, United Nations Commission on Genomics Ethics, 2047.

"Daddy, what does regret mean?" –Video meme, origin approximated to the Orbital Surf Video Channel, 2014.

"The Lord and Lady of Mictlán do not care. They will eat your dog, your grandmother and your newborn child. They will eat you, too. They devour everything." –Arkangel, "Tunnels that Lead from the City of the Dead to the City of Dust", *The Golden Architect: Full Sequence,* 2010, Reckless Records.

Arms exploded outward with every step we took inside Minerva's house. Mom and I were the insects, they were the Venus flytraps.

"Clara!"

"Juliana!"

"Clarita!"

"Juliana and Clara!"

Every hug came with kisses on the cheek, the forehead, and just as I finished that hug with a cousin, aunt or uncle, those arms ushered me toward another. We had to move around the dance floor, which had exploded into applause. All adults and most of the grandchildren danced, but when the toddlers decided to join in for the cumbia, all of my relatives went wild. Whooping, hollering, laughing. I soon lost sight of my mother, who ended up at the back of the house, near the kitchen, while I looked for my aunt Minerva and her newborn.

Minerva was the youngest of my father's six sisters. She and my father had always been inseparable, and now they sat on a sofa, side by side. He took her newborn from her arms and brought him over to me. My father kissed me on the cheek during the exchange, and then he was gone, to go drink beers with the men in the living room. He kept his eyes distant, far away from mine. He didn't want to let on that anything was different.

I took the baby in my arms, and he stirred for a moment, brushing his nose and then falling back into sleep. He was still red and lumpy, but his clean smell and the big eyes on his round head stirred something in me. He was a beautiful baby cousin. Jonas.

"He's so pretty," I said.

"He'll be a lawyer, just like his dad," Minerva said. She liked to predict, and often.

(There's only one prediction that's true. You're learning that now, aren't you?)

I pushed the thoughts aside, and I squinted under the throbbing colors of the blue baby blanket and the walls of the green living room.

Just days before, this tiny infant had emerged from my aunt's body. I had never stopped to think much about babies, not until now. After everything I had seen and witnessed, I wanted to find a place where there were only brand new babies and their smells. If I could forget about places like Pritzker or the gate to Mictlán, I would do so now.

"Maybe you'll let me babysit sometime," I said.

"Only when you are off during the summer. You have school to think about," Minerva said. "After all, you're going to go law school, too."

I let her words hang in the air for a moment. I gritted my teeth. I had never talked to my aunt Minerva about what I intended to do when I finished school.

"Well actually, I was thinking of changing majors—"

"Don't even think of it. You'll be just like your uncle Horacio. Where is he? Go get him, would you, Clara?"

I didn't particularly want to go find her husband Horacio, but I sure did want a break from her. I sniffed my hands as I walked away. *Keep that baby smell.*

"Hey, Clara—" Minerva said, one hand in the air to make sure I didn't stray too far. "You doing okay after, you know—the tragedy—"

"Yes, I am. Thanks for asking."

"The plastic surgeon did an incredible job, and—"

"I'm still not used to it."

"And your eye? How is your eye?"

I had explained to all of my father's sisters many times over, but it never seemed to stick.

I don't want to talk about my blind eye.

"It's dead," I said. "But the other one still works."

Minerva recoiled, and satisfaction allowed me to keep walking away from my aunt. Problem solved for now, but she'd be back later to prod me some more.

"You know, your father knows a lot of things about dead things," she said. That caught my attention. I glanced over my shoulder, playing with my cell phone to pretend my interest was low. However, my ears were alert for every syllable she spoke.

"What things are those, Minerva?"

"He learned the old ways from our mother, Abuela Blanca. You know, the very old ways, from Oaxaca. Surely Abuela showed you some of that when she was alive—"

"No, she never showed me *anything*," I said. It was true.

In my mind, spirals of lichen and fungus exploded, expelling the fumes of death, stink and rot. I heard the sound of bells, the sound of the Xolotl ringing from the top of the mountain with his black human eyes set into his dog head.

"Well, I am surprised," Minerva said. "Your father knows those old ways best. Can't forget them."

"Guess you're right," I said.

"You sure he hasn't taught you the songs your abuela used to sing? Those songs could help you after the tragedy from Millennium—"

She's getting bolder. She wants to get right down to it.

Jonas kicked in Minerva's arms, and she brought him closer to her breast. She flipped down the flap in her blouse and fed him. He suckled with his eyes shut, in absolute innocence. Jealousy and revulsion churned inside me. But my curiosity burned.

"What songs?" I said.

"Well, after a tragic death, or in this case, many tragic deaths, you sing special songs to send the souls off to the next place."

"What place is that?" I said.

"You should ask your father. He'll tell you. Then come and tell me what he said, okay?"

She suspects already. Mom was right.

I had no idea why my father asked me to conceal things from his sisters, and it made no sense to me. This was a family of paradoxes.

I squeezed past relatives through several rooms, looking for José María. I found him in the den, kneeling before an Xbox, surrounded by eight other cousins around the glow of the screen. José María ignored me.

Uncle Pirulí nursed his tenth rum and Coke in the La-Z-Boy in the corner. He traveled for a living, selling marketing services to insurance companies, but he was more of a fixture in this room than the Xbox or the furniture. When he didn't travel, he lived in this basement, and though he tolerated nephews and nieces during parties, this was his kingdom, and we all knew it. I still wasn't sure why my aunt Minerva allowed him to live in the basement this way.

"Clara," croaked Pirulí. "Go get me another cuba libre?"

Even at nineteen years of age, I still hadn't shaken off the obligation to run small errands for all my uncles and aunts in this way. No one needed maids as long as the kids were there to refill ice buckets and deliver bowls of chili peanuts to the adults at the party.

I glanced one more time at my brother. I was invisible to him while he lanced demons through the flat screen.

At the top of the stairs, I ran into Minerva again. I thought of making an excuse for not going to find my father, but instead, I just scooted past her, hoping to avoid more questions. In the hall, I walked past the portrait of my grandparents, which took up the whole surface of an ebony mantel.

Just as soon as I thought I was free from her gaze, she said, "Did you go ask your father yet?"

I bumped into a doorway, and I stumbled forward.

Man, I want to go back to school right now. Get me out of here.

This monster of a house went on forever. It was easily triple the number of rooms of my parents' house in the city, and I knew I could go sit for a moment in the TV room upstairs. The magnetism of the Xbox would ensure none of my cousins would be up this far in the house. My head was starting to pound, and gray spots floated in my vision. Headache time.

In the 1980s, every single one of my father's sisters had left Little Village, trading in their bungalow rentals and apartments for homes in the suburbs.

Even when they had the chance, my father and mother refused to leave our house on 26th Street and Kedvale.

"It's a love for cities," my father had told me once when I asked when they were going to move to a nice neighborhood. At the time, I was only about nine, and I coveted the giant bedrooms of my cousin's homes and the long driveways where they could play without fear of a car or a bullet.

But now that I was at the university, I was glad my parents had stayed put in the city. Every single one of my new friends at school had grown up in suburbs like the one Minerva chose when she bought this house. They were homes filled with space and light, dramatic and filled with Pottery Barn furniture, but I no longer related to those things. Maybe I was like my father. Maybe a city was better. As a result, I still felt at home in Chicago, in its alleys and its anonymity.

Was my father upstairs, perhaps? I took the stairs.

Most of the lights were turned off in the upstairs portion of the house.

My footsteps echoed, and beneath them, the bunny-hop beat of the cumbia vibrated through my shoes and socks.

Minerva decorated every room in the house with two types of images: Monet prints or cats. Jungle cats. House cats. Siamese. Garfield. Every room except the TV room. In this room, the walls were bare, and the TV and DVD player's black surfaces made austere shadows. Portraits of her cats dotted the bookshelves, and I got ready to flick off the light and head back downstairs when an object caught my attention.

At the far end, I spotted the rocking chair.

My grandmother Blanca's rocking chair.

When she had been alive, she planted me in her lap in this very chair, and I screamed. I screamed again, and I kicked out my legs. I jammed my elbows in her soft belly, and my sobs finally forced her to let me off.

I had been scared of Abuela Blanca back then. Her face looked old and different. And the chair's creaking noises reminded me of the dark gap in the basement of my parent's house.

But she was dead now.

Now I was alone with the chair. I brushed my fingertips on its arm rests and relished the smooth feel.

BUT SHE'S DOWN THERE.

ABUELA BLANCA WAS THERE, IN THE DARK WORLD.

YOU KNOW WHERE, DON'T YOU?

SHE WAS DEAD AS DIRT.

SOMEWHERE IN THAT WORLD OF SOOT AND STINK.

SHE WAS DOWN THERE.

"These are shitty thoughts," I said out loud to myself. "Stop it."

Of course she was dead. But was I to believe she had gone down into that land of black mountains, black dirt and air?

Even if my grandmother had scared me, I didn't want to think of her as a corpse or a trapped soul moving into the vast abyss in the bottom of a world shaped like a spiral.

She had been my father's mother, after all. The woman who taught him everything he knew.

But your father will go down there too, you see, and he'll rot belly first, split open like a melon, and he'll sink into the stench of that place. You know this, too.

Had that been one of my thoughts? Could I really think that? Or was there someone else saying those words?

Was it a voice? It was a voice.

Though I heard no sound, that voice that spoke to me felt close and real, as if it were whispering in my ear. Its rhythms were lascivious, and its tones like the sound of night swamp.

The way it filled my head reminded me of the language of music that the Xolotl initiated me into with his blood. It had felt that close to my thoughts.

I took a seat in my grandmother's rocking chair. My feet pushed me back, and I rocked for a few moments.

For the first time, I considered that it was only mental illness—a progression of mental illness—that was making me hear voices. A mental illness that had started when I had the shit kicked out of me at Pritzker.

But it's not in your head, Clara. I'm right here. Can't you hear me?

I'm in the room with you.

Don't you see my teeth?

Can't you hear the rumble in my gut?

Can't you feel my blood thumping in my body?

I caught a movement in the bookcases, and I stopped the chair from rocking by planting my feet on the hardwood.

A shadow stretched over the bookcase next to me, and it shifted, bulging outward, like a fist through pantyhose. The shadow floated at eye level, where Minerva kept her cat encyclopedias and her ceramic doll collection. It throbbed, defying the light that created it, and I heard a rustling sound, like leaves in the month of October. Just like the voice, the sound came from inside of me, clear as anything I could hear with my ears.

I*'ve been here with you, nuzzling you. Why do you hide from me, Clara?*

I took in long breaths, trying to calm myself down.

Fight the fear.

Another shadow shifted next to the first one, and the triangular shape bent itself like taffy. They were twin shadows now, dancing just about ten feet in front of me. They formed into a shape.

I was looking at a pair of eyes, blinking, staring at me. They were big eyes, and I didn't dare imagine just how big their owner would be.

I could see the details in the dark, just like I had learned to see every shade of the color black inside Mictlán. The eyes glistened with wetness, and veins marbled their surface. It had no eyelids, just a membrane that flicked over the eyeballs as if it were blinking.

You gonna bring me your little cousin Jonas, too? You'll let me suck on those little eyeballs? I will squeeze them between my teeth like grapes.

Jonas, I thought.

I can have the infant, and your uncles, and your aunts. Bring them all to me, Wanderer?

The voice had used that word: "Wanderer."

I let out a scream, but my hand muffled it quickly. I rose from the chair. I had no idea if I would run away, but I would be ready if I had to.

I needed the comfort of something familiar, something from this world. Something good.

The voice spoke again, and its speech grew harder, more clipped. I heard nails scraping on a hard surface. Thousands of nails.

You like Abuela Blanca's chair. She did, too. I ate her up after she had the stroke. Your father Adán was right there in the room with her, and he watched her go while I bloomed in her head like the marigolds that flower down inside the valley of spines. Your grandmother, so old, so ready. She was praying to Jesus Christ when she died; did you know that? When I took her, she forgot about everything but *the Jesus. Funny, because she used to believe more in us, the citizens of Mictlán, than in that other god. She understood we were very real, but at the last moment, she turned back toward that man on the wood. Her flesh became mine.*

Did you know most of them wet themselves when I come and touch them on the shoulder to take them to the next world, Clara?

"Stop it," I said. I was talking to no one and nothing. "Stop this now."

But it doesn't stop, Clara.

Did you like it when you set the wheels in motion, Clara? When the gas blinded everyone in that hollow dome and the men were free to shoot them like cattle? When their heads exploded, round after round? When those women and teenagers got shot?

The eyes blinked, and I recognized something in them. Something feral and big.

"Xolotl!" I said, invoking the name of the creature. I had called its name once, and it stunned him. Perhaps—

Thunderous music sprouted from the bookshelves. It was angry music, full of metal and acrid tones. The music died and the sound of clicking nails returned.

I am not Xolotl, Wanderer. But I can send the Xolotl to fetch you. He can do my bidding, too. He knows your scent well.

"Who are you, then?" I said.

I am the keeper of the law in Mictlán. You don't know my name? You should know my name. LET ME WHISPER IT TO YOU.

My eardrums burst with pain from the needles of sound that stabbed my brain. My breasts stung like fire and I felt things, like cockroaches, all over my body. The sound was music, and its melody was built of sandpaper, belches and the tearing sound of teeth on flesh.

The name I heard was nothing like Xolotl's true name when he had given it to me at the gate of Mictlán.

Send me more tribute, Wanderer. Millennium Park was not enough.

I took slow steps backward, ready to bolt out of the room as soon as I got close enough to the doorway. I wanted Xbox, I wanted Corona, I wanted cumbia, I wanted my mother's prying eyes and anything else that was happening downstairs. I wanted away from this thing.

"I am imagining this," I said.

Interesting idea, the shadow said. *But how can you imagine me? Those without a tonal do not have imagination.*

But one thing is true… THEY *know you who you are.*

"Who are…*they?*" I demanded. My hand was on the doorway finally.

The Lady and the Lord. The Lords that live inside the black heart beneath the coil. Come see their faces. You will never forget their faces. They will kiss you long and hard, and you will feel the pleasures of the body, and the ejaculation of your mind. Come, Clara.

I bolted out the door. *Fuck this*, I thought. I pivoted on my heel and darted into the hallway.

I slammed into limbs and breasts, and the soft textures of a knitted sweater.

We tumbled to the ground, and I kicked out my legs and my arms, and I kept my screaming quiet, my fear tight inside my belly.

"Clara!" shouted my mother. Her hair was tangled in mine, and she tossed me off her. She was flat on her back, and she got onto her knees to inspect me.

"Get up," she said. I was stunned and my head ached, and she lifted me up in what José María called "Mexican Mother Move." She put a hand under my armpit and then hooked the other at my hip and lifted me as if I were made of paper.

"Cálmate, niña!" she said, and she slapped me. That was also part of the Mexican Mother Move.

"Clara Hortensia Montes Olmedo!" she hissed.

She said my full name. Now I knew she was angry.

I felt the shadow back in the TV room, and I wanted out. But my mother held her eye contact. Soon, I was breathing slowly again.

"I saw it."

"Saw what?"

"Black eyes," I said. I blubbered, and all of it spilled out. "This *other* thing talked to me—it's not the Xolotl, it's something else—and it says I have no tonal, I have no tonal, and is that like not having a soul? Mom!"

She smacked me hard again.

My cheek stung from her slap, but then I was crying into my mother's hair, and

(you have no tonal)

WANDERER.

"Come with me," my mother said.

She moved fast through the hallway. She opened the last door on the left, the one that led up to Minerva's attic on the third level of the house. I looked up into the white stairway and saw many hard triangular shadows, and I knew that thing I saw could move through them, bend them so it could make a pair of eyes, and I didn't want him to take my mother, or me, or anyone in the house.

But I had to trust her. She was my mother.

There was a baby below, for God's sake. And this monster up here wanted to eat everyone in the house.

It had said it would take even the baby.

I followed my mother and the folds of her gray dress.

That was the last time my mother and I climbed a set of stairs together.

This was the way my mother fit into the tapestry of the Montes clan.

She had been born Juliana Olmedo, the sole daughter of Francisco Olmedo and Antonieta Haciendas, grandparents I had only met once but who still lived in Guadalajara. My grandfather Francisco ran his own shoemaking business, and as his factories expanded from Mexico City to Monterrey, so did his wealth. My mother had been sent to the United States for university, and she met my father while she visited Los Angeles.

Their Los Angeles affair was short, their long-distance relationship long. By the time my father got on his knee for her hand, my grandparents had made up their mind that my father's family was much too vulgar and low class for my mother to marry him. When my mother married my father, she essentially said goodbye to her life in Guadalajara.

And that meant that my mother had found a home in every single one of my aunts' houses. The Montes sisters took her in as one of their own, for better or for worse, and that meant that over the years, my mother made a new family in multiple houses across Chicago: Minerva in Palos Hills. Paca and Olguita, both in Berwyn. Pati in Bridgeport, and Dolores in Tinley Park.

And then there was the oldest sister, La Negra.

Her house was in Logan Square, but none of us—not my father, nor me, nor José María, much less my mother—had set foot in there as far as I could remember.

Le Negra was absent from today's party.

She was not a party person.

You would think that having an aunt called "La Negra" would be a very racist thing, and it was.

It also wasn't.

I had tried explaining this to friends on campus, and I had run around my own words in circles and silly politically correct excuses.

The Montes called their oldest sister Veronica La Negra because she was indeed "negra." Our great-grandparents had originally hailed from Veracruz, a place filled with Caribbean blood and African ancestry. Veronica's hair and skin stood out in stark contrast to the siblings'. Even our grandmother had called her La Negra. I had witnessed our uncles crack jokes about her skin and kinky hair, and they had held their bellies to contain their cackles.

Our great-uncle often suggested La Negra should take up a career in dance, because "you know, it's in your blood, Negra." When La Negra still used to attend parties, and hip-hop songs came on the stereo at our birthday parties, hands ushered La Negra to hit the dance floor, and even my father told her she should show us what that "Veracruz blood" was made of.

La Negra had never taken well to these comments, and so she stayed away from pretty much all of us. And yet, she was closest to my father. If my partner in crime was José María, my father had La Negra.

La Negra steered wide berths around my mother, and in essence, she only chose to communicate with my father. I knew cross words had been exchanged between them at José María's baptism in 1990, but like many of the grudges that existed inside the Montes clan, they remained for years without being spoken about explicitly.

My mother and I emerged into the attic, which had been carefully painted in white. Cheap IKEA furniture provided places to sit and relax, though the space functioned more like a giant warehouse. The belongings of my grandmother Blanca were stored up here, as were those of our great-uncles and more. It was impossible to ignore the power of La Negra in this chilly corridor.

When my Abuela Blanca and my grandfather Darío died, La Negra had collected all their things and brought them up to this attic. But no one touched any of these things without La Negra's permission. She might not attend the family gatherings, but she was the keeper of these things.

"Grab that box, Clara, and bring it over here," my mother said. "Hurry."

I brought down the box on the mantle. It was an old tin sewing kit. Its circular shape felt good under my hands, and the old-time lettering on the top had faded away. Now it just shined in a dull gray under the track lighting.

I set it down on a side table next to my mother's chair.

"Mom, all this secrecy is—well, I'm just gonna say it—annoying as hell. We can't tell any of my aunts about Mictlán because…."

"Because it's more serious than you think."

You don't know the half of it. You didn't go there like I did.

"It's the worst place I've ever been," I said.

My mother considered my words and nodded. She ran a hand through my hair.

"You are intent on *not* following instructions, so I thought I'd try talking to you my way, away from your father. Woman to woman."

"Mom, I don't know what to do."

"Did the Xolotl give you any instructions?"

"No, it just wanted tribute." I didn't tell her he asked for José María as this tribute.

"And your tonal? Did you see it? Your father believes that if you find your tonal, that the shadow that hovers near you would stop haunting you."

"Ha, don't I wish. I saw nothing."

"No tonal?"

"The Xolotl dragged us, Mom; it tried eating me. But it told me its name, in the language they speak down there."

"In Náhuatl."

"No, it wasn't Náhuatl."

My mother looked confused now.

"That can't be right. No one in your father's family ever got direct experience in Mictlán—it's forbidden. But nevertheless, we expected Náhuatl to be spoken there."

Now that I thought about this, I had no way to explain how I actually felt and heard the language of the Xolotl. I knew that our blood pact had allowed me to hear it, but I couldn't even string one sentence together to explain how I experienced its language of music and inner sound.

I was only nineteen years old. I would need more time, and more experience, to one day be able to explain the language of Mictlán to another human being. I would need decades of time to do so, in fact. I failed my mother that day.

"Their language sounds, like—uh—sound," I said.

"All the stories and all the myths I learned from your father's sisters—explain that the Xolotl should speak Náhuatl, Toltec at least."

"I didn't even know what a Xolotl was until I saw it."

"I was convinced that the Xolotl is what visited you on your thirteenth birthday, but your father is not so sure anymore. I have my doubts, too."

"And just a few moments ago, I thought I saw a shadow, and it talked about seeing my grandmother when she had her stroke."

"When I married your father, his mother terrified me. Her eyes were the deepest shade of green I had ever seen, and her skin, brown and wrinkled, looked like a mask. But over time, she taught me about these traditions, and I realized she was unlike any woman I had ever met. She was a generous, smart and wise woman."

"Was she the one that taught you about all this?"

"Yes, but not at first. She didn't take well to me, not for years."

"Why didn't she like you at first?"

"These are things you only learn when you marry."

Lightning flashed through the windows as the snow storm built up power.

"What am I supposed to do now?" I said. "Just a moment ago, something spoke to me in the TV room—"

"I remember a story your grandmother told me when I was pregnant with you, and it's helped me remember things that shouldn't be remembered. But I think I know now what it is you saw in the library."

"And it's not the Xolotl?"

"It's worse. Your grandmother called it a spirit. The Ocullín."

The word sounded hard, like a knife striking through flesh and into bone. *Oh-coo-yeen.*

How can there be something worse than the Xolotl?

"The Ocullín is the servant of the Lady and Lord of Mictlán," my mother said. "He is the other side of death, the part that's difficult to celebrate. He is raw hunger for blood—he's disease."

"What does he look like?"

"We don't know. I only have stories from your grandmother. She never described it. She just said it was a terrible presence."

"What does he want with me?"

My mother cocked her head for a moment, to make sure she heard the sounds from the floors below. She lit a cigarette, cracked the window open and shut her eyes in ecstasy as she puffed into the frigid air.

"You've started smoking again," I said.

My mother laughed, beaming inside the curls of smoke.

"Your father and I thought it would be easy for you to go find your tonal in Mictlán. It's not a place we're supposed to fear, since we will all go there someday. In fact, we should celebrate Mictlán. But we had no idea how closely something like the Ocullín would follow you. It's worse than being followed by a serial murderer, or an executioner."

"What does Ocullín mean?"

"Worm. But he's worse than anything a worm could ever be."

"I'll just go back one more time then. Find it."

My mother shook her head.

"No. No more trips."

"I can do it. To make this stop."

"We regret sending you there."

My mom draped a rosary over my neck.

"From my first communion," she said. "Maybe it's time to get all the help you need."

I wanted to laugh at my mother. Despite all the madness from the past few weeks, this felt ridiculous. Seriously, a rosary? But it was typically my mother, too.

My mother took down a few cardboard boxes from the shelves, and she systematically opened and closed several until she found what she was looking for. She brought the tiny object to show it to me in her cupped hands. I expected to see something delicate and alive, like a hummingbird.

A tiny obsidian knife lay in the folds of her skin. Its handle zigzagged like the tail of a snake, and it glistened with tiny green mosaic patterns. The blade's obsidian edge absorbed light instead of reflecting it, as if it were made of shadow. The obsidian looked fragile, like glass.

"This knife belonged to your grandmother Blanca. She used it for everything. For cleaning out chilies, for cutting umbilical cords when she was a midwife, for removing splinters and for rituals, too. She also used it for contacting the spirits from her house in Oaxaca."

"Where did it come from?"

"Where all our things come from. Our ancestors," my mother said.

"So, I take this with me back to the Aragon?" I said.

My mother shook her head. She glanced at the door to make sure we were alone.

"No. No more travel through mirrors."

"What then?"

"Lake Michigan," she said. "That's the place you need to go to. Your father and his sisters can't come to an agreement on whether the Lake should be avoided or not, and by the time they decide on a course of action, it will be too late. I want you to be able to solve this as quickly as possible. And the quickest way back to Mictlán will be through Lake Michigan."

"Why the lake?"

"Terrible magic has been performed in that lake for centuries. That's why death rolls from it like a perfume. The Chicago Eastland disaster, the serial murders at the World Fairs—"

"The Millennium Riot."

"And it happens again and again. It can't be stopped."

"José María would think you're talking about his Japanese horror movies right now."

"Do NOT tell him any of this. "

"But he knows so much about Mictlán and then the way the music—"

"No. He's done enough. He shouldn't have gone with you to Mictlán. Just like the journey to find the tonal, it must be done alone."

"José María's tonal is the flint knife—shouldn't he be the one to use this thing?" I said.

"I don't know where I went wrong when you were growing up. I tried teaching you these rules, these lessons. Your tonal acts as a link to the spirit world, as a protector. And that's all. The job you have to do with this knife is different."

"How far down do I have to go?"

"Your father said all the way to the end. To the ninth level. He believes your tonal is down there."

I saw what was down at the bottom of that spiral-shaped canyon. A beating mass of darkness that pumped like a heart.

I don't want to do this anymore.

"This knife was used for sacred rituals. And you should take it to Mictlán when you go find your tonal. For good."

"I don't want to go back."

I wasn't going to cry. So I didn't.

"Put the knife away. And don't tell any of your aunts that you took it. Don't tell your father, either."

My father had been the one who wanted me to go to Mictlán, and now things were very different. I didn't understand why my mother would send me down there like this—so suddenly. But I wanted to find an end soon so I could return to daily life, to the things that actually mattered to me.

And I also trusted my mother when it came to emergencies, and this felt like an emergency.

My mother finished her smoke and put it out in an Altoids tin in her pocket.

"Let me tell you something," she said. "Even good men like your father stray, Clara. I want you to be prepared for the hardness of life."

"What does this have to do with Mictlán?"

"Your father met a woman at work years ago. They worked together at the Botanical Gardens, and she didn't leave his department until the affair was over. That lasted six years. All those years, I pretended not to know."

My headache intensified.

"Her name was Elizabeth—she knew about the history of the lake, too. That's how I knew he was cheating. Because he couldn't stop gushing about her knowledge about the magic that floated above the water.

"Elizabeth told your father that at the time—and this was around 2007—a terrible thing happened in the water of the lake.

Someone performed magic that drew on the bloody history of the city's past and made it into a solid object. According to her, that object is still there, under the water."

"If I smoked cigarettes, I'd ask you for one now," I said.

"Stop talking like that. You're wishing for what you do not want and what you do not need."

My mother closed the book, placed it in the bookcase, and walked me back to the top of the stairs. She shut off the lights, and I realized that we were actually stealing things from my aunt Minerva's house.

Things controlled by La Negra. She will find out she took it.

"Just like every house has a door, Mictlán has doors, too," my mother said.

"Yes, the Xolotl said he guards the gate."

"Yes, and doors can be opened from our side, too. The person who opened the gate in Lake Michigan was a terrible man."

"What kind of man?"

"A wizard. A corrupt wizard. He taught at the university in Guanajuato for years, but he disappeared. No one knows where—or what—he might be anymore."

"What's his name?"

"He was once called Guillermo Villa. But he's disappeared now. His only legacy is the gate he made in the lake."

It occurred to me that the glass of the Aragon's doors had functioned as a gate, too. Was that bad magic, and if so, was I responsible for it? Was José María?

"Your father will say differently, but I think you will need to go through that gate," my mother said. "It will be safer than the one you entered with José María. More stable. The citizens of Mictlán won't be able to kick you out like the Xolotl did, because they'll never even know you arrived."

"It's a side entrance?"

"That's what I'm hoping. You'll be able to travel through the nine levels and find your tonal."

"I don't see why the tonal matters so much."

"If you don't find your tonal, death will trail after you like a stench. Misery and tragedy will be your companions. And death will corrupt you."

We passed the TV room, where the Ocullín had promised me everyone in this suburban house would die, and I felt a chill race down my spine.

"And why can't we tell my dad?" I said, as darkness cloaked our shoulders but the light of the hallway lit our chins in the stairway.

"He doesn't think you're ready for a journey of this scale. He's decided it's best if he regroups with his sisters to decide your fate. I disagree."

My mother and I split when we reached the first floor. As I crept down the carpeted stairs, the music stopped. Someone fired curse words in Spanish like rounds of a machine gun.

I did my best to make it seem as if I hadn't just had my world turned upside down one more time, and squeezed past my cousins, who gathered around the fight.

My father spat out words at Minerva's husband, Horacio. My dad curled his hand around a beer. He towered over Horacio's wheelchair, but Horacio didn't care. My dad's face had gone red, and his eyes shrank into little brown pinpoints. Uncles and cousins tried to ease my father away from Horacio.

"Your medals and that wheelchair don't give you the right to run this place like it's all yours," my father said.

"Look at yourself, you hypocrite," Horacio said. "Didn't Clara herself get the shit beat out of her just weeks ago? You have a kid in the OLF, for God's sake. Your mother would be ashamed of you and that *mocosa*."

Suddenly, eyes were on me, then back on the fight before us.

"You weren't there, and you weren't either at Tlatelolco," my father said.

"Where the what?" Horacio said. He had married Minerva in Chicago, but he was fourth generation Mexican-American, with a little Irish thrown in. I suspected he didn't know what happened in Tlatelolco.

"Learn your history," my father said. He shook off the men's hands and straightened the collar on his jean jacket.

"None of you people who didn't serve know shit," Horacio said. "Look at these nubs on my hands. They used to be fingers. Five of them. And this wheelchair—the result of Fallujah. Five years serving, to protect you, and you, and you. What you got, desk jockey?"

Horacio was talking about my father and his job in the development office of the Botanic Gardens.

I had never seen my father lunge in a rage, and as he plunged forward, I was reminded of the way José María had pounced last night on the driver on Lawrence Avenue. Same animal energy.

My father swiped, and he got close, grabbing a handful of Horacio's T-shirt. He pulled it hard, and it ripped. The wheelchair started to tip over, but the men on Horacio's side righted the chair. Both men were drunk beyond belief.

"You let that girl keep on terrorizing the US and you'll see she'll end up behind bars like a damn *cholo* from 26th Street," Horacio said.

Horacio's just knocking one, after the other.

My parents still lived near 26th Street. That neighborhood had split the family in many ways. It was the place we came from, but for some of us, we never wanted to go back there.

My father brushed off the hands that held him back and stuffed his hands into his jean jacket. The gesture said, *It's safe not to touch me,* and it worked. The cousins receded and let him walk over to the rows of beers and soda on the table.

My father tossed back a plastic cup full of Patrón and he walked away, stumbling, talking to himself.

"Where is your mother?" he shouted at me. I wasn't scared of his tone. I pointed over behind him. She stood behind him with her arms crossed, and she didn't have to say a single word. Her look was enough to bring him to a neutral state, even if he was wasted.

Horacio continued to shout in the corner of the room. He had married Minerva at the age of eighteen, and three years later, he had served in Iraq. After an improvised explosive device blew off his fingers, he came back to Chicago. He attended law school, and somewhere during that time, he became bolder in his words. Very bold. I envied that.

Someone turned the cumbia back on the stereo, and suddenly, toddlers were scurrying past my legs again, screaming, smiling.

And that is how the men used to fight in our family. Just thirty minutes after the shouting match, Horacio looped an arm over my father's shoulders. My father crouched next to the wheelchair, and they shared a can of Old Style, reminiscing about things that made them laugh. This pairing created distance between them and the women, who had seen this type of behavior many times over.

I ate some cake, and the pink sprinkles on its surface sparkled like jewels. Colors continued to throb, but I was learning how to live with their intense flashes in my eye.

A hand grabbed my by the elbow. Even in his sixties, my father's wiry strength coursed through his hands.

"Follow me," he said. "You won't believe who's here."

He smiled like a child. Now that I had seen the vastness of Mictlán, I began to worry that he would go down there one day, and he would no longer be here. No more smiles, no more trips into the redwoods, no more mushroom trivia.

Stop thinking about that. It's morbid.

But it's true. He'll be gone one day. And he's not a young man, either.

The Lords at the bottom can consume him, too.

I pulled a lock of his long hair back from his brow, which was hot to the touch. It warmed up every time he drank tequila.

We walked to the back porch of the house, which overlooked a gigantic wooden deck for summer parties. Snow covered the deck. The porch was lined with narrow couches. My aunt Veronica stood up when she saw me enter the enclosed porch. She and my father exchanged smiles, sly and fun smiles.

Her arms enclosed me with the same strength of my father's. She led me back to a spot next to her on the couch.

"I need to see this girl more often, Adán," she said to my father. He was sipping water now that he had established he had drunk too much booze.

La Negra did things her own way. After working as an actuary for decades, she had quit to become a playwright. She took no shit, and though she commanded respect from all her brothers and sisters, she put distance between herself and the siblings. That's about as much as I knew about her. Her plays popped up sometimes in the city, and she had even broken into a season of the Steppenwolf Theater on Halsted. But she remained a recluse in her Logan Square apartment, accompanied by her husband, Octavio, and the plants she raised. Octavio did not attend parties, and he wasn't here tonight.

"Your father told me what happened to you after the Millennium incident," she said. Her eyes evaluated me with serenity. She made me feel nervous sometimes, but never judged.

"It's been pretty bad. I have to find my tonal, and maybe then all this weird stuff won't trail me anymore." I said.

Be vague but useful in your answer, I thought. *Be precise.*

"Well, not stuff; it's more like visions and bad luck," I said. "And I am missing my tonal."

"That's the problem," La Negra said. "Traveling to find the tonal at thirteen *may* take a child to Mictlán, but dream travel is safe in that way. You are not meant to go there with your physical body."

"But is it possible to do so?"

"Anything is possible, Clara," She said. "But it doesn't mean it should be done."

"What would happen if someone did so? What if they went into Mictlán on purpose?"

My father moved in closer to our corner. His T-shirt glowed with a deep crimson color, like blood. I wanted to stop the colors for a moment, but I bored through it.

"You shouldn't even speak of that," La Negra said.

"Your aunt is right," he said. "My first impulse was to send you there, but Veronica reminded me that our mother taught us differently."

"It's okay; I knew her longer and better than the rest of us," La Negra said.

"What do I do, then?" I said.

"You wait for us to figure this out. Together. As a family."

After everything that had happened to my body, my mind and to actual people inside and outside of this world, I had had enough of the secrets of this family, and the elephant in the room.

"Is this a family of witches, then? Why won't anyone tell me anything?" I said. I kept my voice controlled, just like my aunt. I would be more authoritative and earn more respect if I built my argument with logic and coolness.

"No, there are no such things are witches here," La Negra said. "But we have a long history of knowledge of the cosmos. And this element of nature that concerns what happens when living things move on—"

"You mean death, Negra," I said. "Let's call a spade a spade."

She liked my response. She nodded and sipped her black tea.

"Yes, I like what you're doing there, Clara. Getting down to the essence of things. Yes, death is indeed an aspect of nature. And the rites we learned from your Abuela Blanca *describe* aspects of death and the beings that live in that realm."

"Then why keep it secret? Why all the hushed words? Shouldn't we tell other people?"

"You haven't looked around outside long enough, have you, Clara? The world is collapsing. The police shot innocent people in Pritzker Pavilion. The president is deporting Mexicans again with a new Immigration Act. The creationists want to take away evolution from the classroom—"

"But creationists believe the Bible is literal and that a God with a white beard made our planet with magic. I mean, doesn't that make us all hypocrites in this house with our stories about a land of the dead? It's anti-science."

"But do the creationists have direct experience with the earth, the mountains, and the energies that move them? Do they really understand that we cannot fight death and the decay of things? Last time I checked, they still buy beauty creams and get hormone replacement therapy. They still think time stands still. If they worked directly with the cosmos, they would understand more about the things that are out there. The *creatures* that are out there."

"I don't understand what you mean," I said.

"That's the reason we stay hidden and we keep the word Mictlán away from prying ears. Because if the outside world understood what's on the other side of the gate, it would flip everything upside down."

"How do you know that? How do you know it wouldn't make things better?" I said.

My father grabbed me by the shoulders, and I was glad.

"This is why heretics were burned at the stake, Clara," he said. "We live in parallel with other beliefs about politics and ethics and religion, and that's okay.

"That's not okay with me, I don't think," I said.

I felt the thin knife poke me in the ribs inside my sweater pocket, and I moved my eyes away from La Negra. Could she know I had stolen it with my mother just minutes ago?

"A slow and methodical approach is best," she said. "If you can hold out and go back to school as if nothing has happened, then we can figure out things for you."

"But don't I get a say in this?"

"You're not twenty-six yet, and frankly, you've shunned all this knowledge for years," La Negra said. The tears in my father's eyes confirmed his agreement with his sister about this statement. "It's probably too late to teach you all you need to know."

But they didn't know what my mother knew, what José Maria knew.

They might never understand what *I* knew.

La Negra and my father didn't know how close I had come to the Xolotl and how he had shown me the chasm of darkness that could eat planets like candy.

"Dad, can I be excused?" I said.

"Sure thing," he said.

"I'm glad I got to see you, Clara," La Negra said.

"Me, too."

"Oh, and by the way," said La Negra, "The Parade of Lights—your father's convinced me to take a break from writing. Want to go together? He and I can tell you by then what we intend for you to do to shake off the stink of death from you."

"Okay," I said.

I'll see you there, for sure. So will the OLF.

I walked around the party like a ghost. None of my cousins asked me about school, my surgery, and definitely not about Millennium. I felt the heat of their young bodies emanate into the room, fogging the windows and reminding me they were full of life.

Now that you heard my name, you can give me each of their names, too.

If you give me their names, I'll know how to welcome them into this kingdom of death. And we can call each and every one tribute. You give me tribute and I give you something back.

That's also called a trade, a swap.

A trueque.

Trueque is what your ancestors called it.

Give them to me, Wanderer.

The alien voice screeched in my head, and I put my hands on a windowsill to keep myself from tipping over. I felt dizzy.

I needed to talk to the voice, but I had nowhere to do it.

I pulled up my cell phone to my face and pretended I got a call. This way, I could talk to the voice out loud without looking batshit crazy.

"What is trueque?"

A trade. A swap. I eat your eyes out, you eat mine. Or my lungs. Your pick, Wanderer.

"Shut up," I said.

Its voice swelled like a symphony in climax.

I like them young. I like their blood, and what do you need all these cousins for? I will take them when they get the deadly flu. Or maybe I'll take that one when she's hit by a car. I'll take the other one when she loses the fight with leukemia.

I walked with the phone up to my ear, pretending to laugh at the caller's joke.

Act as natural as you can.

I was almost at my destination. I marveled at the sheer size of this house.

"Tell me more, okay?" I said.

You think you'll come and find me, but the truth is, I'm going to find you, the way I find everyone. I find them when they are not looking for me. I find them, and I caress their hair, and I cut the skin, just a little at first, and—

I jammed the phone in my pocket and shook off the voice from my thoughts.

I found the room I was looking for.

There he was.

José María hadn't changed positions since I had last been here. He was shooting arrows in the last level of an epic, and the cousins around him hovered, waiting for the outcome. His fingers danced on the black controller. Of course, Gregorio, who trailed José María like a puppy, would be my target.

"Time to switch," I said. "Everyone gets a turn."

I hit the pause button on José María's controller, and he snapped out of his trance. A roar of boos from the five-year-olds on the sofa crashed in on us. Without hesitation, I handed the controller to Gregorio.

"You finish the game. Don't mess it up," I said.

Gregorio licked his lips and got to it.

Giving orders like this was easy if you were one of the older grandchildren.

"Let me guess," José María said, "things just got cray cray?"

"Oh they're cray, all right. Crazier than Dad trying to punch Horacio."

"What?"

"You missed it."

"For real? Who won?"

"That's all you care about," I said as we walked back out of the crowded room and its stink of Cheetos, apple juice and beer.

"Will you help me go back inside?" I asked José María. "No one can know."

"Sure, I'm up for some more world of tar-craft."

"No, just me this time. You stay outside, keep guard while I go into Mictlán."

"Oh, that sounds way too simple. Come on, spill it. What's the *whole* plan?"

"Mom told me what we have to do. What *I* have to do."

I showed my brother the green handle of the knife in my pocket.

"I think it's time that you had your first sleepover to visit your big sister on campus," I said.

José María smiled like a Cheshire Cat.

"I'll bring the weed."

"You're going to have to pay me so much money," José María said as he sipped a can of PBR in my dorm room. He took slow, methodical sips from the beer, trying to stay composed as the alcohol hit his liver.

"I will have to owe you," Dennis Cho said.

The game of poker was ending, and Dennis was dozing off. He scratched his balls through his basketball shorts and shuffled off to his room.

"Nice meeting you, José," he said.

José María glanced sideways in the room, as if invisible friends were there, meeting his approval. He took another sip and let out a belch.

Trying to be a grown little man among us. Always ready to prove something.

My roommate Morgan was gone for the night, so he took her bunk.

"Now, *you* are going to have to pay *me*, *reina*," José María said.

"Pay you for what?"

"For being like Reddit to you. I am an Aztec myth nerd. Ask me anything."

He was insufferable.

"I need you to tell me all you know," I said. "We don't have a lot of time before we have to go down there."

"I realize that," José María said.

"Your tonal—how did you find it?"

"I dunno—it was in my dream. On my thirteenth birthday. Just like everyone else. I fell into a dream of red-and-white clouds, and then it was next to me. A flint knife."

One of the twenty tonales.

My mother's tonal was grass. My father's was movement.

And none of it made any sense to me.

"The tonalpohualli should tell us," my brother said. He pulled out books from the stacks next to the bed. This was his collection. The tonalpohualli was the sacred Aztec calendar. Anyone could find their tonal there, like a zodiac sign. We had looked mine up. Technically, it was supposed to be the house.

"Why didn't Mom and Dad just tell us our tonal *before* we turned thirteen? Why all the mystery?"

"You don't get it, do you?" José María said. "You can know it, but you have to find it. Really find it."

"I have never seen a house. I have never felt a house. And I certainly saw nothing like a house at the gate."

"Well, you at least know what you need to find," José María said.

"Do you know how this wizard would have opened a gate in Lake Michigan?"

"Not exactly, but there is something out of the norm with stats for that year. Lake-related murders and deaths in the lake happen in the years before and after 2007. In fact, 2007 remains mostly death-free as far as I can tell. Unless you don't count the people that off themselves. There's a few suicides in the lake that year."

"You sure are casual about all this death," I said.

"Hey can we order a pizza? Munchies."

I ignored this request for a moment.

"One thing bothers me," I said. "Why isn't the gate in Mexico City itself?"

"Maybe these are gates out of space and time," José María said. "Like wormholes. You know, from physics. You open a door in one place, and it appears in another place and time This gate in Lake Michigan is secret, I think."

José María looked older suddenly, and I could really imagine him as a man, maybe with a family and a trustworthy wife someday.

José María had real imagination and a lot of heart. Not to mention all this knowledge he jammed in his memory.

"Tell me about secret gates," I said.

"No, not yet," he said, sounding even more adult than before. "Let me sleep on it, and when we get downtown tomorrow, I'll tell you my theory."

"Fine," I said. I went to brush my teeth, and he followed after me.

We both slept soundly, though I don't know how. We were more wired than ever.

Snow pelted the streets and the roof of the El train. José María wore his hoodie over his down jacket, and he looked like a puffy doll.

"If I told anybody this, they would laugh me off the street," he said, "but I think Arkangel was right. Mictlán is just a place. One of many."

"Many what?" I said.

"Many cities. Cities in other worlds. Places out of space and time, but cities nonetheless. Cities that can be *visited*."

"And what does Arkangel have to say about Mictlán? It's too late for me to learn all their music," I said.

"Well, all their songs are stories, you see," he said, "and according to the trilogy of albums, the gates opened not too long ago."

"They were sealed before?"

"Not exactly, not how you think," José María said. "Gates to the other worlds were always accessible, but that was a place for the priests and the wizards to squeeze through. According to the second album, *The Golden Architect,* a change in the cosmos is allowing more stuff to seep back and forth in our time."

"When did that happen?" I said.

"It started in late 2012, but it's almost irrelevant, because Arkangel says it's gradual. It doesn't just open up overnight."

"That means more people can step into the other worlds more easily," I said.

"Yes."

"So if a wizard made a gate in Lake Michigan in 2006, maybe

it's easier to open smaller ones, like the one at the Aragon."

"I can't believe this all sounds so normal to me, but hey, I'm listening with full attention," José María said.

"And how many worlds are there?"

"Thirteen. Says it right there in the liner notes, and the closing song."

He showed me the Arkangel CD and its kaleidoscope of red and purple shapes, the liquid lettering dripping off the edges. Its gold border.

"And that would mean there are—" I said.

"Yes, *that many* cities."

"And are all the cities in…the Aztec world?" I said. I knew that there was also an overworld for the Aztecs, and other gods and creatures that lived there.

"Oh, no," José María said, giggling. "The only city that maps to the Aztec myths is Mictlán. The other cities are—more terrifying than that. And not Aztec at all."

"How can that be?" I said.

"According to Arkangel, some of the cities are friendly to visitors. Those places can get a little spooky, but—"

I knew I could complete his sentence, because that was definitely one Arkangel chorus I knew by heart.

"Some of the thirteen cities are much, much worse than the others."

It was my suggestion to walk through Millennium Park, and even now, after everything that has happened, and all that pain, I still regret having done so.

We were stopped twice as we walked across the park. Once by security. A second time by police. They checked out our IDs, and for now, I wasn't yet flagged in their database. My heart didn't stop racing until we reached the center of the park.

The city had announced that the park would be remodeled into a memorial for freedom in 2017. The Pritzker dome was already being dismantled to make way for the spear-shaped tower that would take its place.

The snow hid the grass, and I was glad. The layer of ice helped me keep some distance from the memories of all that death on the ground. The color green was an instant reminder of the Millennium Riot, and I welcomed the lie that the snow told me.

Temperatures were dropping fast, and we inched along the BP bridge. Memories blasted my mind, and the colors of the city screamed as if they were made of neon and fire. I shut my eyes for a few seconds at a time.

Breathe.

I fought off nausea and fear, and José María smoked a joint, whistling to himself and sliding down the last twenty feet of the bridge as if on a slide. The rock salt on the ground impeded his movement, but he looked happy anyway.

We walked along the bike path, headed to the very spot where my father had burned twigs over the water on my birthday. We didn't talk as the gray clouds rolled over the water of the lake.

"If that is where we go to die, it seems too sad," I said.

"Mictlán, you mean?" said José María.

I nodded.

"Well, other Gods have been down there; you know that," he said.

"Quetzalcóatl?"

Quetzalcóatl. The most iconic of all Aztec gods. Perhaps the only one that people recognized in America. He was the feathered snake. The bearded white man. The progeny of the sun.

"They called him the White Tezcatlipoca," José María said. "He's one of the four Tezcatlipocas."

"That makes no sense. How could four separate gods be the incarnation of a single god?" I said.

"Well, you heard of the trinity in the Catholic Church. Doesn't take a genius to see how it works."

"And he went down to Mictlán, then?"

"Sure, he went down there to restore life to humankind. Because all the humans had died out already."

The way they die when a flu pandemic wipes them out. Or when meteors hit the Earth. Or when nuclear blasts pulverize us off the planet.

"But he's not down there at all now, is he?"

"He went there once, and whatever he did there allowed man to be reborn. He got the fuck out, like any sane god with superpowers would do."

I laughed, but I had to know for sure.

"Couldn't he *still* be there?" José María said.

"Not sure what Quetzalcoatl looks like, so I don't know."

"Well, he's not made of darkness, so if you saw him, you would know. He'd maybe be radiating light. And you know, it's not like he could hide—being a feathered serpent and all—"

"Shut up," I said. "If he was down there ages ago, it doesn't matter. That's not gonna help us. I have one thing to do, and it's my tonal."

"Good deal," my brother said, respecting my anger and confusion.

We rolled off our packs from our shoulders and found a spot right north of Chicago Avenue. From this curved part of the bike path, we could lean over the concrete and see the gray waves leap toward us.

"You'll wait for me here, then," I said. "If I'm gone too long, well, you'll know what happened."

"You're coming back; don't worry."

I wanted to believe everything my brother said.

He removed his winter coat and got down to his hoodie. He rolled up the sleeves and his tattooed arms got to work. He set a thin blanket on the ground and placed a set of tools on it in even rows.

We performed the ritual according to what we remembered hearing from our grandmother Blanca when we were children, stories my father told us and the books that José María carried in his L.L. Bean pack.

The ritual hurt. We sat cross-legged, drumming the concrete at first with wooden spatulas—it's all we could find—José María smoking his cigarette and invoking words in the best Náhuatl he could muster. We burned herbs that José María stole from our parents' house.

It was weak drumming in terms of volume, but we both felt it and heard it.

And the longer we drummed, the more the sounds of Lakeshore Drive faded away.

We drummed in a steady beat, and the waves of the lake got quieter.

I worried we'd break the wooden spoons, but they skittered on the concrete over and over.

I was scared of the Xolotl and even more scared of the creature called the Ocullín, but I saw the face of the woman at the Pritzker haunting me. I saw her eyes go flat again, and I wanted to fix the emptiness I saw in them.

The drumming felt steady, but our arms grew tired. What was I supposed to hear or see?

We gave it a go this way, risking hypothermia and frostbite for an hour. Nothing worked. The sun would rise soon, and I felt frustrated.

"Not working, *reina*," José María said. He laughed.

"Stop laughing; fix this."

"Fine," he said.

He reached into his pack for a headphone splitter, and he jacked both of us into his iPod. He put his giant headphones over his head, and I stuffed earbuds into my ear canals.

He tapped the playlist named "#13SC," and it started to play.

We had drummed on the concrete, convinced that would help us find the entrance, but we had been wrong. What we needed besides beats was to *feel* the sound, to feel music.

The first few bars of "Plainsong" by Arkangel pirouetted inside our ears.

The music swelled in our brains, and the withering guitars and the thunder of the synthesizers pulled us into its depths. We moved on from song one to song two and on and on, until we couldn't keep track.

The songs put us in a trance. José María's Parliament Lights and the weed he packed into them wafted in our noses, and suddenly, we were moving in a mental space that was quiet, punctuated by drums, and soft, so soft.

We didn't drum anymore. We sat on the blanket, shivering, listening.

We fell into this place for what seemed like hours, and we climbed down into the very structures of Arkangel's music, as if it were a solid ladder leading us up a tree and into the woods.

When the playlist ended, I opened my eyes. José María was there, still as a statue, with his eyes closed, as if in meditation. I stared in front of me at the Lake beneath.

Below our patch of concrete, a large crevasse had opened on the surface of Lake Michigan. A set of iridescent stairs led downward, and the light that shone from its walls was so brilliant, it glowed.

The hole in the water defied the laws of gravity. It was just wide enough for a person to walk through, and even as small splashes of water surged up to its edge, I saw the droplets of water strike the interior of the opening. Even the floor shimmered in an emerald color.

I stood up, and I took a step down. Then another. And another. Soon, the water level of the lake was up to my waist, but I was dry as ever. The water held its shape around the hole. A perfect tunnel with stairs.

I touched one the walls with my fingers and gasped when it moved as if it were alive.

It was made of living things.

One by one, millions of green butterflies overlapped, silently vibrating. They made perfect patterns, forming a surface made of what seemed like scales.

Like dragon scales.

No!

Like snake scales, wanderer.

And as I took a step into the tunnel, the walls shimmered in long waves. I put my feet on the green floor and stared off into its depths. It continued forward seemingly forever but pointing toward the center of Lake Michigan.

"This is the object that the wizard built," José María said from behind me. I could still see him behind me, standing on the concrete at the top of the butterfly stairs.

"Stay here," I said. "You know what you need to do."

"Sure thing, boss," rang my brother's voice.

When all of this is over, I can't wait to go back to the plans we have for the Parade of Lights with the OFA. This will all be over, and I can go back to school and the things I love. That will be my reward for doing this.

Each step I took made a soft sound, like a cat's purr, and soon, the sunlight from above had disappeared, and my skin was bathed in emerald light.

I felt in my winter coat for La Negra's knife. I had no idea why this entrance to Mictlán would be safer than the passage we found in the Aragon, but it sure was more beautiful.

Then I heard the wings flutter behind me by the thousands, and I snapped my neck around.

The gate is closing.

I felt the anxiety of suffocation come over me, and I tried to calm down.

You'll drown in here, bonita. *Drowned forever, and under thousands of pounds of pressure from the water.*

You'll never leave. But you sure will be mine.

The bits of sunlight that filtered through the gate above dimmed.

José María was outside, and now I was down here. There was no going back.

I turned back toward the place where the entrance had opened up.

It was sealed up tight now, and the gray light of late autumn was done.

I tried taking a step into the tunnel, but I couldn't move my feet. I was too scared.

The walls shimmered in green, and their light felt alien, cold.

I needed to do something to calm my nerves that could help me keep going. I covered my good eye with one hand. The open dead eye returned nothing to me but darkness. That dark wasn't as scary anymore. I knew what darkness could really be.

I can't do this.

I took several breaths to calm myself down.

And then I felt a hand on my shoulder, and I shrieked as loud as I could.

"Relax, *reina*!" I heard my brother's voice and in a blur, I saw his long face , his whiskered chin. He had snuck down next to me, slinking behind me.

You have a blind spot, Miss Cyclops. He took advantage of your blind spot.

"José María!"

"Now, you didn't think I was going to let you go get autographs from the gods of death and I would stay behind just to text and play on Instagram, did you?"

The gods of death. The masters of the thing called Ocullín.

The Lady is Mictecacíhuatl. The Lord is Mictlantecuhtli.

They are the Lords of death.

Suddenly, I realized I had learned the names of the things called "Lords." And knowing their names felt like power.

I wanted to rattle my brother by the neck, though.

"You were supposed to stay up there, fool!" I said. "How will we reopen the door?"

"Shut up and let's get moving," he said. "Who knows how solid this tunnel actually is? I mean, look at it. It's *old*."

He was right. Many of the butterflies' wings looked nicked, as if they had been here so long that their tiny scales had fallen off.

From inside the green corridor, we heard a roar, like that of an animal. The walls gave off a slight emerald strobe effect. My brother's face looked goblin green and his hair reddish under the shimmer of the tunnel.

"Come on," I said, leading the way. "Before these butterflies collapse on us."

We stepped on metallic insect bodies, and they provided support for our feet. The butterflies stayed glued to the surface of the tunnel even as our feet murdered them by the dozens. Green scales caked the edges of my boot. Each step we took caused the wings of the butterflies to whisper, like an animal taking its last breath.

The corridor stretched on for what seemed like forever. As I walked, I saw at least two distinct sets of footprints on the ground. People had been here before.

PART THREE
BLUE TEZCATLIPOCA

BLUE HUMMINGBIRD, SORCERER OF MY HEART

"At the age of nineteen, I demonstrated for my mother my camera obscura, and she screamed in terror. It is the work of the devil, she said. She didn't want to look through it ever again.. That's one of my strongest memories of her during my youth in Philadelphia." – Photographer Harvey De Castille, in an 1899 letter to George Eastman, Eastman Kodak Company private archive, New Jersey.

"If you want to glimpse at the god Huitzilopochtli, all you have to do is play a sport, play a match of chess, or go to war. To call Huitzilopochtli's name is to invoke battles. He has that power. But I think I misunderstood your question, child. What do his mommy and daddy call him, you say? Oh, that's simple. His parents call him Blue Tezcatlipoca." – Q&A by children's author Paolo Verdi at the Global Children's Book Summit, Mexico City, September 2013.

"Even the gods abandon the places where they once thrived." – Arkangel, "My Name is Dita", *The Violet Album,* 2008, Reckless Records.

The tunnel of green butterflies curved, which meant that we couldn't see how far it stretched into Lake Michigan. As soon as we advanced a few more hundred feet, we still had more ground to cover. I felt guilty stepping over so many insects with my winter boots, but the butterflies never took off in flight.

Above us, thousands of pounds of water bore down on us, ready to crush our bodies, but the wall was as firm to the touch as wood. My fingers came away with green stains from wing scales.

The cylindrical shape shimmered and pulsed each time its musical tones echoed in the hall. The steamy air was making me sweat, and I shrugged off my wool coat. I re-slung my backpack over my shoulders and wiped my forehead with the back of my hand.

"This is insane," José María said. "How was this thing built?"

"Mom said a wizard built it," I said. I felt vulnerable saying this out loud. Could the walls hear me? Was it wrong to talk this way inside this tunnel?

"What kind of wizard?" my brother said.

"I don't know what kind of wizards there are."

We had been walking for twenty minutes now. Roughly a mile by my estimate.

"So, a tunnel into Mictlán…" José María said. "Why would that wizard leave it behind for anyone to find?"

"Maybe it was so much work to put up that it would be even more work to collapse again," I said.

"Like building a house."

We stopped for a moment for my brother to tie his shoelaces and take off his parka. He took my coat from my arms and laid it flat on the ground. Then he placed his parka on top. He folded once, twice, and then he tied the bundle using the sleeves. He stuffed the bundle into his backpack.

"How do you know how to do that?" I said.

"Dad showed us when we went to the Redwoods, remember?"

I did remember. My father took us by the hand to forage for berries and photograph mushrooms. Mom had stayed up in the tent, making dinner. My dad had draped our coats over a tree log and folded it several times. He spoke the directions out loud to me, but José María had been the one to learn.

"Wish I had paid attention." I said.

"Don't worry; I'll show you."

My brother repeated the process, and he guided my hands over the sleeves to make sure I had learned it. Within minutes, he taught me how to pack my coat like a tiny brick, just like him. We dusted the green streaks of butterfly scales off the pack and continued again in silence, and I checked the time every twenty minutes or so.

Three miles.

An animal's bellow traveled inside the walls of the tunnel, and I remembered the savage dog face of the creature Xolotl.

In this deeper stretch of the tunnel, the butterfly wings took on a purplish hue, and streaks of violet swirled in the semicircular corridor. We didn't carry flashlights with us, yet the walls emitted their own glow, as if each scale gave off a tiny bit of sunshine.

The path before us curved more sharply now, and I pictured the shape of a hook curled inside the lake like an animal tail.

I looked at my watch. Six miles.

We came upon a sharper bend, and as we walked through it, light stung my eyes. The ground felt a little softer here, and my feet sank deeper into the floor. I grabbed José María's hand as we stepped into the room.

Light filled my eyes, and I raised a hand to my brow to keep the glare out.

"Daaaaaaaaaaaaaaaaamn," José María said.

We had entered a dome. It rose for about 300 feet, and the iridescence blasted our eyes in green and violet.

"This is like Arkangel's tunnel!" my brother said. He might be Chicago's resident expert on all things Arkangel, but he often forgot that *I* didn't know the Norwegian band as well as he did.

"How so?" I said.

"The song says that a tunnel connects Mictlán to the City of Dust. And the City of Dust connects to the City of Stone Spirits. The gods build tunnels shaped like webs. The tunnels that men build are different. They are shaped like domes."

"Mom said the wizard Guillermo Villa wanted to enter Mictlán," I said. "He left this structure behind after he disappeared."

I did not fully understand how Arkangel's music could provide clues about the city of Mictlán, but José María had made connections that thus far had proved to be true.

Azul vs. Fibonacci, the second album in Arkangel's trilogy of albums about the 13 Secret Cities, said that the web tunnels of the gods pre-dated the existence of time.

The brother-and-sister duo of Arkangel always performed live while wearing monster masks, and they ended every concert by crowd-surfing down onto the dance floor. It was there that they wailed into their mics, dancing in ecstasy, writhing like lunatics. Their music thundered through a mix of the most cutting-edge electronic instruments, and guitars that shimmered like polished glass. The siblings' names were Sergio and Karyn Andersson.

No one had ever seen what the brother-and-sister duo looked like in real life.

"I have to admit, Arkangel has always scared me a little," I said.

"Good," José María said, smiling.

I slapped his arm and ran my hand over the walls of the dome. The butterflies shifted under my palm, and the animal sound we heard before came through again.

"You're upsetting the green pets, *reina*," my brother said.

"No, I don't think so," I said. I pressed again, and the howl subsided. "I think the dome is making sound, together—all the bugs together as a unit."

I couldn't imagine how many butterflies it took to make a tunnel and dome like this one, but indeed, if I pressed on the walls, the dome grunted like a sleeping beast.

"Can you talk to it like you did with the Xolotl?" José María said.

"We can try," I said. "But I have to tell you something about how I was finally able to talk to it."

"Shoot."

"It requires a blood sacrifice. He cut me, and he cut himself too, with his knife. He made us go through a blood exchange. Once I had his blood in me, we could communicate. Brings a whole new meaning to the human sacrifices of the Aztecs."

José María shivered, and for once, he didn't have a sardonic comeback. He was spooked.

The butterflies' shine blinded me, just like most colors were hurting my single good eye lately. When the colors flooded my vision this way, I sometimes had to lie down from the migraines they induced. But I was learning to cope with the headaches. And I needed to see these green walls in order to try out my next idea.

I may have been damaged by the memories of the bloodshed I witnessed in Millennium Park and the world without light called Mictlán, but I wasn't stupid. I had paid attention to what I learned in Mictlán.

I withdrew the obsidian knife from my backpack.

"Where'd you get that?" said my brother.

"Mom gave it to me."

"Impossible! It's supposed to be up in Minerva's house."

"You know about it?"

"Dad showed it to me last year when we helped her organize

boxes up there."

"So, besides organizing our attic three times over, he's also organizing Minerva's house?"

"You know that's what he does when he's stressed out," he said, rolling his eyes.

"I wish I had an activity like organizing boxes for when shit gets heavy," I said.

José María blinked and adjusted the sleeves on his T-shirt. He didn't seem to buckle under *any* pressure.

We moved close to the wall and I plunged the knife into it. The dome grunted, and I detected its own musical voice. It made the tiny chirps we had heard before as we walked through its length. The wall of butterflies split under the blade, and black blood ran in a single droplet down the cut I made in the wall.

But the structure held strong. I tried peering into the cut, but all I saw were more butterflies.

Good.

José María cringed.

"You know I don't like blood," he said. The color drained from his face, and squatted on his haunches and panted.

"Relax," I told him.

The knife's jade handle felt right for the palm of my hand. I had enjoyed plunging its sharp edge into the living wall.

I took a deep breath and I rolled up the sleeve of my T-shirt. I put the blade on the meaty part of my shoulder, and I sliced across the muscle. Heat bloomed in a straight line on my skin.

Now that my eyes sensed colors so intensely, the red liquid that came up to the surface of the cut looked like molten lava. It ran fast, moving down my brown arm and onto my hand. I wiped as much of it as I could with my free hand, and when it was bathed in red, I plunged it into the cut I made into the wall.

A flash of green light blinded me, and then a thousand black spots detonated in my brain.

I waited a second, and soon, I lost track of my body, but I felt the dome speak to me in a skittering musical voice. And I spoke to it in blood, the way the Xolotl taught me. Speaking in blood allowed me to think in English, while my lips spoke words in another language I did not know.

"She speaks," the dome said.

"Hi," I said.

A hand yanked at my T-shirt sleeve.

"Oh, no, you dork," José María said. "You're not leaving me out of the conversation this time."

"Just a second," I said to the green wall, and turned to my brother. "You sure? You don't like blood and—"

"I know, but some shit is worth it," he said, and he yanked the knife from me. His eyes watered at the sight of my own bloody skin, and for a second, I thought he might cry, just like he used to when he got vaccinated as a toddler.

He sliced himself across his hand, and he jammed it into the cut I had carved in the dome.

He's so reckless, I thought.

My brother's scrawny body jolted, and for a moment, I thought he might be having a seizure. He arched his back, and his eyes took on a watery appearance. And then he did cry a little. His skin flickered into a darker shade of brown, and then it came back to its original color.

José María withdrew his hand and sat down cross legged in front of the wall. He pressed his hand into a fist, and kept it as far from his sight as he could. I knew that if he saw more blood, he'd faint.

"Well, aren't you a little chatterbox?" he said, and the skittering chirps from the dome turned into words.

"Humans," the dome said. "We meet."

"We need to go farther," I said to the dome.

"You need to continue onward through the gate, then," said the dome. "My path is free."

"There are no doors here," I said.

"Yes, there are," said the voice. "You are standing in front of all of them."

"How many are there?" I said.

The high notes of the wall turned into a screech, and silence fell on the circular room. For a moment, I felt as if the presence that lived in the wall had gone away.

"Don't make her angry," José María said. "You gotta learn how to talk *her* way."

"Can you tell us who made you?" I said.

"Indeed. The Black Wings made me," said the dome.

"My mother told me a wizard made you." I said. A flash of purple swelled through the dome.

"Yes, the Black Wings called us to this place. You call him wizard, but my name for him is Black Wings. He built this structure, and the dome invoked my spirit to inhabit it. If you look down, you can see the footsteps the Black Wings left."

On the other side of the dome's circular floor, I spotted them. Black indentations made by men's dress shoes. I guessed they must have been a size ten.

"And where is the wizard now?" I said.

"You don't understand, do you?" the dome said, and I felt afraid.

"Understand what?" I said.

"Time will press down on you."

"Can you repeat that?" I said.

"Time will crush you, and then you will see how there are beings that watch our every move. You will learn this. And it will be then that *he* will find you."

"Who?" José María and I said at the same time.

"The wizard who goes by the name of Black Wings will," the dome said. "He will find you one day."

I didn't like this riddle. José María held up his index finger to signal for me to wait. He was going to say something.

"Did the Black Wings wizard travel to Mictlán through your gate?" José María asked.

The wall's chirps softened. It looked like the wound in my brother's hand was clotting up, and now that he felt a little more confident, he put his hand on the wall. The butterflies remained frozen in their catatonic state, but José Maria looked pleased.

"Your male counterpart is clever," the dome said to me. Its voice flowed out from the walls slowly, like a river of honey. "Very clever. No, the wizard Black Wings never reached Mictlán through this tunnel. He didn't have enough power to go there. After he built this tunnel and dome, he returned to the world above. I have been abandoned down here alone for years in this kingdom of water."

"Did he go by the name Guillermo?" I asked.

The dome hissed so loudly, I felt the sound brush my shoulders. It sounded like the word "yes."

"And why would the wizard leave you down here?" I asked.

"To leave his legacy behind. He thought he would be remembered if he made me. Most men seek this type of legacy.

This is why they build temples, towers and domes. To cheat time. That wizard used me for that purpose."

The dome spoke to me through images then, and it showed me a sequence of them, one after the other. They were images of eggs, thousands of them, colored blue, like the color of the sky. More images followed: water, stones in water, and then a coiled nest that looked like a loop of ropes, sitting on the floor of Lake Michigan.

"Oh my god," I said to José María. "She thinks—"

"Yes, she's definitely a she, isn't she?" he said.

"But how could she think that she is a female? I mean, she's a—"

"But why not?"

"Clara, the dome thinks she's a snake," José María said.

Now I understood what the dome was trying to tell me. This long butterfly tunnel was under the delusion that she was a snake. A female snake.

"But who are we to say what she is or she isn't?" my brother said.

"I don't know," I said. "I don't know at all."

I supposed my brother was right. But how could this thing made of butterflies think she was something or someone else?

The dome sparkled in green and violet, and then it went silent again.

"What happened?" I said.

"She's straining. It takes too much effort to talk through the dome," José María said. "That's what she said."

"I didn't hear her say anything."

"Well, she said it to *me, reina.* Through its blood. This bloodletting language works after all."

José María's been having a separate conversation with the dome all this time.

"She said we have to go now," José María said. "She'll be waiting for us to come back through when we're done, but for now, talking is too difficult for her."

"How do we enter the gate, then?" I said.

"She told me. Like this!" José María said, as he grabbed me by the wrist. We sprinted toward the center of the floor.

"No, no, no!" I said. I wanted my little squirrel of a brother to stop, to stop and think, to wait just one second—

"Jump!" my brother commanded, and I used all the strength in my legs to leap. We jumped.

In midair, the dome's voice filled our ears with a long, deep sound. As our feet approached the ground, the butterflies that formed the walls of this place shifted and folded like origami, and before I knew it, millions of insects rushed toward us, devouring us in green. As their tiny wings fluttered around us, I spotted white light bursting through the spaces between each butterfly.

And then, in the way in which my mind had exploded once as I had traveled through a glass door at the Aragon, my vision got pulled apart until I burst. This time, I fell into a sea of white light, and soon, I forgot the sensation of my brother's arm wrapped around my wrist.

I moved through the gate and beyond.

Before I reached Mictlán, I glimpsed three cities. Ever since I saw those shocking cities, my life has never been the same.

It was a short journey, but as I soared through a white expanse, I caught glimpses through my peripheral vision. Though I could not see José María next to me nor feel his hand in mine, his presence moved alongside me. It was like seeing scenery roll by from a train, except that each image floated near me in a flurry of music, building up in my ears, then fading fast.

The first city was not much more than an image of flat lines that rose like a wall before me, and each of the lines went on forever, like a fence that ascended into infinity. The music in my ears informed me that the lines were only a protective structure, like a wall. The lines did not look solid but thin and ethereal, like gas. Beneath the lines lay the city, gnarled and rusty, like a junk heap. For a second, I caught a glimpse of an animal's face staring at me from one of the towers in that city.

And then that city was gone.

I soared faster now, but I didn't move forward. Instead, I twisted sideways, as if I might be expanding like a balloon. As I lost all sense of my body, I saw it: in the distance, a new city lay suspended in the air. The city was completely deserted but decked out in the most lavish gold architecture I had ever seen in my life. The metropolis was shaped like a nautilus shell, and it hung in space like a miniature planet.

It was deserted.

I felt the loneliness inside its steeples and its towers, and I felt very afraid.

And then that city disappeared, too.

The whiteness shrank, and I shrank with it. Soon, I was tiny, microscopic, and out of the corner of my eye, I spotted two pairs of eyes watching me. They belonged to a creature that looked hundreds of feet long, snakelike and watery. The animal's four eyes emitted a cymbal sound, and then the animal crawled up a structure built like a spider web. I understood then that the web structure was a city, too, and that other four-eyed creatures lived there. Hiding inside the tiny houses, I spotted little human figures with tiny pinpoints of light as eyes. They were watching me. I knew this, because I caught them staring at me from the corners. Soon, millions of eyes were looking at me. Both the animals and the humanoids took me in, analyzed me, sought me… They blinked in unison, and they spoke to me. *Come join us,* they said to me.

The sounds died, and then the web structure blew apart, as if made of dust. I had no body and no face, and yet I hung in this fast-moving white place.

And then, the white space of the gate spat me out into Mictlán.

To my surprise, I could still feel José María's hand wrapped around mine, and the way in which I rushed back into my body turned my stomach. Nausea churned in my gut, and I wanted to vomit, but the scream in my lungs made me forget.

Just like before, we were bathed in the darkness of Mictlán.

We rushed downward, and our clothes flapped around us. My hair was plastered to my face, and I felt the yank of my brother's arm. He grabbed my other free hand.

"Open your *ears*, *tonta*!" my brother screamed.

I relaxed and allowed the sounds of Mictlán to show me things around me. My open eyes took in the vast blackness of the place, but through the sound, I could feel and pinpoint the details of my body and its relation to the world around us. José María emitted twin cones of sound, like the Xolotl had done so before, and I also had my own cones. My brother's charcoal skin, eyes and clothes came into sharp detail, and I realized why his thin T-shirt flapped with fury.

We're free-falling like skydivers.

I turned my attention below, and I felt a familiar landscape. The mountain we had climbed during our first trip lay to our right, but it was tiny now. We fell toward the spiral-shaped canyon next to it, and I gasped at the sheer size of it. The canyon looked like it could contain a thousand earths.

"Ohhhh!" I heard my brother scream as we plummeted. We were headed toward large objects inside the canyon.

"Are those things alive?" I screamed.

We were about to land on top of two animals the size of mountains. One creature was shaped like a pitchfork, with curling hairs and blades of bone that adorned its body like tattoos.

The pitchfork creature jammed its thin limbs into another creature. They both roared and screamed.

The adversary was just as tall as the pitchfork animal but shaped instead like a triceratops head without eyes—like a beak with a plate and two horns. Each one of these creatures was bound to the earth and legless. It was only their heads and limbs that rose through their volcano-like bodies.

The animals clashed, and they drew blood. They roared again, took a quick breath, and then they clashed again, driving their horns and claws into each other's flesh. They ripped out whole chunks, and the flesh crumbled like dry clay. We were headed straight for the head of the triceratops creature.

Our bodies accelerated toward the ground, and I knew that the hard, bony surfaces of the triceratops head would crush our bones on impact.

José María whistled to get my attention, and he drew my body in tighter. We interlaced our arms. We braced for impact on top of the gigantic monster, which could have been the size of the whole city of Chicago.

The two creatures locked their heads together, and as we rushed the last hundred feet to strike, the giants broke their lock on each other. They pulled apart, screeching like violins out of tune, and they recoiled away from each other.

We fell through the space between them. As I did so, I felt the details of these creatures come into sharper detail.

The triceratops monster was covered with tiny orbs. From up high, the creature had looked eyeless, but now that I was close, my sonar ability told me that the rows of tiny orbs were eyes. Those eyes were made up of thousands more eyes, and inside each one, I heard scorpions, crawling around inside the eyeballs like a prize. Each orb had an ancient presence, and I distinctly felt each of those eyes evaluate us as we flew past them.

The pitchfork creature had no mouth, but it sang a long bellow of rage and fury. As we flew past it, I could almost feel the velvety touch of the creature's tendrils and the prongs that made up its mountain-like body.

I never wanted to see things so alien and so foreign again.

There was a sense of freedom as we free-fell, and I could feel my brother's excitement in his heartbeat as we sped through the gap between the fighting mountains.

José María's screams were pure joy, like a thumping R&B jam, while the wet fear in my vocal cords made the music from my body howl and screech without a single bit of melody.

We would strike the land below the monster very soon.

"They have no feet," my brother said. "Those monsters have no feet!"

My heartbeat thumped, and the ground rushed at us. We struck it facedown, and the smack of earth on my arms, belly and face made my whole body shake. Surely I would break my bones instantly.

But my brother and I held. I hurt from the fall, but I felt a softness in the ground beneath me, and I was grateful to

(Who, god?)

whatever broke our fall. José María

We fell into brambles that looked as sharp as rose thorns but instead were gauzy and feathery like dandelion heads.

I scrambled up to my feet, and José María got up from the ground with the same sense of urgency. Above us, I could hear the rumbling that the giants made, and I wanted to get as far from them as I could. They were going to clash again, and the crumbling rocks and earthquakes they made might kill us. They were so large that running away from them could easily takes us many hours to get away from them, but I didn't care. We pummeled the ground as fast as we could.

As we ran, the terrain around us came alive. The sounds I emitted from my body let me see all around me as the sonar that existed in Mictlán revealed details around me. Above us, the two monsters continued to clash, oblivious of our escape.

We ran for a good half hour, and though we hadn't cleared the valley between the mountain monsters, they continued to recede from each other, as if taking a break from their clash.

The road beneath began to change the farther we moved. From this spot in the canyon, I could see across to the other side, where the spiral shape of its walls led downward. We slowed down to a walk a few times, but we never stopped.

We eventually reached the outskirts of the monsters' bodies. As I peeked behind them, I realized they were cemented to the ground.

"They're the clashing mountains just like the Aztecs described," José María said. "Mictlán, level one, COMPLETE."

"Shut up," I said. We ran a little more.

As we ran, my shoes skidded on pebbles. Eventually, the stings of the pebbles were fewer and farther between, and the ground below felt clean and smooth.

It felt good to be on more stable ground, and I hoped that the mountain creatures would continue to ignore us.

We were now traveling along a road. It was paved with more precision than a German highway. It stretched on, several hundreds of feet in width, and the way that sound bounced on it told me that its smooth surface glistened as if made of glass. Our feet did not slip on its surface. Instead, the ground gave our winter boots just the right amount of slickness and friction so that running felt effortless. Behind us, the two colossi continued to fight, and chunks of rock were pulverized into dust around them, creating sounds like a war zone. I smelled the blood on their claws, even from our miles in distance.

We took a short walking break until we could jog again. As we picked up speed again, I felt full of movement, as if a gentle hand propelled us to become faster runners in the dark.

"We can't run like this," I said. "We're not marathoners. We have to figure out where to rest, and find some food."

My brother nodded. But there was no safe place to rest, not if the giants found us with their million eyes again. Our packs bobbed up and down and their straps cut into our shoulders, but we were not going to get rid of our stuff.

My calves burned from exertion, and my brow was sticky with sweat. But slowing down allowed me to notice the other things on the wall that flanked this road.

Things that seemed alive, even in this world of the dead.

Slowing down let me appreciate the smaller details of the landscape. I could see tiny plants and insects on the canyon walls on our right. When I glanced at them on the wall, they dispersed in tiny clouds, and when I looked away, they returned to their perching spot.

Though our pace was very slow, I noticed that the animals on the wall seemed to move past us very quickly.

This speed was impossible.

"This feels amazing," José María said, and he took a few hops in his jog, as the trees on our left side began to whiz by and blur.

I looked behind me, and the clashing mountains were now very far away, nothing more than pinpoints in the distance. How had traveled so far, so fast?

Then I felt it. Something throbbed under the ground beneath us. The force below made the smooth road shift in a very tight rhythm, like the surface of a drum vibrating. As we moved farther along the valley, I got the sense of freedom I felt back in Chicago at O'Hare on the moving walkways.

The ground below us didn't make any music. Instead, it throbbed and pulsed.

We were finally leaving behind the vastness of the giants. I could no longer feel them with my sonar, and all I sensed from that direction were tiny peaks.

"The legends talk about those mountains," I said to José María.

"Yes, passing through them is supposed to be one of the trials for those who visit Mictlán," José María said.

"But no mountains should ever have eyes, and no mountain with eyes should look into the dark with such knowledge, with such presence."

"Why not?"

"Because it's scary, that's why."

"And those eyes… Millions of them, Clara."

"In a place that has no light, no color and no sun, why would these giant mountains have the need for vision? Why have eyes at all?"

"Dunno," my brother said.

The uncertainty of the possible answers to that question terrified me.

I was glad the mountains were gone from our range of hearing.

The road on which we ran cut a path through a thick jungle. A canopy of their leaves floated above our heads, and meanwhile, the ground pulsed with more intensity. The rubbery leaves of the canopy above us made a latticework of hexagons and octagons. On our right, the wall continued to host a variety of intricate-looking birds and mushrooms, none of which I dared touch.

The road was as wide as the length of a football field, but so far, we hadn't ventured to its inner edge. I grabbed my brother's hand, and as we walked forward, we drifted across its width until we reached the edge.

The cones of sound that projected from our heads and shoulders spilled into the darkness, and using their sound, we tried to pinpoint our location.

This wall followed the shape of the canyon of Mictlán, and from the ledge of this smooth road, I stared deep into the spiral canyon.

We were located along the outer edges of the spiral, moving downward into its core. The canyon remained as breathtaking as the first time I had experienced it. It moved for thousands of miles downward, into the dark, and along its path, I spotted more trees and, off in the distance, structures like buildings, punctuating the path down the coil.

"I am thirsty," I said.

José María slowed his jog down to a walk and handed me the water bottle from his pack. I had no choice but to slow down, too. The trees made no noise, no music. The ground, which continued to move us through at amazing speed like a conveyor belt, also made no noise, other than its occasional throb.

"That's the best water I have ever had in my life." I said.

"You don't get out much, do you?" my brother said.

"I was hoping we would enter in a place far away from the Xolotl," I said.

"You got your wish. Looks like we came down right in the upper levels of the place. We bypassed the mountain above the canyon."

"I've never seen monsters like those mountain things, José María."

"They're not monsters. They're in the legends. Those were mountains that clash in the first level of Mictlán, Clara. Mountains with hands."

And eyes. Too many eyes.

Up ahead, down the slope of the road, a voice hummed a melody, forlorn and silken.

"Those mountains have names," the voice said. Its timbre was deep, its pitch glossy and dark. "You have forgotten to implore the mountain's names as you passed through them. They will not be pleased with you."

"Who said that?" I shouted.

Suddenly, I no longer wanted to walk forward. I turned my body to allow the cones of sound to see behind me, and I felt the mountains screech as they continued to fight. No clue as to who was talking to us.

"Clara, you hear that voice, too?" José María said.

I grunted to say yes. José María grunted back in acknowledgment.

Before us lay darkness. I could sense the jungle around the path, but beyond that, not much else. Not an animal, and not another human. To our right lay a flat wall that rose thousands of feet. The insect hives that had risen along our right side on the wall were gone. Only rock was left. And to our left, a chasm with those throbbing pods of blackness at the bottom.

"Come forward; don't be afraid," the voice said. Its source had now become distant, as if it had moved from a position in front of us to a new location hundreds of miles away. Even though the voice felt like it had moved off and away from us, I was still scared. It was tracking us.

"We're headed straight for where that voice is. It's up ahead," I said.

"I know. But that's the waaaay down the path," José María.

"Sigh," I said.

"I don't want to go, either," my brother said. "But we don't have much of a choice. You want that tonal, yeah?"

"It's what we came for."

We walked for what seemed like a half hour without hearing the voice again. We stopped a few times to stretch our legs, drink water. We ate the Clif Bars in our bag in small bites to ration them for the trip. For a long stretch, we walked in silence. Neither of needed to fill our time with chatter. That was one of the advantages of having a brother. Plus, I needed time to think by myself.

I tried checking my watch, but I couldn't sense the hands along its dial through the glass, and I gave up. I guessed that we had been walking for three hours, but in my head, I felt like we had been walking for much longer.

My feet began to ache, and sometime around what I thought was our fourth hour, I patted José María on the shoulder.

"You would think our ancestors would have made a map of this place," I said. "Make it easy to visit."

"Oh, they probably did make maps," he said. "But they probably got destroyed during the conquest. Lost forever."

"You love buried treasure."

"Because I love Indiana Jones." José María said.

"And who doesn't?" I said. "He's fine."

José María giggled.

"Whatever happened to that girl who used to come over to the house?" I said. "You two watched sat there watching YouTube all day."

She was the only girl I had ever seen my brother hang out with. I couldn't remember her name. I had met her once, in my senior year of high school, but after that, José María had returned to his favorite home companions: his headphones, his books and his laptop.

"Ah, you mean Joy," he said. "She was all right."

That answer meant he had been crazy about her.

"Why'd you stop hanging out?"

"She got boring, dunno."

In translation, this meant he had gotten dumped. I couldn't speak of a lick of the endless syllables and music that made up the language inside Mictlán, but I could read José María quickly and well. And I barely needed English to do this.

"Ever want to get married?" I said.

"Yep," he said, hunching his shoulders, deep, becoming thin and sleek like a fox.

"And kids?" I said.

"Oh, my god, you're tireless with your questions," he said, but he wasn't angry. He wanted to keep talking. "No kids, I don't think. I think I'd rather just hang out, you know, if I was married?"

I nodded.

"A house?"

"Nah. My wife and I will be drifters. Live in a trailer in

California. Hike. Live on berries."

"A dog?"

"Freakin' twenty. No cats."

"You hate cats."

"More than bros."

"What job would you have?" I said.

"Clara, over there!" José María said, and ran to the right edge of the road. He peered up at the immense wall, and I saw both the wall and the rubbery plants move past me like a carnival ride.

"Where?" I said, and as I turned my head up, I didn't see, but I heard, what he wanted me to see.

A sound like an electric guitar, followed by deep bells, like those of a cathedral.

On a cliff set into the wall above us, I caught the long jawline of a canine peering into the dark from a jutting rock on the canyon wall above us.

The Xolotl howled, and my brother and I dove onto the ground. The Xolotl cut through the air like a blade, ready to land on top of us.

A cloud of rotting fumes expanded above us, and the sound of the deep bells of the Xolotl became as loud as bombs. He roared.

The night before in my dorm room, José María had explained that the Xolotl greeted the dead to begin their journey into Mictlán. I had gone inside its throat once, and the despair I had felt inside made me never want to come close to such a creature. His eyes had scanned me, seen through me, and now, I feared he may take his final bite of us.

The humanoid shape of the Xolotl left a trail of smoke in the air above us. As he fell down toward us, feet-first, I braced for the worst.

But a long, thin flying object intercepted the Xolotl. The Xolotl wrestled with the object for a moment, and the two became entangled in a ball of smoke. Then two figures burst forth and up into air, joined together. The Xolotl emerged from the smoke riding a creature like a jockey, and I finally understood what I saw.

The Xolotl rode a hummingbird made of smoke, so thick it was as solid as flesh. The bird's round eye flickered, and its wings emitted a thin layer of music as its powerful muscles defied the air currents. The hummingbird and the Xolotl dove around in a few circles, and then it became clear that the Xolotl hadn't spotted us yet.

"Shh," I said to my brother. I tapped my temple and waved my hands to make a gesture of emptiness.

Quiet your thoughts, I mouthed to him. I knew the Xolotl had heard our thoughts before.

José María nodded, and he took out his portable camera from his back pocket.

No!

I shook my head, but it was too late. He clicked the shutter button.

The flash on the camera burned for a fraction of a second, and I expected it to fill the space around me, to perhaps burn through this darkness, maybe reveal more monsters.

But instead, the white light that poured from the tiny halogen spilled forth like liquid. It poured out of the camera and down onto the floor, as if the camera had sneezed a gob of snot. The liquid pulsed with a weak silvery color, and it gathered itself like a worm, as if it had a consciousness. Then it dried up, until it dissolved back into the smooth ground that transported us.

"What the heck—" José María said.

"Hell." I said. "He must have seen us."

Then the Xolotl and the smoke hummingbird nose-dived. They flew just a few dozen feet above us, then moved past us.

"What the hell?" I said.

The Xolotl rode his bird like a jockey down into the canyon.

The sound of the bells grew fatter, thicker, and then they were down in the canyon so deep that they only looked like pinpoints. I kept my hands at the edge of the moving road. I didn't want to get too close to the lip. A fall from up here would surely kill us.

"See? I told you to trust in me," said the voice we heard earlier coming from the depths of the road. "You're safe now."

"Hmm, okay, tell me more," José María said into the dark.

"You'll be safer this way," the voice said. "Just walk closer, you two. Come toward me. You'll see everything is fine down *here*."

"*Down there*?" José María said as turned to me and bit his lip.

"Bring your box with its light magic. I want you to show it to me," the voice said.

It's strange to think one could fall in love with just a voice, but it's true.

When I was 31 years old, I got a phone call late at night after coming home late from work in the Loop. My hair was tangled by the winter air, and my belly ached with hunger. My lips had split from the cold as I stepped out of my car, and as I ran my tongue over the wound in my lip, my phone rang. I didn't recognize the number, and to this day, I am not sure why I picked up the line.

"Is Morgan there?" the voice said. The silky, deep texture of sound that insinuated itself into my ear made me sit up as I poured myself a tall glass of water and multitasked to order takeout.

"You must have the wrong number," I said. "There's no Morgan here."

"Morgan who went to Western Chicago University," he said. "This isn't her number?"

I had a roommate at the university once, and her name had been Morgan. I explained this to the caller.

What I didn't say then was that Morgan had also been patient with me when I had been part of the OLF, and she had been kind when my face emerged from the bandages after the Millennium Riot. Morgan had been there when I needed her most, and though her life in teaching meant that we lost touch over the years, she had been important to me. She had met José María the night before we went into Mictlán as she prepared to visit her boyfriend across campus. Morgan had been red-headed, bold, a good friend.

"So, she's not there?" the stranger said. I wanted to hear that voice, to know it.

"Morgan has never lived at my address," I said.

"But clearly it's the same Morgan."

"Honestly, this feels like coincidence," I said. I should have been alarmed. Instead, I was intrigued.

"Well, it's a good coincidence. Surely you must be a good person, if you know her. I was hoping to get a group of people together to go to dinner for the holidays, for those of us who don't have family in Chicago."

Chicago winters were searingly cold and lonely, if you let them be.

"You live here?" I said.

"It's where I do my work, and I have an apartment in the south Loop. You could say that, yeah."

"What's your name?" I said.

"Ken."

His voice danced through the mobile phone. I wanted that voice the way that people want to smoke a second, third, and fourth cigarette.

And so Ken and I started a conversation. Our relationship started during that call, and it continued for a decade, in all its forms and shapes. He was a good lover, despite the things he did when he learned my history. But on that day, it was his voice that brought him into my life. Ken's actual words came second.

His throaty voice, the way the sound unfurled from the speaker into my ears, had intoxicated me.

And just like I fell in love with Ken's voice, I saw how the voice coming from the darkness in the path below seduced my brother José María in the upper parts of that canyon in Mictlán.

"We have to see *who* she is," José María said. He yanked up his jeans from his hips and ran a hand through his nonexistent beard. The textures of his skin remained smooth, hairless, and the color of onyx.

"I think we should be careful," I said.

"That's not like you," he said.

"Is that so?"

"Of course. I can't think of anytime you were actually careful., You always act on impulse."

"Strange that you see me that way," I said. It was true. I had always thought of myself as cautious, but José María saw me another way.

"Hell, you went to that protest at Millennium, and you stole a family heirloom," he said. "All I can say is badass."

He had no idea what I saw in Millennium.

"Well, I still think we should be careful of the thing down there," I said. "When I was at Minerva's house, something else spoke to me, through the walls. And it wasn't good."

"Oh, snap, and what did it say?" my brother said.

"'Give them to me, Wanderer,' among other things. Terrible things."

"The Xolotl also called you a Wanderer," José María said.

"What does that mean?"

"I wish I knew."

"Our family also warned me about the Lords," I said.

"Well, duh!" José María said. "They have to. The Lords are the kind of things you only see once, if you catch my drift."

"Are the Lords really down there, at the bottom of that canyon, you think?" My own words felt thin,and brittle. I was not prepared for this journey.

The Lords of Mictlán were supposed to be a couple, a man and wife. I hoped I could find my tonal without actually having to face them.

José María walked to the edge of the road, and he pushed a few of the rubbery plants aside so he could get closer to the voice. As we glided along, he let out a bellow.

"Yo!" he said.

The cones around his head swelled in size, and though we couldn't see a single shard of light, I could suddenly *understand* the objects around us better, and in more detail. José María's voice was lighting the way around us in the sonar of the music.

"You sound like those dinosaurs in that movie," I said.

"*Raptor World?*" he said. He bellowed again.

"But that thing with the voice will hear us—the Xolotl will hear us, too! I told you to be quiet!"

"Not loud enough," he said. "Wish I had Dad's voice. Needs to be deep."

I pulled at José María's shirt, but he fought me.

"Do you want to see what's up ahead or not?" he screamed.

"But how?"

"The louder we can get, the louder we can sing, the better we can see in this world. Bats and whales do it; why can't we?"

And it made sense.

"But to call attention to ourselves—" I said.

"We won't get killed, silly. We just need to shout a little to get more details. But you need to sing it like you mean it."

He was right. The deeper he went in making his sounds, the farther the cones expanded. Thanks to José María, I could now see farther down the canyon, as if a fog had lifted from it. The immensity of the place gave me the chills, and the soft scents of the place rose all the way from its depths. I expected the smell of dead flesh, but instead, the notes of flower petals and moss rose from the canyon. Much to my surprise, I liked this smell.

Those were the smells of the specimens on my father's desk at the house in Little Village. All the petri dishes with fungi, lichen and many fuzzy things I couldn't name.

José María's voice was strong enough: More details came into relief. The spiral of Mictlán's topography was thousands of miles wide, but I could suddenly *feel* its ridges, its walls and the things that lived there. José María's voice provided the map I needed.

I could now feel the cities that dotted the roads on the way down, and the forests, and the desert-like plains. This place was populated by trillions of things that I couldn't name, but I felt their heartbeats and smelled their breath.

Now that I could feel that far into the canyon, I could now also understand our position in its nine levels.

"Oh, my god," I said. "We're in the upper parts of this place. This road goes so deep into the ground, so far down."

"And not a single star in this world. Freeeeeeeeeeaky!" sang my brother.

A wind kicked up from inside the canyon, and it reached us in our upper level. It bit at my shoulders, and it felt completely different than any wind from Chicago. It was filled with the scent of tree sap and applewood smoke. I heard a buzz. Objects were rising from the canyon, moving up toward us. They were probably thousands of miles away, yet I heard their approach. They would be here soon. My heart pounded, and I broke into a jog again.

"The Xolotl's coming back," I said. "Run!"

"I hear them, too," José María said.

Our boots held fast on the glasslike surface, and as we ran, we picked up more speed, just like before. The angle of our descent became steeper, and I struggled to not tumble forward as we traveled downward. The wall on our right whizzed by. We covered lots of distance in very little time.

And off to our left, I saw the Xolotl glide past us, seated on the hummingbird and leading a flock of the smoking birds, streaming smoke by the thousands, diving deep into the canyon. And then they were gone again.

The road curved around the wall, and I could no longer see around the bend. We would reach the bend within a few seconds.

"I see that you listened to your brother," the voice at the bottom of the road said. The syrupy voice shimmered with a series of sharp sounds, like the vacuuming sound of opening a tennis ball canister.

"I am waiting for you," the voice purred.

José María ran faster as the voice beckoned us further. He dropped his backpack.

"Hey!" I screamed. I stopped to pick it up. "You idiot!" I said. I slung the pack across my shoulder by its strap. By the time I got back up to a jog, José María was already heading around the corner and into the depths. My own cones were losing my brother's location. If he ran farther, I would lose him.

No, I can't lose him.

But José María ran fast, because he knew where the voice was coming from. It was a voice he needed to feel. He was gone. I heard him give out a yelp, and then he went silent.

I needed to go further to see where my brother had disappeared, and the wall curved. In my rudimentary sonar-like vision, I could see how it turned, like a highway.

I didn't dare run around that corner, but I had no choice.

My feet pivoted on the smooth ground as I ran, and then I turned through the bend.

I pulled back before it was too late. The road dropped off in front of us, and below, I looked down on the tallest drop I had ever seen. And José María was completely gone.

I slid forward on the smooth road, and I wondered, if there were light, would this road have a color? In this place, only black ruled, and not even gray survived down here.

And then the voice at the end of the road hissed at me.

"You want to see your brother, yes?" it said.

I was hundreds of feet away from the drop, but since the floor moved, I would fall off the edge within seconds.

And then it hit me.

This is not a conveyor belt.

It's not a road.

It's not even a floor.

And it's not made of glass.

"José María!" I shouted. "Get back! We have to go back! Where are you?"

He was nowhere to be seen, but it was too late for me. The ground slid forward, moving me to the precipice, and off in the distance, maybe ten miles away, I felt a single body move in the distance. It flowed gracefully in an undulating line, and it rose into the sky. It reached a point high up in the air, many miles above. And then it came toward me like a question mark.

This was the thing I hated the most. The thing I couldn't tolerate in zoos, or the desert, or the woods.

The undulating shape beneath us—the very living thing that made this road possible—was a snake.

And all that time we had jogged on the smooth road, we had been traveling along her back. And if that back was big enough to make a flat surface, that meant that she had to be the size of—

Her head zoomed toward me.

She had four pairs of eyes, two on each side of her head. They emanated a hard sound from deep within their orbs, but even from this distance, I had a sense that her nostrils were more skilled at detecting my moves. Those nostrils were large enough for a grown man to walk through. The snake pulled its jaws apart, revealing a perfect, interlocking-triangle mouth made only for killing.

So many teeth.

She was unlike any snake I had ever seen on Earth. Inside her mouth, I counted ten rows of teeth, filling her gums and even her palate.

We had been traveling for hours on the back of this giant snake, and now this was the end. And who was "we," anyway? I was now alone.

José María was gone, probably fallen into the pit beneath the precipice. The snake cocked her head to the side. Her eyes grew wide, and I cringed from the presence—the consciousness—I felt in them. Just one of the fangs in that mouth was easily three or four times my height.

"Welcome to the Coil, Wanderer," she said.

MY MOTHER'S SKIRT OF SNAKES

"No, you wouldn't actually want to glimpse one of these gods. The act would be too terrifying." – Director Robert Hanig, on his film tetralogy *Kieślowski's Dream in Four Colors.* New Yorker Video Channel, 2036.

"How do we rescue that which we do not know we lost?" – Arkangel, "Heartbreak of the Colossus That Moves Through the Water", *Millennium Recedes,* 2009, Reckless Records.

"Your problem isn't that you've been beaten down by a racist, sexist government, motherfucker. Your problem is one of scale. You're not *imagining* big enough. If you can imagine yourself out of this ghetto, your shit's free. Now get." – *Englewood and Dickens.* HBO series, 2015.

"I've been waiting for you," said the snake. "I'm open and ready."

"For what?" I asked.

"To have you share your knowledge with me," the snake said. Her neck swelled, and her skin took on a braided appearance, as if her muscles were flexed so hard, they serrated. The head weaved around me, and her eyes locked in on mine.

"I don't have much to share," I lied. My heart raced in my

chest, and my legs felt rubbery.

"Every being has much to share," she said. "I don't understand your tone. Surely you will share your knowledge with me?"

"First tell me what the Coil is," I said.

"Why it's this canyon of poetry, flowers and blood. The Coil is what we citizens call Mictlán."

"I need you to take me to my brother," I said in my hardest, coldest tone.

"You speak to me in a strange manner," the snake said. "A guarded manner. Because you *fear* me. Odd."

The absolute darkness of this world reminded me that my parents' Catholicism said nothing about what Mictlán could really be. Was this hell? I couldn't be sure. Was this snake like the snake of the Garden of Eden? I began to think I should believe in something good, something filled with light. Maybe it was better to believe in a God up in the clouds, a God who could take people away from places as dark as this one. I still had the little laminated Virgin of Guadalupe in my pocket.

Cold air whipped around me, and I remembered how adept my father had always been at meeting strangers when we traveled. He did this with charm and wit, and I had an idea.

I opened up my backpack. I removed my cell phone, my notebook and the knife. I also took out the remainder of my clothes. I took my time, despite the impatient breath of the animal. Her breath was imbued with the smell of the ocean, and it rolled over me in waves. Surprisingly, it was a pleasant smell, long-lasting and clean. My heart screamed in my chest.

Her eight eyes blinked, and I felt the air shift as their membranes flickered over her eyeballs.

I wanted to cry in frustration at not knowing where José María had gone, but I had never felt a presence so powerful inspect me in the way the snake did.

"These are my things," I said, and I held each object up. "My phone. My notebook. The shawl my mother gave me. My sweater."

The snake emitted pulsing bursts of music, and as she did so, her eyes widened. She was understanding these objects, even if she wasn't seeing them with her eyes. As the pulses of sound filled the air, her skin emanated a sound sparkle that made my mental representation of her skin look like polished stone.

"These tools you show me—they are hard objects, vibrating

objects," she said. "Are you a warrior?" she said.

"I am confused by your question," I said. "I am just a person. You don't have tools down here?"

"This place —what you call Mictlán—has no objects. All we have down here are *beings*. The mountain, the trees, the smoke owls. Every being here has a spirit, or what you might call an essence. But we have no *objects* to speak of."

I felt the snake's body shift beneath my feet, and the conveyor-belt motion almost toppled me off my feet. She was bringing me closer to her, and I had no choice. I wouldn't be able to move off the back of her body in time.

"I would like to travel with you, friend," the snake said.

Friend?

What the hell. Maybe you can work with this. Just play along, Clara, play along.

Her tone confused me. Her face was the most terrifying reptilian horror I had ever seen, but the velvety tones of her words made me feel as if she were asking me for something private and intimate.

That snake head and its movements reminded me of the currents in the depths of the ocean. Moving slowly, in the dark. Gargantuan.

"Sure, take me with you. I want to learn more about this place—the Coil," I said.

This seemed to make the snake very happy. Her head dove down into the canyon, and soon, the length of her body closest to her head was gone. The thick body beneath shifted, and we were gliding over the cliff. We were about to slide straight down the wall.

I had nothing to grip, and if I went over the precipice, I would slide off the smooth scales and tumble down to my death. But as soon as I came close to the edge, the snake's body throbbed and its flesh liquefied in front of me.

Two bony ridges, covered in tiny scales, rose up from her back. I grabbed onto them, and they grew longer, sliding under my armpits and wrapping around my legs like limbs.

We slid over the wall, and I screamed as we dove. The ridges held me in place like a harness.

How to describe the terrible vision of the depths of the canyon? I felt my stomach tighten and quiver, and adrenaline shot through my body. We slid past several thousand miles of canyon wall. I saw more hummingbirds made of smoke in a structure that looked like a beehive, and farther down, we passed a lake swimming with scorpions. We zigzagged through a vast plain inhabited by mushrooms the size of skyscrapers, and we even came upon a grotto of creatures that resembled rabbits on stilts.

She lowered me to a clearing, and I drank water from the grotto. My thirst was incredible, and I felt the coolness ease my throat. I felt hungry, and I ate from a plant shaped like starfish. Its flesh was sweet and salty, like a pineapple dusted with lime and salt.

"We rest here until you're satiated. Then we continue," she said.

The snake did not speak while I rested in the grotto. Her head floated about fifty feet above me, still as stone. She blinked and came toward me.

She returned me to her back, and the ridges and protuberances held me in place. We traveled along the walls of the canyon again, and flowers sprouted from its wall by the billions. Black flowers, whose petals looked as soft as baby skin.

The snake's flesh felt good under my hand, and I stroked her scales. Was I the first human ever to do this? I felt electricity in my arms and a tingle in my breastbone.

I still had too many questions, and though José María's safety was still on my mind, I didn't want to anger this being.

She spoke again, and the proximity of her voice felt good. She said, "Tell me about your mother, eh…—"

"Clara," I said.

"Clara," she repeated. The way she said my name sounded like a flock of seagulls combined with a lullaby. The word left her jaw and spun through the air in waves of sound.

"My mother's name is Juliana. She lives in Chicago, where I'm from."

The snake flicked her tongue up and over her head, and it came right near my breast. The triangular tips looked sharp enough to cut my skin.

"This path on the canyon is the place where I remember my experiences with my own mother," the snake said. "I come here often to remember it. Your description of your mother is curious. She has so much hair, so much life and red blood inside her limbs. She has strange eyes. Do you know that?"

"How do you know what my mother looks like?" I said.

"You spoke her name, Juliana." The way the snake spoke my mother's name became a short symphony in the dark. "In that single word, you told me her tale in your music and in your voice."

I considered quieting my thoughts, but instead, I relaxed. I felt like the snake was really listening to every thought that I emitted through my speech and my movement.

"Are you a mother?" I asked.

I heard a hollow cracking sound behind me, and I turned around. The snake was coiling her body from the tip of her rattled tail forward, covering thousands of miles as it approached our spot. She was making herself comfortable, coiling herself around me. I wanted to scream.

"No, I am not a mother," the snake said. "Not yet. Maybe not ever."

"Why?" I said.

"Because that is my role down here. To transport beings throughout the Coil. I do not make life."

"I see," I said. I got down on my knees to get a better grip on the snake's skin in case she decided to yank me. I still couldn't hear or feel any trace of my brother.

"But I have a mother, and we share our love sometimes," the snake said.

"What is your name?" I said.

The word that flowed out from the snake was long, twisted, gnarled and gorgeous. Its sound made an image in my mind, and I saw a dazzling bird with wings that sparkled like jewels. That bird was as blue as Lake Michigan.

"Your name is Blue Hummingbird?" I said.

The snake flexed her muscles beneath me and sent out a thick pulse of music. It was a yes.

"What is your mother's name?" I said.

Blue Hummingbird sang, using her body and the hiss inside her jaw. And in just a few bars of that song, I could suddenly grasp the memories of the snake's mother. The music showed me an image of a monster, bigger than Blue Hummingbird, a planet-sized giant made of bone and hard muscle, with several limbs that exploded like needles from her stomach and her lower back, radiating in shimmering waves. That body looked nothing like a human's. Her upper body had four arms, and on her lower body, six muscled limbs lunged forward, covering thousands of miles with each step.

This gigantic mother moved on a vast plain, alone, radiating music around her in cones, just like the Xolotl and the other beings in Mictlán. Water circled the mother's neck like a collar, and it sparkled in kaleidoscope colors, some which I had never seen before. At the mother's waist, thousands of snakes curled, forming a skirt. Many of these looked just like the snake poised in front of me now. And instead of a head, two thick rattlesnakes sprouted from the colossus' bleeding neck.

I know her. I know her name. She was in José María's books!

"Is your mother Coatlicue?" I said.

The snake quivered, and she pulled back her lips, revealing the hundreds of teeth in her mouth. The sound she made was a definite yes.

Coatlicue, whose name meant Skirt of Snakes, had captivated me in those books, with her monstrous appearance. Yet, the image of Coatlicue that the snake showed me shocked me more than I could imagine.

I knew that the Nahuatl names for these gods that José María and I brought with us into this world didn't exactly match the names of these creatures, but in the case of the Xolotl, he had acknowledged the name. Perhaps in the time of the Aztecs, this was as close as their language could come to describing these beings.

"Your word 'Coatlicue' is close enough, Clara. My mother's real name is too long to say to you. You do not have enough wheels to understand that name, but yes. Coatlicue will do."

"Does your mother live down here in Mictlán?" I said. I hoped the answer was no. The giant I saw in the vision felt foreign, like something beyond time.

"Oh, no, there's not many of my mother's kind down here, Clara," Blue Hummingbird said. "Ironically, Mictlán welcomes all children and siblings, and their parents. But the Major Beings, those that are like my mother—they left this canyon a long time ago. You may not understand this, but those elder beings are still evacuating now. There are only two parents who still live in the Coil: the Lords."

"But the Lords are not your parents?" I said.

"That's correct. They have no real children. They were here before all the other beings. All they do is eat other people's children. You know the Lords?"

I took a deep breath as I shivered.

"Yes, I have heard about them. They're at the bottom of the Coil. Mictlantecuhtli and Mictecacíhuatl—the Lords. I am trying to find them."

"Then surely you are ready to die," the snake said. "Are you filled with the joy of death, Clara?"

The question scared me. I felt my skin grow cold.

"Why would I be filled with joy over death?" I said. Suddenly, the small hedges of black plants stirred, and I felt a presence in them, as if they too could feel me standing next to them. The jungles and the woods of this part of the canyon looked hungry, feral. If it was possible for plants to want to eat me, this was that time. By now, I had really grown used to being able to locate and understand all the beings and the topography in Mictlán based on how their music bounced off of their surfaces.

"You will be happy when the Lords tear your limbs apart, Clara."

No, thanks.

"I'd like to give you my phone in exchange for a favor," I said.

The snake rose into the air, singing, growing thicker. She smacked her mouth open and shut, evaluating me each time she flickered her tongue.

"You want to trade, Clara. I love trades. What do you want in return for your weapon object?" she said.

"You tell me where my brother might be, since you seem to know so much."

"Your sibling… Yes. Yes. This is a pleasurable exchange. Give me your object."

Blue Hummingbird traveled down toward me again. Her mouth gaped open, as if she wanted me to step into it.

No way.

"Okay, but first, you have to explain something to me," I said, holding the phone behind my back. "Why does the Xolotl have an object? He carried one too, in his loincloth. That means that you lied when you told me there were no object here in the Coil," I said.

Blue Hummingbird flexed and spat sideways. The gob struck the wall and made a hole in it as if the saliva were made of acid. Her eyes grew wide in rage.

"His arrogance," she screamed. "So much arrogance. You have

seen that dog-headed intruder, I take it."

"Yes, I have. He tried to eat me," I said.

"Of course he did. And Xolotl gave you the power of speech—"

"Yes, with his knife. He cut me, and he cut himself. And since then, I could speak in this place."

"He brings objects from your world, because he's always been in love with your kind," Blue Hummingbird said. "Now that I have seen you and your sibling up close…I can see why."

"But why a knife?"

"To tear his way into your world. There are gates that lead to other worlds, and he's mastered his gate by tearing a hole at the top of the mountain with his knife."

"Are there other kinds of travel through the worlds?" I said.

The snake's musculature swelled, and her brow descended, as if she were considering a thought.

"Beware of mirrors," the snake said. "Because they offer access to gates, too."

The snake hissed, and she put her head down directly in front of me so I could see right into her multiple eyes. Her teeth had the texture of glass, but I knew they were as hard as steel. They rose about twelve feet into the air. Too high for me to reach. I had to toss my iPhone over the fangs, like throwing a ball over a fence. It landed inside her mouth with a wet sound.

The snake hummed like a live wire while she inspected the mobile phone in her mouth. Then she tossed it back into her throat.

She grunted and flicked her tongue, lashing the empty air hundreds of times.

"This object has no real knowledge inside of it, Clara."

"In our world, it does."

"I will need to think about this."

"Can you tell me why the Xolotl would attack me?"

"He plays with what he loves, child."

It occurred to me then that I had been wrong to think of the Xolotl as a being with human attributes.

"Now, why would that filthy cur give you the power of speech?" the snake said.

"I don't know. He called me a Wanderer."

The snake raised her head to taste the air with her forked

tongue. Its lashes were alert, full of energy.

"We haven't seen a Wanderer here in millions of wheels," the snake said. "And you claim to be a mere human?"

I nodded.

"Then you can't be a Wanderer. Speech is only given to Wanderers, and there has *never* been a human Wanderer in Mictlán. Only the Major Beings can be Wanderers."

"That's what Xolotl called me. And he gave me speech."

"He gave you blood, and you gave him yours. So sensuous. So irresponsible."

"Well, I don't care," I said. "I came here to find my tonal, and I demand that you help me find it," I said.

I only spoke this way in the outside world when I dealt with oppressive right wingers, with homophobes and racists. The tone of voice came from somewhere deep in me, and it always got my point across. I mean to hold it until I got some answers.

"The Feathered Snake *was* a Wanderer, Clara," the snake said. Her voice filled me with its music, and I felt drawn toward her. What would it be like to touch the ridges on top of her head?

But then my mind returned to the clue she had given me.

The Feathered Snake.

"Quetzalcóatl," I said.

"He's one of four children who grew up in the Coil but left the canyon. They were four babies, each bathed in one of four colors. Most of those children seem to have forgotten Mictlán. Except for Quetzalcóatl, as you call him. Quetzalcóatl came back to the Spiral Canyon to stay with us. But the neglect of the other three brothers—it's lamentable."

She talks as if they are family, I thought. *Back at home, this could very well be the same conversation about how La Negra stopped going to family gatherings.*

"Do you have siblings?" I said.

"Sure, many. But I am the only one that lives down here, with the Lords. The rest live in the outer worlds, beyond the Mountain Above The Coil. Many of my siblings still live with my mother. *In my mother.*"

I didn't understand exactly what this meant. Just as soon as I seemed to find a trace of something human in this snake, she surprised me with the utter alienness of her personality.

"Well, then, maybe you can tell me where to find my sibling,

José María."

The snake squealed and rose in the air, thickening as she flexed her muscular body in rage.

Blue Hummingbird's flesh lost some of its solidity, and I realized she wasn't made of conventional flesh and bone.

She's braided. She's made of billions of snakes. Woven so tight that they form this snake.

The woven snakes parted, and for a second, I could see right into her flesh as if a butcher had made an incision. Buried inside, cocooned, lay José María. He looked dazed, as if he were high, and he waved from the gap in the snake. It was a lazy wave, full of pleasure and relaxation.

"Hey, *reina*," he said, winking. Then the snakes covered him up again.

"Bring him back!" I demanded.

I sprinted and jumped off the ground, lending inside the aperture in the snake, just in time to slam into my brother.

And then the snakes knitted themselves together to seal us in like linens around a corpse in a grave.

None of the snakes bit me, but they ran their bodies over every bit of exposed skin, and in some cases, they slithered up my jeans and into my shirt sleeves.

But I didn't scream. I didn't want to upset the snakes. They each made their own song, and though I lost my ability to feel objects around me, I could tell there was a solid human body not far from mine.

"José María, can you hear me?"

"Yep," he said. "Loud and clear."

"How'd you get in here?" I said.

"I asked her if I could step inside her folds."

"But why?" I said.

"It was her voice," he said. "I couldn't resist."

My body felt as if it had been suspended in a thick liquid, and I discovered that if I relaxed, my fear of the snakebites receded. They flowed over my lips and my hair, slow as lava.

"There are giants that move through the cosmos," said the snake. She was speaking through us right inside her flesh, without the need for a voice. Her words felt closer than ever before.

"And those giants move through the gates," José María said. His phrase rhymed with the snake's words, and I realized they were singing together.

He's in love.

"Like the gate we walked through in Lake Michigan," I said.

"Yes," replied my brother and the snake together, in a chorus of gauzy music.

They were singing a song together, even as her flesh of snakes imprisoned us.

"Many wheels ago, this canyon unfurled itself from the navel of the darkness. The Coil wound unto itself, while at the same time it expanded outward, up to the highest levels, close to the ground. That is how things began. And the Lords of Mictlán took residence inside its center," the snake sang.

"Mictlán was just a home." José María added. "A home made of flowers and rivers that run like veins."

"Just one home in the cosmos," the snake said. "A home for us."

"A home for us," José María said, as if he had known this song all his life.

"Two Great Beings, older than old, became lovers. The female swelled with pregnancy. And she bore four children, as the wheels rotated, touched and collapsed. Four children, four colors," José María continued.

"Those beings are so old that we cannot see them anymore. They are even older than the Lords," Blue Hummingbird said. "But they are there always, beyond this spiral canyon."

I felt my brother stir inside this sea of reptiles. He was turning around to face me.

"And those four were powerful gods—" José María whispered to me. He was close, maybe just two or three feet in front of me.

"Four children, all of them Tezcatlipocas," Blue Hummingbird said.

"And three of those children left Mictlán. They didn't visit often."

"But the Lords continued to devour," the snake said.

The music continued, but the lyrics faded off to an echo.

"Clara," the snake said. "Can you hear me?"

"Of course," I said.

"You are here for reparations, yes?"

"To reclaim my tonal," I said.

"And you know how your tonal got lost, don't you? You felt the presence of the Ocullín, did you not? You felt his cold body, his roving eyes and his need for violence?"

"What are you talking about?" I said.

"I will take you there, I will show you what the Ocullín did. I will show you why the gates are opening and why the Ocullín followed you. I will show you what he can do if you don't stop him."

"Show me, yes, show me." I said.

"I will help you find your tonal," the snake said as she looped her body over cliffs in the distance.

"Thank you" was all I could think to say.

"But first, our trade," Blue Hummingbird said. "You can keep your metal object from your world, Clara. Those objects are dull and useless. They contain no real knowledge. What I want is *you*."

Music swelled inside the snake's body, and though my eyes were blinded by the snakes that enveloped my body, I felt my body flow forward and *through* the snake, into the brightest flash of sapphire I ever saw in my life.

Edgar's body had been lanky, marked by moles at his shoulders, and during the times we had sex, my hands had explored his back, his face and even his eyelids. That's what I remembered most about the times we made love: his skin. Those sensations on my skin and in my nose and eyes had made me orgasm several times when I touched him. And now, as I fell into a thousand shards of the color blue, my skin came alive, just like it did during those early mornings with Edgar. Thousands of electrodes had been turned on over every inch of my body.

The snake called my name, and the two syllables—the way she caressed the sound—made my stomach tingle.

"Clara," she said. "*Crawl with me.*"

I felt hollow, as if I was just a shell made of skin. But this feeling—the way it made me feel free, as if gentle air currents inhabited my insides instead of organs made of carbon and water—was a taste of something sacred. The brushes of the air against my neck, my toes, my legs—they felt as if they were coming from a windmill inside my heart.

I let out a deep breath, and as I inhaled, I felt the essence of the snake move through my lungs, stomach and organs, on a journey with purpose.

She's moving through my cells, I thought. The thought made no sense from a biological standpoint, but my heart felt it. The snake was in me, swelling inside my head, and pressing into me with her blue beauty. She was now seeing through me, as if she had infiltrated me from the space behind my eyes.

In my ears, a wash of sound, velvety and sharp.

But warmer, so much warmer, so much more like blood in my veins.

My body swelled, crested, and then it ran in rivers of liquid. I felt the same rush of an orgasm that I might have given myself with my own hands. Stars flooded my vision and my skin bloomed with heat. I panted inside the sea of snakes.

The blue intensified, and it became thicker, darker. Its music spread itself apart, like a siren going off in the night, and the snake and I became one being, connected by oceans and galaxies of blue color.

It was in this blueness that I understood where I was.

You're inside the snake's eyes. You're literally inside her eyes. Outside, in the circular valley of Mictlán, those eyes are nothing but useless black orbs, but if you ever saw Blue Hummingbird in the sun, those eyes would be as blue as the heart of the Pacific Ocean.

"Thank you, Clara," the snake said. "We have communed. And now I can show tell you the story of the Ocullín, if you will let me."

I sang "yes," and the music of that word flitted off, like a bird, into the blue.

I saw a new vision through Blue Hummingbird's eyes, and she was nothing but a baby. She peered up from the lower levels of the spiral canyon, and up above, a war took place. Thousands of owls and hummingbirds surrounded an animal that had cut through the circular opening of the canyon. The being disobeyed the natural spiral flow of the walls of the canyon, and instead, it cut across its thousands of miles, like a knife puncturing an onion. The animal was segmented, and covered in thick fur. It ate through the swarm of owls with its five mouths, gathering force as it moved through space.

"That was the first time I ever saw the Ocullín," the snake said. "He Who Murders Worlds."

The Ocullín embodied every thrust of a rapist, every hand that slit a throat, every cell of cancer that ate a body from the inside out. The Ocullín felt as putrid as the vision I had seen of Richard Speck walking throughout that house. The Ocullín was the explosion of bone and muscle when guns had shot us down in Pritzker Pavilion.

The Ocullín consumed the hummingbirds and cracked their bones. Their attacks with their talons on his bulbous body did nothing to stop him.

The Ocullín made no song in his path through the empty space of the canyon. In a place where even the cliffs and the stones gave off music, its silence made the young snake take cover in a hollow cave near the fields of poppies.

The snake witnessed this battle of the Ocullín against the citizens of Mictlán. It lasted many wheels, and she lay helpless, just an infant, in her nest hear the bottom of the Coil. I saw it in a simple flash of images, but I understood that it was a war that had gone on for centuries or maybe millennia.

A flash of light broke through the sky, and two shards of white light lit the spiral canyon for a moment. The forests and cities and the creatures of Mictlán were bathed in the white light for a moment, and I gasped, even through the snake's vision.

And then the Ocullín clashed with the two beams of light. They turned and twirled, and the Ocullín emitted a howl full of rage and pain.

The beams of light grew thicker, brighter, and a sharp screech came from their very core. Spiraling sparks blew out from the beams by the millions, and even the smoke owls flinched, flapping in fear back toward the mountain as the white spirals ripped the darkness open.

The largest of the white beams took on a slender, fluid shape, and its tip swelled in size, forming a head, a mouth and dozens of sharp teeth. It was a head that looked just like that of a snake, at least until horns and feathers grew from the back of its skull like a radiant headdress in brilliant reds and oranges. The beast dove into the canyon, down toward the black heart at its center, and for a moment, it looked like it had disappeared, spirals and all.

Then a roar detonated from the heart of the canyon, and the snake of light rose like a spear through the thousands of miles between the black heart and the Ocullín above. The snake pierced the worm's skin, and the Ocullín gross body began to absorb and eat the spiraling sparks. They wrestled, turning and biting. This battle continued for several years, until the snake opened its jaw wide enough to swallow the Ocullín. The music of the white snake turned moody and blue as it wrapped its jaws over the worm, and eventually, he swallowed most of it. The white snake's body bristled in colored feathers that stood up like spikes all over its back.

Just as the feathered snake closed in on the last segment of the Ocullín, this remainder of the worm ripped itself away from the white jaws that sliced its body. The runaway segment was nothing more than a set of mouths reeking of pus and rot, and it flew up, away from the canyon, while the feathered snake lay in the upper walls of the canyon, fat and bloated as it tried to digest the murderer. What was left of the Ocullín flew up and out of the canyon, and up toward the tip of the mountain, where the gate to Mictlán stood inside its snowflakes.

Then the feathered snake slithered into a cave at the foot of the mountain next to the Coil. Years passed while it lay in silence.

A familiar figure emerged from the flocks of hummingbirds that raged through the air. The Xolotl, draped in his tiny loincloth, clutching his knife, burst from the hordes of birds, seeking the last of the Ocullín.

They used to be inseparable, the snake reminded Clara. Xolotl and Quetzalcoatl, twin brothers. But that was the last time they fought together.

The Ocullín's last segment sat on top of the mountain, murdering the beings that lived there.

The Xolotl reached the tip of the mountain, and there he slashed the Ocullín's mouth, and the thick fur that was left on its flesh. But the Ocullín bit back as the snowflakes bristled with music around them. The Ocullín bit the Xolotl in the arm, wounding it, and with a single fluid movement, stepped out of Mictlán and into another world through the reflections in the snow. The smoke owls tried to stop the Ocullín, but it was too late. The Ocullín was gone.

"That is my story," Blue Hummingbird said.

Then I felt essence of Blue Hummingbird swirl inside me in an ocean of blue color and alien music, and my body melted into hers.

I lost track of where my body ended and hers began, and my vision rolled back into a vast, open plane of sapphire.

The snake ejected me from her body onto a field of flowers in Mictlán. The flowers recoiled from my body as I hit the flowerbed. I felt relaxed but exhausted, and I turned to face up toward the animal. José María was also sliding out from the weave of her body, and he landed sideways, gently, on a cluster of flat rocks off to my right.

José María crawled on his elbows toward me, his eyes wide as saucers, sweat streaking the thick hair on his forehead.

"I think I'm in love," he said.

Blue Hummingbird was leaving us.

"We have covered many more levels of the Coil," she hissed. "This should help you continue. There are places in Mictlán that even I can't go to."

The snake rolled off of the wide plain where she dropped us off. Her coils flipped over the jagged edge, one after another, and soon, she was gone without saying another word to us. Though she had spoken a kind of syntax that I could understand as sentences, what I knew about her from being inside her flesh made me think that she was very far from human.

"Even without daylight, I felt like she could see us with her eight eyes," I said.

"The things she showed me," José María said. He sat cross-legged at the edge of the flower bed. Roses. Black as night, their petals dewy and graced with a velvety touch. José María began to eat their petals, and instinctively, I did too. Their taste was opulence, sugar and something akin to blood. The experience inside the snake's blue eye had left me so hungry.

"She showed me the Ocullín," I said. "From a long time ago, when he tried to eat his way through Mictlán."

"That's not the story she showed me. She showed me things that I don't have words for." José María said. "But she spoke to us individually. Again."

"Again?" I said.

"Yes, she was back there, in Chicago. She was talking to us through the tunnel of butterflies. She was manifesting through the tunnel."

"Holy shit," I said. He was right. That's why I had thought it so strange that the tunnel could have thought she was a snake.

"Don't you see, Clara?" José María said. "The creatures—the gods—inside Mictlán, we catch glimpses of them in our world sometimes, just tiny little glimpses. They can inhabit buildings, and maybe living things, too. They manifest there, and well, we got lucky when the snake spoke to us through the wizard's tunnel."

"And you're sure Blue Hummingbird didn't make that tunnel?" I said.

"One hundred percent," my brother said. "She showed me. The wizard named Black Wings was Guillermo. He tried so hard for so many years to get into Mictlán, and he never could. All that time, he talk to Blue Hummingbird, begging to be let into the Coil. And then he disappeared. He left that tunnel down in Chicago, like a haunted house."

"If we heard the snake speak to us through the tunnel—" I said.

"Then maybe you really did see the Ocullín through the bookcase in Minerva's attic, too," José María said.

I ate more flowers, hoping my belly would get full. Food was a comfort right now, the only thing that could quell my fear from having been seen by something as horrible as the Ocullín back in Chicago.

I walked to the edge of the ground we stood on to get a glimpse of the canyon around us. In this lower part of the spiral canyon, flowers invaded every wall and even the roads. Even the wasp nests were covered in flowers of every shape and kind. They dripped down like lazy diamonds and thick trumpets.

The intoxicating shapes and scents of so many flowers was something I had never expected to see in this place without light. Part of me wanted to keep those flowers with me forever.

A forest of marigolds pulsed with music and their scent just about a quarter mile from us. We walked through their trumpet-like howls, and I brushed their tops the way I might pet a dog. Afterward, we reached a clearing. I unpacked the shawl from my pack, and I placed several dozen roses in it to save for eating later.

"Let's see if we can find a place to rest up there," I said. "Where we won't be so exposed."

The taste of the flowers haunted my mouth. Mictlán had nothing that resembled weather. There was only wind and breezes.

As we approached the forest of marigolds, their subtle music took on a brighter note. With each step of our approach, the flowers sang, and they released more perfume. Their song startled me.

I know this song.

I had heard *Abuela* Blanca sing this to us when I was a toddler, and its sweet melody filled my chest with warmth.

"That's just like the song we're supposed to learn for the journey to Mictlán," I said to José María. He nodded, listening to every note.

The carpets of marigolds formed several peaks and folds, and I could see there were openings in some of its surfaces, as if someone had constructed a new architecture out of living flowers. We walked through a canopy of trees and arrived in a plaza. In its midst, an impossibly tall structure, constructed of marigolds, roses, orchids and corpse flowers, stabbed the open air of the canyon.

It was a castle, a temple of flowers.

It rose about a mile into the air, with twin stairways that led up to small conical rooms at the top. The flowers hissed and bellowed in their song, and though the building looked like it could eat us alive, I knew I should not be afraid. Even in this place without any colors, I could feel the vibrant, soft textures of all those petals, and the firm, smooth surfaces of the stalks and the stamens.

The architecture of the temple looked very familiar, but I couldn't place it.

I tried speaking to the flowers of the building, but they only responded in song. I couldn't understand what they were singing.

"If we get to the top, we can get a handle on how far down we've made it," José María said. "Maybe we can see how much farther we have to go down the canyon, too."

"Perhaps," I said.

We climbed slowly, because the steps were steep and the scent of the flowers made us sleepy, but we took swigs of the water in our water bottles. José María helped me up the risers when I became afraid of the heights, and we did our best to not disturb the smoke owls that swooped above our heads. They did not attack us. Rather, I felt that the smoke owls were keeping us safe.

For now.

"Are you really going to go to that protest on Michigan Avenue when we get back?" José María said.

"If we get out, yes. This time, we're going to make a big

difference," I said.

Nothing delighted me more than my brother's innocence. This trip down here was just a game to him. Nothing but a romp. He was already planning on our return. I wanted to be as hopeful as him, but I knew I could not. If I found my tonal in the bottom of the Coil, I had no idea how we would ever get back.

We may be dead already for all we know, making the trip that everyone makes when their time is up.

"Do you hear that?" José María said as he put his arm on my elbow. We had almost reached the top of the temple.

I listened. Floating like a whisper, beneath the bell tones of the rocks and the ringing screech of the owls, I heard something. I also *felt* something.

It was viscous liquid. Heavy and with intention. Rushing, crashing, sparkling in waves. It was water.

"Sounds like a river," my brother said.

"It's coming from *inside* the temple," I said.

We took a few more steps up the temple, and I swooned with nausea. We were so high up in the air, I was reminded of the times my father took us to the Willis Tower to the observation deck. I felt afraid but alive.

And alive was good.

José María let out a few hard noises, like a human beat box, and the sounds he emitted permitted us to see down below us. There, just over the edge of the temple, I could see thick, rubbery grasses flanking a wide river. The force of the water crashed and swelled. Inside the current of the river, tiny objects like sparkles emitted their sound signature through the liquid. Without light, I shouldn't have been able to see anything sparkle in the river, but I could see billions of the tiny metal particles flow through the water.

"We must be moving in the right direction," José María said.

"Which of the rivers do you think this is?"

There were nine rivers in Mictlán, all of them interconnected like a braid. They flowed in a spiral downward along the walls of the canyon. There was something about the sheen of the water, the twinkle inside the river that felt familiar, and good, something that felt like the safety of home.

"Clara, get your ass up here," José María said. My brother was standing at the top of the temple with his hands on his hips. The flowers provided him a firm surface to stand on, despite the petals' delicate appearance. "You're never going to believe what's up here."

I clambered up the last riser and walked onto the flat landing. It spread before me in an area of about 300 feet by 300 feet. At its center, two shrines stood like twins. They had triangular openings but no doors. Though I could sense many of the details around me, I couldn't feel anything that was inside those conical towers.

"No, fool, not inside the rooms; turn around!" José María said, and he yanked me by the shoulders so I could see the landscape below the temples.

I could see very far with ears instead of eyes, and there, maybe two thousand miles in the distance, I could feel *all* of it. I gasped.

A lake spread out below me for miles, almost as big as an ocean. Its waters were as still as a stone. I could see the way in which the river we had just seen fed into the lake, and the opening on the other side, where the river continued on, as it dove under a mountain and continued its underground journey.

Situated on top of the lake, in a perfect cross shape, stood a small city made of thorns, flowers and the bones of animals. Four roads connected the shore to the center, and at the center, a flat circular stone rotated, emitting multiple symphonies of music. The structures of the bridges and the island throbbed with life. The thorns swelled, and poison rose to their tips. The bones bent their shape as the flowers bloomed and swelled in the darkness.

It's a city floating on top of the water.

Blue Hummingbird had promised that there were no objects down here, and she was right. Even the city below me was made of things that seemed to be alive.

Beyond the lake, snow fields spread out for thousands more miles, and somewhere in the distance, they fell off into a thicker darkness.

But the city floating on top of the lake before me made so much music, it was as if the city wanted to be noticed.

"Is that—" I said.

"It's the place we showed you and your ancestors many wheels ago, Wanderer," a familiar voice said behind us, and its music pounced in our ears while its stench of maggots and pus grew in our nostrils. I turned over my shoulder, and in doorway of the right-hand shrine, I heard him.

I felt his lean but ferocious presence. I felt the textures of his dog head, his erect ears, the milky eyes, and the ragged body. His sharp claws.

"It's what you came here for, Wanderer. The city of Mictlán," the Xolotl growled, and he lunged at me. He struck me hard in the gut, and we flew off the ledge of the temple as his jaws snapped at me through the air.

The temple of flowers grew distant, and the Xolotl clamped his jaws over my right arm. The pain was fiery hot, but my skin maintained its integrity. I screamed, and as I saw the walls of the temple rise past me, I cried.

I told myself I wouldn't do this. But I want to be home now. I want to be back as soon as I can, however I can.

I have a mother, a father. I have a bed that I sleep in.

I was an ingrate.

Just as soon as I let out a sob, a skittering music blasted my left ear, and a fast-moving object approached us. I could hear it moving, so fast that I couldn't understand its shape, just its force.

And then it was under me, cradling me, and the Xolotl was screaming lines of a song, lines that called forth the name of this creature beneath us.

We were no longer falling, but instead, we were rising again, even though this spiral canyon had no sky.

The Xolotl released my arm from his jaws, and I realized that he was playing with me again.

But he also held on to you for safety. For your safety.

The Xolotl grabbed me by the shoulders, and he turned me around, so I could face forward and ride the creature like a horse. Below me, I could see three sets of slanted eyes, feathers so slick they looked like fish scales, and a beak that elongated into the shape of a very long and sharp needle. The wings at its sides beat so fast that I lost the texture of their music.

"To ride her, you must speak her name," he said. "It goes like this."

The song he sang spoke her name. It was a song filled with honey, cactus quills and shards of amethyst. I did my best to speak it with my tongue and throat.

I had never felt an animal so powerful and graceful respond to its name in the way the hummingbird did. Her feathers grew slicker and she emitted wider cones of sound. Suddenly, I could get my bearings on where we were going.

We were circling the temple of flowers, and each time we passed its walls, the temple's song groaned an aching song.

"The flowers in that building don't want you here," the Xolotl said. "That dissent is not a surprise. They have never wanted visitors here."

The stench of the Xolotl made me gag, but he was no longer trying to bite me, and he had taught me how to ride the hummingbird. And I was grateful.

"Why wouldn't they want visitors?" I said.

"That's the way the flowers in the canyon think. They have long been the strongest political force in the lower levels of Mictlán, and it's because of a simple fact: they don't want knowledge to escape the canyon. They want it to stay hidden here."

"Knowledge of what, exactly?" I said.

"That's my very point," the Xolotl said. "They have gathered so much of it, they no longer know what knowledge is sacred and what isn't. They just have too much of it. They hoard, Wanderer."

"Can they tell me how to find my tonal?" I said.

"Yes," the Xolotl said in a howl, and his voice echoed through the walls of the canyon. It was a lonely, horrible sound.

"My parents said if I find my tonal, the shadows of death will leave me alone," I said.

The Xolotl grunted, and then he snorted. "That's what they said?"

"Yes."

"Then you should return home now. You will never be free of those shadows."

He laughed, while I wanted to cry. I bit my lip instead.

"But why?" I said.

"Because you and your brother are the first visitors we've had in many wheels. You have felt and heard too much of Mictlán."

"But it can't be," I said. "Don't all the souls of the dead pass through here? Don't they get to see the Coil, too?"

When I said this, the hummingbird let out a howl too, and as she joined the Xolotl, I felt in their cries the fear of children who see monsters inside the woods at night, and the chill that young women feel in the dark when they walk in an empty parking lot in the city at 2 a.m.

"We will collect the creature you call your brother," the Xolotl said. "It's time that you saw the dead you speak of."

And then the hummingbird spoke, too, in a voice that sounded like water, and like steel bending under thousands of pounds of force.

"But once we show you these wonders," the hummingbird said, "you will forever know the taste of death, the way it cools the back of your neck, the way it steals the breath."

"Once you see the dead, don't ever say you're sorry," the Xolotl screamed, and we soared up above the temple. José María waved at us as we approached him, and then suddenly the world—this place of black lakes, thick canyons and gigantic snakes—felt like the worst place I had ever experienced in my life.

"Why would I be sorry?" I said.

"Because the Ocullín is following you," the Xolotl said. "And he's got your name on his lips."

THE OCULLÍN

"Dahmer, Speck and Gacy: They all set foot in Chicago, and each one of them carried an evil that felt like it was from another world." – *Inside the Mind of the Serial Killer,* Sathomé Harrison, Grand Monarch Press, 1991.

"We used evil to build a city. Its resulting buildings, plumbing systems, highways and public parks became an automatic sequence. Day by day, we built a metropolis. We enjoyed prosperity in the city of Chicago, until the fire interrupted it Death did not look too kindly upon us, but what a story she told." – Jonathan O'Clanaghan, City Commissioner, regarding the recovery of bodies after the Great Chicago Fire. Stefan Muth, *The American Occult City: Profiles of Five Men.* October 11, 1871, Velocifero Press.

"They're all going to laugh at you." – Nursery rhyme and meme. Era of origin unknown.

José María did not fear the ride on the back of the hummingbird. In fact, he was too quick to jump on its back. The animal bristled, and her feathers grew coarse and sharp until he had learned to sing her name.

José María rode up front, while I sat sandwiched between him and the Xolotl.

We flew right in through one of the open doors of the temple of flowers, and soon, we were lost inside.

The grace of the creature we rode, and the music that it made from the way it beat its wings hundreds of times per second took my breath away. I wondered why I had never stopped to marvel at a hummingbird back on Earth. My father had certainly wanted me to stop and look at them many times. So many opportunities wasted.

I used the cones of sound emanating from my shoulders to see where we were going. The places outside this temple—the canyons, rivers and jungles that made up Mictlán—had come into sharp relief because sound illuminated the spiral canyon of this world. I didn't need eyesight in Mictlán to know the size of the eagles and the smoke owls, or to know that the canyon spanned for thousands of miles. They were full of texture and as vivid as if I could see them with my good eye.

The air became cooler as we took a dive into the lower rooms of the temple.

The cones of sound that radiated from our heads gave us a limited sense of the narrow hallways of this place, but I noticed that this sonar was not as strong down in the depths of this building.

Soon, our cones began to diminish, and it was harder to feel and see what was up ahead.

Then my nose began to twitch. Deep scents vibrated inside it, and suddenly, I could smell so deeply and so far inside this pyramid that I *felt* its walls, its ceilings, its corridors and the pools built into its deepest rooms. I didn't see the rooms. My nose saw them.

My cones receded down to nothing, but I didn't panic. My sense of smell illuminated the way now.

This temple was vast, expanding forever, floor after floor, winding like a maze. As I relaxed into the flood of information that my nose gave me, my sense of hearing came back, too. I heard the faint music of the hummingbird wings, the breathing of the Xolotl, and my brother's grunts as the bird jostled us through our flight through the stairways of the temple.

"José María," I said, "Can you smell this place like I'm doing right now?"

"My mind is officially blown," José María said.

The walls around us, the foundations below and the ceilings above our heads left a signature of their makers. As I took in deeper breaths infused with sulfur, berries and the metallic stink of blood, the scents told me who had created this place.

The flowers had built this temple, and the flowers reminded me with the soft music they made, as well as with their smells. The scents there contained notes of daffodils, mignonettes, heliotropes and violets, but other scents wrapped around them. These were smells I had never encountered in my life. They were fragile, pungent and glorious.

Inside this temple, the flowers sang a deep chorus that created rooms, floors and hallways. The architecture of this place was something ancient and completely foreign to any building I had ever been to in my life.

We traveled through many rooms, and we buzzed through many mazes. The wonders inside that temple were more priceless than any gold on earth. The flowers—trillions of them—sang, mourned, cried and made love in this deep dark that smelled of three thousand things, but which was just as black as the outer levels of Mictlán.

"How do you measure time here?" José María said. His voice didn't echo inside these halls. Instead, the walls ate up his words and garbled them up, retuning their musicality and turning them into mockeries of the originals. The playfulness of the flowers inside this place unsettled me.

The Xolotl snorted, and he sat up straight as he rode the bird. His scent of carrion threaded itself into the air. I could feel his ferocious mouth and his lips peel back to reveal his sharp teeth as he spoke.

"The wheels interlock, one on top of another," the Xolotl growled. "And from other planes—other angles—many other wheels come together at several points. Then they disperse again. The wheels fly off, and they kiss each other."

That sounds like poetry, not like the nature of time, I thought.

"That makes sense up near the mountain where we entered, but I call bullshit," José María said. The Xolotl's gnashed his teeth , and the wound-like slits in his chest flared open.

"In fact, if I am not mistaken," José María continued, "it feels like time is moving at a different pace down *here,* in the lower levels of Mictlán. I have measured it; I know." He waved his iPhone in his hand.

"The wheels always turn, but time ceases to matter in the lower parts of the Coil," the Xolotl said. "Your ancestors knew this. Why don't you? Are you not their children?"

"The Toltecs? The Maya? The Aztecs? We're supposed to be

their children, but, well, we couldn't tell you exactly how." I said. "Many generations have passed."

I had tossed away the notion so many times when my father pressed me to acknowledge it, but now—

"That info got lost, Scooby," José María said. "The shit got burned by the Spaniards. Didn't *you* get *that* memo?"

The Xolotl emitted the mournful bell sounds from deep in his belly. The multiple rows of teeth in his mouth flared outward as he drew his jaw open. He licked his lips in hunger.

"The deeper you go in the nine levels of Mictlán, the farther away time will feel for you," the Xolotl said. "And that's because time dissolves as we get closer to the Lords. This is how things have always been."

The hummingbird bucked, and for a moment, it looked as if we might crash into one of the walls of the temple. The flowers sang in a deeper register here, informing me we had traveled miles below the outer shell of the temple. In this level, the flowers gave off the scent of bitter chocolate, blood-red chilies, and sea foam.

"We found our spot," the Xolotl said. "Step off the hummingbird."

Our feet sank into layers of flower smells, and their wet juices stained the legs of our jeans. I began to worry about time. How long had we been gone from Chicago?

If time doesn't matter as much here, will we forget to return?

"Keep up, *reina*," José María said. "We're about to see the main event."

The Xolotl led the way through the dark. His feet also sank into the wet floor, which extended roughly fifty feet ahead of us, where it suddenly stopped. Above us, a massive hall rose hundreds of feet into the air.

And beneath the eerie quietness, I heard the murmur of music beyond the edge of the floor we stood on.

We knelt at the edge of the floor of the temple, next to the Xolotl. I tuned my ears to catch the music around us, the sounds that built images for me. And there it was: beneath us, a giant waterfall hidden inside this temple like treasure. The waterfall rang its music in millions of chords.

We stayed there for several minutes, listening to the waterfall. Slowly, a soft hue entered my vision, and for a second I thought it might be made of sound, but—

"José María" I whispered. "Is that—"

"Yes, it is," he said. "It's the real thing. Holy crap."

For the first time in all my journeys inside Mictlán, I saw light.

The light came from the waterfall itself, which originated from a steep wall on our left and flowed downward into the cavern beneath us. Its waters roared out into the wide room and fell hundreds of miles into the depths of the palace.

I let out a long sigh of exhilaration and awe.

Tiny particles of light traveled in the currents of the waterfall, and they twisted and turned like stars inside a galaxy. They emitted a soft light in shades of sapphire, ruby and rose.

José María let out a long sigh. With his back turned to me, I could see how the lights from inside the water turned him into a shadow and lit the sharp angles of his face. His face glowed pink, violet and blue. Music rushed from his body in a soft hum.

The tiny pinpoints of light that flowed in the waters turned and rotated, twinkling from every angle, sweeping the room with washes of soft light.

He was weeping. He cupped his face in his hands, and as he did so, I felt what he felt, too. There was a sadness beneath this riverbed and waterfall, but dancing over that foundation was something else. Something bright, wide and ample. Something that made me feel I could fly. There was a joy in these particles and the tiny coils of music they gave off from inside the waterfall.

"You see them, Wanderer?" the Xolotl said as his body rang out in bells.

"There's so many of them," I said. "It's like jewel dust."

"So now you understand my duty in the Coil," the Xolotl said. "It's my job to ensure that they travel down the nine rivers to meet the Lords."

The Xolotl erupted in laughter, and now that I could see his body in the faint glow of the river, I marveled at how old his skin looked. His skin was the same shade of black as that of his dog head, but his claws were white as snow.

Why was he laughing? It made me uneasy. Did they eat souls down here? Were the Lords more monstrous than this dog-headed man?

José María wept openly, but he gathered himself up to a standing position. "Clara. Clara!" he said as he tugged at my shirt.

"What?"

"Arkangel got a couple of details wrong, but this one is spot on. This river, this waterfall, Clara—"

"What is it?"

"Those twinkling particles are *souls*."

The music of the waterfall intensified. The smells of linen and copper intensified.

"Wanderer," the Xolotl said. "Perhaps you should stay down in the Coil with us a bit longer. It seems you have much to learn about this place."

This prospect tempted me, but a voice inside me, deep inside—it told me it would be a one-way ticket.

"This is more complicated than what my parents taught me about the nine levels of Mictlán," I said. "I must admit, I don't understand exactly what I'm seeing."

"Of course you don't," the Xolotl said. "The knowledge that you humans have learned about our citizens and our architecture in the Coil is *refracted*."

"That's an actual line from a song!" José María screamed. My brother was literally shaking, tapping his feet, running his hands through his coarse hair. "Do you know Arkangel, Xolotl?"

"I know no such word, and I have no knowledge of what you call Arkangel," the Xolotl said.

José María spread his legs apart and put his hands on his belly. I knew that stance. It was his karaoke warrior pose. It was coming.

Nothing could stop my brother from singing "Cissoid of Diocles" by Arkangel.

"The line goes *They traveled far and wide, and when they visited the thirteen secret cities, the visions they felt were galactic and refracted.*"

My brother had a good voice; I had always known that. In this temple made of smells, and in this world of sounds that lit up places like light, he sounded glorious. He sang the line from Arkangel's song again.

The Xolotl cocked his head and leaned forward to inspect José María. "You are a poet?" he said.

"No, the singers from Arkangel are," José María said. 'They sang that line in 2009."

"That word—two thousand nine—is that the time in your wheels?" the Xolotl said.

"No, not wheels, Scooby. We measure our time in a flat line, like a flower stem."

The Xolotl opened his jaw wide and licked his lips. He seemed satisfied by my brother's answer. When he interacted with José María, he was a creature of few words. When he spoke to me, he was full of questions, full of words.

Perhaps he was always constantly evaluating my brother as prey. I hoped this wasn't the case, but I knew better.

The walls of the temple groaned, and I felt a presence there, something thick and oppressive, observe us. I never thought it would be possible to fear flowers, but these were more ancient things than Earth's flowers.

The Xolotl dripped thick pus from his gums, and he licked it with his rope-like tongue.

"You see," José María said, turning to me, "the little particles—the souls, they can see glimpses of Mictlán as they travel. They can see the temples of the creatures of the canyon. They can even probably see us as they travel inside that water."

"Is this true?" I said to the Xolotl. He sat on his haunches, and now that he was closer to my height, I didn't think he was so menacing.

"Your sibling is right," the Xolotl said. "This is how your ancestors discovered our faces and heard faint traces of our songs. That's how they learned about the Lords. And the other family members who left this canyon long ago."

"And tell her, Scooby, tell her," José María said.

The Xolotl was annoyed by José María, but he continued. He said, "That is also how those of us in the Coil—the citizens of cities like Mictlán—can see out into your world, Clara. We see and learn much when you travel through the nine rivers. We see you."

I felt a chill run down my back, and the walls groaned again.

"And so each of those bits of glitter is a human—"

"Wrong, Wanderer," the Xolotl said. "It's every being from your world. The frogs, the trees, the jungle animals and the sea beings. Each becomes a particle in the river."

"I could stare at these waters forever," I said. The liquid looked cool and refreshing, and I marveled at the fact that a tree might have a soul. In what color did it shine inside that stream?

"Your brother Quetzalcóatl left you here, didn't he?" José María said.

The Xolotl groaned, and smoke escaped the slits in his chest.

"My brother has abandoned many," the Xolotl said. "I was not surprised that he would neglect me. It's in his nature."

"So it's true," I said as I elbowed José María.

"You saw Scooby's brother in the snake's eyes memory, Clara," José María said. "He's the Feathered Snake. Quetzalcóatl, who fought the Ocullín."

"That makes no sense," I said. "There's four Tezcatlipocas. The feathered snake is the white one, Huitzilopochtli the god of war is the blue one, the Flayed One is the red—"

"And yes, the Smoking Mirror is the Black Tezcatlipoca," José María said. "But that doesn't explain *you*, Scooby."

The Xolotl drew his sharp claws along his left arm, and he drew blood. Now that we had a glimmer of light from the waterfall, I could see that it sparkled in hundreds of shades of red. In his bare chest, the thin slits that took in air swelled, then closed shut. Their narrow passageways made smaller music, the kind that creeps in your ear and never lets go.

The Xolotl dug his claws into his chest cavity, and he split the flesh apart. It was a simple gesture, and one without violence. He simply reached in as a mother would pull two halves of a papaya apart so she could scoop out the seeds with her fingers.

We saw the Xolotl's breast. It was made of a thick heart, arteries and bits of his bones. Blood pumped, and the flesh pulsed with life. He kept on pulling until his chest began to split in two, and the seam undid itself, traveling up toward his neck and down toward his groin.

"Every living thing has a duality, Wanderer. You and your sibling, what shall we call him?"

"You can call me Bangin' Master of the Universe," José María said.

"Yes, Bangin' Master of the Universe, then. Understand that my brother Quetzalcóatl and I are dual expressions of each other, even if we are both a single White Tezcatlipoca. In a way, we are just like you and the Bangin' Master of the Universe."

Inside his knotted flesh, wrapped around his beating heart, a snake with colorful feathers and white scales encircled the creature's heart.

The Xolotl stopped pulling his flesh, and the wound knitted itself until his skin was smooth and all that was left were the slits on his pecs.

"So you can now see that my brother and I are separate but

often the same," the Xolotl said.

"That I can understand," José María said. "Clara understands that, too. Two in one, one in two. We're Catholic, after all."

"What is *Catholic*?" the Xolotl said.

"Our religion," I said.

"You must explain religion, Wanderer. We have no such word here."

"You know—what you believe made the universe—who made the universe. What makes things right or wrong."

"You need a *Catholic* for this knowledge?" Xolotl said.

"Well, no, but the priests, they're the ones that teach us," José María said.

"Ah yes, your priests," the Xolotl said. "Odd things, those priests. Even the men who glimpsed us through the waters made up priests to ask me for favors. We have seen the priests, as well as the wicked wizards, many times, floating inside the waterfall. Begging, full of greed. I despise them."

"Who makes it through to tell the tale, then?" José María said.

"Some of the clever priests glimpse us from the waters, that's true. But the children—they flow down the nine rivers, and they return several times in their lifetime. These are their journeys to find and commune with their tonal."

"That's a trip I should have made," I said. I bit my lip. "At thirteen."

"But things went wrong, as you know, Scooby," José María said.

"But my brother has a point—we did learn about duality, or something like it, from the Catholics."

"I see, Wanderer. Your *Catholics*, do they ask for knowledge, then?"

"No, no, no," José María said. "What Clara means is that the Catholics taught us about God, and the son of God, and how the Holy Spirit—all three of them—are expressions of a single God."

"This feels relevant, then," the Xolotl said. "And true. Tell me more. I have never seen this God that you say travels in the waters of the nine rivers. What makes this human named 'God' so special?"

"No, he's not human; he's a god." I said.

"I don't understand. God is not a human?" the Xolotl said.

He doesn't know the word 'god,' I thought.

Suddenly, a bitter smell, like burning wood and acrid oil, made the walls around us quiver. The flowers of the temple spoke.

"You must leave now," the flowers said. They shared a single voice made up of billions of individuals. The sound was terrifying.

"The flowers do not like our exchange of words and ideas," Xolotl said. "We must depart. We can continue elsewhere."

We mounted the hummingbird, and I took one last glimpse at the crimson-blue waterfall. It warmed my heart, but it also filled me with sadness. Its specks made me smile, and I didn't want to leave them behind. But I remembered the pressure exerted by the flowers of the temple, and I was glad we were leaving.

We rose as the hummingbird beat its wings millions of times, and we approached the top of the temple.

"Xolotl, I said. "In Chicago—on Earth, in our world—they have taught us that you and Quetzalcóatl are gods."

"Did the flowers teach you this in your world?"

José María laughed. "Hell, no! It's other humans that teach that to each other."

"Then your human teachers are wrong. We do not have *gods* here, and we do not have any *Catholics.* Things inside the Coil simply *are.*"

"In our world, we use flowers for ornamentation or to show love," I said.

"Or to mourn the dead," José María said.

"But we don't talk to the flowers," I said.

"You don't talk to the flowers," the Xolotl said.

"No," we replied in unison.

"And you don't consult the plants," the Xolotl growled.

"Maybe some people do; don't know," I said.

"You are imbeciles in your world, then," roared the Xolotl.

The Xolotl's inner sound changed from a baritone melody into a melancholy but frightening song. He extended both his arms, and he let the hummingbird's wings brush the claws at their tips. More frightening sounds erupted from their contact.

"I cannot fathom a world where you do not consult with the flowers and the moss," Xolotl said. "Down here in the Coil, plants move history through the wheels, and flowers are the keepers of all knowledge."

It began to occur to me that the lowest levels of Mictlán belonged to the flowers. All of them eyeless, trillions of them.

"But the flowers don't like to share knowledge, do they?" I said.

"That is correct. They believe the rift that is opening the gates between worlds is caused by knowledge coming through."

We flew out of the temple and into darkness, and we dove toward the lake and the city on top of its surface. I didn't have to turn my head around to feel the temple of flowers behind me, but I turned my head anyway, out of sheer habit. The structure was immense. Now that we had emerged from the shrine's opening, my cones were working again. It felt good to breathe in air that was no longer flooded with the strong smells of the temple.

As we sped away, I recalled how my father had taken José María and me to the Templo Mayor archeological site in Mexico City when I was twelve. There we walked through the ruins of the center of the Aztec empire. I had spent an hour sketching the maquette inside the museum's center. On this maquette, one could see the city of Tenochtitlán, its wide plazas, its cylindrical buildings, the bright reds and blues the Aztecs had used to paint their walls. At the very center of this maquette, I had learned about Templo Mayor, the most important religious and war temple of the Aztecs. One tower was red, the other blue, and each one was dedicated to a different god.

This memory rolled over in my head until I understood why I was recalling it. I let out a scream of joy and partial terror.

I leaned in close to my brother, hovering over his neck.

"If souls traveled through these rivers, and for some reason they were able to travel *back* to our world—like wizards might—that means they would have been able to imitate the architecture they saw," I said. "That means Templo Mayor would have been modeled after the temple of flowers."

"Holy crap," José María said.

José María gave out a hoarse shout, and then another. He was doing so to get better information about the temple of flowers behind us.

"Clara, it looks just like Templo Mayor. Only twenty times as tall. And if that's what they modeled it after—"

We approached the spinning disc set on top of the still lake.

"That means Mexico City was modeled after the city of Mictlán."

"And inside the city we will find the palace of skulls," I said. "Right in there."

The disc rotated as the thorns and plants that gave it structure pulsed with the sound of fireworks, oboes and insect wings.

We landed on a soft patch of grass at the very shore of the lake. Before us, one of the roads that led to its center went off into the distance. The hummingbird flew off, and we walked behind the Xolotl, whose claws made hollow scraping sounds on the road as he scrambled to a standing position. The water on each of the sides of the roads was still, unmoving. The sonar-like ability I had in Mictlán told me that not even one single ripple blemished the lake's surface.

"Do you get lonely down here?" I asked the Xolotl. I couldn't believe I was talking to him this way, but he seemed so different from the first time I ever heard and felt him, in the mountain above the canyon.

"I feel loneliness only when people ask me how lonely I've been." He said. He had cried the first time I had asked his name. His human eyes blinked in the dark, and no tears rolled off his face this time.

"But you're not alone here," José María said. "There's the flowers, the smoke owls, and surely the snake—"

"Blue Hummingbird asks me often if I am lonely. That is when I take leave and fly off to get away from her. She likes to wallow in self-pity. She is haunted by the events from the past."

My father is, too, I thought.

And so is my mother.

And me.

"Wanderer and Bangin' Master of the Universe," the Xolotl said, "listen carefully. You will travel through the palace of skulls alone. I cannot complete that journey for you. At its end, you will exit onto the northern road of Mictlán. You will follow this road until you encounter the Snow Fields of the Lords. The journey through the snow may kill you, in which case you will be forever lost in the spaces between the wheels."

I felt sick at hearing this possibility.

"Will there be other beings like you?" I said. I wanted to say "gods," but I decided against it.

"You mean brothers and sisters?" The Xolotl said. "You will

see none. The last of my kin to visit Mictlán was the Black Tezcatlipoca, and he's long since gone. The only thing he left behind is his Ocullín."

"The Black Tezcatlipoca owns that thing?" José María said. "Now that is some bullshit right there."

"The Black Tezcatlipoca is the most dangerous of the four brothers. We do not invoke his name often. And for those that do, the act can often summon the Ocullín. So be warned."

"Xolotl, why would the Black Tezcatlipoca keep such a monster?" I said. "The Ocullín—it's the worst thing I have ever seen, ever felt."

The Xolotl shook his head at me. The expression on his face was that of pity and disdain. He thought my question was a stupid one. He didn't humor it.

"I have to return to the snow caps at the top the mountain," the Xolotl said, "where the rivers begin. Maybe the flowers of your world can teach you about the Ocullín someday."

I felt a presence above us, in the open air of the canyon, and I remembered how the Ocullín had eaten through the walls, through the snow owls, and how it had promised me the worst kind of murder. The murder of my family.

"Well, then, how far do we need to go in the Snow Fields?" I asked.

"You must walk the snow until you hear the song of your tonal. And be sure not to fall in the last of the nine rivers. That river feeds the lake on which the city rests. It runs deep, and you must *never* touch its waters."

"How will I know I have found the Lords?" I said.

The Xolotl cackled and ran his claw through my hair, as he widened his jaw.

"I recommend not perishing in the Snow Fields, Wanderer," he said.

"Uhm, OK," José María said. He tapped me on my shoulder. "This is freakin' nuts, Clara."

"I heard you, Bangin' Master of the Universe," the Xolotl said.

"And then what happens?" I said. My voice and its music took on the texture of steel and platinum. I wanted answers.

"Then you can ask the Lords for your tonal. And just be sure that they don't devour you. The Lords will see you as dead souls, no matter what you say to persuade them otherwise."

"And then you'll take us back to our world?" I said.

The Xolotl grunted. "Yes. You'll have to meet me back here, at the southern road to Mictlán. I'll be waiting."

The Xolotl turned on his heel and walked away from us.

I suppose we should have been insulted, but I don't think he had the concept of rudeness down here. As he walked back toward the lake shore, he broke into a run, and he roared. Two smoke owls dove toward him and grabbed him by the shoulders with their talons, and soon, they were gone, up into the higher levels of the canyon.

"He's a real charmer," José María said.

"Yes." I said.

"I'm hungry," José María said.

I dug in my pack for the last of the energy bars we had packed, and we ate in silence as we walked toward the palace. As we did, the silence of the lake began to fill me with dread. Unlike the other realms of Mictlán, there was a silence that floated over this water, and even though the city of Mictlán gave off its song, the water around it seemed to mute it from our ears.

"I'm thirsty," I said. I knelt over the water and approached the lake's surface. It gave off no single note of sound or music.

The beauty of this city atop the water brought tears to my eyes. A few miles away, I could see the cylindrical shape of the city, rotating.

But my thirst was tearing at my throat, and my tongue was puffy and dry. If I could just have a sip of water, I could continue this journey. And the stillness of that lake water felt so inviting.

"We should wait," José María said. "That water doesn't look quite right. It looks stagnant."

"Are you always going to be so annoying? I said. "Even when we're little old people?"

I'm trying to be more reckless like you, little brother. Less structured. Less stiff.

"When we're little old people, I will set your wig on fire and steal your dentures." José María said. "You know that's the river water in this lake."

Something about the stillness of the water of this lake, and its lack of ripples, made my thoughts hazy, and as I stared at the liquid, I felt intoxicated, drowsy, unable to resist the mirror-like planes of this lake. I felt a little scared, but more than anything, I felt as if I were under a thick mental fog. I had been warned about the water, but I felt an attraction – an addiction to it. I had to touch it.

I put my hands into the water, and as soon as they plunged into the icy liquid, I knew I had made a mistake.

A face stared at me in the murky liquid. Her eye was half shut, and her hair was disheveled. I saw her in shades of black inside the water. Her flesh was bloated, and pitted where fish had eaten little bits.

"You came to save me," the face said. She was the woman I had lain next to in Pritzker Pavilion, while paramedics rushed to save us.

While the police shuffled bodies off into piles. Like her.

I let the water slip from my hands and back into lake. The first few ripples started to move off into the distance, and suddenly I wished that the water had stayed smooth and undisturbed. The ripples would let any fish, any plant, any creature inside these waters know my location. But the dead woman was now with me.

"You came to save me, too," said a new voice, and a new face emerged, replacing that of the young woman from Pritzker. This new face spoke in Spanish, and I recognized the nose, the shape of the lips, the deep brow. I had seen it hundreds of times in a photograph, next to my father.

"Tío Jorge," I said. This was a person I had never met but which my father mourned for every day. Those times when the tequila ran deep in my father's blood, and he collapsed in a chair in our back porch to sob, they were because of this face. I spotted a thin hairline crack in his skin where the bullet had entered his face at the riot in Tlatelolco in 1968.

"Clara," he said. "I have always wanted to meet you."

Tío Jorge's voice resembled my father's. His eyes had a milky quality. They stared up at me, through me.

"José María, get over here," I said. Soon, my brother kneeled next to me over the water. "Look."

We peered at the face. José María could see it, too.

"Our father misses you," I said. What else could I say?

"I miss him, too. But no worries; he'll come down here into the water soon. The water is nice and cool, like a kiss of ice." he said.

The music of the giant stone turning down the road faded off, and suddenly, I only felt silence around me as I stared at my uncle.

"What is it like to be dead?" I asked. The paradox of the question was not lost on me. I presumably might already be dead if I made this far down Mictlán, but I didn't think that really was the case. I had seen the river of souls, and I wanted to believe the Xolotl that the river carried the spirits of the dead.

My uncle crinkled his eyebrows just like my father did when he worked on organizing shelves at home. The wounds in his face looked soft like putty. They were spotless, as if the blood had been removed from his flesh.

"What it feels like to be dead, children," he said. "What it feels…is good. Pleasurable. Moist. Dark. Surely you want to feel these joys, no? Why wait when you can taste it now?"

His eyes flickered, and I wished I could verify their color. Were they like my father's? Or lighter in color, like La Negra's eyes? Suddenly, they didn't match my memories of his eyes from the family photographs. They looked *wrong*.

"Tell me about your father, Clara," Tío Jorge said. "Is he still lost in his memories?"

"I suppose you could say that," I said. "He's sort of stuck, I suppose. Or lost. Or both."

"Good," *Tío* Jorge said. "That means he's still a little fucking bastard."

That response didn't feel right. I elbowed José María, who was fishing something out of his backpack. He never took his eyes off our dead uncle.

"I don't think you would want our father to be haunted," José María said. I felt him shiver and shake. He was holding back tears. "Would you?"

"I don't see why not. Death is nothing but pain, children. Dark, nagging pain. We live in pain down here."

My uncle's head turned sideways, first to the left, and then to the right, as if he were on the other end of a teleconference and he was checking to make sure he was alone in the room. I could see tiny maggots crawl along his Adam's apple.

"Will you help us find Clara's tonal?" José María said.

"Of course," our uncle said. "No woman should be without her tonal. She would be a monster without it. Clara, if you'll help me out of the water, I'll travel with you to get your tonal. Just take my hand and help your uncle out."

The limb that emerged from the water was smooth, hairless and strong. His oval nails had grown long (and I remembered that hair and nails continued to grow after death). The arm entered the space right between José María and me. Behind the image of my uncle, I could see the modern high-rises of the apartment buildings in Tlatelolco, where he had been gunned down. The clouds in the image drifted, forming long strands like taffy, and suddenly I felt swept in their long shapes, lazy and undulating. They became a siren song and—

STOP IT, I heard myself think.

José María had plunged his arm into the water, hoping to free our uncle from the confines of the lake.

"No!" I screamed, but it was too late.

The being crawled out, changing its shape with flesh that bristled with murderous energy. It roared our names as it aimed to scoop out our eyes.

Tío Jorge emerged with a human torso connected to arms and legs, but as he did so, I realized why he had made me feel uneasy. He made no music, unlike the other creatures inside Mictlán.

He emerged naked, a fully grown man, and his skinny leg took hold of the road above the water. As he brought his other leg forward, he frowned, and his face collapsed in a series of thick folds. His lips and nose fell into each other, and the flesh re-knitted itself before our eyes as its human fleshiness disappeared, and hard lines and creases took over its structure. He stood over us, and we backed up, as thick branch-like structures rose from his shoulders. His naked belly and his flaccid penis gave the transformation an even more horrible twist. Soon, they were gone, too, transformed into a writhing mass of legs and bristles that resembled fur.

"Thanks for playing my game, children," said the thing, and the rest of our uncle's body folded over, like origami, into the hard spikes of the thing that lay beneath. "Now if you'll direct me back to your homes in the other world, I will murder you and murder them. As I promised you, Wanderer."

The thing turned toward me with a hundred eyes that lay

hidden beneath the spikes of its true shape. Its voice was as ancient as that of Blue Hummingbird or Xolotl, but its sounds were those of blades scraping against metal and the growls inside a carnivore's throat.

"Take me to your mother and father first, girl," the entity said, "Because I want to take them first."

José María darted toward the creature, and with a single click, he turned on the flashlight on his phone. The light that poured out melted and fell onto the road. José María scooped it up and tossed it at the face of the creature. The tiny gob of light was limp and pale, like snot, but it was solid.

The thing recoiled, and it folded itself up into something that looked like a shrimp carapace. Its legs bristled, and then it spat out the gob of light, which faded into droplets of liquid, and then evaporated into dust.

"Time to die," the creature said, and it lunged at José María. I was ready with the knife I carried in my coat pocket, and I plunged the blade into the folds and spikes of the thing. It didn't bleed. Instead, darkness poured out of its wounds. A sick darkness, nothing the smooth dark of Mictlán. Its thick tendrils wrapped around my hand, and as it touched my skin, it spoke its name through his touch in a long guttural roar.

Our direct contact was brief, because I yanked the knife back from the seeping dark, but as I learned its name, I saw through its eyes. Millions of eyes, all of them malevolent, hungry and with an intelligence that frightened me more than anything I had ever felt. It was very old and ready to kill us any way it could.

I grabbed José María by the arm and covered him from the path of the creature. I slashed in the air, hoping to fight of the spikes from the shapeless body and the sense of desolation and despair that seeped from its dark. It had emerged onto the floating road and stepped toward us.

"Your parents are next," the Ocullín roared, and it plunged a spike deep in my thigh. It was then that I screamed with all the power I could muster, and the song that erupted from my scream turned the canyon of Mictlán into a bed of fire.

My scream sparked balls of black fire above the still waters of the lake, and in the distance, I felt spiders and owls fly off in fright from the music my throat made. Each time I swept the knife in the air, it left long trails of sound like whispers. The Ocullín flinched at the blade, and he was genuinely afraid.

At least, he seemed afraid. Beneath the dark folds of his body, I spotted many mouths of all shapes and sizes. All of them were smiling.

"You don't need a tonal, Wanderer. Don't bother trying."

Get to the water, the reflection in the water.

I remembered something my mother had said. "No more travel through mirrors," she had said. And she was right. No more travel through mirrors.

I grabbed my brother by the collar and I dragged him with me as we dove into the still surface of the water on the lake of Mictlán.

I had come to this place to find my tonal, and I would get it any way that I could.

As we approached the mirror-like surface of the lake, I noticed small columns of smoke drifting from it. My face, that terrible misshapen, plastic surgery monster face, stared at me as I tumbled toward it with my brother, his eyes peeled back in fear.

When we struck the surface, the knife in my right fist went red-hot, and I felt the Ocullín scream as it chased after us.

I swung the knife to the left, to the right, and in any direction, hoping it would tear through our attacker.

We exploded into the smoking mirror.

José María and I traveled through the glassy material of the water, and as we pushed through its jagged prisms, the Ocullín followed us.

I had been here before, and as the swaths of white light engulfed me, I knew we were returning in the very same way in which we came.

The Ocullín tore through the air, making the sounds of a bottle rocket, darting to keep up with us.

We fought without bodies, and we used the sound that came from inside us to cast off the ferocious anger and savagery of the monster behind us. As we spun through the vast crystal landscape, I spotted a nautilus shell in the distance. Farther back, beyond it, a vast field of black stripes. I had seen three cities in this transitory place, but now I wanted to see none.

Farther in the distance, I saw more pinpoints, like stars. In my heart, I knew they were cities, too.

This was the tunnel that connected the cities.

The Ocullín roared behind us. He was all at once a jet engine, the sound of metal shears and the angriest screech of a predator.

Inside the glass, the Ocullín slashed at me with claw and bristle, and he sliced my arms, my legs. The gashes I felt were worse than any I had ever experienced when I had a body. I came close to the Ocullín, and it wasn't until I willed myself to escape his dark body that I felt myself gather my brother José María to shoot us up and out of the white glass.

We burst through the center of the dome, and we stumbled on the floor of butterflies. Hundreds of them took off in flight, and a wet sound sloshed around us.

"José María," I screamed. He had landed on the far end of the dome, and he scrambled to where I stood. "The dome—run!"

As we ran for the door, the wet sound became a roar. The butterflies lost their solidity, and water poured through the top of the dome. Icy drops hit my face, and I knew that people didn't survive the waters of Lake Michigan in late fall.

We ran as well as we could. My pack cut into my shoulders, and my legs burned with soreness. We had a long way to cover in the tunnel.

"We're not going to make it," José María said. "It's too long to go."

He was crying as we stomped on the butterflies. Cracks were appearing in the walls, and butterflies danced in the air, in a stupor.

Then we heard the crash behind us.

"The lake," I said.

Water and foam, crusted in white and blue, barreled through the tunnel. It would reach us within seconds, and then it would be all over.

And inside that form, I spotted a black mass made of black needles and hungry mouths. Thousands of legs and no heart.

"Thanks for the ticket back," the Ocullín screamed at me. "I owe you, Wanderer."

"Call her, José María," I said. "Call her!"

"Call who?"

"Blue Hummingbird."

José María laughed out loud, with pure joy and a youthful candor. He winked at me. He opened up his mouth and sang a word, made of long syllables and sensuous utterances.

And she appeared then.

The tunnel roared to life with the sick butterflies that held up its structure, and we stumbled. The path behind us sloped backward and we he had to scramble to get a foothold. More cracks appeared in the wall, and water seeped through the insects.

But we were moving, and something was happening.

The Ocullín receded in the foam behind us, and a single blue eye opened up in the wall, a membrane flickering over it. We felt thousands of pounds of pressure shift as our ears popped, and then water poured over us as sunlight burst through the walls.

The butterflies were now dead, and they washed over us as we got tossed onto a hard surface and the sun blinded us.

Sun, glorious sun.

I gasped for air and got on my hands and knees. Two people on bikes stared at us as they rode on the bike path, and the jagged metal of the skyline cut out the fading sun. We were back in the place where we began, at the lakeshore.

"Call 911," I heard the biker say to the other. The water was so cold it burned, and José María coughed, on his side. I looked back at the water, and I saw a single line of green fade into the water, dissolving into the current of the lake. The tunnel of butterflies was gone.

But the Ocullín is here.

I gathered all my will to live and dragged my brother away from the water. That deadly water. We hobbled all the way to where the bikers stood. Sirens wailed, and I saw an ambulance whiz toward us.

If I told the EMTs the right lies, they would take us to the ER without alerting our parents.

José María and I parted ways that afternoon, and my return to school became a fever dream. I was behind on my coursework, and every one of my senses was on fire. I felt a hunger that tore at my insides. I ate six full trays of pasta, meat, fruit and desserts three times a day, and after eating all that food, it was still not enough.

At night, I sweated through the sheets, and I feared the moonlight coming through the blinds. I considered playing music, but I feared that my playlists would lead me back to my playlists that featured Arkangel. I knew if I listened, I might never sleep again.

I also bit down on the meaty part of my thumb at night in a rage. I choked back tears of my failure, and just as I got close to chewing through the bone, I got up to bandage my digit.

I stayed up until dawn reading for my classes. That became easier than trying to fool myself into thinking I could sleep.

In those few times I drifted into sleep, I did not dream.

Each night, I vomited bile into the toilet in the shared bathroom at the end of the hall, and every time I looked down into the yellow liquid, I expected to find snakes swimming in it.

Morgan urged me to go to the university clinic. Instead, I swaddled my thoughts around the way I had failed in my journey through the Coil.

José María emailed me and sent me private messages every day. I ignored all of them.

Colors screamed, and smells roared. I didn't know how to make any of it stop.

At the end of that week, I walked with José María from the top of Michigan Avenue. He had met me at the Belmont stop on the Red Line, and he had offered me a hot coffee on our way down to Michigan Avenue. I had taken one sip and vomited right at the station.

The intensity of the colors of the world was worse. They hurt my good eye, and all sounds had become so amplified that even laughter made me cringe in pain.

But we didn't talk about why I vomited.

I was having a hard time talking to my brother since our return.

We got off on Chicago Avenue and walked east toward the top of Michigan Avenue. My heavy breathing sounded like songs of despair and sadness. I heard the music of my breath now, and the music of all things.

The music of the real world was not always one of beauty.

We wore several layers as the wind bit into our skin. I handed José María a container of flyers I brought to hand out at the rally while I Instagrammed photos to our OLF group.

"You look like shit," José María said to me.

Nightmares had filled my dreams every night since I came back from Mictlán, and I had caught a terrible cold that brought wet coughs each time I tried to talk.

"Why are you still going through the motions with this plan?" José María said.

"I'm like a zombie," I said. "The truth is, I don't want to go to this OLF thing anymore, but—"

"I know, staying home and thinking about what happened in the Coil—"

"—Is worse."

"I'm sorry you didn't find your tonal. Maybe you don't really need it," José María said.

The rapport we shared—the way we bounced language back and forth—was gone today.

I shrugged.

"Even if that's true, the Ocullín wants us," I said. "It wants our family. I don't want them to die."

"Why are you so stubborn, then?" José María said. "Let's go back to the Coil and get it. You have that knife."

"Why is everything so reductive with you?" I said. My anger stung my brother, and he reacted with anger, too.

His words, his breathing, the colors of his face, were stinging every facet of my mind and senses. I wanted it to stop.

"Hey, just trying to help," he said. "No need to take it out on me."

"Well, screw you, not everything is a game. *Nothing* is a game."

José María looked different since we had come back, and I realized now what the change was. He continued to smile and laugh as he always did. But his face was harder, the jaw more square. Lines cut grooves into his forehead.

He's aged.

I felt I had aged too, but I could really see it in my brother. In fact he looked taller, more muscular, as if he had moved through puberty and exited at the same time the tunnel of butterflies delivered us to the shore.

It can't be. How long were we down in Mictlán?

But I knew. I knew. José María had told me that the journey through Mictlán lasts years.

"You'll need to help me bring the flyers up the tower. We're going to deliver them in a very unusual way."

José María dropped the box of flyers on the sidewalk. People behind us stumbled into him, but he didn't care.

"You can carry your own flyers, bitch," he said. "I'm done helping you out."

He had never called me names. Ever.

"That's fine. What the OLF has planned for today is much bigger than parades for some damn *kids*."

"You think I don't read the backdoor messages in the Internet, *reina*? I know you and those terrorists are planning a blackout today. You're not that special."

"Whatever."

"You want to keep playing games with these anarchist fools in Chicago while that *thing* is after us."

"You need to listen to me," I said.

"No, you need to stop telling me what to do."

"You know what? I hate you, José María. I hate you and your stupidity. You're so naive."

He lit a cigarette and dragged on it until the cherry went bright red in the dim November daylight.

He cocked his head to the west.

"I see Dad and La Negra," he said. "Looks like they just parked. See you after your game of hide-and-seek. And keep your bullshit to yourself, because I am tired of you."

And he walked off down Ohio Street, where my father, my aunt Veronica and several of our cousins filed out of his Honda.

I checked my watch. We would target the websites of every major news outlet at the start of the parade, and that was just the beginning. This morning in bed, I had wanted to quit my membership to the OLF, but now that José María had spat in my face, I felt a rage like boiling water in my veins. I had never been so angry in my life, and as I stared at the Tribune Tower and the Trump Tower a mile down the avenue, I knew I could fuel the rally with my rage.

As I cut through the hundreds of sightseers, children and tourists, I should have paid attention to the hungry mouths that shimmered inside the shadows cast by the buildings, the hard eyes encrusted behind the concrete of the Magnificent Mile.

But I didn't. My focus was hard and brittle, like a pinpoint in the distance, and no hallucinatory vision, no night of nightmares and cold sweat was going to stop me from doing something tangible in the real world.

I was going to change the history of Chicago forever.

PART FOUR
BLACK TEZCATLIPOCA

0.13.26

"What if we could confirm that entities from another place could actually see us? Would their gaze change us? Could ours change them?" – Playwright Veronica Montes, *Miss World: Somebody Kill Me,* Chavela Vargas Publishing, 2035, fourth edition. (Editor's Note: This line of dialogue was performed on the Pritzker Stage in 2033 and co-opted into Montes' script by her estate shortly after her death in 2034.)

"Nobody knows me." *Philosophy of Dr. Yu-Tsun,* p. 266, Edited by Wang Yang-Ming. Kays Press, 2001.

"In later years, I was lucky enough to get to know Clara Montes beyond my role as biographer. If you knew her like I knew her, you would understand that she was motivated by fire in her belly. As a result, she left black smoke in her wake." — Jane Morrigan, *Clara Montes: A Biography in Four Parts,* 2074, p. 875, Castor Books.

Did it matter why the police had shot the protesters in the Millennium Riot? After all, they were already dead, and the damage had already been done.

But it did matter. It mattered because on the day of the Millennium Riot, we gathered in downtown Chicago to help the people of our city.

The OLF scheduled the march on October 4, 2013, in Millennium Park to bring attention to a fire that had broken out in Englewood earlier that year. The city had not only been slow to respond, they had let that whole community languish. Poverty, gang violence, and oppression had made that neighborhood as prominent to the world as Willis Tower, but when Englewood burned, it remained as invisible as air. We had marched up to Pritzker Pavilion, ready to change something, and as far as I was concerned, we had failed. We failed when the law enforcement officers shot us, corralled us, and gassed us like animals.

We failed, but worst of all, I failed.

The way I dealt with failure was to win the next round.

I also failed my father's side of the family in another place: down in Mictlán. I had meant to complete a task in that nightmare world, and I came back empty-handed.

Nothing had gone as planned.

I re-emerged from that failure onto the plaza that overlooks the Chicago River on a cold November day, ready to triumph.

No more failures.

Dennis and Mercy met me on the black marble benches beneath the hard lines of the Equitable building and the gothic arches of Tribune Tower. This is what I liked most about Chicago's late fall and winter: the long shadows cast by a forlorn star.

"Clara, why the shades?" Mercy said. "There's no sun. Are you trying to draw *all* the attention to us?"

"Migraine," I said.

Everything hurt. The shimmer of makeup on Mercy's eyes stabbed my optic nerves. The roaring motorcycles and sirens throbbing down Wacker Drive stung my ears. The taste of coffee swelled into scorching bitterness on my tongue . Since escaping

(no, bitch, you mean FAILING)

from the Coil, my nervous system, and all the feedback it got from the world, were on fire. Puking often relieved this for a moment, but I could only puke so much.

"Well, just lie low, okay?" Mercy said. "For now."

Dennis looped his arm around me, hanging off my shoulders, both a trooper and a confidant. I needed his company, and I was glad to have it. He knew nothing about canyons filled with flowers that sang in the dark, and his ignorance allowed me to focus on this world and what lay ahead.

"Okay, let's get moving. We only have a couple of hours before things get started," I said.

Mercy slid her backpack over to me. I unzipped the bag and

found a compact video camera and three MiFi cards.

"Okay, just remember to keep the camera rolling, no matter what. If your live video feed goes down, you have two more data lines as backup."

"Sounds good," I said. "But let me ask you—why are you doing this? I mean, what does this all mean to you?"

Mercy clicked her tongue, but then she realized my question was earnest.

"My mom was a dyke, just like me," Mercy explained. "After her divorce, she raised me in L.A. That's where she got diagnosed with her neuro disorder. When she was at her worst and could no longer make decisions for herself, her girlfriend sent her to a Los Angeles mental hospital. It was the worst mistake she could have made. Her girlfriend had zero legal rights when it came to my mother's medical decisions. My mother's ex-husband arrived shortly thereafter, and it was he who called the shots about her care. And in the end, their lack of a marriage license meant that my mother died in a hospital room with a soiled diaper, alone and rambling in her last moments, while he went back to his suburban life on the East Coast. My mom's girlfriend could do nothing about it. Even after she passed away, my father's family wouldn't let us see her. I was a minor at the time. And all because of what the laws say about people like me and my mother. I fight this fight because of the assholes who won't give us basic human rights. Plain and simple."

"You?" I said to Dennis.

"All of it. Nothing seems to be getting any better, does it? Fires in Englewood, a high-tech army deployed to Millennium Park, and more surveillance than we even know."

"Well, good. Let's go show them we're not afraid, then," I said.

My words made solemn, angry music, and I lamented that my two friends couldn't hear the way the language clanged like a steel drum.

Mercy split off and headed north, to the top of Michigan Avenue, where the parade would start. The anticipation in the streets was tangible as families sipped coffee and hot chocolate, trying to find the best spots in the sidewalk to see the Parade of Lights.

At 2 p.m., the city would kick off the parade, and as the floats drove south on Michigan Avenue, every tree, shrub, lightpost and facade on the Magnificent Mile would burst into thousands of electric colors. The tiny light bulbs had been especially designed just for the city of Chicago at Mayor Amadeo's request. To the children, the sparkling lights were like a drug. For the parents, they were a touch of nostalgia. And for us in the OLF, they were the perfect stage for our one-act.

We met our university group at the arches of Tribune Tower.

"Ah, there you are. We're just waiting for a couple more people," said the tour leader. She was a tall redhead, earnest, devoid of irony. Her T-shirt read "Wildcat Club: Parade of Lights Realness 2013." She led our school's press club, which printed this sort of commemorative t-shirt of our club for this visit to the Parade was sponsored by the newspaper as a way to recruit students. Our tour of the tower would give us a very exclusive view of the parade while we networked with recruiters.

She didn't know that Dennis and I were part of the OLF.

My phone buzzed in my pocket. I glanced at the notification. It was from José María. I ignored it.

We rode up the elevator banks in two separate groups, since there were about twenty of us. The smells and sights of all those faces, all of those beating hearts making music, made me grit my teeth. I heard them loud and clear, and the flow of blood in their veins made a bubbling noise that turned my stomach. I wanted to cup my ears with my hands, but I knew I had to feign some normalcy. I caught my reflection in the polished brass interior of the elevator: my second face, its lines smooth, its brow clear.

We rose, and the yellow plastic numbers lit up one at a time, signaling our ascent through the levels. Those buttons were perfect little circles, machine-made. I relished the beauty of their curves and the soft yellow light behind each number.

My face insisted on staring back at me in the gold surface of that elevator.

I no longer cursed that strange face the plastic surgeons had given me. I was okay with it. It was a mask of sorts, and it occurred to me that many of the students in this tour might have recognized me from the Millennium Riot if I didn't have this mask keep me hidden.

Perhaps something good had come out of the riot.

We poured out on the 35th floor, where the executive suite was located. We entered a room furnished in red leather, lined with expensive bookcases and double doors that seemed to defy visitors, as if to keep them out.

But we were very welcome here.

"My name is Roger. I am the director of the Freedom Museum and Tribune Tower liaison," said a voice at the end of the long room where we stood. Heads parted, and Roger, a thin black man in his forties, walked along the massive windows that overlooked Michigan Avenue.

"We're glad to have visitors like you today. You'll have the best view of the Parade of Lights. Better than anyone else, in fact. Something to really brag about."

Our university (and in turn, our group) was full of overachievers, and I could see them salivate at the thought of making a connection here with the director, of one day working at the museum, or for Tribune media.

Catering staff brought out coffee and snacks, and those of us closest to it flocked to the carts like flies on shit.

The director paused as he exited the room; his hand grazed me at the elbow.

"Nothing for you?" he said.

"Maybe later," I said. "I'm just waiting for the parade."

"Roger Washington."

"Clara Montes; nice to meet you."

"What is your major?"

"Political science."

"Wonderful. We need more people like you in the world. We need that diversity."

Something about Roger, his narrow, tailored suit, and his ease in a world of the privileged felt insincere to me. He sounded scripted, like an actor on a TV show. Anger rose in my throat.

"Let me ask you something," I said. "You're a person of color, yes?"

"What a strange question. Why, yes, I am."

"And do you work with people of color here at the museum?"

"We have a great diverse team," he said. He crossed his arms and took a half step toward me. I was not afraid.

"Is that what they teach you to say? I asked, do you work with people of color here?"

He began to walk away. I could hear disgust in the song that his beating heart made. I was like a gnat to him.

"So, can you count how many people of color you actually work with, then?"

He turned. This time, he actually looked angry.

"Well, there's me, and we have plenty of people in many departments, such as marketing, development—"

"Okay, so tell me about the executive level," I said. "Are you the only black person at your level?"

"Yes, I am."

"The rest are…white men?"

"Well, yes."

"Any women?"

He was thinking about it. He stayed silent.

"And you're okay with this, then."

"Listen, Clara, I am not sure what you're getting at—"

"There's no need. You told me all I need to know. I see how little has actually changed."

I turned my back on him, and I pressed my hands on the cold glass of the windows. A family of spiders had made a home in the nooks and crannies of the window frame, and I marveled at the tiger stripes on their bodies, the way they clung together as the wind whipped them.

I had felt and heard spiders like this in the walls of Mictlán, living in the tall cliffs above the woods. Those spiders had lived in thick colonies, the babies suspended in silk pods from the trees while the parents sang poetry without words. The Mictlán spiders had been the size of a house.

But these spiders were not citizens of Mictlán. And neither was I. We were stuck in this city.

Roger checked his watch, and after saying a few words to our tour guide, he left the conference room.

I counted ten minutes on my watch after he left. 1:27 p.m.

It was time.

I walked back toward the elevator, and when the door opened, a tall figure loomed over me.

"Never thought we'd *really* meet in person," he said. He resembled a boxer with his Irish good looks and muscular build. But the lines on his face told me he was probably in his fifties. The burst capillaries in his nose and cheeks told me he was perhaps an alcoholic, too.

"Glad we could make this happen," I said, with a new

confidence that made me stand tall next to this man.

"Is it okay if I call you by something other than your screen name?" he said.

He was smiling at me; the creases in his eyes reminded me of better times. In IRC and other forums, I only knew him as Snowy. He knew me only as She-Ra.

I shook my head. He didn't press me any further.

"Let's go; we have a train to catch," he said.

Snowy ran his building ID over the scanner. Once the light shone green on the pad, we could rise to the top two levels of the tower. Snowy had worked inside this building for a long time. I had chatted with him for years inside our chat channel. He had arrived at the paper in the '80s, and he worked as an investigative journalist for many years. Over time, he had been relegated to covering more lifestyle pieces and fewer hard reports. He wasn't the most powerful person inside the power structure of the news company, but he had been there so long that people didn't mind if he dropped in on everyone's business. This had made him a perfect insider for us to see our plan to fruition.

"Be sure to turn off your smartphone, She-Ra. The GPS on that thing will reveal your location right away."

"Sure did. I'm running all my gear off the MiFi cards now. And I'll toss them afterward."

"Good. Once you are up there, you'll be on your own. I cannot follow you. But I will be there to escort you back down. Make sense?"

"Lots. Where will you be when it happens?"

"Just a few floors below, in the newsroom. I'll be happier than I have been for years."

"Do you expect this place to change?"

"This time, I do. That's why I am helping you."

Mercy and I had talked for a long time about the frustration we all felt with old newspapers like this one. These companies didn't report on the actual events. Instead, they defended their self-interests, which were driven by a lot of money and a lot of political campaigns. Snowy had written to us in chat so many times anecdotes of cover-ups and corruption inside the tower.

"Clara, they're buying me out," Snowy said as he put his lips on an electronic cigarette. His fingers and hands were delicate, hairless, and smooth. "I get to retire early, and they can get us dinosaurs out of here. And then they can continues to provide 'content' without any investigative journalism."

The newspapers and TV stations inside this tower had never shown the user-generated videos of the Millennium Riot. In some of those clips, it was possible to get a sense of who shot first in the clouds of tear gas, but the Tribune ignored those clips, as if they didn't exist at all. They never aired or appeared as links on any of their broadcasts or sites.

In most of those YouTube videos, the SWAT teams shot at the crowd without mercy.

"And once you take the buyout?" I said.

"Belize. I have a tiny house there, and my lady will come with me. Then I can dive as often as I want."

"But I thought you'd go back to harder reporting."

"We all get a little tired as time passes. Some of us get more tired than others. I think this will be my swan song today."

For once, I could relate to these kinds of words. I did feel a tiredness, something heavy, tugging at me, and I thought that perhaps I would come to envy Snowy's situation one day.

We emerged into a narrow hall, which led into another boardroom lined with more books. Snowy led me through a locked door with a key he kept in his pocket. I stepped out onto a balcony that overlooked Michigan Avenue. Off to my left, I could see the jagged steel lines of the skyscrapers, and down to my right, a valley of streets and commercial buildings. The wind buffeted my face and arms at this height. I leaned over the railing and I felt a rush of adrenaline at the height. The parade would come through here in just minutes. People filled the sidewalks.

"I probably won't see you in person again, Montes," Snowy said.

"Seeing really isn't everything," I said. "But it doesn't mean we won't cross paths in some way."

"Your tour group is scheduled to exit the building at 3 p.m. I imagine it's not going to go as planned."

"We'll see," I said. "Thanks for bringing me here."

"Enjoy the parade," Snowy said, and the elevator doors slid shut. I was now alone in the highest level of the tower.

The event was coordinated simply but covertly: The parade was scheduled to start at 2 pm, and it would take an estimated sixty minutes for the floats to cover the length of Michigan Avenue down to the bridge over the Chicago River. The tower was located right next to this bridge.

At 2:10, I would begin recording using my camera.

At 2:20, I would begin transmitting my live feed to four different video streaming sites.

At 2:25 p.m, the web attacks would begin. OLF had three sites on its list: the City of Chicago, the mayor's political fundraising site, and the Tribune's site.

At 2:27 p.m., the computer-based controls for turning on the decorations throughout Michigan Avenue would be cut over to control by the OLF.

At 2:30 p.m., the operations on the ground would begin.

The time was now 2:09. I steadied my camera on a portable tripod, and checked the sound and the image one more time. Above me, the clouds swirled as the wind picked up speed.

2:21 pm.

The adrenaline in my veins quickened my heartbeat, and for the first time since the return from the Coil, I felt what it meant to be older. I had a nineteen-year-old mind but a twenty-three-year-old body. Inside my heart, nothing had changed, though. I wanted change with a touch of revenge.

My live feed had kicked off, and I tested them on my laptop. Anyone with a web browser could watch these feeds at sites like Ustream and through other hosted sites. I wished we had thought of this before we attended Millennium.

I tried to spot Mercy on Ohio Street, but I had to squint, and my eye gave me nothing more than a cluster of tiny heads.

Dennis was positioned much farther north, and I gave up on trying to spot him.

The sites where I fed the video showed users were starting to log on to watch. I knew these were probably just OLF members on the ground.

The numbers would rise soon.

The floats gave off tiny clicks like camera shutters as they traveled south on Michigan Avenue. The familiar characters of my youth crowned each one. Cartoon characters that had entertained me for years at the movies and on DVD at home with my parents. The corporations that owned these characters put them on top of the motorized floats, and they waved endlessly, some waving hankies, and the crowds on the sidewalk roared. They were anthropomorphic darlings: mice, ducks, dogs and even a woodpecker. They smiled forever from their large masks, and the familiar theme songs of their shows and movies played on the float speakers.

The floats of the Parade of Lights had been outfitted with the most expensive LED technology possible. These digital caravans were molded into shapes of corkscrews, mountains, and giant bubbles, and their surfaces shone with textures and shapes that made them elongate, turn purple and red, and set them on fire. It was magic for the eyes and a wonder of technology. Sunlight was still not penetrating the clouds, and the grayness of the day allowed the LED floats to shine to their brightest.

Their colors and intensities burned my eye, but I couldn't stop staring at them.

It was the LED floats, all of them full of surfaces that could show any image, and any video on them that interested me most.

My eye grew hot, and I relished the passage of the floats coming down Michigan Avenue.

It was like seeing blood pour into a vein for the first time.

2:24 p.m.

I spotted Mayor Amadeo on top of the 10th float, and I laughed.

He looked so tiny from up here.

He's just like any of the rest of us, I thought. *Just a tiny man.*

2:25 p.m.

As the web attacks began, but I fought the urge to turn on my phone to check Twitter. I had to trust the rest of us citizens who had a job to do. They had theirs; I had mine.

2:26 p.m.

The number of users of my feeds spiked from 1 viewer to 50.

Right now, the three web sites would be taken over by OLF, defaced and filled with images of the Millennium Riot, the Englewood Fire of 2012, and the murders of teenagers by corrupt police. The fundraising campaign for Mayor Amadeo was also taken down, and we replaced it with a full archive of his own emails, where he brokered deals with the NRA and pharmaceutical conglomerates to secure his election, and eventual run for governor.

As the websites got taken down, the numbers on my video feeds rose. Someone was sharing the link to the feeds.

1,100 viewers.

2:28 p.m.

The first of the floats went dark. Gone, like an old light bulb.

Pop.

Then, in perfect succession, another float went dark.

And another.

And another.

The luxury shops set amid the valley of concrete and glass of Michigan Avenue dimmed.

And that's when the floats popped off.

Just as soon as they had been, there, those LEDs were gone.

The lack of light soothed me. Soon, all the floats had gone dark, and the throbbing pain in my optic nerve lessened. The LED surfaces of the cars were black, matte, and opaque.

As the floats blacked out, about two thousand people were

watching each of my feeds.

By now, Twitter would be on fire with the missives from people on the ground witnessing the blackout. And surely, the TV news crews covering the parade would also begin to cover the event. As messages poured into people's smartphones, the eerie silence on the street began to expand, and I felt it. It felt good.

People started to shout on the ground. I could hear them, even from this high up in the balcony.

I smiled.

2:29 p.m.

Every LED float went back online. The OLF used all the electric power available to turn up the brightness of the screens.

We hijacked each of those floats, 30 of them to be exact.

Our video hijack used the LED screens of the floats to play the videos of every police brutality we had lived through in the Millennium Riot. The images were often out of sequence and shaky, just like I remembered.

I saw the aftermath in one of the bubble floats, as the FBI investigated the grounds of Pritzker Pavilion in the weeks after the event. Then images of the early stages of the march showed on the screens. In these I saw the thousands of us that had marched from Roosevelt and Michigan up to Millennium on October 4, 2013. The LEDs then showed the YouTube clips of the faces frozen in fear, the white clouds of tear gas blooming, and the wounded on the ground. The sound of screams and shouts filled Michigan Avenue as the floats replayed the dozens of clips. The words "SWAT KILLS" and "WE DON'T FORGET WHAT YOU DID" flickered through every screen as OLF hacked their displays.

Some of the drivers of the floats stopped their vehicles, and they rear-ended the floats in front of them. A couple of the drivers successfully shut off the LEDS on their floats, but the other twenty-eight remained on, reliving the events. I heard police sirens, and near me, beneath the tower, policemen on horseback moved in on the chaos that was starting to erupt on the ground.

About ten thousand people were watching each of my feeds.

Just one minute until moment zero.

2:30 p.m.

At that exact moment, our main event started.

Each intersection along Michigan Avenue had been staked out by pairs of OLF members. We called these pairs our "dancers."

No one noticed how they quickly jumped into the street and began to climb the floats. Why would they? The video of the feeds was hypnotic, and they were unable to tear themselves away.

Our dancers unfurled banners, and they draped them over the floats, working quickly to make sure the banner could be seen from both the east and the west sides of the street.

The banners read things like "Most corrupt state" and "Bring our Schools Back." Others read "Police Brutality is what Chicago is good at."

Each of our dancers was masked, and most were able to jump off the floats and run back down the side streets. Of course, they knew their chances of escaping might be very low, but they were ready for being apprehended.

My HD camera caught all of this in its eye and fed it back out to the world.

We had relied on the broadcast media to show our struggle during the Millennium Riot, and they had shown us nothing. Instead, we broadcast the event ourselves. We outnumbered them, and we always would.

Each of the feeds now had forty thousand viewers. That was roughly a hundred and twenty viewers in total.

I ran my hands through my hair and pulled it back into a ponytail, and I celebrated our victory. I hadn't been this happy in a very long time. I let the cameras roll while I leaned over the railing of the balcony.

And that's when I spotted the men with the rifles across the way.

They were lying low on the roof of 436 N. Michigan Avenue, directly across from the Tribune Tower. Their hard helmets formed masks, and their dark uniforms covered every inch of their bodies like a second skin.

They held aimed their rifles down into the street, locking in on targets as they squinted at the telescopic viewfinder.

Our display below — the video displays, our dancers, the banners — had sent out a message, but the implications of what we did were real to me now.

I felt afraid — not for myself, but for the people down below. My own family was watching the parade, and it wouldn't take much to hit them with a round from those rifles.

I considered my hidden position in the balcony of the tower, and I gathered all my strength, telling myself to be brave.

Then the wind picked up, whistling, and the men in the uniforms stirred.

As if someone had whispered to them in their earpieces *heads up,* all three of them looked up at me.

I had seen those helmets and those visors before. Men in those helmets had struck my face under the overpass on Michigan Avenue once. Tiny badges marked their breasts. Their eyeless stare felt endless.

"Hey!" one of them shouted at me.

In the air above those men, I spotted a thick shadow that drew itself into folds, draping itself over the men like a blanket. And as the trio evaluated me, their target, a pair of eyes emerged through the shadow, and a voice filled with needles and hate spoke across the way.

"It's time to do this all over again," the Ocullín said.

And then one of the uniformed men fired at me.

I should have remembered the camera. I should have grabbed it by the handle of its tripod, and swung that merciless video eye toward them, to capture them forever in my video feeds.

But when their first shot rang out at me, I forgot about the camcorder.

The rifle burst in a hollow pop, and it gave off a gnarled sort of music, atonal and thick. Behind me, the limestone exploded and bits of the wall struck me in the back of the head.

I covered my head and ducked behind the railing.

Weeks ago, I had obsessed and pored over tweet after tweet

from witnesses at Pritzker who claimed to have seen troops with guns situated on the northern side of the park, above the stage of the pavilion. That was the conspiracy theory that had never been resolved, even after hundreds of viewings of YouTube clips and photographs.

I had seen the pixelated pictures showing these men in dark clothing, and now here they were again, working covertly, armed and ready.

I peeked out at the small gaps on the limestone balcony.

Even if these three people weren't those same gunmen, in my mind, on that balcony, they were.

"Freeze!" they shouted. "Hands up!"

Then another shot rang through the air, and it struck just two feet from the tripod. They could see the camera.

I had to keep it running.

I curled over, into a ball, snail-like.

(spiral-like Clara, you recall the spiral, don't you?)

And I realized that I was crouching like a cowardly animal. Crouching the way I did when more uniformed men split my face open and changed my face forever as I ran from the Millennium Riot.

If I crouched, I would be repeating the same story, again and again.

I would be weak one more time.

I shut my eyes, and things went dark for a brief moment, and I enjoyed the sound that the city made around me. I felt my own two cones of sound radiate out from my head and shoulders, and I heard the music of the heartbeats in the street, the trill of the starlings arriving from the east, and the clanking symphony of cars, turnstiles and phones.

Inside this darkness, I found what I needed. The anger I had felt for so long but never allowed myself to touch.

My eyes flew open, and though I could only see out of one, I focused hard, first at the limestone floor, and my hands splayed out on the floor like a sprinter ready to start.

I came up to standing and clamped my hands on the railing, letting my upper body lean forward into the open air.

I shouted a song that I didn't know I knew, and across the way, the three people in uniform cocked their rifles to shoot me again.

What emerged from my lips into the air currents above

Michigan Avenue was a song made of a single word — it was long, very long. It had a diamond form, but its edges changed shape, forming crystals of sound, undulating, releasing its musical notes.

As the music expanded out from my throat, two of the men across the way fired directly at me.

Syllable after syllable poured from my lips. Their hard edges and flute-like whistles made the air shimmer around me, and as I said this word, time began to slow down.

In that word, something secret was embedded, but as it emerged, I came to know it.

I couldn't see the bullets that were coming my way, but I saw the kickback throw the troops' shoulders backward, and the bounce of their helmets. Surely those bullets would kill me.

The shimmer in the air grew hot, and I felt a pressure come through on the balcony where I stood, but also in the empty air between us.

I got ready for what might happen if they struck me, as I finished singing my lone, single word.

As I neared its last dozen syllables, memories of a dog-headed creature flooded back. He, the Xolotl, had given me his name once, like a gift, and it had sounded like this, long, musical, and forlorn, replete with syllables.

And when I finished the last syllable on my lips, I knew that what I had spoken was my own name. My name spoken out loud in the language of Mictlán.

I heard a buzz, like that of a thousand bees, coming from somewhere above, and I feared some high-tech drone had come to piggyback on the lethal shots that would surely hit my stomach or my chest any second now.

The word I sang hung in the air, like the drone of a musical instrument, and the insect buzzing intensified.

I had said my name, and someone had heard me.

I looked up, and just twenty feet above us, large shapes with spear-like beaks burst through the very fabric of the atmosphere. Each had a sleek body with feathers slick as black steel, and their multiple sets of eyes throbbed with excitement as they entered the space. Their wings were the ones making the sound of a million beehives, and I knew then who was here.

The hummingbirds of Mictlán, hummingbirds made of smoke, burst into the world.

The hummingbirds intercepted the bullets with their smoky flesh, which left thick trails behind. The word I spoke slowed down time, but now that I was done saying it, time sped up back again to the pace I understood on Earth.

Four hummingbirds had entered the airspace, and each one was easily the size of an SUV. They flew in the path between the two buildings, and they made circles around the flying buttresses of the tower, staining the air.

The men in the uniforms shouted and turned their rifles upward, shooting at the birds. The hummingbirds seemed to be made of the darkness I had experienced in the lower levels of Mictlán, because they sucked sound and light toward them, stretching the air like taffy. The gunshots were dim, and soon, the word I had spoken and its trailing music got suctioned into the bodies of the birds.

The largest of the animals hovered in front of me at the lip of the balcony. It had eight pairs of eyes on each side of its head, and I recognized him. I had ridden his back with the Xolotl. Out here under the weak November sun, his smoky flesh shifted and pulsed, as if a hot bubbling liquid ran beneath his feathers. He had a deep intelligence inside his many eyes, one that I knew I could never tame.

"Help me," I said. I could only try.

Two of the men dropped their rifles and ran back into the building, and as they did so, a thick voice spoke to me from up above.

"YOU," the voice roared.

The third man held his ground and continued to shoot until one of the hummingbirds plucked the rifle right from his arms. The bird swallowed the weapon, and the gunman screamed as he crawled back toward the door.

Two eyes peered at me through the smoke. Each was the size of an automobile.

"I'm never going to leave you, Wanderer," the Ocullín said. "As long as there are men with soft minds like these, I will always be there to corrupt them, and their dark deeds will eat you and everyone else alive."

"But why?" I said.

"Every corridor or the universe has me in it. You go through life and death, and then, off to the side, I sit in wait. I am the winding side road that you shouldn't have chosen. I am the disease in the cosmos's liver, Wanderer."

"I am not a Wanderer," I said. "Stop calling me that."

And then its long laugh echoed toward me.

"Imbecile. How do you think you invoked the hummingbirds? You spoke your true name for the first time, and it's confirmed. You are a Wanderer, too. Just like that damned dog and his filthy white brother."

I put my foot on the edge of the balcony, and I leapt into the air, ready to break the Ocullín with my own hands if I could. Instead, I fell down toward the street.

As I began to fall, the hummingbird caught me. I grabbed at the feathers on his back to find any sort of grip. The windows of Tribune Tower were just inches away from my face. I looked down and saw the street more than thirty stories below.

"Take me up to the Ocullín," I screamed. "I am through with this shit."

The hummingbird rose toward the voice of the Ocullín. The air shimmered at the spot on the roof where the voice originated, and I pointed the hummingbird toward it. As I approached, I wished for my grandmother's knife, but I would have to live without it.

As I approached the shimmer, I heard a final laugh, and I knew it was all too late.

The Ocullín escaped this plane of existence , and as he moved through into another realm, he left his calling card: a hard ball of thick, savage sound, concentrated on that roof like a bomb about to detonate.

The Ocullín's sound bomb exploded. I felt a shock toss me back, and pain rang in my ears.

The hummingbird recoiled from the soundwave, and it and I fell backward onto the concrete roof. The smoke animal landed on top of me. His black blood of smoke ran down in my face, and I slid out from under his body and onto the roof to see if I could still catch The Ocullín. The bird was dead.

The Ocullín was gone.

I wiped the black blood from my face, and I tasted the earthy sweetness of the hummingbird's blood. His blood turned into smoke immediately, making me choke and burning my good eye.

My skin was dry, as if the bird's death had never happened. I beckoned another bird, and he took me back to the Tribune's balcony. I jumped off the bird and ran to the spot where the camera had fallen over. Its lens was pointed straight down at the surface of the roof.

I placed it back on its tripod and made sure it kept on recording.. Below, more shouting emerged, and ambulances stained the city streets in red.

The air shimmered again, and the essence of the remaining three hummingbirds faded, and the vacuum of sound lost its power. I could hear noises a little better now, and the shapes of those gigantic birds vanished in the smoke. And within a second or two, all trails of that black smoke disappeared.

I looked down at the street, panting. The LEDs were returning to their previous displays of Christmas trees, advertisements, and cartoon characters. Police circled the Golden Mile, and pretty soon, I would be missed in the tour below. I grabbed the camera from the tripod, folded the steel legs, and made sure I left no traces of myself on this balcony. Thick, acrid smoke filled the air, and I was glad to return into the building, where I could breathe a little easier.

I ran back into the elevator, where Snowy waited for me, tugging on his e-cigarette.

"You stink, Montes. Did you barbecue hot dogs out there? What the hell?"

"We won," I said. "I have it all on tape, and you saw the video streams, like everyone else."

"Half a million viewers," he said.

I hugged Snowy, and for the first time in my life, I wanted to go get a beer to celebrate.

"What happened out there was pure theater. Egg on the city's face, and a showcase of the corruption that we live in. I can retire now," Snowy said.

That night, I reveled in the bitter notes of a dark ale that was much too fancy for me, but which tasted of victory. Mercy had chosen this Rogers Park pub, making sure it had a private section of booths where we could rejoice.

"What a damn success," Mercy said. "And we would be nothing without our She-Ra. The newspapers and broadcasters still can't figure out how someone got up on the roof of the Tribune to shoot the whole event."

"Phantom hero," Dennis whispered to us with both thumbs up.

My phone vibrated over and over. Surely it was José María. My anger for him had not subsided and I wasn't ready to deal with him again. I muted his texts without glancing at what he was writing. This was my victory, and if he didn't want to recognize how important the OLF was to me, then I wasn't going to deal with him until later.

We ordered more beer, and we did shots of whiskey. We replayed the YouTube clips of our feed on our phones, and we laughed at how the mayor's approval rating went down to fifteen percent in a single day.

"So, Montes," Dennis said, "where was the fire?"

I had been dreading this question. I couldn't get anything past Dennis.

"What fire?" Mercy said.

"CNN reported that while the parade got shut down by OLF, a fire erupted on top of one of the buildings by Trump and Tribune Tower."

Think quick, girl. Think real quick.

"Yes, I saw it and smelled it," I said.

"Where was it?"

"I don't know, but if the wind had been blowing the other way, our perfect video feed would have been nothing but smoke."

"They showed the footage from helicopters above the street," Dennis said. "It was like a big ball of smoke. For a second, I thought those cameras would spot you, but the smoke was too thick."

"But they never determined the source of the fire?" Dennis said. "That's weird."

This was just like him. He wasn't going to drop it, because all his life he had been thorough.

"Whatever or wherever it was, it helped us get some cover. I'm just grateful."

"Grateful — to whom, God?" Mercy said.

"I don't know," I said. "Just grateful."

"Montes is our hero," Mercy said.

"You guys, I saw something else in the building across the way," I said.

There it was. I knew I couldn't keep every secret to myself. I had to tell someone.

"Uniformed men, with badges, pointing rifles."

"Just like at Millennium. Snipers," Mercy said.

"Did you get it on video?" Dennis asked.

"There wasn't any time," I lied.

There's always time. It moves in the vastness, wheels gnashing and gliding past each other.

"Save that info for now," Mercy said. "That's serious. Very serious."

We went to get something to eat at the Golden Nugget, and afterward, we went to a small Polish tavern on Broadway. I felt victory in my veins. I could forget about Mictlán for a few moments. Now that I had said my own name, I hoped the Ocullín would stay put away, to let me rejoice in this real victory.

By 2 a.m, we were squealing, doubled over at the bar, drunk off our assess and feeling like kings. The coverage of the Parade of Lights would be going on for many days, and we would relish every moment of embarrassment from the corrupt powers.

My phone continued to vibrate, and finally, I got fed up. I muted my text messages, and instead, I posted a series of selfies of all of us to Instagram, one after another, our smiles wide and our eyes bright, and I knew that doing this would take my battery from five percent down to nothing.

After posting the selfies, I tucked the phone into my coat pocket.

We still had a four o'clock bar to hit.

We rode the Blue Line up to Logan Square, and as we exited the station, a dozen cops stopped us to inspect our IDs. It was a Saturday night, and the bars were bursting even at this late hour, but the cops didn't care.

Our driver's licenses passed their inspection, until they got to me.

"Don't I know you from somewhere?" said a tall cop as he turned my driver's license over and over in his hands. He shone a flashlight in my eyes, and I recoiled. The light beam felt like a block of ice bursting into shards in my brain.

"No, I don't think you do," I said.

"I'd advise you all to get back to the university tonight after you're done partying. After what happened today, I wouldn't be surprised if a curfew is put into effect."

In that dim light under the street lamps, I could hear the blood rushing through the cop's jugular, and the roar of his stomach. The music he made was faint and fading, and I knew then, from the song his body made, that he had an internal disease. He continued to stare at me as if I were a fish in an aquarium.

"Are we done, officer?" Mercy said, stepping between the cop and me.

"If you see any suspicious activity — terrorist activity — you come find me, okay?"

"Sure thing," I said.

"This city's going to turn into a very dangerous place to live," he said. "Don't contribute to it."

"Have a good night," Dennis said.

"Fucker," Mercy said under her breath as we stepped into the bar.

I could still hear the damaged song of that cop's body. Since my return from Mictlán with José María, I had never felt the songs inside of people as sharply as I could now.

At 4:15 a.m., we wandered back up to the train station, but by then, police had shut down the El train, and we were told we needed to find alternate routes to go home. Helicopters filled the sky.

Mercy and I split a taxi, and we rode in drunken silence most of the way. When she dropped me off in front of the dorm, I fumbled to get the key in the lock, but I made it. I fell hard into the bed with my clothes on, and I drifted off into dreamless sleep.

The next day, my face lay buried in the pillow, and I heard a faraway drumming sound. Tiny. Three bursts, followed by silence. And then it repeated.

It came through clear, and sharp. Three knocks. Again.

My door.

I felt dizzy, but I did my best to run my hand through my hair. I answered the door, still wearing the clothes from the night before.

It was Morgan, my roommate. She wore her sleek running pants and jacket.

"What time is it?" I said.

"It's 3 pm. Clara, I was hoping I'd find you."

My mouth tasted like hops and stale, cheap whiskey.

"Can it wait?" I said.

"Your family's been calling since last night, but I slept overnight at Tom's. I was just coming back now, and security at the front desk asked me to find you."

"What do they want?"

"Something happened to your brother."

WANDERER

"We took many trips on the railroad when I was a boy, but for some reason, the journey back was always the most enjoyable for my grandfather." – Adán Montes's journal, 1967.

"There are no chosen ones. There are no special people. And there are no special rock bands. We're all just sound waves in the orchestra pit." – Sergio Andersson, lead singer of Arkangel, addressing the audience before the #13SC tour in 2016, Oslo, Norway.

"Chicago came into its own in fits and spurts. By the time the 1920s arrived, the city left behind its murderous legacy. It was reborn as a crib of new life." – Historian Belinda Ronstadt, *Songs of My Father's City,* Colibrí Books, 2052.

Life never prepares you for a true moment of change. Just like a snake bites down and injects neurotoxins into a mouse in the jungle, the transfer of new knowledge can have the same effect on a person. Your flesh paralyzes, and your brain does things that you wish it wouldn't.

Morgan went back out to run some errands, and I went back into our room.

My phone was out of battery, so I video-called my father from my laptop. For some reason, I thought he would know what I had done at the Parade of Lights, and that's the first question I expected to hear from him.

"Clara, I've been calling you all day."

"What's going on?"

The music my father's breathing made through the video screen was something I had heard before, in a place shaped like a seashell.

"I sent him out to get menudo for breakfast. It was just six blocks away—"

More ragged music emerged from my father's lungs and heart.

"A driver ran him over."

"Where is he?" I said.

"The doctors pronounced him dead at noon."

I choked and took hold of the armrest on my chair. I couldn't look at my father's tears through the screen, but I had to.

"But are you sure—"

"I'm very sure, Clarita. We need you to come down to the house later today."

"I'm leaving now."

The taxi cruised through the streets. The ride was nothing I could afford, but my father had instructed me leave the university right away. I left the lake breezes of Rogers Park and blew past downtown Chicago, and then back out toward the southwest.

We got stuck in traffic just a half mile from my parents' house, and there, on 26th Street, I felt the urge to cry, yet nothing happened.

Not a tear, not a single whimper.

Little Village had not yet been gentrified, and in those days, its large *farmacias*, sprawling restaurants, and quinceañera boutiques for cotillion dresses still gave off echoes of the places in Mexico that had inspired the communities that lived here. The three-story walk-ups and short bungalows were singularly Chicago architecture, but the people in these streets spoke only in Spanish, and the smells of home cooking scented the air with something that I could never find in other parts of the city.

I walked out the taxi and faced the house. José María had been born in this house, arriving much too soon to make it to the hospital back in 1990. He had never left it, either. It was a two-story walkup, drenched in beige. Solemn and quiet, like my father's taste in everything except his clothes.

My face was hot, and the cramps in my gut were pure hangover. The heat in my brain and in my eye came from somewhere else.

As I put my key into the lock on the side door, pain shot

through both of my legs. It hurt to stand. But I took a deep breath, and I turned the knob on the door to let myself in.

I don't know why I expected José María to be there, waiting for me, as if it had all been one very long and involved prank in his repertoire.

Instead, my father ran to me, and my mother followed suit. Behind them, all my aunts stood in the kitchen.

That day, I made physical contact with every single relative. Through these hugs and holds, I heard the music in their bellies and the songs in their bones. Though their words were about being sorry and the loss in our family, the sound waves of their bodies gave off music that only I could hear. Inside this music there were songs of princes, kings, and loves lost. I remembered the song that the police officer had given off last night, and I realized that I didn't drunkenly imagine it. I could hear the music inside these bodies clearly, as if I were still in the Coil.

This new knowledge I kept to myself.

"How did it happen?" I said. My mother and father sat with me in their tiny living room, and Minerva and La Negra remained in the room. The rest of the relatives were in the back, cooking and drinking.

"It doesn't matter how it happened," my father said. His tone was harsh, excited.

"They think it was a drunk driver that hit him," my mother said, "but the witnesses said it was random, very random."

"No matter how it happens, *it* always feels random," my father said.

My mother drew me into her arms, and her smell filled my nostrils. I wished for those tears, and they didn't arrive. Instead, my insides were hollowing out.

"I was so angry the last time I talked to him," I said.

"José María said he saw you the afternoon of the parade," my mother said. "He was also very upset."

My face flushed, and I felt shame in every inch of my skin.

"Yes, I thought I might see you guys after the parade," I said.

"We waited for you for a while. José María texted you for a long time to meet us," my mother said. She was not angry about this fact.

She doesn't know. She doesn't know what you really said to him the last time we saw each other. She doesn't know about the angry note between us.

La Negra came over to the sofa and sandwiched me together with my mother.

"I am sorry, Clara," said La Negra, and she held me for a long time. "He will be in a good place now. And remember he helped you so much to find your tonal."

I loved my aunt, but I no longer wanted her comfort about tonales, especially since I had failed to find mine.

"I found it; I don't know if I had mentioned it earlier."

"Really?"

"It's true," I lied.

"That's strange, I don't *feel* a tonal around you."

"Well, you just have to try harder," I said.

She drew me in tighter into her bosom, and I let myself enjoy the embrace.

I moaned, but no tears arrived.

The rest of that day was a series of rote performances. Wash my hair, apply eyeliner, smooth out the wrinkles in my skirt.

Kiss my aunt, hug my uncle. Attend mass with Mom.

I wanted to eat, but I skipped that night's meal.

I read back through all the text messages José María had sent me on the night of our victory at the Parade of Lights.

"Everyone's waiting for you."

"Did you see that crazy bullshit on the screens?"

"Tsk, tsk, *reina.* I know your secret."

"Hey, why aren't you answering your phone?"

"Check your texts, Clara."

On and on they went, pestering me. I had ignored them all, but reading them now made my stomach turn, and I had to force myself to finish reading every last one. I knew by their tone that he was still angry. And then they stopped.

Then they stopped forever.

At the funeral, I chose not to look at the open casket. My father pulled me out into the parking lot to shout at me, and I shouted something back, but the exact words faded quickly from my memory.

My father escorted me back into the narrow funeral parlor, and when he asked me again to look at the body to say good-bye, I shook my head and took a seat at the opposite end of the room.

I knew too much, and I knew too little.

Returning to my everyday life was what hurt the most. I survived the wake, the funeral, and the shitty condolence cards from Hallmark.

José María wasn't coming back.

Sometimes, I wished I were just dreaming it, but I wasn't.

My parents didn't let me go back to school right away, and I stayed in Little Village with them. I went to mass daily with my mother, and I went through all the rituals, prayed all the prayers. I did this for her, and she was happy.

My father mostly kept to himself. He talked to my aunts every day, whispering sometimes, crying at others.

"He's lost his little best friend," my mother said one day as she beat pancake batter in a frenzy. She didn't even look up when she said this. She never mentioned my father's mourning after that.

I survived the two weeks I stayed at my parents, and I even brought my grades up by the end of that semester.

But I didn't want to go back to classes, to my part-time job, or to anything. I just wanted to hide, to lie inert on a patch of grass, stone-like.

My mother was the person who forced me to go back to my routine. She packed up my things and drove me back to school, and I am glad she did. I spent more time with Dennis and less with Mercy. In fact, Mercy and I drifted apart, and something inside me felt okay with that.

When I came home for the Christmas holiday that year, I managed to get through a meal without that spiky-haired runt at the table.

I went through my day staring at television shows that had no point, and noodling on Facebook as if there might be a stopping point. I visited my cousins, and at night, I helped my dad cook dinner. I pretended like everything that had started since my birthday in 2013 had never happened at all.

It's very easy for any of us to do this, and if we pretend hard enough, we can fool ourselves into almost anything. As humans, we like to pretend that the dead ones aren't actually dead.

Until we are reminded by outside forces.

I spent New Year's Eve wasted on cheap beer via a fake driver's license at the Hideout, and I puked so hard that night that I vomited blood. I think I cursed out Mercy in the women's bathroom, but I don't actually remember. Dennis claims I also broke up a fight of big men, but that I also don't recall.

I spent the next four days nursing a massive hangover, and I went back to classes on January 5th. By now, I was pretty good at staying out late, slogging through a hangover, and avoiding the dreadful nights.

It wasn't until then that my dreams about the Lords of Mictlán began in full.

The first dream was a tiny knife tearing into the darkness of my dreamless nights.

The knife plunged and then it sliced, and blood the color of snow poured out of black skin.

After the cut, the sounds started.

They were drums. They drummed and drummed, like twin heartbeats that syncopated and throbbed in the same time signature, and in the darkness of my sleep, I felt a cool rush of air on my skin.

You owe us a visit still, said a voice that was distinctly female. It was a voice the size of a continent, deep as the ocean.

And we expect you to be here. Soon, said another voice. This one was more shrill, yet more masculine than the first.

And then, in the dream, I had the vision that I could never have had inside Mictlán. I could see through the dark and into a deep pit that smelled of wet moss and that pulled light toward it like a magnet.

Mictlántecuhtli and Mictecacíhuatl were in the pit, and I

approached within a few feet, without a body. I came close to a thin blue membrane, metallic and in movement, like the beautiful swirls on a soap bubble in summertime. And behind the blue sheath, the drumming grew bigger.

Wanderer, we are waiting.

The two voices said this in unison, and it occurred to me then that they could help me.

Give my brother back to me, I said, but the membrane was already fading, and the drumming picked up speed, and before I knew it, I had fallen out of my bed and onto the floor.

Morgan shook me awake. I tore at her face and yanked her hair and kicked her in the knee.

"Give him back," I screamed.

I dreamt a variation of this dream every single night for weeks.

In February, Mayor Amadeo resigned from his position as mayor after the scandal of his leaked documents became bigger and bigger. The Parade of Lights became a success inside OLF, and we patted ourselves on the back for a long time.

But not everything went according to plan. Our dancers, those brave people who leapt onto floats to toss banners, were eventually tried and convicted. They were all sentenced to multiple life sentences for acts of treason against the state. The police that apprehended them became heroes for the city, despite all our protests.

The city did agree to channel more money to Englewood to help rebuild the city, and Little Village, my parents' neighborhood, received the first Spotlight Grant from the federal government to help residents buy homes first to prevent gentrification. In the spring of 2015, the city re-inaugurated Pritzker Pavilion, and its new drone-based camera system became the first in the country to monitor all angles of public events through the use of tiny robots shaped like dragonflies.

Despite several investigations, no one ever found out who recorded the footage of the Parade of Lights from the top of the Tribune Building. Tribune folded in May, after repeated bankruptcies, but the Freedom Museum remained open. The rest of the tower was sold to developers to be converted into condominiums.

For me, each month that went by drew me further away from Mictlán, as if that too had been a dream, just like the dream of a blue membrane and its sound of drums. It was easier to forget, to forget deeply, and to just go back to classes, exams, and papers that kept me up late into the middle of the night.

Every night, though, I dreamed again about the Lords, and each time, I awoke terrorized, unsure of who I was or where I was.

Spring passed and summer grew hot on my skin, and both of them came through like a series of short breaths.

And before I knew it, I was back for my second year of university.

In early October, my father called me back to the house.

"I'll pick you up tonight, and I'll have you back tomorrow."

He showed up promptly that night.

"You don't come home anymore," he said.

"Okay, and your point?"

"What did you do for your birthday?"

"I ordered pizza with Morgan and Dennis." It was the truth. Together, we drank PBR while watching old *X-Files* reruns on our laptops.

"I suppose that's pretty fun," my father said.

My father took my bags to my room. I found my mother in the hall. She was preparing an ofrenda. I had seen her build them a million times with my father, but for the first time, I paid attention to every detail.

They put it in the hallway, on a side table. My father stacked several long wooden cabinets to create a series of levels, and my mother draped each of the boxes with pristine white linens. At its skirt, she placed two of her best dishes: lasagna and mole verde, made with pumpkin seeds. Between these two dishes, she places several packages of gummy worms in bright wooden bowls. These had all been my brother's favorite foods. On the next level, my father draped several dozen marigolds, and he handed me one of the dozens he had wrapped in butcher paper.

"You do it," he said.

To look deeply inside the structure of a flower like the marigold can be a dizzying thing. Inside it, the petals form ridges, one laid on top of each other. So many, in fact, that when you pull the flower away from you, a pattern emerges. A pattern inspired by a circle, but not quite a circle. And there, in the center, is its sex organs, its stamens, also arranged like a spiral and the little spaces between them deep, like cuts.

Like slits on a shark.

Or like gills underneath a mushroom cap.

I had never really taken the time to see these structures on a marigold, but my father brought his magnifying glass and showed me.

I was grateful that he did, but seeing the internal parts, that flat bed of spikes moving about in a spiral, made me want to vomit.

These tiny spirals, inside this place were small, smaller than me, but they made a very structured coil.

A COIL, Clara. They make a COIL.

The music wafting from the flower was too familiar, too deep, and too real.

My father could see into the flower, but he could not hear it. I moaned under my breath.

"Hold still and stop your twitching," he told me.

I arranged the marigolds on the linens. They bled in shades of crimson and gold.

On the third level we placed five framed photographs of José María. One as a baby, one as a toddler in his tricycle, and three from the last year he was alive. His hair extended from his brow like spikes on a porcupine, and his thin arms crossed his narrow chest. Every photo revealed his grin, his hidden smirk.

My father put the last photograph, a school portrait, at the top level of the altar, like a snow-capped peak on a mountain.

"Now, you know that in just a few weeks, your brother will return, and we put this ofrenda up to welcome him back. He'll be here so soon, and we'll be glad to spend some time with him."

This was our tradition for Día de Los Muertos.

It had been almost a year, and my father still didn't know what José María and I had done in the tunnel of butterflies and in the places that lay beyond it.

There are the secret lives of parents, but there are also the secret lives of their children.

To tell my father about Mictlán meant I would tell him about the Ocullín's promise to find me, and that was something I would never do.

Minerva and La Negra were still convinced that I had eradicated my problem of "the stench of death" when I announced I found my tonal, but now, as my father showed me this yearly rite, I felt like the world's biggest clown.

I could do better than this, and I knew it.

When we finished the ofrenda, I went into José María's room and rummaged through his drawers. I took his iPod, his hoodie, and as many of his books as I could carry out in my backpack.

"Clara, are you ready to drive back?" my father shouted.

"Yes, gimme a minute."

On my way out the back door, a hand tugged at my sleeve.

"Mom, you scared me!"

"Clara," my mother said. "You don't want to forget this one."

She placed a copy of *The Popol Vuh* — José María's copy of the book of Maya creation stories — in my hands.

"I am not sure what you're up to, but I want you to succeed."

"Thanks, Mom."

"And your tonal?"

"We'll need to discuss, but much later."

"If you need more of his books, you tell me. I'll get them to you."

"Mom, do you think we can really atone for things we have done? You know, after we die?"

My mother smiled to herself and reconfigured her shawl. She pulled out a fresh laminated card of the Virgin of Guadalupe and tucked it into the book. She kissed me on the forehead and ushered me out the door.

I met my father in the car, which was idling in the garage. His hands wiped the dashboard with even strokes. Not a single speck of dust escaped his movements.

"How long have you been wiping down the car, Dad?" I said.

"It's just a touch-up. Your mother's mad at me, Clarita. Do you know why?"

"There's very little I actually know anymore," I said.

My mother walked into the garage a few seconds later to say goodbye.

"Juliana, are you staying?" he said.

"Yes, I am. You two have a good drive back. I'll see you at

Thanksgiving, Clara."

My mother winked.

On the morning of November 1, 2014, I was alert, in case José María indeed came back the way I expected — and the way our family expected him to return. That's what our traditions told us would happen.

That day I felt energetic and full of health. Otherwise, I didn't get a single sign of José María's return.

After everything I knew about Mictlán and the beings from that place, I had expected my brother to return, even just for that day. But instead, nothing.

I did want him to come back. He *had to* come back.

I was going to make sure it happened.

November 3, 2015, turned out to be much too cold for the outdoors. Arctic winds arrived early, and the wind chill factor was ten degrees below as ice pelted Randolph Street. I kept my steps short and firm to prevent myself from slipping on the ice, but I skidded more than a few times.

I cut through Millennium Park on Monroe Street. I kept my eyes lowered as I passed through the security scanner that read my driver's license. The uniformed cop nodded and I passed on to the park. I stayed on the sidewalk, walking east until I reached Columbus Drive. From this point, I turned around to make sure I wasn't being followed. At 4 pm on a Monday during an ice storm, I had most of the park to myself.

Drones swept the perimeter of the park like toy UFOs. The whined as they soared in the sky about every ten minutes or so. And then they were gone again.

I walked up the pathway that ran parallel to Columbus Drive on my right, and as I moved north, the tinfoil wings of Pritzker Pavilion unfurled, as they always did when tourists walked toward the structure.

I was no longer scared of the memories of the dome or its grass.

I had come here to find the bridge. The pavilion was besides the point, but I still felt proud of myself as I glimpsed it from the corner of my eye.

Off to my right, behind a set of trees, I found the gate I was looking for. The BP Bridge was made of sheet metal was so smoothly made that it seemed to melt right into the ground. I took the bridge step by step, careful not to fall on the ice, and I stuffed my hands in my coat pockets.

I was sweating inside my coat, but I didn't care. I had layered myself with silk long underwear, ski pants, jeans, and two wool sweaters. I had covered myself with a thin down coat, followed by a heavy wool pea coat.

This time, my return to Mictlán would be far more comfortable than before.

At the end of the BP Bridge, six metal poles marked the gate of the eastern end of the snaking structure. I turned around and caught the first threads of red and orange as the sun began to set.

From this angle, I could see the Chicago skyline and the wings of Pritzker Pavilion, like jagged teeth on the lower jaw of an animal whose head was a ravenous, gaping blue sky.

I put the headphones over my head and I smoked a joint, breaking the rule my father and his sisters had made about these rituals. In fact, I made my own ritual, the way José María would have wanted.

I put his playlist on repeat. When I finished the joint, I tasted licorice and antifreeze on my tongue, and I heard the music of my brother's playlist in my body.

I couldn't make this trip alone, so I decided to call out for help.

Once, a long time ago, my brother and I had felt the essence of a creature that lived beyond time through the walls of a green tunnel underwater. That creature had allowed us safe passage through her walls. This time, I listened, and I hoped that I could hear the throbbing music of Blue Hummingbird embedded in the Pritzker Pavilion.

But the bridge made not a single noise.

I looked behind me at the water, and I felt foolish for a moment, standing alone in a backpack during an ice storm.

Next, I tried listening for the Xolotl. If there was someone who could get me in, it would be him.

I spoke his name, and when I did, I felt the sheet metal of the

BP bridge vibrate to the point of almost shattering. A murder of crows flew off into the air and left me even more alone than I had been before.

Two down, one to go.

I only had the one choice I didn't want to make. But I just had to enter Mictlán.

"I'm here; come find me," I said. I held my grandmother's tiny obsidian knife in my hand, and I ran my gloved thumb over its edge.

And then I shouted the name of the Ocullín.

The wind screamed, but I heard nothing.

The right side of the BP Bridge's entrance looked as sharp as a blade, and it was right along this thin edge that I heard music. It was a low murmur, filled with white and red. It was so faint, it sounded like an old radio, but it was there.

I walked up to the railing, and I leaned in.

There, reflected on the sheet metal was a girl of 19 years of age.

She had a face that I recognized. A face like mine, but better. Symmetrical and natural.

I was staring at myself before I got my involuntary facelift and nose job. And just like I had witnessed once before at the Aragon ballroom, I saw the flesh on that face melt, stripping away its skin to reveal a tattered skull, while its flesh came off in red ribbons.

I had always wondered why a door had opened up inside the Aragon, and now I had my answer. The being that made these doors wanted me to step through it, to lure me into Mictlán.

This time, instead of fearing the reflection, I checked myself in it to make sure I showed no signs of fear.

I wanted my brother back.

I plunged myself into the mirror and left Millennium Park behind.

I didn't glimpse any of the other secret cities in this journey through the sheet metal mirror, and I remembered that the green butterfly bridge had been built by a wizard. The reflections at the Aragon and the BP Bridge perhaps belonged to someone else.

I dissolved into darkness, and when I emerged again, I felt a breeze whip my legs, and I heard the sound of a million songs encircle me.

I had walked out into a short patch of flowers, and the wasps that hovered over their petals made music together with the plants. Darkness enveloped me, like an old friend, and my ears, nose and skin took the place of my vision.

The fullness of the sounds and the intensity of the smells of this place felt welcome. I cocked my head and let my ears guide me. I could feel the vast height of the canyon, and I felt the way its nooks and crannies rose for thousands — maybe millions—of miles into the air.

I listened to the space behind me, and I recognized the pyramid of flowers in the distance. In front of me lay a long road that floated on top of the lake. And at the center, a column that rotated in the dark. This was not the place where I had fought the Ocullín, but I recognized the road. This was one of the three roads that led to the city of Mictlán.

The city of Mictlán sat exactly in the cross shape that the four roads made as they led into its heart.

I walked toward the entrance of the city, and I let my thoughts drift into the intake and release of my breath.

Up close, I marveled at the rotation of the city. It didn't just turn on an axis. It danced. Its walls were made of tendrils of moss, linked like a spiderweb membrane, and it teemed with life. Scorpions, snakes, and even fluted birds had woven their bodies together, sacrificing their individuality to make this structure that eclipsed me. The city was easily the size of all of Chicago but contained by a living body of things.

The paradox of life supporting a place of dead things was not lost on me, but I pressed on toward the end of the road to find an entrance.

Up close, the cylinder took on new life, as every texture in the universe came together to meet the palm of my hand. I needed a door, and I found none.

And then the city sang to me. It was a low murmur, but a song nonetheless.

"Seeking entry?" it said.

"Who are you?"

"I am the House of the Canyon. The Belly Button of the Coil. I can tell you met the children who grew up in my rooms."

"What children are those?"

"The four Tezcatlipocas."

"When did I meet them? I heard they left the Coil a long time ago."

"Just because they're gone doesn't mean you can't *feel* them or hear the songs they left behind."

"You were their caretaker?"

"The first to leave was the Red Tezcatlipoca, the flayed one. He's the one who rejoiced in the skin peeling off your face in the world above when men beat you with sticks."

"So, you were a nanny of sorts."

"Sure, I like that word. You can use it, friend."

"And the White Tezcatlipoca?"

"He's Quetzalcóatl, the Deserter. I also knew him when he was just a baby. Surely you saw his white plumage and his snake teeth, his face white as bone?"

"No, only in a memory. Someone else's memory."

I wondered where Blue Hummingbird might be now, in this vast Canyon.

"Well, you're standing on the entrance of the White Tezcatlipoca, child. Each of the Tezcatlipocas has their own road into the city. This is the white road."

"Funny you should say that. How can it be white if there's no light in this place?"

The city let out a series of hard hisses.

"For a clever Wanderer, you have a very limited consciousness," the city said. "And you surely don't know how to really open your eyes."

"And the Blue Road?"

"Yes, the Blue Tezcatlipoca. He was my favorite of all those babies. His road is the southern Road, where you once walked. Or where you will, depending on where the wheels take you."

"But how would I have met the Blue Tezcatlipoca?"

"His name is Huitzilopochtli, and don't you forget it," said the city, and I felt a sharp scent of carrion escape its walls. Its presence possessed the air.

"He's the god of war," I said.

"And how fitting that you started a war on his southern road, child. Did you enjoy slashing the Ocullín with your blade? Did it make your skin prickle with excitement when you began your vendetta on the people of your own city? That is the essence of the Blue Tezcatlipoca, who is almost like a son to me."

The cylinder sped up, and its music grew stern, sharper.

"I think you were a good nanny," I said.

"One day, you too will know these joys. But I see you have come here to ask me for something. I feel it in your voice. I hear it inside of you."

"I'm on my way to the Lords. And I need to take the northern road into the snow fields. The only way through is by traveling through the city."

The city whispered, and several strands of thick moss reached out to me. They brushed my hands and my fingertips, seeking my skin.

"Let's take you to the northern road, then, and I'll tell you a story."

With each step that I took into the cylindrical city, the moss and the bones that held it together rearranged themselves to create spacious halls for me to tread. As I moved forward, the path behind me knitted itself shut. I heard whispers from the walls by the millions, and the corridors and rooms sang tiny songs with questions at the end of their lines. The insects that formed the walls of this place were talking amongst themselves and wondering who I was.

I counted many living things in the walls, including crocodiles, lizards, snakes, deer, rabbits, dogs, monkeys, jaguars, eagles, vultures, and animals that looked like living rainstorms.

And in front of me, a soft purple glow led the way, like a tiny sparkler in the distance. It made music in the same voice as the city, and I eased into my journey.

"You don't know how happy I am to have another person here," the city said. "There are abandoned cribs and playrooms in this city. Maybe when you return, you will let me show them to you."

The corridors spread for miles. Just as soon as I glimpsed one or felt one with the sonar of my cones, it was gone.

Then, down the long passageways, I felt us move toward something very tall.

The city showed me tall doors along the hallway. Each door was the size of a mountain. Whatever baby would have lived there would have been gigantic.

"No child is identical to another. You have been very close to the White Tezcatlipoca. You smell of his white light."

"But I have never seen him. Just the Xolotl."

"Close enough."

"Why did they all leave?" I said.

"The children? Because that's what they do. Children grow; they leave. Their parents entrusted me with their care, and eventually, the parents, the Elders, left too."

"The snake — Blue Hummingbird — says she gets lonely in the canyon."

"She's sentimental. I am not. I do not mourn and I enjoy my new children. The vines in my walls and the rabbits that weave the ceilings inside this city — they are like babies to me."

We made a turn. I hoped we were heading north.

How absurd that this hole in the cosmos has cardinal directions.

"I hear you, Wanderer," the city said. "We do indeed have cardinal directions. In the depths of the Coil, we need to know our way, too."

"Sorry," I said. I forgot that I could quiet my thoughts, and that I *should* quiet my thoughts.

"There's only one child who visits Mictlán often. Do you know him?" the city said.

"Can't say I do."

The lizard eyes embedded in the walls shifted, as if they blinked in unison.

"He's the Black Tezcatlipoca; I am surprised you wouldn't know him in your city."

I laughed. "There's a lot of info about you that we don't receive in my city."

"The Black Tezcatlipoca is the Smoking Mirror, girl. He's the very reason you made it this far."

"Why do you say that?"

"He's pleased to see you disrupt the Coil."

"I never saw my tonal at the age of thirteen," I said. "Instead, I saw a presence in my bedroom."

"That was a familiar being, the Ocullín. He was there under the permission of his creator, the Black Tezcatlipoca."

"What's worse, the Ocullín or its master?" I said.

The city's music tinkled. In between the notes, I felt a deep silence.

"Remember this, Wanderer. The Black Tezcatlipoca wields the deepest powers inside and outside the Coil."

The dim purple light ahead blinked a couple of times, and I put my hand on the walls to steady myself through a narrow passageway. My palm came away wet with a sticky resin.

"Hurry, child, this way. If you walk too slowly, the gastric juices under your feet will begin to consume you."

My feet squished in the dark, and I put terrible thoughts out of my head.

"The Black Tezcatlipoca sent the Ocullín to find me?"

"Yes, that's what he does. He likes to play savior at times, and at others, he is a destroyer."

"You mean he sent that thing after me just for fun?"

"He was always the most unruly of the four."

"Will I ever see him down here? Or has he abandoned Mictlán forever, too?"

"You don't understand that your link to the Black Tezcatlipoca grows inside many wheels, do you?"

Tendrils caressed my neck in the dark, and I let them. The city was one of the few beings who were willing to answer my questions. In fact, she was the only thing down here that resembled something human.

"We've come to the end of my body, child. You'll need to step into the palace so you can exit onto the northern road. But before you do, there's the matter of payment. Consider it a toll."

"What do you think of this?" I said. I took out my wallet and handed it to a tendril. I had no use for money down here.

The city seemed satisfied with this, because her tendrils took it away and the purple glow expanded, revealing another tall door, shaped like a giant star with jagged edges. As I approached it, it shrank into itself, like a sponge, until it made an opening for me to step through.

As I entered the palace, I realized that the wallet had contained my tiny laminated icon of the Virgin. I wanted it now, not because of the Virgin, but more that because it reminded me of home.

But it was gone, and there was no turning back.

I walked into the biggest hall that my mind could possibly comprehend.

The Palace of Skulls was a room that shone in pearly black liquid walls that stretched like taffy into the heavens. It felt open and claustrophobic at the same time, and I marveled at the way in which its liquid walls flowed slowly, like lava.

And then from the walls, I heard a rattle. At first it was soft, like a child's toy, but then it grew into the sound of a snake's tail, and soon it was big enough to shake the ground under me.

Inside the molten black walls, I spotted hundreds — no, thousands — of skulls. They came in all shapes and sizes, some curled over like a corkscrew, many of them humanoid. They slid downward, while some others flowed upward. And from each one of them, music sprang.

Every skull spoke its name in a shard of music, and they formed a chorus of millions that made my heart quicken. These were the songs of things that had once been alive, but their skulls rang out their glory like faded vinyl recordings on a record player.

I felt very afraid and so foreign. I knew the skulls on these walls were of creatures that had never been on earth, and that would probably never be. Creatures from this dimension and not mine. Feral, intelligent, dead, and still staring at me through their eye holes.

And I remembered what my mother had said.

When you step inside the palace of the skulls.

"I guess I made it," I said.

Hundreds of voices echoed my words inside the slick walls.

"I guess I made it," they said.

I walked faster.

"And the story, you owe me the story," I said to the city.

"Oh, I did not forget." Down at the end of the hall, a tiny opening the size of a pinpoint let in a breeze. As we approached, it widened, and the skulls around me chattered their teeth. "The Black Tezcatlipoca always antagonized his brother White Tezcatlipoca. Each of them was so beautiful in his own way. The White, so glorious in his feathered snake body, while the Black

Tezcatlipoca shifted in shape so often, not much more than a blur. His face always shone in black, and the two brothers fought through many wheels. And one day, as they played inside the gardens on my rooftop, they heard the monster approach. The monster was named Cipactli, and he was almost the size of this canyon. Would you like to see my memory of the Cipactli?"

"No." The fact that most of the four Tezcatlipocas had abandoned this city scared me, but the notion of a monster much larger than the brothers scared me more.

"Well, the White and the Black Tezcatlipocas realized that this Cipactli monster would destroy everything in the canyon if they didn't stop him. And once, just that once, the brothers worked together to defeat the monster."

"How?"

"They used Black Tezcatlipoca's foot as bait. And the Cipactli monster took it. As chewed it like an egg, the brothers captured the beast. They used the Cipactli's flesh to make dirt, and to build roads inside Mictlán. The very roads you used to cross the lake and reach my doors are made from this monster, a being made of crocodile and teeth hard as stone."

"Freaky!" I said, and I wondered what made me say that. José María would have made such an exclamation before. Not me.

"The two brothers saved the world. For this reason, the northern road, which is the road of Mictlán and the road that leads to the lords, was given to Black Tezcatlipoca."

"And the Ocullín?"

"That monster came from the worst emotions inside of Black Tezcatlipoca. Haven't you ever felt an anger that you thought might consume your very flesh, girl?"

"Yes. I have felt it."

"That type of anger is what the Ocullín is made from."

"One last question," I said. "When I was last here, and I touched the waters of the lake—"

"That was the Ocullín waiting for you beneath the waters. He had been waiting there for you there for many wheels."

"And my dead ancestor that emerged from the water?"

"That was the Ocullín's trickery, too. Draped in a cloak of illusion. Surely you have seen this cloak?"

"Many times, unfortunately."

"The Ocullín thrives on lies and fear."

The door had widened to the size of a building, and I walked out onto the Northern Road. I felt the city trailing after me. I put my fingers on the mossy tendrils and smelled millennia of time on those vines.

"Thank you for letting me come through," I said.

"I like your gift. To reach the Lords, just continue through the Snow Fields."

"Thank you."

"Watch your step. There are beings that can see you when you walk through the Snow Fields."

I turned around, and the opening in the city was gone, and the cylinder resumed its rotation on top of the lake.

I walked on the snow, and I was grateful that I had worn so many layers for the trip.

During my walk, I didn't encounter a single animal, insect, or plant. I walked for a long time, and time dissolved. But my mind didn't fret over the loss of time, because I knew the Lords were the ones eating it. The snow under my boots chilled my feet, and I walked into a silence that was deeper than a dead galaxy.

I heard the throb of the Lords, and I knew that they could hear me, too.

MICTECACÍHUATL AND MICTLANTECUHTLI

"Empty cities are scary cities." – Ron Amadeo, exclusive WTTW interview regarding his memoir *I Continue to Be the King,* 2017.

"Everything you need to know is in Frida Kahlo's painting *The Two Fridas.*" – Clara Montes, *A Kiss in the Dreamhouse,* Aleph Digital Press, Paris/Mexico, 2034.

"There are cities made of gold, and there are cities drenched in dew. There's a city in a coil; it eats me, and it eats you." Arkangel, "Rhapsody," *The Violet Album,* 2008, Reckless Records.

The Snow Fields spanned thousands of miles, and I walked them. The air kissed my forehead, and at this depth in the Coil, the scents of flowers became very faint. Instead, I tasted something like sea water in the air.

I only heard the sound of my breathing and the crunch under my boots.

I didn't notice someone had been walking next to me. I felt his body heat, and I heard the deep bell sounds that rang from his body.

"Just a few more steps, Wanderer," the Xolotl said.

Suddenly, he looked comical to me. Skinny legs, a caved-in chest, and the head of a hairless dog.

"Am I going to have give you a tip after this little tour?" I said.

"What is a tip, Wanderer?"

"I could explain, but the joke's already gone."

"Tell me about your 'jokes,' then."

"You know, when things don't go as you expected, sometimes, you laugh. That's humor."

"I don't understand your meaning, Wanderer."

"Haven't you ever laughed?" I said. Down in the distance, I felt the ground slope upward. We were coming up on a shallow hill.

"Wanderer, how often will you be returning to the Coil?"

"I have no intention on coming back. I've come for my tonal and to retrieve my brother."

"Is this when *I* should laugh?" he said.

I bit my lip and shook my head.

The slits in the Xolotl's chest emitted tiny echoes, and he dug his claws into my shoulder. It was a gesture that felt friendly but also territorial, like an eagle digging its talons into a mouse before devouring it. I would never understand the feral nature of this being.

"I enjoyed our adventure, Wanderer. You can always call for the hummingbirds in your city of towers."

"Thank you."

"And your brother? Where is he?" I said.

"You have seen his traces wrapped inside my body, but there are things that I don't know. But if he returns, I will know. He blazes."

I took the Xolotl's right hand in mine, and I did my best to shake it. The sharp edges of his claws grazed the palm of my hand, and I had to put my left hand over his to let him know I was saying goodbye.

I heard the Xolotl turn back, and his bells rang off in the distance. Now I stood on the lip of a shallow crater, and beneath it, a hard drumming began, thick as a heartbeat. I had heard it many times before.

The pit beneath my feet was covered by a thin membrane, swirling in shades of blue ranging from cobalt to cornflower blue.

This is the third time you've seen color down here. If you're this deep in the canyon, how can color exist?

The first time had been next to the waterfall inside the temple of flowers. The second time happened when I had walked through the city of Mictlán, the Heart of the City had showed me its faint purple light, and that had been the first time I ever saw color inside the Coil.

The membrane beneath me was split down the middle by a thick vein, and from where I stood, the structure that throbbed inside this pit in a snow field looked like a giant beating heart bathed in cobalt.

"Why color, and why now?" I said.

"ENTER," a voice roared. It shook my body, and as the drums pounded, I felt the snow stir beneath me.

The snow slid forward and backward toward the crater, and at first, I noticed a soft edge in my field of vision. Nothing solid, just a hint of gray.

But then I saw another edge on my left.

The snow was going gray. An actual gray.

And further below, I saw tiny threads, like gossamer. They glowed.

There were pink and purple threads, and green ones, too. Some were ruby-colored, and some sparkled in colors that I had no name for.

More light radiated from the tiny rivulets, and the snow went from gray to white.

The threads ran like veins on the flat ground, up the tiny hill, and down into the blue membrane.

"ENTER," said the voice.

"But how?" I said.

"ENTER."

The membrane grew transparent, and beneath the pit, I saw them.

The Lords were a marvel. They gave off black light just as bright as the sun's, and it was only if I squinted that I could see their shapes in the pit. Two beings, colossal in size, flowed into each other like the roots of a tree. They were faceless, smooth as glass. Inside their limbs, I saw stars thick and bright — whole constellations that knitted together to form flesh. The Lords had teeth and beaks, snouts and antennae, and I could feel how one was distinctly male, and the other female. Each of these intertwined beings was the size of a planet, and I stared down at them from my crater.

"You look nothing like what I saw in José María's books," I said.

They spoke back to me in a music that was full of knowledge, but which contained no words.

The edges of the pit dripped with the luminous streams of shining particles, and they dripped onto the Lord's bodies, shimmering.

Each of the Lords had a pair of human lips, and they met at the center of their embrace. The kiss was sensuous, and I could see spiral galaxies beneath their transparent skin.

The Lords unlocked from their kiss, and as they took a break, they turned these human mouths upward, to take a moment to drink the multicolored particles.

Their drinking swallowed all light, and it released endless music out from the snow pit.

After satiating their thirst, the Lords returned to their lovers' kiss.

"I want my tonal," I said. The membrane grew so transparent that it virtually disappeared.

"You already have it," they spoke. "Our daughter handed it to you."

"Your daughter?"

"Tonalpohualli, the Heart of the Mictlán City. She rotates over the lake."

"Yes, I do know her."

"She says you gave her a gift. You are kind."

"And what is my tonal, then?"

"Your tonal is the symbol of the house, just like our daughter. You are like her in so many ways."

The rivulets of sparkling liquid thickened. The Lords were beginning to consume the liquid faster, and I felt my feet slipping on the snow.

I fell on my ass, and the snow slid beneath me. Tiny colored particles clung to my coat and my boots.

They're pulling you in.

If I didn't find a foothold, I would fall into the limitless bodies of the Lords.

They will eat me.

"One more thing," I said, and the pit echoed back my words like a parrot. "I want to talk to my brother. I didn't leave things okay with him."

The gravitational pull on my flesh eased up for a moment, and I felt their attention turn to me.

The Lords pulsed with music, but without anything even close to eyes, I had no real signs of their having heard my request.

"I want to see my brother. I *need to see* my brother."

The Lords emitted a long musical note, forlorn and alien.

The Lords continued consuming liquid, then embracing and kissing. The galaxies inside their translucent skin exploded, bloomed, and then faded into an inky darkness.

Is this all there is?

"It can't be," I said. "It can't."

The beings beneath me flooded my eyes and ears with fright and beauty, but I had come here for a reason, and I wanted answers.

I felt an anger rise. I had wanted to see José María in corporeal form, right inside the Coil, just like he had been there with me the other two times before.

"I came to bring my brother back to my world," I said.

He was nowhere to be seen.

The glow of the snow intensified, and for a moment, it lit up the snow field around me. It burned so bright, in fact, that suddenly I could see up into the vastness of the canyon of Mictlán. From my spot at the heart of the canyon, I could see the top of the city of Mictlán, and the temple of flowers, and much farther up, a series of blue eyes on the head of Blue Hummingbird as she nestled in the upper levels of the Coil.

"This is the mouth of the river, Wanderer," the Lords said. "The nine rivers lead here. Your sibling has swum in their waters."

José María had been a particle in this snow, flowing into the pit, but how would I know which one?

I got down on my knees and plunged my hands into my snow, hoping to recognize something, anything in the flecks of snow.

Which one is he, dammit?

I shoveled snow in big handfuls, and its rainbow light turned my clothes red, green, and violet. But in these tiny specks I found nothing that could help me find the speck I was looking for.

"Give him to me," I said, raking my hands through the snow. I lowered my face so I could see the flakes up close, but I didn't see him. I didn't hear him.

But the sense of peace in this place continued, and the Lords ignored me. Their gravitational pull was still making me slide toward the edge of the pit. I stood up and took a few steps back.

"So, you will agree to your task?" the Lords said.

"What task?"

"To widen the gates between worlds?"

Even though time had come to a standstill in this pit, my heartbeat quickened in fear.

"I thought you didn't want that to happen."

"It is the flowers that would deny the gates, but my wife agrees," the Lord said.

"And my husband feels the same," the Lady continued, "that we can't stop the gates from opening. And we love you too much to deny you that journey."

"But opening gates and all this death—does this mean you will kill everyone on Earth if I do this?"

"We do not kill. We only transfer souls into the other side. Once we take them in, they emerge on the other side of our consciousness."

"And who kills then?"

"Well, it's the creatures in your world that do. The plants, the insects, the cats, and the men. You all kill. You all die."

"Why don't *you* open the gates?" I said. I was very angry with these two beings.

"Because we are too old, too far inside the wheels. That is not our role."

I considered everything I learned inside the Coil, and I wished for a moment that I too could be dead and turned into a particle of colored light in one of these rivers.

And then a word froze my thoughts: *Reina.*

Reina.

José María would never have walked away from such a challenge from the Lords of Death. I knew this. He would have thought it was cool as shit and easy to do. And he never would have wished he was dead.

I took a deep breath.

"Sure, I'll accept."

"It is decided. And thus, you will need to defeat the Ocullín,

Wanderer. Because opening the gates allows his passage, too."

The membrane grew thick and blue again, and the incomprehensible bodies of Mictecacíhuatl and Mictlántecuhtli disappeared beneath the shield. And the snow returned to its still state as darkness crept back over me.

Time was frozen down here, yet I could still understand for a moment — for a fraction of a second — how beautiful the Lords really were.

I now understood what my parents had meant about rites of passage. Despite the travels I had made inside this crib of darkness, I still only felt like I was just nineteen, and deep down inside I feared I was not ready for the Lords' task.

But I had no choice. I gave the things in the pit my word, and their music had only shown me kindness. And I had seen that rainbow-colored snow that melted into their mouths. I would never want to destroy that.

I walked back toward the northern road and the city of Mictlán.

I did some quick math as my footsteps echoed along the Northern Road, and I realized that if I emerged from Mictlán again, I would be twenty years old on Earth, but I would be closer to twenty-eight years old from the two journeys I had already made here. The numerals looked beautiful in my mind as I saw them lined up next to each other, and as I moved in the darkness toward the city, I stopped paying attention to my surroundings.

I could see the cylinder of the city about three miles in the distance when I felt a stir in the waters of the lake.

"I will be happy to see you when your teeth fall out, girl," said a gnarled voice beneath the water. "Weathered, old, ready to die."

The water's surface remained smooth, but I knew what lay down there, inside the surface. Whatever magic the Ocullín used made reflections possible on this lake, despite the lack of any light.

This time, instead of letting him chase me like an animal, I sharpened myself to greet him. Now that I was out of the Snow Fields, I removed my coats and wrapped my mother's shawl around my hips like a sarong. In my right hand I held the tiny knife I had brought with me.

I dragged the knife along the surface of the lake and it sliced open, letting out sharp notes of music and the smell of fresh blood.

"I see you in there," I said. "Show me how you travel."

"Stupid girl," roared the Ocullín. "It's as simple as mirrors. The doorways of mirrors belong to my father, Black Tezcatlipoca. Maybe you'd like to meet him someday?"

I turned my blade in front of my eyes, and I stood next to the water as the sound of thousands of legs scuttled toward me.

If the sound was accurate, the Ocullín would tear my back within seconds.

But I called his bluff. No attack came. He only wanted me to fear such a thing.

I knelt on the ground and stabbed the water again, and with my free hand, I reached in.

I emerged with something resembling a wet caterpillar, and it spat in my face. It cut my skin, and it burned.

I wrestled the creature on that road, and I lost my breath as I clawed at it and slashed it as hard as I could.

I screamed the names of the hummingbirds, and two of them flew down to my location. One distracted the Ocullín, slashing him with its beak, while I rode the other. The Ocullín sprouted moth wings and flew upward, chasing after us.

It screamed in a thousand unique voices:

"BITCH"

"CUNT"

"PUTA"

I swatted its caterpillar hairs away from my face, and I sang my own name, just like I did in Chicago at the Parade of Lights. The Ocullín recoiled, and it slashed at my arms, making tiny cuts that stung like fire.

"HELL IS REAL; COME SEE IT"

"YOU'LL DIE BURNED AND MUTILATED"

"JOSÉ MARÍABURNS IN HELL"

The creature's tongue lapped the blood from my wounds, despite the hummingbird's attempts to shake off the invader.

We tumbled through a jungle in the upper levels of the Coil, and I crashed into the leaves. The trees shrieked as I slashed at the Ocullín, and the Hummingbird plucked me out with its beak to resume our flight.

We flew past the layered levels of the canyon and emerged onto a flat land dotted only with a mountain with a snowy peak.

"Take me to the top," I commanded, and the bird beneath me soared to the destination as the smoke trail that he left with his tail screamed like a bottle rocket.

As we approached the Snow Fields, the Ocullín crawled over my body, and its caterpillar barbs raked my skin.

I knew we were headed toward the gate, where the snow of the mountain began. As we neared it, I stabbed the Ocullín many times in its face, which was both insect and human. It recoiled and shrieked, and as we dove through the gate, it called me more names, fading into the darkness as I exploded out of Mictlán through the gate at the top of the mountain.

I took in big gasps of air, and the scents of car exhaust filled my lungs. The Chicago skyline filled my vision, and I slid forward on the BP Bridge, just a couple of feet from where I had entered through its reflection.

"Hey, bitch, I'm still here," said a voice behind me.

He was dressed just like the men that struck my face until it cracked on the day of the Millennium Riot, but he wore no helmet. He wore the face of my uncle Jorge, and the eyes of a feral cat, and a mouth lined with hundreds of needle-like teeth.

"No," I yelled, and I lopped off his head with a single swipe of my hand, which had a force it never had before.

The headless body turned into thick liquid, and then smoke. The head stared up at me and winked.

"We're not done with each other, Wanderer."

I stomped on the head until it was pulp and my boots were covered in its pus, blood, and feces.

I ran in my T-shirt through the remainder of the ice storm. I didn't care if I got frostbite; I was going home.

I dropped out of school that fall due to "illness" and I moved back in with my parents for a couple of months while I lay in bed. Fevers and sores raked my body, and I spoke to no one.

During those weeks in my parents' house, I discovered

something.

My father was more fragile than I had ever imagined. To touch José María's room caused him physical discomfort, and even through his shouting matches with my mother, I knew that his obsession with keeping my brother's room impeccably clean would never end.

At night, I heard my father walk through the attic. The sounds I heard sounded like coughs or sobs. I am not sure which.

I assured my mother that things would go back to normal, but she had many questions.

"Would you want to take a trip with your aunts to Mexico?"

"What for?"

"To keep learning. To learn from a teacher."

My heart said yes. My mind said no.

"I'd be a danger to them, Mom. Trust me."

"You need people," she said.

And she was right. I probably did.

It was impossible to explain to her how I could physically look close to thirty while remaining twenty years old on the surface. But I tried.

"I see real age in my face," I said.

She ran her fingers over my brow to smooth out the wrinkles in my skin.

"I would never tell anyone if you got a little more surgery to fix this," she said.

"Are you saying get a facelift?"

We both laughed, though my casual tone left my mother looking hurt and sullen.

"Mom, what you need is a joint so you can relax."

"Excuse me?" she said.

"Get the good stuff. You'll feel oh so sweet!"

"You don't sound like yourself."

She was right. I noticed that over the weeks of my stay in their house, the sick sense of humor — something irreverent and wild — had found its way into my speech. In José María's absence, I was learning how to find levity in things — including my relationship with my mother. Just like he did.

When I handed my mother a joint at Christmastime, she took my temperature again, shaking her head. I hope she smoked it when she had some time alone.

I went back to the university during the last semester, and on my way up to the campus, my father hummed a song to himself as we cruised along Lakeshore Drive.

"Minerva's having another baby," he said.

"Good, I love babies."

"Maybe she'll make you the godmother."

"I'd pencil that in my calendar, sure." I laughed.

"Promise me you'll never leave Chicago, Clara," he said.

"Promise."

This was a promise I never kept.

Many of the things I did during and after university are not a big secret, and anyone who takes the time to look at the public record, or chooses to read books, can learn of what became of my life.

But of course, they won't ever have the full story. I am not sure myself that I even have the full story.

I traveled far to continue to investigate the mystery of the gates that connect between our world and that of the Coil. To do this, I forced myself to go live in Mexico, the place that none of my aunts wanted me go permanently. *You can learn from your relatives there; just don't actually stay and live there, OK?,* they said.

But I lived in Mexico City for two decades, and in between, I traveled to other places that showed me glimpses of the *other* cities, those thirteen places that José María and I knew existed, currently exist, and *will* exist. These glimpses were seen sideways through a ramen stall in Shibuya, or inside a dirty hut in the Himalayas. That's when I saw shadows, reflections, and blurs of places. Sometimes, I could glimpse these cities in a single gold reflection of the sun on the Black Sea, and in an instant, it would vanish.

During the twenty years I lived in Mexico City, I searched for a young man named Alan. His uncle Guillermo had disappeared years ago, and like me, he was in search of knowledge. I will one day write a book about how I finally found this young man, and how he found me. We had his uncle in common, a man who built a living tunnel of insects that he shouldn't have.

I will also write one day about how I discovered symmetrical slits on my breastbone, and how they make music when I dream at night and the sun goes down. These slits don't bleed, and they give me no pain.

I have lived long.

Time has become my ally, but as a result, it has been painful to outlive many of my relatives. This is pain no one should ever feel.

This is the first time I have ever written about what I did atop the Tribune Tower, so in a sense, it's a bit of a confession. The only crime was trespassing, I suppose, but it doesn't matter. The video footage I shot lives on. Of course, those who could complain, and those who might seek retribution against me for what I did by broadcasting those images, are dead as of the time of this writing. All of them.

DOTS AND LOOPS

"Food nourished my body; travel fed my soul." – Tumblr meme, origin circa 2019.

"Heartache smells of moss, licorice, and flowers." – *Princess Kami: A Horror Tale for Children,* Studio Gibri Films, 2017.

"We are bold and bright. We are a celebration." – Karyn Andersson, lead singer of Arkangel, upon the announcement of the band's breakup, Twitter, 2020.

In the spring of 2017, almost four years after the Millennium Riot, Arkangel announced a single stop in the Midwest for their world tour. I read about the update on my computer, and though I was in the middle of a lecture, I stood up and walked out into the street. Using my smartphone, I ordered myself a ticket for their concert.

I kept the ticket in my phone for weeks, and I stared at it every day. I dreamt about that ticket often, and though I was tempted, I didn't sell it.

On June 19, 2017, I rode my bike down to Millennium Park, and I entered the Pritzker Pavilion from its western side. The attendant scanned my phone, and I moved up to the front, directly in front of the stage. The metal wings of the pavilion shone bright, and the hot air on my bare shoulders meant summer was actually arriving. I was the only person there.

Above me, tiny little dragonflies made of aluminum, glass, and silicone swept through the air, fighting the Chicago air currents and glinting in the sun.

An attendant in a ponytail inspected the aisles, glancing at me a few times until I noticed her.

"You must be a big fan to arrive this early," she said.

"It's Arkangel or nothing," I said.

"I used to listen to them, until I started having strange dreams. Now I listen to nicer music," she said.

Over the next three hours, thousands of people filled the seats and the lawn beyond the turtle shell of the pavilion.

When Arkangel arrived on the stage at 9 p.m., the crowd's screams reached a hysterical pitch, and the purple lights on the stage bloomed into the night. Arkangel used new holographic LEDs, and that meant they could project images into the air above the stage.

Their favorite image, a mouth filled with many buildings instead of teeth, opened and closed.

It took the brother-and-sister duo a full thirty minutes to arrive on stage, and by the time they strolled on stage, I felt electric shocks on the back of my neck. The warmth of all these bodies in the pavilion felt right, and I heard the music of all their heartbeats.

Sergio and Karyn's masks lit up in green, and they stared out at the audience, arms at their sides, like two colossal figures.

When the first strums of guitar from "Plainsong" fell over us, I knew I was missing something. The deep movement of sound was full of soul and adrenaline, like I remembered, but I knew that it wasn't until later in the song that the stakes went higher.

I let a few bars flood my ears, and then there it was.

The second movement of the song allowed the synthesizers to trickle in, and suddenly, Arkangel's music took me back through time, to places I had been to before.

I should have bought two tickets, dammit.

That was my thought.

I never expected for someone to answer it, right inside my head.

I felt a soft voice inside of me. A voice other than my own. Male, young, just over the hill of puberty.

Stop, fussing, reina. *Shut up and enjoy the show.*

The music from the stage flowed over my skin and seeped into my bones, and for the first time in the three years since my brother had died, I felt real tears arrive in my eyes. My vision was dead in one, and the other felt alive and ready to absorb the lights from the stage. Both orbs filled with water, and saline rivers ran from my tear ducts and down my cheeks in long trails.

The lights from the stage made endless circles in the air. Their loops interlocked, came apart, then moved away from each other again. They were endless.

As I cried inside the sound waves of the music, I smiled, and I laughed, too. These were tears of joy, and of a certain release. Indeed, there was a festive melody found in the return trip of dead souls. And it sounded like this.

There was so much I still couldn't understand, but I felt the molecules of water slide down my skin, while at the same time I felt other particles — sparking particles — rise back up, defying the laws of gravity and screaming their song of joy into the night.

AFTERWORD

The novel you hold in your hands was originally serialized on Kindle in four parts. The serial was part of an experiment to find a new form for my narratives. I am publishing both the serial and the paperback through my imprint Solar Six Books, which places emphasis on digital. Both formats have been edited to mostly mirror each other, but it's in the digital edition that you will find all sorts of bonuses: glossaries, alternate covers, and more. The experiences of the digital book shaped the final form of both the final e-book and the paperback.

The themes and mythological elements of this novel are explorations that I have been making in my writing for decades. I welcome all reader feedback, and rest assured, readers will get more glimpses and visits to the 13 secret cities volumes to come. If you had asked me just five years ago if I could write a novel about multiple generations of parents, children and families of the human and non-human kind, I am not sure I could have said yes. And it's better that way. The universe is better when it has the element of surprise and novelty.

We live in an interesting time for adventure books — the young-adult genre (or rather, marketing category) is going strong, and we are seeing many new amazing stories being told by some great authors. And yet, diversity is lacking. I have two nieces under the age of five, and it is my hope that in a novel like this one, they will one day see their culture, heritage and story, even if it's through the refraction of a fiction. Perhaps they will be inspired to tell their own fictions one day, too.

Cesar Torres
New York City
December 2014

ABOUT THE AUTHOR

Cesar Torres was born in Mexico City and studied journalism at Northwestern University. He is the publisher of Solar Six Books. He lives in New York City.

OTHER WORKS

The 12 Burning Wheels (2010)
13 Secret Cities (2014)
Cesar is currently at work on a new novel, due out in 2015.

For updates, please visit:
cesartorres.net
13secretcities.com
Labyrinth podcast on YouTube

www.ingramcontent.com/pod-product-compliance
Lightning Source LLC
LaVergne TN
LVHW091117080826
845145LV00008B/1948

* 9 7 8 0 9 9 1 0 3 6 3 4 9 *